PARAGON LOST

DAVE DUNCAN

A
CHRONICLE
OF THE
KING'S BLADES

PARAGON LOST

BCA

This edition published 2004
by BCA
by arrangement with EOS
an imprint of HarperCollins*Publishers*

CN 127008

EOS
An Imprint of HarperCollins*Publishers*
10 East 53rd Street
New York, New York 10022-5299

First Eos paperback printing: August 2003
First Eos hardcover printing: October 2002

Eos Trademark Reg. U.S. Pat. Off. and in Other Countries, Marca
Registrada, Hecho en U.S.A.
HarperCollins ® is a trademark of HarperCollins Publishers Inc.

Printed and bound in Great Britain by
Mackays of Chatham plc, Chatham, Kent

*This one is for
Tony King,
reader, writer, webmaster,
and (most important) friend.*

Contents

The three "Tales of the King's Blades" formed a set, although possibly not a true series because they were not sequential. The present book is independent of them and complete in itself. It recounts some curious events that occurred about a dozen years later, during the reign of King Athelgar.

◆ ◆

Thousands of swords hang overhead in the great hall, each one a memorial to the Blade who bore it. For his own hand and style it was crafted, into his heart it was plunged in the ritual that bound him, and its touch on his shoulder ultimately released him when the King dubbed him knight. After his death it was brought back to Ironhall, to hang forever with its sisters in the place where it was made. Swords of all types and styles hang there, as fashions have changed through the centuries, but each hilt bears a shining yellow gem as its pommel—with one exception. On one sword alone the cat's-eye stone has been replaced with a plain white pebble.

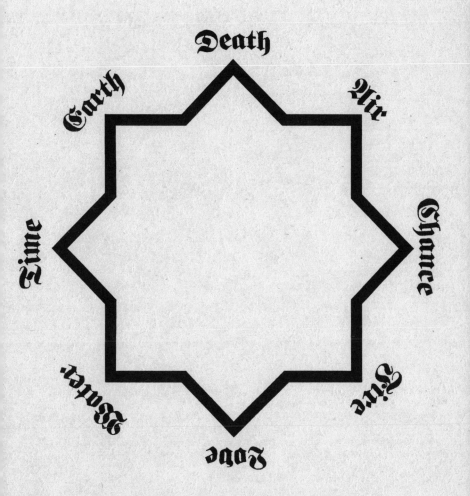

I

At Gossips' Corner

♦ 1 ♦

"Isabelle!" Mistress Snider screeched. "Are you deaf?"

Isabelle was not deaf, but she would have had good cause to be, working in this kitchen. On one side of her Nel was chopping up salt pork with a hatchet, on the other Ed pounded dried fish with a mallet—it took hours of pounding and soaking to make it even close to edible. At her back, Lackwit was powdering salt just as loudly. Lids danced and clattered on boiling pots, the pump handle squeaked, drudges were rattling sea coal into the great brick ovens and raking out ashes. The door, left open to admit cool air and flies, led to the stable yard where the farrier was shoeing a horse. Deaf? Not at all.

"And what're you doing with all that cinnamon?" The old harpy waxed louder and shriller. Mistress Snider was tall and stooped, tapering from grotesquely wide hips up to a small, mean face shriveled around a beak nose.

"I am making a dipping sauce as you told me to!" Isabelle

shouted back. "Cameline sauce, with ginger and raisins and nuts, with cinnamon and pepper, but how you expect me to do it with no cloves, no cardamon—"

"Not so much cinnamon! You think we're made of money here? Stale bread and vinegar, that's what makes a sauce, girl. Use up some of those herbs before they rot completely. A man wants you! A *gentleman* is asking for your husband." The old horror canted her head to peer at Isabelle with one glittery eye, oozing dislike. "And be quick back. I need that sauce done right. And *soon!*"

With difficulty, Isabelle held back some truths as unpalatable as Mistress Snider's food. The woman skimped ridiculously, but all Chivians tried to get by with inferior ingredients smothered in peppery sauces. In Isilond, one began with a good piece of meat and used only enough seasoning to bring out its natural flavor. She wiped her hands on her apron.

"Yes, mistress."

"He's waiting in the King's Room. You hurry back. Don't expect me to pay you when you're not working."

No, Isabelle would be paying *her* for the privilege of speaking with a potential client. She set off on the perilous trek to the door, watching out for scavenging dogs and people hurrying with hot pans, for her balance was not as certain as it used to be. Fortunately, the baby never made her nauseated, although she lived in that horrible kitchen from before dawn until after nightfall. She had nightmares of giving birth there. But a *gentleman* looking for Beau might mean a client and real wages, instead of the pittance he earned in the yard by day and serving beer at night.

Leaving the reek of boiling cabbage, she went into the big taproom with its smoky fog of yeast, people, and cheap candles. Gossips' Corner was, first and last, a tavern, where beer flowed like water—"and for good reason," Beau said. Located in the heart of Grandon, not far from Greymere Palace, Gossips' Corner was a universally recognized address for people to rendezvous or leave messages or even dine, although Isabelle could never understand why anyone who had any choice should choose to do that. It offered rooms by the night or the week or the hour—she and Beau lived there, in a garret five floors up. It provided music and singing and gambling. Those who sought to buy a horse, hire a servant, pick pockets, or contract odd jobs could usually be accommodated.

The City Watch, bought off by Master Snider, turned blind eyes to shadier services: girl or boy companions in the rooms, sinister conjurations not offered by honest elementaries, recovery of recently stolen goods, collection of debts, or other forms of assault. Today the taproom was as noisy as the kitchen, with a dozen carpenters competing in hammering. Riots were commonplace in Gossips' Corner, but last week's had been unusually vigorous, climaxing in a party of public-spirited Baelish sailors attempting to burn the place down.

The King's Room was a cubicle for private conversation. Furnished with a timber table and two benches, it was just as cramped and pungent as the taproom outside, but the pebbly glass in its diamond-pane windows let in a fair light. The solitary occupant rose as she entered, an unexpected courtesy. A gentleman, certainly. His hose, doublet, and skirted jerkin were of fine stuff and beautifully tailored—not quite in the latest mode sported by court dandies, but quite acceptable on an older man—and his knee-length cloak was a magnificent gold brocade, trimmed with a collar of soft brown fur that tapered all the way down the edges. Yet he was clean-shaven, in defiance of current fashion, and the silver hair visible below his halo bonnet seemed clumsily cut. He bore his years well, standing straight and tall.

He bowed. "Lady Beaumont? Good chance to you, my lady."

Isabelle shut the door. "I am Mistress Cookson, may it please your lordship." People who claimed a rank above their station could land in the stocks. Was he one of the King's spies?

He pursed his lips in disapproval. "Then pray be seated, mistress. I do believe we have business to discuss. And if you are to be Mistress Cookson, then I shall remain Master Harvest for the nonce. May I offer you some wine, or order some other refreshment?"

He would have paid dearly for the bottle of Snider's best that stood on the table with four goblets. Isabelle declined the wine, but she did sit down, determined to get her money's worth. The Sniders would dock half her day's pay for allowing her a few minutes to meet with this man under their roof, despite having charged him for the use of the room.

The man not-named-Harvest returned to his bench and studied her with coal-dark eyes that age had not dulled. "I need speak with your husband, my lady. The matter is urgent."

"It is about lessons?" He was too old to fence, but he might have grandsons.

A smile flickered and was gone. From his pocket came a paper that she recognized instantly as one of Beau's handbills. She had helped him design it and was still furious that Master Snider's printer had ruined it by setting *Available At Gossips' Corner* in the largest type. The visitor spread it on the table and her suspicion flamed higher.

"That is outdated, my lord. We have a newer version. I can fetch one." She began to rise.

"Pray do not trouble. I have seen that, also. The only difference is that Sir Beaumont's name was changed to 'Ned Cookson.' Will you tell me why?"

Long-smoldering anger made her blurt out the truth. "He was ordered not to claim to be a gentleman, my lord."

"Ordered by whom?"

"By Blades from the palace! The Royal Guard! They harass him! They threaten to report him to the Watch for wearing a sword when he is not of rank. They frighten his pupils away. Is that why you are here, master? To cause us more trouble?"

Master Harvest shook his head vigorously. "Mistress, I am shocked by this. I thought I had put a stop to it."

"They are not so bad now as they were last year," she conceded. "But by any name he is still the same expert fencer, my lord. His time is almost all spoken for just now, but I am sure he would be honored to wait upon your lordship at your convenience."

The visitor sighed and laid his hands on the table. He stared at them, not at her. "Mistress, I truly believe it is in Beau's interest that I speak with him as soon as possible."

"He is currently instructing at a noble house not very far away from here. I could send a boy and have him call on you at your residence."

Another sigh. "Lady Beaumont, pardon my doubts. Your husband is far from the first man to try teaching Ironhall fencing outside the school itself. In four centuries, very few have succeeded in earning a living at it. It is the best system, of course, but it needs great dedication. At Ironhall we pound the boys' heads with mallets of honor and service and tradition, day in and day out, all through their adolescence. Anything less than that and it won't work."

"He teaches many styles, my lord. Long sword, bastard sword, short sword, sword and buckler, backsword, rapier—"

"—rapier and cloak, rapier and target, two rapiers, rapier and dagger—" the man said, quoting from the handbill.

They finished the list in unison: "—sword and buckler, sword and sword-breaker."

He laughed. "I am sure he teaches them all very well. The juniors used to fight over him. Unfortunately, fencing is out of style now. Old King Ambrose was a devotee of the noble art, but King Athelgar does not care for it and kings set fashions. Henchmen with staves are in; fencing is out. And now you tell me that the Royal Guard is driving away his clients! Lady Beaumont, has he any pupils at all?"

"If you will not tell me your business, I must be about mine."

"I wish to offer your husband a job. I will pay well."

That was more like it! "Pray forgive my suspicions, my lord. Beaumont has served the Duke of Permouth, and His Grace gave him a very good reference. The Earl of Mayewort also—" She distrusted the intelligence behind those penetrating dark eyes.

"Last year. For about a month in each case, just long enough for the King to find out about it and apply pressure."

"Who are you?" she shouted, heaving herself up. "Why are you spying on us? What harm is he doing, trying to earn an honest living?"

"None, mistress. But the King bears Beau a grudge. He had him fired from those positions and probably others, is that not so?"

"No," Beau said. "I quit because they expected me to eat in the kitchen."

Isabelle wondered how long he had been standing behind her. The visitor should have noticed—must have done! He looked up now, dark eyes studying the newcomer.

"Where do you eat these days, then?"

"I have given up eating. It is a disgusting habit." Beau closed the door almost as silently as he had opened it. He sat, pulling Isabelle down beside him, then reached across for the wine bottle. He poured, filling three goblets.

His boots had brought a powerful odor of stable into the room. He was a compact man, and his filthy, shabby leather jerkin and breeches made him seem small compared to the padded and pleated visitor—those were emphatically not the clothes he normally wore when meeting potential clients. He was bareheaded, which no gentleman ever was, but the wind that could never ruffle his ash-blond curls had flushed his fair cheeks. Or his color might be from anger, for certainly his pale eyes were steely as he regarded the stranger.

"I recognized Destrier." Beau set a glass in front of Isabelle. "He's too old now for such a long ride. He has an ingrown lash in his right eye that should be seen to." In a world where every man prized himself on his horsemanship, that was first point to Beau.

The visitor could be just as inscrutable. "He doesn't live on Starkmoor any more and I'll tell my son to have the eye looked at."

Starkmoor was the site of Ironhall, the Blades' headquarters and school, and now Isabelle recalled this stranger's curious remark, "I thought I had put a stop to it." Only three men could hope to stop the King's Blades doing anything they pleased, and since he was neither the King nor Commander Vicious, he must be Grand Master, the legendary Durendal, Earl Roland, of whom Beau normally spoke with awe and reverence, quite unlike his current biting mockery. Roland had been the finest fencer of his generation and King Ambrose's Lord Chancellor for another. She had just offered him fencing lessons.

"Are you truly forbidden to use your Blade name?" he asked.

Beau shrugged. "Title. It was always only honorary and a

stable hand claiming knightly rank is unseemly. 'Beaumont Cookson' lacks euphony, don't you agree?"

"Some say that you brought much of your trouble on yourself."

"Who does not cry for just deserts, when all he really wants is pity?"

Grand Master showed his teeth. "You had orders to leave town. That's what the harassment is about. Why don't you do as you're told—go away and start over somewhere else?"

"I enjoy listening to the gossip here."

"Why didn't you enter the King's Cup this year?"

"You came for lessons? A man of your years will find fencing strenuous."

They were fencing with words—feinting, parrying, riposting, and never quite saying what they meant. His lordship tapped the handbill spread on the table.

"This says that you won the King's Cup two years ago against competitors from four kingdoms. Last year, of course, you were elsewhere. Why did you not compete this spring?"

"I might have lost. Who wants lessons from the third or fourth best swordsman in the world?"

"Then you need not have mentioned it."

Isobel sniffed at her wine glass and set it down hastily. She should go back to work. Nosy Mistress Snider would know that Beau was here and selling fencing lessons did not need both of them. But she wanted to know what spite the Blades were plotting against Beau this time.

Lord Roland tasted his wine. Without comment, he set the glass down and folded his arms as if he had reached a decision. "You are not the first Blade to end up working as a stable hand, but you will never convince me that you enjoy it. I came here to offer you a job."

"I happen to be married."

"I did not mean an Ironhall post. This would be a favor to me personally, not His Majesty."

"An assassination, is it?"

Roland glared. "No. I have a serious problem and I believe you may be able to solve it for me."

Beau rose, ignoring the wine he had not touched. His mocking smile did not waver. "I do appreciate your concern, my lord, but my work is piling up even while we speak."

Isabelle kicked his messy boot under the table. They needed the money! Men! Why would a man do anything rather than accept help when it was offered?

"Sit down," Grand Master said. "This is very confidential."

"Then it would be safer not to tell anyone." Beau shaped a slight bow. "I must rush and prepare bran mash for my charges, and my wife likewise, for hers. It has been fun reminiscing about old—"

"I have lost a Blade. He has been stolen."

After a moment Beau said, "That is a totally ridiculous statement!" and sat down again.

◆ 2 ◆

"Do try the wine, Lady Beaumont," Grand Master said. "It is not what its label says it is, but quite drinkable."

"I must attend to my duties, my lord. And if the matter is as confidential as you—"

"Please stay! I am very happy to meet you at last, and just wish the times were happier. Mine is a very curious problem. It has me baffled, and that snaky grin on your husband was always a sign that he was out of his mental depth. Perhaps you will be able to shed some light on the path for both of us."

Lord Roland had won a point and was enjoying it. He knew how to charm. She returned his smile, acknowledging that few people could fence words with Beau and win.

Beau, quite unabashed, moved Isabelle's glass a little closer to her and took a sip from his own. "Forgery?"

"Of course."

"But *why?*"

"That is the question. As you probably know, Lady Beaumont, Ironhall boys always leave in the same order in which they were admitted. There are good reasons for this, but it can cause difficulty, especially now, when we train fewer boys than we used to. I send regular reports to the Commander of the Royal Guard, advising him how many we have ready for binding. Sir Vicious, in turn, advises His Majesty. Two or three times a year, the King comes to Ironhall and harvests the next batch. He cannot delegate that duty; it must be his hand on the sword that binds them."

Isabelle suppressed a shiver, thinking of the deadly white scar over Beau's heart.

"Of course the King may also assign Blades to other persons." Lord Roland regarded her darkly. "You will not remember the Thencaster Plot, but one of its more distressing results was that some Blades were put in impossible conflicts of loyalty. Many went insane when their wards turned traitor. Others died fighting against their king. Ever since then, His Majesty has been reluctant to gift Blades to others. The Royal Guard absorbs almost our entire output nowadays; that is why we admit so few. But the King has not completely given up assigning private Blades."

Like Beau. She nodded.

"Consequently," Grand Master continued, "I had no reason to be suspicious a few days ago when a man rode into Ironhall with a warrant from the King. He gave his name as Sir Osric Oswaldson. I was mildly surprised that I had never heard of him, nor had Master of Protocol, but he dropped hints of a secret mission and the King wishing him to have a Blade guardian."

"Is that usual, my lord?"

Lord Roland smiled. "No, but possible. It happened to me, about half a century ago."

And Beau, who was positively leering. He hated mysteries he had not created himself.

"I was unhappy that the warrant required me to bind only one Blade, because His Majesty knows my concerns about that and has never ignored them before. But kings do as they please."

"Osric," Beau said. "Baelish name. *Was* he a Bael?"

"He could be. His hair was more sandy than red, but it did have a reddish tinge and he was the right age to be one of Athelgar's childhood friends. He volunteered no personal information and brought no attendants who might have gossiped in the kitchens. The King sent most of his cronies home after the Thencaster Affair, but he could well have chosen one for some confidential mission. It all made sense."

When his audience did not comment, Lord Roland continued. "I gave him my usual lecture on the care and upkeep of Blades. In all good faith I summoned Prime and introduced him to his ward-to-be. Swithin? Remember him?"

Beau nodded. "Gangly lad, with a shock of black hair? Always looked surprised, as if his eyebrows had been stuck on too high."

"He has a nasty surprise coming to him now, if he hasn't had it already. He was late developing, but he turned out very well, excellent man, wonderful on a horse. I like to keep one of the best to be Prime so that no one thinks he's a reject. The following night he was bound."

Beau drummed fingers on the table. "I suppose . . . the

oath is part of the binding. There's no question that the conjuration would work if the ward used a false name?"

"If it hadn't, Swithin would have died. And if it was possible to bind by proxy, the King would not come to Ironhall. No, it's whose hand holds the sword that counts."

"Osric knew how to wield a sword?"

"No," Grand Master said. "I doubt if he'd ever touched one before, but he got the point in Swithin's heart, which is all that matters. Before dawn they rode off over the moor together, Aragon succeeded as Prime, and Ironhall carried on as it always does."

"But?" Isabelle prompted in the silence.

Grand Master scowled. "A few hours later a couple of guardsmen came by. Sir Valiant and Sir Hazard—you remember them, Beau? They were on their way to Nythia to inspect renovations at a royal hunting lodge, so of course they dropped in at Ironhall. Hazard mentioned that the King had gone off to Avonglade for a week's hunting and would be back on the ninth. That's today."

"Loose lips!" Beau said scornfully. "Does dear King Athelgar not keep his movements secret?"

Roland shrugged. "He tries to. He keeps everything secret. He's said to keep secrets from himself. But if he had gone for a week, then he must have left on the first or second . . ."

Beau emptied his goblet and pulled a face. "So you retrieved Osric's warrant from the archives and took another look."

Grand Master produced a paper and passed it across. Isabelle leaned against Beau's shoulder to study it. It was a common octavo sheet, printed in heavy black type, with a few gaps where additions had been inserted in a hasty scrawl.

We, Athelgar, King of Chivial and Nostrimia, Prince of Nythia, Lord of the Three Seas, fount of Justice, &c. to our trusty Durendal, Earl Roland of Waterby, Companion of the White Star, &c., Grand Master of our Loyal and Ancient Order of the King's Blades: Greeting! We do request and require that you cause the most senior *one* Candidates to be bound as Companions in the aforesaid Order by its Secret and Ancient Rituals to serve our Royal Intents by defending our well-beloved *Osric Oswaldson, Bart* against all Perils and Persons Whatsoever for as long as he shall live.

Done by our hand at *our Palace of Greymere* this *3rd* Day of *Eighthmoon* in this *13th* year of our Reign.

Athelgar

As a warrant for a man's life it was singularly unimpressive, not unlike Beau's handbill. He took that up also, as if to compare them.

"You said His Majesty was not in Grandon on the third," Isabelle said. "He made a mistake on the date?"

"Kings are very careful over dates, Lady Beaumont," Grand Master said. A former chancellor would know that. "A wrong date on a royal signature could have grave consequences."

"Then he postdated the warrant."

Beau's smile was more catlike than ever. "What possible reason can a king ever have for postdating anything, love?"

She had no answer to that.

"So you suspected a forgery," Beau said. "Is it conjured? You had a White Sister sniff it?"

"No need," Roland growled. "The writing is a purely secular forgery. The seal may be a conjurement. I can't tell the seal from the real thing—it's only the royal signet, of course, not even the privy seal, but that is standard. The hand is not the King's. A good copy, good enough to fool me at first sight, but when I compared it with others, I could see the discrepancies."

The old man spoke calmly, but he must be seething. A long lifetime of public service would end in ridicule. The King might impose a cover-up, but that would not save Grand Master from the royal wrath.

Beau smiled. Neither man spoke.

"I don't understand," Isabelle said. "How can the imposter hope to get away with this? A Blade is not a silver dish to be fenced or hocked. A Blade has a tongue. He talks."

"If a man can be hanged for stealing a sheep," Lord Roland inquired acidly, "will the penalty for stealing one of the King's Blades be less?"

She should have seen that.

"So the loot will not testify against the looter," Beau said. "I'm not sure if a Blade's binding prevents him from pounding his ward to mush in a non-fatal sort of way. Were I Swithin, I should be inclined to try."

A private Blade was bound until death. Only the Guard could be dubbed knights and released.

"A Blade is not invisible," Beau continued. "Dress a Blade in rags and he does not lose his . . ."

"Arrogance," Isabelle murmured helpfully.

His knee nudged hers under the table. "Distinctive poise. And our friend Osric can never go anywhere without taking his ill-gotten guardian along. He can never risk visiting Grandon, certainly."

"He's gone abroad, then," she said. "Back to Baelmark."

Roland shrugged. "Or anywhere in Eurania."

"And you cannot even hazard a guess who he was?" Beau asked.

"I had never seen him before."

"So why bring your gaffe to me?"

They were playing word games again, feinting at meanings. Of course they must know each other very well, so they could jump the gaps, but there was also danger looming. Kidnapping a Blade was certainly crime enough to involve the Dark Chamber. Since no lie could deceive inquisitors, conversations must be deniable.

"What can Beau do about it?" Isabelle demanded. "What can anyone do? Swithin will die before he will desert his ward. If you catch Osric and lock him up, you'll have to lock up Swithin, too. If you chop off his head, Swithin will go insane, won't he?"

"This could be more serious than that," Beau muttered.

"Much more!" Roland said.

"What can Beau *do,* though?" Isabelle repeated.

The two men stared at each other as if they were now communicating without any words at all. They still did not answer her question.

Lord Roland rose. "Swithin has been kidnapped! Tricked into dedicating his existence to safeguarding a thief! His entire life has been stolen from him. I want that boy found and compensated. Somehow. I cannot imagine how. And in secret. I think you are the man to do it for me, Beaumont. I will provide expenses." The wash-leather bag he tossed down landed with a metallic thud that shook the heavy table.

Beau jumped up. "I will not take your—"

"You will need a good sword." Lord Roland was not only taller, he was louder. "Fortunately, I have one I can lend you." He reached down and produced a sword in a battered, well-used scabbard—it must have been lying on the bench beside him all the time. He laid it on the table, as if raising the stakes in a wager.

Beau stared, shocked into silence; the wind-burn flush on his face fading to pallor.

Even Isabelle knew that hilt, with the silver cage around the leather-bound grip, but the pommel was wrong. The cat's-eye cabochon that had once gleamed there had been replaced with a simple white stone, like a pebble off a beach. She leaned across the table to draw the blade just far enough to expose the name inscribed on the ricasso: *Just Desert*.

Beau licked his lips, then said hoarsely, "I will not take your gold, my lord!"

Isabelle was seized by a potent urge to kick him or shake him. They *needed* that gold! *Desperately!* It would buy them passage back to Isilond, or provide a start of a decent life here in Chivial. She had a baby coming. Beau was being wilful again, crazy-proud again, ruining everything again, just as he had when he defied the King. She forced down her anger, clenching her fists. *Loyalty! Trust him!*

Grand Master said, "Sir Beaumont—"

"No!" His voice was soft, his smile hard. "I do not need your charity."

"You need someone's!"

"*No!* I refuse. I was expelled from the Blades in disgrace. They miss no chance to show their contempt for what I did. I won't wipe their noses for them. Take your gold, and your warrant, too." He thrust purse and paper back at the frowning Roland. "Good chance to you, my lord. You can find your own way out."

Lord Roland bowed stiffly and stalked away, cloak swirling.

But the sword still lay on the table.

◆ 3 ◆

Isabelle opened her mouth to start asking questions and Beau kissed it. He might still not be the best swordsman in the world, because in the two years since he won the King's Cup he had been deprived of the intense daily practice that experts needed to keep up their skills. She never doubted that he was the world's best kisser.

He was far stronger than he looked, and she could do nothing but cooperate. Her swelling breasts spread against his hard chest and her belly could just still fit in the concave curve of his. When the world spun at a crazy angle and her knees buckled, he lowered her carefully to sit on the bench. She was giddy and breathless. He was flushed.

Only then did he take up the sword.

"Why didn't you accept his gold?" she asked bitterly.

"Because I will have nothing to do with treason."

"Treason?" She thought of the horrible things they did to traitors.

"Tampering with the King's Blades could certainly be construed as treason." His eyes flickered a steely warning, and she remembered the cryptic hints that there might be more to the crime than Roland and he had said. "Sooner or later the inquisitors will bay." He peered along the blade.

The first time he proposed to her, he had warned her that a Blade's ward must always come first, promising she would always be second. He had lied, although unwittingly. *Just Desert* had been second. He had always spoken of his sword as female, *she*. She was a schiavona sword, two-edged, tapered, basket hilt—not a large, clumsy weapon, but neat, like him. Also deadly, like him. The only time Isabelle had ever seen tears in his eyes was when they took her away. And now she was back. Roland had known the one coin that would buy her husband for whatever his real purpose was.

"It's yours, isn't it?" She was still breathless.

"Oh, no." He smiled thinly. "His Majesty ordered mine destroyed, remember? But Master Armorer keeps records of every sword he makes, so Roland could have ordered a replica. He would pay for it himself, too."

She could see the nicks on the edge, many of which tallied men's lives. This was the original *Just Desert,* the one he had slaughtered with on the ghastly Skyrrian quest. The King had been defied. Roland had not destroyed the sword as commanded, but if the Dark Chamber asked, Isabelle could say, "I hardly know one sword from another. My husband told me it was a replica."

She hugged herself and the child she carried. "What was he after? You believe this absurd story of a stolen Blade? You think there's any way you can find him, this Swithin? Wherever he is? Why did you turn down Roland's money? Where could you even start? How could you possibly find Osric, when that won't even be his real name?"

"I know his real name. So does Grand Master."

"What!?" Isabelle cried. "Don't give me shocks like that! It's bad for the baby."

"I said I know who 'Osric' is," Beau repeated, "and so does Lord Roland. The problem will be catching him in time. The warrant was dated the third. Assume Osric rode posthaste from Grandon to Ironhall—"

"How do you know he was ever in Grandon?"

Beau grinned approvingly. "He was, but what I mean is that the date had to seem reasonable to Grand Master. The warrant is addressed to him, but it's a royal command to the bearer, too—if the King gives you a commission like that, you do not drop it in a drawer and forget about it! You move. You act! So Osric probably arrived at Ironhall late on the fourth or on the fifth. The binding ritual begins with a daylong fast, so the actual binding could not have been done before midnight on the fifth or sixth. He and Swithin left early on the sixth or seventh; Valiant and Hazard arrived later, probably around noon. Today's the ninth, so old Durendal did very well to get here in just two days. Well for his age, I mean. But where are Osric and Swithin?"

She was lost in this labyrinth. "What are you going to do?"

Beau's laugh showed all his teeth. "I'm not going to do anything. You are."

"Me? You are out of your mind."

"No, love." He slid *Just Desert* back in her scabbard. "You are going to put on your best bonnet and head over to the palace. I wonder if the King is back from Avonglade yet?"

II

The Ironhall Road

◆ 1 ◆

"Terrible thing, old age," Andy said. He heaved himself into the roan's saddle like a miller loading meal sacks. "I'll see you on the right way. Hate for you to get lost."

"Sir, honor may require satisfaction for that remark." Aided by a groom's hand-up, Durendal swung himself into the gray's saddle with (in his opinion) considerably more grace. His son was an ungainly horseman, although a proficient one.

The sky was bright, awaiting its lord the sun like a court gathered to greet a monarch. Hooves stamped in the stable yard mire; breath smoked. The children still slept, but Maud and many of the servants had come out to exchange last farewells, and whinnies from the stalls sounded like old Destrier bidding good chance to his lifelong friend. The two riders headed for the gate.

Neither spoke until they emerged from the trees at the top of the rise, where they could look back at the big house sheltering in its hollow, amid its own woods and fields and orchards. For Durendal Ivywalls was full of bittersweet memories of Kate, of his days of power, of happiness with grandchildren she had never seen.

The road snaked back into the trees again.

"I'm glad you found the right sword today, Father. Yesterday, when you put on the wrong one and then lost it, you worried me."

Andy's nosiness worried Durendal, although it should not surprise him—as a child Andy had pried into everything. As a young man he had gained renown as an explorer.

The Blades' Grand Master was skating on paper-thin ice in the Swithin affair. That nasty little atrocity was not just about the theft of his reputation or a boy's freedom; it had the potential to shake the Kingdom of Chivial to its foundations or even plunge half Eurania into war. For himself, Durendal did not care—he was old enough to do his duty as he saw it without counting the cost—but he was determined to keep his family out of harm's way. Earthquakes splattered innocent bystanders with falling masonry, and no one would be safe if accusations of treason started flying. Against the inquisitors' ability to detect falsehood, ignorance was the only defense. So how to answer his son's query?

Down on the flats, Andy urged his roan into a trot and Durendal kept pace. Joking aside, he was well aware of age creeping up on him. Still stiff from his ride in from Ironhall, he now faced another two days' return, even if the weather held. He would happily stay longer at Ivywalls, but the briefer his absence from Ironhall the less chance it would come to the attention of those with the power to demand an accounting of what he had been up to.

"You made a mistake, Son. *Harvest* is my sword and always has been."

Andy shot his father a thoughtful glance. He was a heavy-set man, who had always been more rugged than handsome, whose blocky face had never quite lost the ruddy tropic weathering gained in his sailor days. He was stolid and deliberate but never predictable. He had made his own fortune trading to far lands, coming home late in life to settle down and start a family. He had taken over Ivywalls, enlarged it, and turned it into a model estate admired by landowners from all over Chivial. He was an authority on crop rotation, fruit trees, and horse breeding. No man likes to see his son reach middle age, but Durendal was enormously proud of Andy.

"Well, my eyes aren't what they used to be."

Durendal laughed. "They're the envy of every hawk in the county." He dared not discuss the Swithin affair, but Beaumont's sad tale was stale news. While it was not exactly public knowledge, the vultures of the court had picked its bones bare long ago. He could talk about that safely. "I'd as soon not have this known, but I was doing a friend a small favor yesterday."

A problem as deadly as the Swithin abduction was a strange favor to drop on anyone's head, but Beau and that fiery little black-eyed wife of his had virtually nothing left to lose. Beau was the only man in Chivial who might find a solution.

Roland counted years. "You must remember Montpurse?"

His son said, "Vaguely. Your predecessor as chancellor."

"Finest man I ever knew. Brilliant swordsman, magnificent statesman. My friend and mentor. My idol."

"And a traitor?"

"No. A patriot. I sent him to the headsman, yes, but that's another story. See, there's a Blade, an ex-Blade, who reminds me very much of Montpurse. Has the same baby-blond hair. Moves like a sunbeam. Utterly deadly with steel, incredible. When we admitted him, he demanded the name of Beaumont; it wasn't on the approved list, but I allowed it. Of course the whole school instantly began calling him Beau."

Andy grinned. "Did he know what it meant?"

"Oh yes! Beau never gets blindsided." Except yesterday, when he set eyes on *Just Desert* again. That moment alone had been worth the ride in from Starkmoor.

"Father, a captain soon learns not to play favorites among his crew. I can't imagine you ever do at Ironhall."

The horses were cantering now, big hooves pounding the rutted trail. A faint veil of smoke over the fields showed where stubble was being burned. Chivial was prospering, and at peace. In all areas except the extreme north, the harvest of 402 had been the best in a generation. King Athelgar would receive much of the credit, for no rational reason. The Thergian war that had threatened for the last two years appeared to have been averted.

The Swithin nonsense must *not* be allowed to upset all this!

"I hope I don't play favorites, son. But Beaumont was like Montpurse—so spectacularly the best that the problem never arose. He made no enemies. He never needed disciplining." In his last few months in the school, the juniors had taken to calling him "the Paragon."

He had been the bright star who rides the heavens in splendor, then falls to earth and shines no more.

✦ 2 ✦

Early one fine morning the first fencing classes were starting to leap and shout in the quad. The beansprout riding class had just gone out the gate like a cavalry charge. So dewy was the spring sunshine that even Starkmoor's barren crags and perfidious bogs could seem gentle, and the wisps of dawn mist that lingered around Ironhall's battlements and towers gave it very nearly the air of antiquity and invincibility its architects had striven to portray. As a castle, it was a monstrous fake, of course; as a prison for delinquent youths, it would have failed utterly without the deadly moors encircling it. As a school for swordsmen, it was unsurpassed in the known world. A hawk was quartering the sky; doves cooed on the rooftops, taunting the stable cats far below. Durendal was just tightening Destrier's girth straps when he heard childish voices yelling, "My lord!" and saw some sopranos, boys of the youngest class, racing toward him.

It was almost five years since he had tired of growing wrinkles, turned Ivywalls over to Andy, and retired to Ironhall to do something useful. His grief for Kate had faded into numbness, an outrage like a missing limb, never forgotten or forgiven, but no longer bleeding. Parsewood had repeatedly offered him any position he wanted—Master of Rapiers, Master of Sabers, Master of Anything. He had insisted on remaining Master of None, a title the candidates found very funny, but he coached their fencing, lectured them on politics, and generally lent a hand.

That was in winter. The rest of the year he had done some of the traveling that Kate had always wanted to try. At that very moment he was on his way to meet Snake and two other close friends for a trek through southern Eurania. Had he been just two minutes faster out the gate, he would have been gone for half a year.

When the white-faced messengers reached him, Durendal listened calmly to their gabble, then said, "Thank you. Cedric, unsaddle my horse, please. Give him some oats as consolation." He set off to view the body.

Parsewood had been a competent, if uninspired, Grand

Master for almost ten years. Not old, though . . . he'd been three years Durendal's junior, so they had not become close friends until childhood was long past. Parsewood had served under Snake during the Monster War; he had held the Order together through the nightmare of the Thencaster Affair, when Blades were required to slaughter Blades. And now . . .

Now the quadrangle had fallen silent. Durendal detoured past a knot of seniors and told them to keep classes going, there would be an announcement shortly. He resumed his trek to First House.

The Order must elect Parsewood's successor, so Lord Roland's traveling days were over. There was no arrogance in that assessment—the outcome was inevitable. Although he wanted the job much less than he wanted paralytic dementia, he knew he could not escape it. If Malinda still reigned, she would veto his election, but Malinda had abdicated and sailed away. Less than two years since the Thencaster Plot almost tore it apart, Chivial was still divided, with half the country cursing the Blades for propping up a "foreigner" king, and the other half hailing them as national saviors. For the eminent Lord Roland, so closely associated with the days of Good King Ambrose, to refuse this service would be a blatant insult.

By the time he had climbed the stair to Grand Master's chamber, half a dozen knights were gathered around the bed muttering. When he walked in they turned to him with obvious relief.

"It must have happened in his sleep," Master of Rituals said. "He looks peaceful, doesn't he?"

"He's earned some peace," Durendal said. "The King must be informed. And then . . . Um, who takes over until the election?"

"You do, my lord." They spoke in chorus, heads nodding

like drinking chickens. He wondered if they had planned that.

He sighed. "For now, if you want. We'll have a general meeting shortly." He knew what it would decide. "Protocol, will you send word to His Majesty, please? Archives, I assume you have records of the proper procedures?"

Of course. Archives had records of everything that had happened there in four centuries.

By the time the reluctant heir escaped and hurried across to King Everard House to change from riding clothes into something more suitable to the dignity of Grand Master Presumptive, the great bell was tolling, summoning everyone to the hall. Even while he was mentally preparing what he would say to the assembly, he noted the hawk still serenely circling. Men came and went; the world endured.

At the steps a slim young man wearing a senior's sword moved to intercept and the abstracted Durendal almost walked into him. They dodged with mutual apologies. Florian had been Prime for almost a month now, doing much better than the masters had expected.

"My lord!" he said. "This . . ."

Durendal looked down with annoyance at *This,* standing at Prime's side. He was too young to be even a soprano, dressed in jerkin and breeches too grand to be school issue. Not today! The bell was tolling. No one had authority to admit a new candidate and current enrollment was over the preferred limit already.

Then he thought, *Montpurse's hair was not curly.* The color was the same, though, and the boy's eyes were similar, ice in sunlight. They showed concern, but no real worry.

"He'll have to come back another day. Who brought him?"

"Well . . . no one, my lord. I mean, the beansprouts found him on the road. He rode in doubled with Calvert."

Applicants were supposed to be sponsored by a parent or guardian, but foundlings on the doorstep were not unknown. This one unprepossessed—a child not yet into his adolescent growth spurt, weedy and city-pale. But a lot of them started like that and he deserved a fair hearing, because his whole future life was at stake. The bell was tolling.

"What's your name?"

"Ned . . . my lord." He was impressed at meeting a lord, but again not excessively so.

"Hungry?" That was always a safe bet.

The ice eyes sparkled. "Yes, my lord."

"Take him to the kitchens, Prime, and tell the cooks to fill him tight as a drum. Wait there for me, Ned."

Watching the two of them hurry off, Durendal noticed: *He walks on springs. Like Montpurse.*

The announcement was a solemn moment, a sudden shadow. To the aging masters and other knights, Parsewood's passing was a reminder of their own mortality. To the candidates he was the man who had admitted them and given their lives new beginnings. By ancient tradition his sword, *Gnat,* was hung beside the founder's *Nightfall* to await the conclave that would elect his successor.

Having led the procession out of the hall, Durendal reached the kitchens before the servants did, finding young Ned perched on a stool beside a teak counter, still eating. By the look of the remains, he had consumed most of a pitcher of milk, half a loaf of fresh bread, about a month's supply of butter, and enough hard-boiled eggs to build a small mountain of shells. He was just reaching into the bowl for another egg when he saw Durendal. He dropped his feet to the floor and bowed. Few applicants knew gentle manners. Most were guttersnipes or churls.

"Feeling better?"

"Yes, thank you, my lord."

Durendal leaned against the bench. "I'm Lord Roland. I'm in charge here at the moment. Tell me about yourself. All I know so far is that you like eggs."

"They're my favorite, my lord . . . I'm a bastard." The wide juvenile eyes stared up at him warily, waiting for reaction.

"So am I. Carry on."

Ned brightened and began speaking with more confidence. His mother had been a cook in the house of a rich and respected alderman in Brimiarde. She had died bearing him and he professed to know nothing about his father. He was being quixotically loyal there, because someone must have paid for a wet nurse, food and shelter, the rudiments of an education, serviceable clothes. Most unwanted babies died or disappeared. Lest there be any doubt who his benefactor had been, just three days after the rich alderman had been returned to the elements, his lawful heirs had loaded the unwanted brat into the family carriage and instructed the coachman to drop him off within sight of Ironhall.

"How old are you?"

"Be twelve next week, my lord."

He looked younger, partly because of his fair coloring, mostly because he was small. The kitchen staff—all male in Ironhall—were drifting back in, carefully avoiding the intruders, but able to hear what was said. The meeting should be adjourned elsewhere, but Durendal had already concluded that Ned the Bastard was too young and too small. It wasn't admitting applicants that was hard, Parsewood had always said; it was turning them away. What to do with this child?

"You think you could be a swordsman?"

"I'm nimble," the boy said, suddenly stubborn. "They said you'd throw coins for me to catch." He reached both hands into the bowl and came out holding four eggs. He threw one up, then two, and in a moment he was juggling all four. His gaze flickered from side to side, following them, full of gleeful triumph.

Durendal had never heard of an applicant auditioning this way, but few applicants ever had a prior chance to query the inmates on what to expect. "Is that as hard as it looks?"

"Um . . . no. It's just a cascade." The eggs disappeared into his hands and then reappeared, moving in another pattern.

"This is harder. This's a shower."

"Can you do five?"

"Not usually . . . my lord . . . but if you throw me one more, I'll try."

"No need. I'm impressed."

The eggs vanished into the little hands and were replaced in the bowl. Ned grinned hugely as the watching cooks applauded. Durendal was tempted to do the same.

"We don't admit boys younger than thirteen. How old are you really?"

The grin vanished. "What I said. I don't tell lies!"

"Good for you! That's the right answer. Can you ride?"

"I rode here, my lord . . . behind Candidate Calvert."

"That's all?"

Ned nodded glumly. "Yes, my lord."

"I admire your honesty." Durendal himself had not been quite honest, because boys of twelve were not always refused; the problem came later, binding a seventeen-year-old. "I'll give you a chance. No, listen before you thank me. There's a farm below the moor could use an extra hand. If they'll keep you for a year, will you work for them?"

"Yes, my lord! I'm a good worker." The grin was back.

"I believe you, but it will be hard work. A year from now, if you've pleased them, we'll take you in. I'll send you down there with Florian. You can double with him."

Durendal was circling like the hawk. No applicant had

ever been granted a delayed admission like that before, so far as he knew. But this Ned was obviously not the average applicant, a juvenile monster who should be chained to a wall. Nor was Durendal the average impoverished Ironhall knight; he had ample money of his own to compensate his friend Giles for taking on an unwanted and probably useless stray.

He would have to prime Prime very carefully in how to explain this arrangement to Ned's still unwitting employer.

The following spring, Grand Master rode Destrier down to the Giles place, leading a saddle horse. It was not much of a farm—sheep, mostly, and some barley, but he had never regretted his brainwave, and since then he had boarded out other future candidates around the moors. Why had nobody ever thought of something so obvious?

The pack of barking dogs was called off by a scantily-clad boy, nutbrown all over and topped by a shaggy mop of sun-bleached curls. He looked thicker, but no taller. He was jumping from foot to foot like someone who has been counting three hundred and sixty backward.

"You still want to be a Blade?" Durendal tried to remember if he'd told Ned all the advantages and disadvantages.

"Yes, my lord!"

"Just call me Grand Master."

"Yes, Grand Master." Ned's teeth shone against his tan. "I can ride a horse now. And juggle *six* eggs, my lord!"

Durendal took him back to Ironhall to became the despised and nameless "Brat," universal scapegoat, lowest of the low.

It took him exactly three days to make his mark.

Most nights the evening meal in the hall was a rowdy affair, with dishes clattering, eighty or so youths gorging and arguing at the same time, and the sky of swords overhead jingling in every stray draft. At high table the masters shouted back and forth through the racket.

"Grand Master!" Rapiers was new and eager and loud. "Tried out that new Brat today. Think you've found a nugget there. Shows real promise! Not like some of—better than most, I mean."

"He's a scrapper, too!" Sabers agreed. "Makes up in ferocity what he lacks in size, mm? Did you see what he did to Cedric? No one else has dared take him on."

"What impresses me," Rituals shouted from the far end, "is the way he treats the hazing. If humiliation's what they want, he just laughs and takes it. You'd think sitting naked in the horse trough quacking like a duck was perfectly normal behavior."

A year auditioning applicants had shown Durendal how lucky he had been with his first recruit, for that is what the current Brat had been in practice, even if not officially so. And Durendal had been within minutes of riding out the gate and missing him!

"It seems to be working for him," Protocol said. "The sopranos are letting him eat with them, see?"

The masters fell silent, staring in astonishment along the hall.

"Fates!" Archives exclaimed. "The *Brat?* Truly? That's never happened before! The Brat *always* eats in the kitchen."

The future Beaumont had arrived in the hall. Year by year his flaxen head moved closer, table by table.

◆ 3 ◆

King Athelgar rode to Ironhall early in Fourthmoon, escorted by eighty Blades of the Royal Guard. He stayed two nights, bound the five most senior candidates, and rode off with his train at dawn.

An hour or so later, Durendal sent the current Brat to find the new Prime. The young man who appeared in the doorway of his study was blond, slight, and as dapper as anyone could be in Ironhall hand-me-downs.

"You sent for me, Grand Master?"

Durendal looked up from his accounts. "Spirits! You still here?"

Beaumont could always be trusted to accept a joke. His smile was rueful but believable. "Apparently. I do hope to join the Royal Guard when I grow up."

Ironhall turned out a single product—a slim, agile, deadly swordsman of standard size, never fat or weedy, tall or short. Beau was shorter than most and did not even manage to look stocky, although he had muscle enough to wield a broadsword. His appeals to Master of Rituals for conjuration to make him grow taller had always received the same answer: "Why?" Sword in his hand, he could butcher any man in Ironhall, even the masters. As the pedantic Master of Protocol put it: *If a matter be unimpaired, seek not to rectify it.*

Durendal had argued more tactfully, pointing out that even simple conjurations could have undesired side-effects and there was no harm in letting prospective opponents underestimate you.

"It's hopeless," he said now, waving the boy to a seat. "Tancred and Sewald will never allow you out of here." Those two were the current Guard fencing champions. "Did either of them give you any trouble this time?"

"Sir Cedric did," Beau said modestly. "They're superb, all of them."

"What I heard was that you drove off their herds, sold their families into slavery, and buried their carcasses in unmarked graves."

"The spectators seemed to believe I won on form."

"Which one will take the cup?"

The contest would be held in a week—in Grandon, of course. Beau's hopes must have soared to the stars when the King arrived, and then crashed to the depths. "I'd bet on Sir Cedric this year, Grand Master."

"I'm not certain I would," Durendal said casually.

Steel-gray eyes flashed. "How so, my lord?"

All Ironhall was agog to know why Athelgar had taken only five seniors when there were so many good men champing bits. The fencing masters had expected to lose at least nine and were delighted to have been proved wrong.

"Just a hunch. No guarantees. Now to business. Since the King has cleared some of the deadwood out of the seniors' dorms, we can glorify a few fuzzies. Who do you fancy for promotion?"

Typically, Beaumont had foreseen the question. He promptly named four fuzzies, six beardless, three beansprouts, and five sopranos. Durendal's own list was so similar that he just nodded.

"Go ahead, then. Tell them to move their kit. Help the new seniors choose swords—and do make them start with short ones! Advise Archives and Master Armorer what you've done."

"Thank you, Grand Master. Anything else?"

"Well . . . that hunch of mine . . . I was thinking I might enjoy a ride up Home Tor this evening—assuming nothing unexpected comes up beforehand. If you and Oak and Arkell would like to join me, I'd welcome your company. We can watch the sunset together."

Even Beaumont could not hide his excitement then. "We shall be honored, Grand Master. So, I am sure, will the sun."

Not one man in a thousand could get away with a smart-alecky reply like that to a superior, but Durendal laughed.

"Ask them to saddle up Cricket for me."

He had not betrayed the King's confidence. He knew almost nothing to betray, for Athelgar had been typically grudging with information. He had not discussed the identity of the three men's future ward, although he had perforce written it on the warrant he left behind. He had not explained why a peaceable, elderly farmer should need a crack team of Blades.

Two days before that, the King had sauntered into Grand Master's study and acknowledged Durendal's bow by offering bejewelled fingers to be kissed. He wore a mud-spattered riding outfit of blue kidskin blazoned over the heart with a royal lion in pearls. His hat sported a white osprey feather.

Athelgar was thirty and seemed younger, being slim and ever restless. He had come to the throne at twenty and very nearly lost it at twenty-two. His enemies whispered that no smile had graced his narrow, bony face since. They also sniggered that the shock had turned his hair brown overnight, and it was certainly not the Baelish red of his eyebrows and goatee. Granted that he had been born and raised in Baelmark, to label him a foreigner was unfair, for his bloodlines were at least seven-eighths Chivian. Such prejudice and his own youthful follies had provoked the Thencaster Plot, which had been betrayed only in the nick of time. The conspirators had died and he had learned from his mistakes. He was secure on his throne now, but the scare had made him secretive and distrustful.

"Who is that hairy horror? Have I seen him before?"

Durendal straightened up. "Probably not, sire. It used to hang in West House. For a Long Night amusement we collected all the pictures in the school and redistributed them. The juniors voted that one mine." As the ugliest, presumably.

The King strode over for a closer look. "Who was he?"

"I suspect your ancestor King Everard IV, Your Grace. It resembles the official portrait in Greymere."

Athelgar nodded and swung around to inspect the room again. Durendal had remade it since Parsewood's day, with marble fireplace, new paneling, furniture, carpets, and drapes. Each time the King came, he remarked on every tiny change, although he never offered to pay for any of them. Currently he was balking at providing lead for the school's leaky roofs. He wandered over to the windows.

Meanwhile Sir Vicious had entered and closed the door. He stood there like a statue, arms folded, only eyes moving. The Commander was lean and very dark, like a walnut icicle, and had earned the King's trust so well that Athelgar kept him bound well past the age at which most guardsmen were released.

"You say you can part with eight?" the King asked the scenery.

"More than that if Leader needs them, sire, but you know I like to hold back a good man as Prime, so—"

"Who's the best man you've got?"

"Beaumont, sire."

"I don't mean with swords. I mean *man*. Steady, dependable. One who will keep his head no matter what."

The old warrior in Durendal pricked up ears. "Still Beaumont. An all-rounder. He's as good as Ironhall has ever turned out." And he was there only because Durendal had not been faster out the gate on a spring morning six years ago.

"How many ahead of him?"

"Five, sire."

The fidgety King toyed with Durendal's favorite porcelain figurine, tossing it idly from hand to hand. It had been one of Kate's treasures. "And the two right behind him?"

"Arkell and Oak, sire. Good men. They'd work well with him. No bad blood there."

So Athelgar, who almost never gave away Blades, was about to deed someone a team of three, was he? After the dire experiences of his own youth, Durendal had worked hard to convince successive royal masters that three was the smallest practical assignment of Blades. One to stand watch while the other two kept up their fencing skills was how he usually expressed it, but less than three was unfair to the men in many ways.

"Forget the order-of-admittance nonsense this time, Grand Master. This matter is dear to our heart. We need the absolutely best trio of Blades you can provide."

Durendal waited a respectful but unnecessary moment before saying, "I stand by my recommendation, sire. Idris is excellent, but a team should have one leader and no more. He is abrasive, too. Remember you are chaining these men together for the rest of their lives."

The King's eyes were pale brown, not the amber of the House of Ranulf, but they could freeze a man to the wall as well as Ambrose's ever had. "Only the next half year or so need concern you. And we do not expect our guards to be distracted from their duty by childish sulks."

Durendal bowed. "Your Grace can do no better than Beaumont, Arkell, and Oak. As a bonus, Arkell is a lefty, which might be handy in case of trouble. If you would consider adding a fourth—"

"I said three, Grand Master."

"Oak's the one with the limp," said Vicious, who rarely opened his mouth except to eat.

"A *limp,* Grand Master?"

"He had a riding accident about a year ago, sire. His leg was so badly crushed that Master of Rituals barely managed to save it. It healed a little short and there is no conjuration to lengthen one leg. It kept him from reaching his full potential, no question, but very few can be Beaumonts. Try him out yourself, Leader."

"I did. Last time," the Commander said curtly. "He was acceptable, just."

"He has improved a lot since then. He'll never win the cup, of course, but give him a saber or broadsword and no foe will pass him. The courage he displayed when his leg—"

"Test him, Commander."

"Yes, sire."

The King turned back to Grand Master. "I'll bind the five, then, and give you a warrant for the three. I expect their ward to arrive here tomorrow; if not, then the day after. There is some urgency."

Durendal bowed. "You are assigning him three exceptional Blades, Your Grace."

"I'd give him all eight if I could." His Majesty did not explain why he couldn't.

◆ 4 ◆

Years flying like autumn leaves had driven Destrier into honorable retirement. His replacement was a young chestnut, known as Cricket because he had never seen an obstacle he didn't think he could jump—even trees, of which there were fortunately none on Starkmoor. His prancing and innovative footwork kept Durendal busy and amused his companions as the little cavalcade wound up Home Tor.

Spring was in full ecstasy. The wild landscape that had so recently glowered out of an armor of ice, was softly gowned now in sunlight and bejewelled with wildflowers. Hawks hunted, baby breezes played in the grass, and one last mad

Thirdmoon hare bounced up and down on the Blackwater slope. Durendal had chosen High Tor because it commanded a fine view of the eastern road, of course. If Wassail was coming today, he should be visible. If he wasn't, his future Blades should perhaps be sent to look for him.

Spirits! Durendal had spent an hour with Master of Protocol, reviewing everything the candidates had been, or might have been, told about the man named on the King's warrant. He had read everything on him in the library, too. Lord Wassail was Athelgar's closest confidant, but sedentary and well past sixty. Andy knew him. They exchanged enthusiastic letters on the rearing of cabbages. Granted that the old man had undoubtedly made enemies in the past who might still plot to do him harm, Durendal was left with the sad suspicion that the King's affection had warped his judgment and three exceptional Blades were going to be wasted.

An elderly ward was good news for the candidates, of course. If he succumbed to natural causes in a suitably lingering fashion, they should recover quickly. It was when a ward died suddenly or by violence that his Blades were liable to run berserk.

As he led his troop up the path, Grand Master was hailed by a bleating sheep. She had three lambs with her. Behind him, Beaumont made some comment and Arkell laughed. It was a curious coincidence that all three of Durendal's current charges were lambs, at least compared to most of the hellions who sought refuge in Ironhall.

All three had been victims of ill chance and all three were exceptional. Indeed, whatever chance brought Wassail to Ironhall was depriving the Royal Guard of a future Leader in Beaumont. Arkell, too, fitted the popular stereotype of a Blade as a human whirlwind with a steel tooth, but he lacked Beaumont's overall brilliance. Exceptional swordsman though he was, a kinder world would have made Arkell a scholar. He had read every book in Ironhall's meager library and many of Archives' dusty records as well. He used his right hand for a pen and his left for his sword. He had been planning to serve out a standard term in the Guard, then embark on a new career in law; now he must just hope that Lord Wassail would have the grace to die quickly.

Oak was the quiet one—black-haired, heavy-set by Blade standards, and solid as a tombstone—the archetype Blade defender who held off the assassins while his ward slipped out the back door. His limp would have kept him out of the Royal Guard in any event, so the Wassail assignment would be a blessing for him, a safe and probably brief posting.

The cavalcade reached the windy summit of Home Tor, casting elongated shadows eastward. Three young men scanned the Blackwater road for traffic. Their silence was comment enough.

Soon these three would ride away forever along that road. The one thing Durendal hated about his work as Grand Master was its reward. He watched caterpillar boys—often nasty, foul-minded little boys—metamorphose into deadly, butterfly-bright swordsmen. He reared them and shaped them, guided and encouraged them. Then they went away. The Guard kept in touch, but private Blades must stay with their wards, so them he never saw again. He knew he should not let himself become so involved—but if he did not, how could he do his best for them?

That they were suitably grateful, he did not doubt. He recalled his own masters of half a century ago with affection—Sir Reynard and Sir Vicious (an earlier Vicious) and above all the great Sir Silver, the greatest Grand Master of them all. But he had never guessed how they must have felt about him. Childlike, he had seen them as little more than furniture, for his eyes had been firmly set on the future.

Like the eyes beside him now, raking the Ironhall road.

Let's dance! Cricket said in body language, doing so. *Let's run all the way back down!* Durendal cursed and brought him under control.

"Wild geese and red herrings," Beau said. "Stretch the varlet out on that boulder. Lucky I brought the horsewhip."

The sun burned scarlet close to the western hills. Durendal had instinctively put himself with his back to it and was a little disappointed that none of the three youngsters had thought to do so. Or perhaps they had and were deferring to him. When he spoke they had to squint against the glare.

"Political lesson time. Let's begin by reviewing what the class knows about the Thencaster Plot."

An exchange of puzzled glances elected Arkell spokesman.

"On his accession, King Athelgar made numerous injudicious decisions—bestowing multitudinous honors on foreigners, alienating the Commons with demands for incremental revenue, and provoking belligerent communications from Thergy."

"Gracious, what big words!" Oak murmured, but of course Arkell was parodying Master of Protocol, who taught such matters.

"You ought to mention the lady," Durendal said. "Never forget that young men can get in trouble faster over women than anything else."

"We just want the chance, Grand Master," Arkell said earnestly.

"Finish the story."

"The King announced his betrothal to a woman of low birth and even lower reputation, with numerous hungry relatives. Realizing that he had alienated two-thirds of the nobility, he sent her packing and thereby upset the rest. The opposition rallied around Neville of Thencaster, who would have had a superior claim had his escutcheon not been marred by the bend sinister. Treason had penetrated the court and even subverted the Office of General Inquiry, whose inquisitors silenced several efforts to betray the conspiracy. Fortunately the plot was exposed and suppressed, but with considerable bloodshed."

I'm going now! Cricket suggested. While bringing him under control, Durendal was able to sneak a glance at the Blackwater road. There was movement there, in the far distance. His companions' younger eyes would make it out better than he could, but they were watching him, waiting to hear what this ancient Thencaster history had to do with them. Probably none of them remembered those days at all.

"His Majesty did not tell me what service he will require of you." But Durendal thought he had just guessed, and now the King's concern made excellent sense. "He did hint that the danger to your future ward is real and immediate. I assure you that you are not just the three left over, although you happened to come in that sequence. He was adamant that he wanted the *very best team* that I could supply, and I nominated you three without hesitation. Whatever service he requires of you will not be merely ornamental."

They brightened at that news.

"No more hints?" Beaumont said wistfully. "Why Thencaster? When I was a kid I saw Neville's left hindquarter displayed on a bridge. It was well rotted then. He can't be much of a threat to anyone now."

The travelers had vanished into a dip.

"Who let the rat out of the bag?"

"Wassail?" Arkell howled. "You're not going to bind us to *him?*"

In the ancient traditions of Ironhall, a candidate was not told the name of his ward until they met. Although Arkell would not have expressed himself so forcibly were the noble lord present, Durendal had seen that horrified look before. That was why he had abolished the silly tradition.

"Lord Wassail has served his country well," he said stiffly. "You cannot question his loyalty to the crown."

Last of an ancient but now insignificant line, Wassail had been invited to join the group conspiring to oust the upstart foreigner and instead had betrayed it, thereby gaining the young King's favor and trust. As a judge in the Vengeance Assizes, he had condemned a dozen former friends to death. Until his recent retirement, he had been the King's do-it-all odd-job henchman—mending fences as ambassador to Thergy, chairing countless committees and commissions, investigating encroachments on royal forests, enforcing maintenance of highways and bridges.

The wind blew. Silence ruled the Tor. Dreams were crumbling.

"If there is one man the King trusts above all others, gentlemen, it is Lord Wassail. I can tell you that he always refused the King's offer of personal Blades, even during the Vengeance, when he was beheading powerful landowners right and left."

That was a little better—he needed them now? Why?

"He's *old,* isn't he?" Oak growled.

"That has its good side."

"But what are we to protect him from? Rampaging lawyers?"

"Rampaging rams, perhaps. He is well known for sheep breeding."

Three young faces managed to smile.

"And—this is in strict confidence—the King hinted that he would prefer to assign his lordship more than just you three, but couldn't. If you can find out what is stopping him, I'd be interested to hear."

Better yet. "I'd like to see what we three can't handle," Oak growled. "Send them up in sixes."

"You go first," Beaumont said. "There hasn't been an entry in the *Litany* recently."

Arkell pulled a face. "They called him Lord Whistle."

"Or Lord Weasel," Beau added softly.

"I don't think you should," Durendal said. "Especially when the wind is blowing in his direction."

Three heads whipped round hard enough to make his neck ache. Even he could make out a lone horseman leading a packhorse.

"Grand Master!" Beaumont's eyes gleamed with mockery. "You tell us that the noble lord is in such extreme danger that the best *three* Ironhall Blades you can find may not be enough to protect him. Yet he is allowed to ride across Starkmoor unattended?"

"The danger must still be only pending. But if that is not your future ward coming to Ironhall, Prime, then I do not know who it can be at this time of day. Why don't you ride down and introduce yourselves, while I head back and put another onion in the pot?"

They turned and shot off at a gallop—except one. Smiling, Beaumont drew his sword and raised it in salute. "Thank you, my lord. I shall always strive to be worthy of your example."

Taken aback, Durendal could say only, "I am sure you will far surpass it. Good chance, Beau!"

He watched him go after the others, all three plunging recklessly through bracken and gorse, youth in search of glory, rapidly dwindling into an unexpected mist. Cricket, unhappy at being deserted, stamped and pranced and whinnied uproariously.

"Stop complaining, you great crybaby!" Grand Master said.

◆ 5 ◆

Alack, no man was as young as he used to be. Three days
in the saddle had warped every joint in Wassail's body and
he could hardly breathe for the pain in his chest. He had
picked up both a flux and a regiment of fleas at the inn last
night, for although his road had taken him past a dozen
noble houses where he might have sought hospitality, he had
not risked doing so. Far too many of the current so-called
nobility were mere trimmers. With no idea what true loyalty
was, they professed allegiance to King Athelgar and privately referred to the man who had saved his throne as Lord
Weasel. They would have enjoyed shutting the door in his
face.

The King understood. The King repaid true loyalty.

Wassail did not approve of the fake castle ahead of him,
which must be his destination. He did not approve of the
Blades at all, because men should not need conjurations to
keep retainers loyal. Back when his ancestors, the Wassarns,
had ruled in Chivial—long before the House of Ranulf—
kings had relied on their followers' sworn word, not sword-
through-the-heart abominations.

Three horsemen came charging down the hill, much too
fast for the safety of their horses. As they drew closer he
noted that they bore swords, like gentlemen, but their
clothes were shabby and mismatched. Two of them were
even bareheaded.

One mousy youth, a blond boy, and a black-haired,
heavy-set man—they reined in across the dusty trail, the
blond one in the center raising his sword in salute. "My lord,
Grand Master sent us to welcome you to Ironhall. I am
Prime Candidate Beaumont. May I introduce—"

Realizing that Wassail was not about to stop, the boy

hastily kneed his mount aside and the mousy one moved even faster, letting Wassail through. Nicely done. They knew horses, obviously.

But pests like them were not to be deterred. They swung into place as he rode through, the blond one at his side, the others behind.

"My name is Wassail," he told them. "If you want to be useful, you can send word ahead to have a hot tub ready for me."

"Arkell, you handle that, please? Oak, why don't you lead his lordship's sumpter?"

The mousy one took off like an arrow. The thick-shouldered one moved his mount close and untied the tether from Wassail's saddle. They had been taught how to handle horses, but not to remain silent in the presence of their betters.

"Grand Master informed us that you were coming, Lord Wassail. We shall have the honor of being bound as your Blades."

Wassail was tired and sore and had nothing to say to children. He would explain to Grand Master. "Then he's wrong. I won't stick a sword through any man's heart."

The stair was high and steep for a man of his stature, but the bedchamber at the top was better than he had expected, and an oaken tub steamed invitingly before the fire. The three pests still lurked, having run upstairs with Wassail's baggage like common porters, and seemingly without even needing to draw breath.

"Ironhall employs no valets, my lord," Curlylocks said. "But we shall be happy to assist you any way we can."

"You can assist me by getting out." He would not let these lambkins see his fleabites.

The kid's smile never wavered. "As you wish, my lord.

Grand Master will receive you at your convenience. When-ever you are ready, you will find one of us waiting outside this door to guide you to him."

Wassail bore the oldest name in the kingdom. His father had been Wassail son of Wassail and so had all their forefathers uncounted, back for nigh on a thousand years. Some of them had ruled wide swathes of what was now Chivial, although since then the ancestral lands had dwindled to a tiny holding at Wasburgh itself. When the present Wassail had come into the King's favor, Athelgar had offered him great titles, but he had declined them all. He had no son to follow him, so the last Lord Wassail had no need to change his name now. He had accepted some grand estates from His Majesty, though, and even a charming young wife, who had been a ward in Chancery and thus the King's to give. She had not produced the needed son.

Lord Roland was a merely an upstart commoner, with no blue blood at all. Still, he had served Ambrose long and well, apparently honestly. Athelgar spoke well of the man.

He certainly had good taste in ale. Leaning back in clean clothes, in a surprisingly comfortable chair, beside a small log fire—just warm enough to make the spring night cosy— Wassail felt considerably better. He had been too late for the school's evening meal, but a supper waited under silver cov-ers on the nearby table, sometimes wafting interesting odors his way. His belly had settled down enough to let him con-sider eating.

He'd met Roland a few times and they had been remi-niscing about that, trying to recall the occasions. It should not have been hard, because Wassail had very rarely left Wasburgh before the Thencaster Plot brought him to the King's eye. He'd hoped to bury himself back there in retire-ment, but the King had found this latest mission for him. He was no trimmer. When his King called, he answered, no matter the cost.

"More porter, my lord?" His host raised a massive copper jug.

"Perhaps one more before we eat. Thank you. Excellent ale." And a traditional drinking horn, no namby glassware. "Your own brew?"

"We brew most of what we need, but I buy this in Prail for my own use. I bribe the old knights with it. My lord, I need to unburden myself of a little speech I deliver to future wards. If you would indulge me for a moment? First, both you and the candidates are required to fast tomorrow until—"

Wassail said, "Hrrumph! Best clear the air here, Grand Master. I have no intention of engaging in any ritual conjurations. His Majesty insists I take Blades along on my mission. Not for my sake, you understand, but for . . . Well, anyway, the King is the King, and I do what he says. That's how society has to be. All of us except the King have our lords above us, and most of us have people under us, true? They obey us, we obey our masters. That's how it should be, must be, so that we all know where we stand. I'm a good master to my tenants, always have been, and I expect them to be good followers, loyal. I work hard to improve my lands—helps me, helps them, true? No need to dabble in conjuration. His Grace told me to take on these boys. Very well, tomorrow I'll accept their oaths, and that'll be that. No sword through the heart nonsense. Not necessary."

Lord Roland leaned back in his chair. "With respect, my lord, this cannot go. His Majesty's warrant specifies that the three Blades are to be bound. If you will not bind them, I will not release them from Ironhall."

The man was stubborn. Wassail had already noticed that. So was he. He'd proved that back in '92.

"I am on the King's business!"

"So am I."

"Don't see why you take that attitude, Grand Master. During the troubles after Thencaster's treason, I hired some Blades as bodyguards. Good men, they were, but also a confounded nuisance, following me around everywhere. They did chop up the hired thugs who came after me, so I suppose they were worth their salt. When things settled down, I paid them off, with a few extra crowns apiece, and that was the end of it."

Roland shrugged. "Former members of the Guard, knights in our Order? Good men I am sure, but obviously His Majesty does not see that solution as adequate in this case."

No, he didn't. This time he had insisted on fresh-minted Blades from Ironhall. But he had not actually used the word *bound*.

"Archers more useful," Wassail said. "Don't hold much truck with fancy swordplay, but I do have a troop of longbowmen lined up to sail with us, and a squad of men-at-arms as well. They settled for money. Didn't need to stick swords through any of them!"

His host smiled. "And every man-jack of them will throw away his life for you or the, er . . . the person you escort?"

Wassail held out his horn for a refill. "I expect them to do their best, of course. Can't ask more than that."

"You can of a Blade, my lord. A Blade will scream out his life in a torture chamber before he will betray his ward. Many have done so, over the centuries. A Blade's loyalty is unlimited."

"I find that notion obscene! Trust 'em, and if they fail you, chop their heads off, that's what I say. Why can't they be loyal without being bound?"

"They are," Grand Master said. "They are not bound now,

but they are loyal to their liege lord the King and will serve
him by submitting to binding, knowing what it may involve.
I'd say that was *impressive* loyalty, Lord Wassail."

Wassail grunted and drained his horn.

Lord Roland refilled it. "And once they are bound . . . You
need understand that a Blade can never be your *servant,* my
lord. He is the King's man, serving His Majesty by defending you. You are expected to feed him, dress him, and grant
him a reasonable private life off-duty. You cannot give your
Blades orders. Normally they will fall in with your desires
without hesitation, but should you ever venture into danger
beyond what they consider wise, they will start issuing orders to *you.* In an emergency they may use force to remove
you to safety."

Wassail grunted again. "That's all well and good, but . . .
but I don't know how much His Grace told you?"

Lord Roland smiled knowingly. "Let's just stipulate that
Beaumont and the others are not intended to defend you so
much as another, someone who cannot come here to bind
them in person?"

So he did know! "True."

"Of course the binding cannot be transferred, but a Blade
is smarter than a mastiff or wolfhound. He can understand
instructions, although if danger does loom on your return
journey, I urge you to make things as easy as possible for
your Blades by staying close to . . . the lady . . . so that by
defending you they can also protect her."

"Hmph! Not very honorable."

"But practical, and what our dear monarch would want,
surely?"

"Suppose so," Wassail agreed grumpily.

Smiling, Lord Roland poured more ale.

"To continue with my care-of-Blades speech—take an
athletic young man, my lord, dress him well, arm him with

a sword and some authority . . . and where will you find him?"

"In a bedroom. Told you I know Blades."

"With *bound* Blades, the problem is even more acute. The binding conjuration has this side effect. No one knows why, but it is a fact that almost none of the fair sex can resist a Blade on the prowl, or vice versa."

Roland would naturally like to think so, having once been one himself. Wassail wondered what Dorothea would say to such nonsense. He did wish she could see this room. This was very much what he wanted for his own nook back at Wasburgh, but she could not seem to get past the nymph-and-shepherd-tapestry style of decorating.

"Beg pardon, my lord?"

"I was just saying that you should appoint one of the three of them to be leader."

"The blond one seems to think—"

"I commend you on your judgment, my lord! Beaumont is the only possible choice, as you so perceptively remark. More ale, or will you attack the venison? Ah!" Lord Roland had just remembered something. "I do not pry into your plans, my lord—knowing that they concern a high affair of state—but I was just wondering if you will be returning to Grandon with your new attendants when you leave here?"

Wassail considered the question and decided it was harmless enough, if impertinent.

"I expect so. Briefly." He would have to dress the boys in his colors, and the King insisted they be given suitable linguistic conjuration.

"Ah. You may not be aware, but the fencing competition known as the King's Cup will be held there next week."

Wassail grunted again, bracing himself for the effort needed to raise his bulk vertical and approach the board. "So? No one ever goes to see that any more."

Lord Roland went to the table and began removing covers. "It still matters very much to Blades. In half a century, only Blades have ever won it, usually men of the Guard. For the last four years, Sir Seward and Sir Tancred have been tossing the title back and forth between them. This year there was much betting that a relative newcomer, Sir Cedric, would take it from them." He stepped across and offered a hand to haul Wassail upright.

Hmmph! Joints creaked. "So?"

"Whenever the Guard bring the King to Ironhall, as it just did, the Blades amuse themselves by instructing the candidates. For a mere soprano to be coached by a royal guardsman is quite an event!"

Wassail sat down and eyed the dishes. "Looks delicious! You feed the boys this well?"

"Pretty much," his host said, handing him the usual slab of bread to use as a trencher. "Not the lampreys; they were a gift from the King. But everything else . . . The pastries contain cod liver and this is eel puree, well spiced. Roast venison. The 'brewer' is beef in cinnamon sauce. Beans here, obviously, with cabbage. And loach in a cold green sauce."

Wassail pulled out his knife, wiped his other hand on his doublet, and set to work.

"Spiced wine, my lord?" Grand Master poured without waiting for an answer. "I was explaining about the Guard teaching the candidates. This time your Blade Beaumont taught the Guard. He raked the quadrangle with Cedric, cleaned the sewers with Sewald, and tanked Tancred. The Royal Guard was, um, *abashed* would be a kind word."

Wassail chuckled into a mouthful of beans. "Did he so?" Arrogant young popinjays, serve them right! He piled loach and cabbage on his trencher and licked his fingers.

"I will make a wager with you, my lord."

"You think this Blade you are going to hang around my neck could win the cup?" Wassail had more important things to worry about than stupid sports.

"That is highly likely, my lord. In fact, between us two, I suspect the reason the contest is so late this year is that it was secretly held back in the hope that Beaumont would become available to compete. A lot of money can ride on the cup and the Guard loves to bet its insider knowledge.

"But what I meant was that young Beaumont wants to enter more than he has ever wanted anything in his life, or perhaps ever will. But I would wager a hundred crowns with you that he won't ever mention it to you unless you bring it up first. If you appoint him commander, he won't let the other two mention it either."

Wassail popped a piece of cold venison in his mouth and wiped his fingers on his sleeve. Mm! Very good! "Then I needn't worry about it, need I?"

"Oh, think, man!" his host said, eying him carefully. "Think about this mission of yours! Won't it become just a little less dangerous if you can tell them that you have brought along *the finest swordsman in the world* to guard the queen?"

"Might," Wassail admitted.

"Thought so," Grand Master said contentedly.

III

The Sport of Kings

✦ 1 ✦

"Here comes the Pirate's Son now," Hazard said, exercising the Royal Guard's self-proclaimed right to use an insulting nickname for the sovereign.

Pennants and bright canopies rippled in the breeze. Drums' deep thunder quivered in listeners' bones, cheering drew closer. When the royal party entered the field, the crowd's roar swelled to drown out the blare of trumpets and snap of banners. Waving acknowledgment, Athelgar led the procession across the sunlit grass, escorted by a dozen blue-clad Blades and a straggle of honored guests. Lumbering along at his side in the place of honor was his aging but trusted favorite, Lord Wassail, with Sir Oak at his back. No one except the Guard bore swords near the monarch, so when their wards attended the King, private Blades had the choice of being close and unarmed, or keeping their swords and their distance. New bindings itched mightily at this restriction, but there was nothing to be done about it. Oak, who had fists like mallets, had chosen the first alternative. Arkell preferred the second and was already in place in the royal box with *Reason* hung at his thigh and three rows of armed Blades between him and the throne.

This was still a fair turn of fortune for a plowman's son who had been accused of stealing the squire's books five years ago. He had *not* been stealing them, only reading them and putting them back, but the squire had threatened to flog him if it happened again. The squire liked to do his flogging personally and had trouble stopping once he got started, so when it did happen again, the miscreant's father had put him on a horse and rushed him to Ironhall. When Grand Master had assured him they had books there and he might read them, that had settled the matter. It had been a good decision.

The King and his guests were seated. Everyone else could sit down also.

"I do believe," Hazard said cheerfully, "that you have the ugliest ward who ever put a sword through a heart."

"How would you like another through yours?"

"Still a little tender, are you?" Hazard had been a year ahead of Arkell at Ironhall. He was a decent enough yokel, but the place had seemed strangely quiet after he left. Hazard chattered continuously. In any row of Blades, he would usually be found at the end, as now, which was why Arkell had eased in next to him for once. If there was any useful gossip around, Hazard would repeat it—endlessly.

But there was no denying that Wassail was an incredible eyesore, with a bloated, puffed face, all inflamed and veined. One of the lippy juniors at Ironhall had whispered to Arkell that his future ward had a head like a cow's stomach full of blood and a body like the rest of the cow. Not being bound then, Arkell had found that funny.

He still did, actually, but wouldn't admit it. The old man

had outfitted his Blades handsomely and so far was paying them well. Despite his age, he rode like a troop of hussars; he ate and drank like their horses. It took four men to carry him up to bed every night. Perpetually bad-tempered, he approved of nothing done in the last four centuries and never let a kind word pass his lips.

Except when he was near the King. Then he fawned, smarmed, toadied, and truckled. "Your Majesty's presence will lift all hearts." Yuck. "How fortunate is Chivial to have a true philosopher ruling it." Double yuck. At royal functions he stayed almost sober.

Cheering began again as Beau and Cedric came out side by side, clad in bright-hued plastrons. They bowed to the royal box. The two umpires helped them don their masks.

"When did you say you were leaving?" Hazard asked in passing.

"I didn't." Arkell still knew nothing about his ward's mission and had been hoping Hazard did.

"Good, they're going to start with sabers," Hazard said, laboring the obvious. "Poor Cedric! He really thought he had the cup on his mantel when Beau wasn't bound last week, didn't he? Um . . . What odds're you offering on your Leader?"

That was a lunge.

Arkell parried. "I spend my money on women."

"You're a Blade, they pay you."

"Really?"

"Sometimes. You realize that this is the first time the Pirate's Son has *ever* come to watch a cup match? Long overdue. First time for your ward, too, isn't it? I expect they're both bored stiff, but a ward can hardly ignore it when his man's in the finals, can he? Beau's a miracle, isn't he, I mean he just mows 'em like hay. Old-timers are comparing him to Durendal in his prime. This bout'll be a pushover, just like it was at Ironhall last week, won't it? You missed the best match of the meet—almost everyone did, actually, and no one's discussing it because it could have been a world-shattering disaster. Even Cedric ought to thank the spirits that Beau was around because otherwise he'd have gone down in history as the first man to let a . . ." and so on.

The contestants circled slowly, mostly keeping their distance. In sabers, first hit won. Once in a while there would be a sudden appel, a flashing cut or feint, a block, and the players would leap apart again. Spectators duly *oohed* and *aahed*. Engrossed in watching the match, Arkell had almost missed something significant. "Brother, *what* are you talking about?"

"Isilondian Sabreur, de Roget. Big man, florid, white scar under his right eye. Expect he's over there in the contestants' bleachers. He offered Cedric a friendly match and made a dung heap of him."

"What?" Arkell howled. "Not Cedric!" The King of Isilond's Household Sabreurs were the Blade's closest imitators, but Blades told Sabreur jokes among themselves: *How many Sabreurs does it take to beat a Blade?* Answer: *Nobody knows*. "A Sabreur beat Cedric?"

"I'm telling you! If it had been up to Cedric, a non-Blade would have been winning here now, and for the first time ever. He's doing well, though, isn't he? Holding Beau off longer than I expected."

"I didn't hear about this. How far did whatsisname get?"

"He didn't." Hazard's leer promised a good tale. "They don't want stumblebums cluttering up the field, so every first-timer has to pass a qualifying round, and this de Roget was unlucky enough to be paired with Beau. Humiliating as it must have been for the national champion of Isilond to fail to—"

Arkell hooted. "Who makes these rules? The Guard?"

"No, no! The Lord Chamberlain's office. They—
Yieaaa!"

A flag waved, Cedric admitted the touch, the crowd
roared. Beau had won the saber contest.

Hazard sighed. "Beautiful!" He began counting on his
fingers, totting up winnings.

Arkell was still considering the Isilondian's convenient
misfortune. "Who determined the lineup?"

"They drew lots. You're not suggesting the draw was
faked, I hope?"

Not likely! This had *Blades* written all over it.

The rapier round had begun.

"Best of five in rapiers," Hazard said unnecessarily. "Lot
of money says Beau'll take him in three straight hits."

There was less circling this time, and the longer weapons
kept the fencers farther apart. Cedric feinted, Beau recovered. Beau feinted, Cedric recovered, and they were back
where they started. And again. Then steel clattered and
flashed, lunge, parry, riposte . . . Beau signaled the touch,
the umpires waved the flag, spectators applauded tepidly.

"Did you see that!" Hazard cried. "Beau's off his form
today." He scanned the crowd. "Look at this mob! Almost no
one came to see the quarterfinals and semis! Just because the
King's here! I like your livery, brother. I hear your ward
bought the store for his Blades. Lots of good winter clothing, was there?"

"Why should we need that?"

They exchanged baffled glances.

"I also heard that your ward had taken you over to
Sycamore Elementary to be conjured in some foreign
tongue . . . ?"

"Did you?" Arkell was not going to reveal secrets and that
secret was no help, anyway. Instead of a run-of-the-mill conjurement to make them fluent in some foreign language,

Wassail had forked out for a full "gift of tongues" that would let them pick up any language in a few hours. Athelgar always tied his purse strings with a double knot; if he had approved that expense, then the expedition was expected to visit several countries.

Guard scuttlebutt had confirmed Grand Master's hunch about a royal bride to be collected. The Thencaster Affair had taught Athelgar that his bachelorhood was a valuable political weapon, and he had wielded it so well and so long that now Parliament was screaming for an heir. At last, the Guard said, he had made his choice and was dispatching his most trusted henchman to finalize the marriage treaty and escort the fortunate bride to her future home.

But even Hazard did not know who she was. "Vicious must know because he attends Privy Council meetings, but Vicious hasn't spoken a complete sentence since he was twelve. We've gone over every possible candidate in Eurania. Discarding ten highly-improbables, who are over forty or have harelips, leaves seventeen maybes. Athelgar likes them young, remember." Another flag. Hazard's wail suggested sudden pain in the money pouch. "Two-nothing!? What is the matter with Beaumont today?"

Not a thing. Beau could have embroidered lazy-daisy stitch all over Cedric by this time, but he had deliberately thrown the first two points so he must now win the next three or lose the match. This would add some zest for the crowd and save Cedric from total humiliation. Arkell had not learned that by analyzing the fencing—these two were far too fast for him. He just knew Beau.

"So you honestly don't know where you're headed?" Hazard complained.

"No. And I don't care." Adventure in foreign lands beat hanging around Grandon all the time. "May be better for Beau if it isn't Isilond, though."

✦ 2 ✦

*L*ord Haywick's scream of agony was audible from the windy attics down to the half-underground kitchens. It died away into curses, interspersed with sobs.

Waiting in the corridor outside, Master William Merrysock was thus advised that Paulet, his lordship's valet, had just thrown open the bed curtains and allowed the fine morning sun to enter. Merrysock stalked into the bedchamber. A litter of glasses, bottles, and garments, plus a lingering fog of wine fumes, explained why Lord Haywick's nervous system was still delicate. The threats grew more lurid, but at least there was no one else in the Ambassador's bed this time.

"Good morning, Your Excellency," Merrysock said, soberly if a little louder than necessary. "I do regret the need to disturb your well-earned rest, but the hour is close to noon, and certain developments require Your Excellency's personal attention."

His lordship groaned. Paulet offered him a goblet of wine.

Merrysock continued over to the window to peer out at the bustling streets of Laville—he preferred not to look his employer in the eye when the eye looked as bad as it must look this morning. Idiot Haywick was the Chivian Ambassador, and Merrysock First Secretary—meaning Merrysock did the work and Haywick got the honor.

And the bills. The Haywick family had escaped the Vengeance only because the previous earl had been clever enough to die before becoming too deeply implicated in the Thencaster Plot and the present one had been too stupid to be trusted. His loyalty had been cast in doubt, though, and recently King Athelgar had appointed the ninny Ambassador to Isilond—a great honor, but a very expensive service if the

King chose to make it so. Haywick was being bled dry. He skimped by ignoring his debts, including Merrysock's salary.

Fortunately, there were remedies. A First Secretary was not without resources.

"What sort of developments?" came a dying whisper from the bedclothes.

"Lord Wassail and his train will be here before sundown."

" . . . ?"

Merrysock sighed. "Your lordship will recall that the Regent granted your request for a safe-conduct for Lord Wassail as Chivian Ambassador-at-Large, accompanied by a train of one hundred."

The next moan sounded like, ". . . for?"

Having set out his lordship's shaving kit, Paulet was making some effort to clean up the room and lay out clothes. His leisurely pace suggested he was memorizing the conversation. Merrysock had good evidence that Paulet was in the pay of both the Gevilians and the Isilondian secret police, known as the Sewer.

"His Majesty did not inform us of Lord Wassail's purpose, Your Excellency, just that he is not expected to stay long in Isilond."

Others might speculate, but Merrysock had no doubt that Athelgar's most trusted crony had been dispatched to collect a royal bride. Not an Isilondian nymph, though. The infant King had no close female relatives, and his uncle the Regent was certainly not going to let any of the great ducal houses promote a daughter, because that would give Chivial an excuse to meddle in Isilondian politics for the next hundred years. So the eyes of Eurania would be watching to see in what direction Lord Wassail departed from Laville. Merrysock had been able to work it out from Grandon's queries about roads, border crossings, and so on.

"Your Excellency will have to ride out to meet him, of course."

Haywick wailed. "Ride?"

"Arrangements for his escort to bivouac outside the city walls have been made, as was stipulated in the safe-conduct. A small reception has been organized for this evening. The extra staff required by Your Excellency for the next few weeks has been hired. An audience will be held at the palace, no doubt . . . Banquets will be hosted by you on three or four successive nights. The library has been converted to a cabinet where His Lordship may privily receive callers." Certain other parties would certainly pay well for their names. "And so on."

The Ambassador choked. "Cost . . . ?"

"It is possible," Merrysock said with relish, "that Lord Wassail will make a fiscal contribution." He let his tone indicate that the sun might turn green, too. Haywick would bleed and bleed. Best of all, he would have to bleed cold cash, because not a victualer in town would give him credit any more.

At that moment an outburst of brass and drums announced that the band had arrived and begun rehearsing unfamiliar Chivian music. His Excellency uttered a heartrending moan.

◆ 3 ◆

Off to the northwest, the procession wending through the farmlands of Isilond was led by polychrome heralds, who carried banners and blew silver trumpets when passing habitations or other excuses. Most of these show-off lovelies were locals hired for the occasion, but their leader was Pursuivant Dinwiddie, Lord Wassail's personal herald.

Behind them marched a squad of men-at-arms with pikes, followed by a creaking, cockling, cumbersome carriage, half a dozen mounted and highly polished knights—mostly for show—eight creaking ox carts of baggage, and a troop of longbowmen on foot. Many of the men had brought their families; camp followers had added themselves. Add in squires, custrels, body servants, the hounds and their handlers, the hawks and theirs, and the total was near a hundred souls and as many animals. The oxen set the funereal pace under a blistering sun.

An attack of what he claimed was gout had forced old sourpuss Lord Walrus to travel by coach, which kept him conveniently safe and out of the way. Oak sat on the box, keeping an eye on the coachman and the scenery, while Arkell rode behind, his back firmly turned on the knights' clanking armor and long fir lances. Beaumont moved up and down the line as he fancied, scouting the road and flirting with the local women.

"Laville," Oak muttered to himself, tasting the word. There was a powerful air of unreality about all this. The winds of chance were blowing.

Two weeks ago he'd been plain Candidate Oak, clad in patched Ironhall castoffs, riding on Starkmoor with his friends. One week ago *Sir* Oak had been watching the finals of the King's Cup in the royal presence. That sign of royal favor had even persuaded the Guard—which regarded the cup as its private property—to forgive Beau for winning, while hinting he had better never do it again.

Then had come a voyage on a real ship to Isilond. In the tavern last night Oak had spoken Isilondian to Isilondian girls and understood their replies. Of course it had been quite obvious what both sides wanted, and there had been satisfaction all round. He'd become quite good at that already.

Oak was the son of a fisherman. When the winds of chance had wrecked the fleet and left his village bereft of both men and boats, he'd been too young to earn his bread in a village full of orphans just like him. The local apothecary had gathered up a dozen and taken them to Ironhall, begging that at least some be granted refuge. Grand Master had accepted only one—although he had given the rest money when they left.

The winds of chance had almost wrecked Oak again, last year, when he fell on rocks with his horse on top of him. He'd really expected to lose that leg, and been quite certain that his fencing days were over. In the end it had all worked out for the best. Things usually did if you let them.

Like his name. The sword of an earlier Sir Oak had been Returned while he was still the nameless Brat, and the juniors had decided that "Oak" suited him. He'd agreed rather than argue, and been Oak ever since. Now *Sir* Oak. He had named his long sword, though—*Sorrow,* he called her. She was deathly beautiful, but he hoped he would never have to draw her in anger.

He was considering growing a beard, a great black bristly monster of a beard. The fiercer he could look, the less chance that he'd ever actually have to hurt anyone.

Behind the coach, Arkell was equally content, riding along in his stylish red and brown livery. One of the heralds had been impudent enough to disapprove of that color combination, and Arkell had enjoyed pointing out that his ward's family had been using it for centuries before there had been any upstart heraldic colleges around to complain.

Riding a fairly decent horse on a day like this, with *Reason* at his thigh and a whole world to explore, life veered very close to perfection. He was heading for the greatest city in Eurania, many times larger than Grandon, just as Isilond was a much larger land than Chivial.

Beaumont came jingling into view, sunlight flashing on his teeth and *Just Desert*'s basket hilt. He wheeled his horse in alongside.

Confident that the knights could not hear him over the racket of their horses and squeaking armor, Arkell said, "Why didn't you warn me last night?"

"Warn you of what?"

"Warn me that the redhead was a fake."

Beau looked pained. "A gentleman never gossips about a lady."

The girl in question had been about as far from true lady-ship as Arkell could imagine, but he had forgiven her little deception when she started demonstrating novelties he had never even read about in a book, let alone experienced in his two weeks of frenzied debauchery. He wondered if she'd introduced Beau to them earlier, but he knew that asking would be a waste of time. He yawned contentedly. "Tell me, brother, would you have stayed at Ironhall if you'd really understood what we were missing? I wouldn't. All those years to make up!"

"About three months in your case."

"You should talk. You can't even raise a shadow on your lip." They shared smirks of happiness. "You happen to know why houses here have tiles instead of honest thatch? And why can't Chivial grow vines like these? It's not much farther north."

"I'll ask the peasants. Any other questions?"

"A million. Why are the cattle brown? Why do Isilondian men wear berets? Are the girls in Laville really as frantic as they say?"

"You can find that out for yourself tonight." Beau's eyes twinkled.

"True. There's a university in Laville. It's *famous,* all over Eurania. Any chance we'll be staying long enough for me to attend some classes? I'll take all the night watches, gladly." The second best part of being a bound Blade was not having to waste time sleeping.

His leader raised a mocking eyebrow. "Isilondian law isn't the same as Chivian."

"Law? Law? Who cares about law? I only read law books at Ironhall because there weren't any others worth reading."

"I doubt we'll be there long enough. I'm appointing you our geographer. I want to know the best route and how long it will take us. And dangers, of course, and—"

"What?" Arkell howled. "He's finally told you where we're going?"

Beau's grin flashed like silver. "No, I just reviewed the evidence and applied logic."

"What evidence?"

"Nothing you don't know, brother, cross my eyes and hope to die."

Beau was superhuman with a sword and as fine a leader as any man could ask for. Solid, dependable Oak was the anchor, the brawn of the team. That left Arkell to do the thinking. If Beau could work it out, he certainly could.

"Will you tell me if I get it right?"

"Don't know what's right, son. I'll tell you if you get where I am." Beau rose in his stirrups to stare up ahead, where the heralds were disappearing around a copse. "Road inspection. Be right back." He dug in heels and shot forward.

What had changed since they left Grandon? Arkell drew his brain from its scabbard. Well, the promising little duchess in Fitain had been hastily married off to an elderly cousin—nudge, wink. Warm cloaks and gloves had been added to their kits at the last minute. The Weasel had crossed the Straits to Isilond and was heading to Laville; that ruled out a lot of destinations.

By the time Beau came trotting back along the line, paused for a chat with Oak, and then returned to Arkell, the expert was ready.

"I'll start at the cradle end," he announced, "because he likes young ones. Sirenea of Garto—she's too young even for Athelgar; won't be bearing for five years yet. The King of Thergy's daughters likewise, *and* the King of Gevily's. We're heading in the wrong direction for those, anyway. Same's true of the girl in Skyrria . . . Why are you leering, brother Beaumont?"

You couldn't trust Beau's face, though. He had it as well trained as his sword arm.

"Me? Leering? Do continue your fascinating discourse, Sir Arkell."

Skyrria? All the way to *Skyrria?* "Princess Tasha," Arkell said. "The Czar's cousin. Fifteen, nubile, and sumptuous, the toast of the steppes. Very strictly reared, virginity guaranteed."

"I can hear the royal drool dripping. Do mention the recent increase in trade . . . Chivian wool for Skyrrian furs, Chivian tin for Skyrrian gold. That's important."

And the politics would fit . . . "Leader!" Arkell said crossly. "In case you weren't watching, we have come to Isilond. To get to Skyrria this way, we'd have to march all the way across Fitain and Dolorth and other great empty spaces on the map. It would kill the Walrus. You go to Skyrria from Chivial on a *ship,* Leader. With sails. A long and dangerous voyage, granted, around Cape Seileen and the Amuels Cliffs, only passable in summer, but that's the way it is done."

Beaumont said, "Ship?"

Arkell groaned.

Numbskull!

"Unless," he admitted, "you have two Baelish thegns for brothers. Not to mention all sorts of childhood friends who are pirates, too." Baelish longships traded to Skyrria, and it would certainly be keeping up a family tradition to steal Athelgar's fiancée. To a Bael ship-lord that would be an irresistible prank.

"Good man. The university will be proud to have you."

"I'll see if I can get into the pastry classes," Arkell said, disgusted. "At this rate we'll die of old age before we get home."

Beau nodded—frowning, joke over. "Quite likely. Brother, I fear that we have fallen into an epochal, almighty royal bungle!"

Arkell's day was suddenly not sunny any more. This was real, not just one of Ironhall's bloodcurdling case histories. Few of those had happy endings. "Bungle? How bad?"

"It's a rook's nest. Vicious warned me it might be. The King was so obsessed with keeping the business secret that he planned it all with Wassail and took no counsel from people with any real experience. They did it on horseback, riding in the woods so they could not be overheard! Athelgar's a *Bael!* He doesn't comprehend land travel. Wassail's a farmer and won't argue with him anyway. Obviously neither of them had the slightest idea how far it is to Kiensk."

Arkell didn't either, except that Skyrria was on the other side of Eurania. "Long!" he said vaguely. "And hard. We'll have to detour around deathtraps. Fitain's a swamp of semi-independent baronies and Dolorth an outlaw's paradise, with no governance at all."

Beau grinned mirthlessly at the prospect. "If you have any helpful suggestions, speak up."

Arkell thought for a while and then said, "Let's just go home and tell the King he's an idiot."

✦ 4 ✦

The Chivian Embassy—Lord Haywick's residence—was dark and silent. The ancient porter snored softly on his chair by the front door, and sometimes rafters creaked uneasily as they settled in the night chill. Only in the high-ceilinged kitchen was there life and a little light, where a great brick oven crackled up a recent charge of logs.

At a bench nearby, a skivvy was making the day's bread, mixing dough, kneading it, letting it rise, punching it down, over and over. She would have a score or so loaves ready to eat before the roosters roused the city and the day shift took over and made more. The household ate a hundred loaves a day.

She jumped. *"Oh!"*

"Be not alarmed!" a man's voice said quickly. "I am one of the Chivians who arrived yesterday." He moved forward, stopping when she could see him clearly. "That I scared you is regrettable. I mean no harm, I swear."

His livery was dark and outlandish; the hilt of his sword flickered stars. He looked too young to be a swordsman, but that might be because he was short and fair-faced, hair shining gold. He was old enough to be dangerous, certainly.

"What are you doing here?" She was angry at having shown fear.

"Guarding. One of us keeps watch all night. I felt hungry, so I came down to scrounge. My name is Beaumont. What's yours?"

"Isabelle."

"Belle and Beau! This is a most fortunate fit."

There was something strange about the way he talked, but she liked the lilt of his voice. Maybe a voice mattered more in the dark.

"Why do Isilondians hide their most beautiful women in dark—"

"Stop! My lord, I am on duty and an honest woman. You keep your sweet words to yourself."

He shrugged. "I can't do anything else. I'm spelled to be loyal to the Conte de Wassail and can do nothing that may harm his interests. I cannot run around attacking helpless servant girls. Not that I think for a moment that a cook is harmless when she has a knife within reach. Here, let me help." He stepped forward, rolling up his sleeves.

"Keep away!" She snatched up the knife and backed away. "Stop! What are you doing?"

It was quite obvious what he was doing. He pushed the dough with the heels of his hands, lifted the flattened part, folded it over. Again. Over and over.

"You've done that before, monseigneur!" she said uncertainly, amazed to see a gentleman working like a drudge.

"Not for a long time." He grinned impishly. "I'd forgotten what hard work it is. And I am not a seigneur. I am not even a real chevalier. My friends call me Beau, which is most appropriate. Why don't you start the next batch?"

His hands were bigger than hers, and stronger. He was skilled. Intrigued but still frightened, she took up the next bowl, checked the yeast, and began to mix flour in with her wooden spoon.

"Tell me about yourself, Belle."

"What is to tell? My family is poor. My father died, my mother is old, and I am the last of many. And you?" she asked shyly.

"Nothing to tell, either. My father died years ago and my half-brothers locked me up in a kennel. Just escaped last month. This could stand now."

He set the dough to rise beside the others, then took the

bowl from her to finish the hard mixing. She fetched an ear-lier loaf and punched it down to knead again.

"I will have all my work done so soon that Mistress Gon-tier will give me twice as much to do tomorrow!"

"Then I will help you again tomorrow." He flashed his little-boy smile. "Is it not nice to have company?"

It was if you trusted the company, smile or not. "Of course, my—"

"Beau."

"Messire Beaumont!" She thumped the dough hard. "Chief Cook Gontier would dismiss me if she knew you were here."

"Why? I am very cheap labor for her."

"I should not encourage you." Her mother had *especially* warned her against beautiful men.

"You haven't so far. When are you off-duty?"

"Never! I know what rich young men want when they come lurking around a working girl while she is alone. Please, monseigneur! I need the job and the money. My mother cannot work now. Please do not get me in trouble."

To her shame, she wondered what she would say if he of-fered her money—a lot of money, of course. A very great lot of money.

"I will get you in no sort of trouble, Belle. Would you walk with me later? I need to learn my way around the city. Will you show me? Name the streets, point out important places?"

She imagined herself strolling along the avenue on the arm of a very handsome, golden-haired swordsman . . . run-ning into someone she knew? Should she laugh or cry?

"Never time off! I work and sleep, no more. Once every three weeks I go home to Deuflamme to visit my mother. I'm an honest girl. I know all about swordsmen. Mistress Gontier warned us. You all think you can do as you like with women."

"Absolutely. I flutter my lashes at them like this and they collapse at my feet." He blinked idiotically at her until she laughed. "I would offer you money to be my guide, but you would suspect me of terrible things. Please, just this morning, as soon as it's light, go for a walk with me? No dark corners, I promise."

To refuse might provoke him to anger, to accept would start something she must not start. "I'll see."

"It was you who almost took out Hercule's eye?"

"Who dared say that?" Truly, this swordsman was a wagonload of surprises.

"Several people. He tried to kiss you in the laundry. I ask a lot of questions."

He began asking more of them, while still kneading the dough with deft, hard thrusts of his hands. How many people lived in this house usually? How many extra had Monseigneur Haywick hired recently? Who went in and out by the back door at night? Many, many more. Twice he broke off as if listening, then darted out of the room, going like a cat, silent and fast. Each time he came back laughing, to say it had been only someone using a chamber pot. She had heard nothing.

But suddenly all the bread was rising and she had no more work to do for a while. She began to tidy up, then remembered.

"You said you were hungry. What would you like?"

"Anything."

His jerkin was streaked with flour. She reached out a hand to brush it, and remembered just in time who she was, who he was.

"No, I can make you something." She looked away as she added, "Let me? I never get to do any proper cooking here, just bread."

"An omelette, please."

She took down a pan and set it on the bricks. "How many eggs?" She turned toward the larder.

"Twelve."

She hung the pan back in its place and took a bigger one. "That's a very big omelette."

He shrugged happily. "This is spring, so there are eggs. When there are eggs, I eat eggs."

She returned with twelve eggs in her apron. "What else do you want in it? Cheese? Shallots?"

"You don't tell me how to kill people, Belle, and I don't tell you how to make omelettes."

She was shocked to realize that she was smiling.

◆ 5 ◆

𝓛ord Wassail did not approve of Laville. No city should be so big and so . . . unpredictable. Most of it was comfortably traditional, like Grandon—poky alleys winding between high buildings, all tight-packed inside ancient walls. That was how a city should be, but whole sections of Laville had been ripped down, or burned up, and replaced with gigantic baroque palaces and open paved areas like gaps in an aging set of teeth.

Not that he was able to concentrate on the scenery much as he was being driven to the elementary. Every jolt of the coach rekindled the fires in his foot. The colic was flaring up much more often these days, too. He could only hope the foreigner conjurers would know what they were doing.

When he arrived at the elementary, he did not approve of that, either. Elementaries should be small and intimate, dim and mysterious, suitable for the solemn invocation of spirits. This one was vast and bright, with every wall carved in fancy curlicues, tinted with gilt and enamel—and all eight walls were the same, so far as he could see, except for the one with the door. Ornate tiling on the floor almost obscured the octogram itself. How were simple elementals to know where to go?

Four stout porters lifted his carrying chair from the coach to bear him in. White-gowned conjurers fussed around. They insisted on removing his cloak, jerkin, and doublet and laying ears on his chest.

"Gout!" he roared. "In my toe! That is not where I keep my toe."

"The toe has some gout," the ancient chief healer agreed, "but it is the enlargements of the heart that give concern."

"Bah. Colic. Fancy foreign wine doesn't agree with me."

"To treat the gout one must oppose the heat spirits with those of the water, yes? But the heart requires the heat and the water elementals and the time elementals, and a strong revocation of the death elementals." They went into the usual mumbled conference, with much rolling and unrolling of scrolls.

The mousy Blade, Arkell, was standing against one wall. Wassail waved him over.

"Where's Commander Beaumont?"

"I do not know, my lord."

"Sir Oak?"

The kid squirmed. "I believe they are together, my lord, but I'm not sure where."

"Hmmph! I have instructions for Beaumont. I'm to wait upon His Highness at the palace tonight."

The boy smiled, comfortable again. "Leader has already warned us. We look forward to the honor of attending you, my lord."

Beaumont had been present yesterday when the herald delivered the summons—standing in a corner playing statue, but obviously his ears had been working like well-whipped churls. "I have not informed him officially. I will not have you Blades eavesdropping and gossiping about what you overhear!"

The boy raised his shaven chin defiantly, exposing a lumpy neck. "Blades never *gossip* about their wards' business, my lord! He told Sir Oak and myself so that we could be prepared, looking our best. None of us would ever mention your plans to outsiders."

Wassail grunted. The conjurers were still arguing. Had they never seen a gouty toe before?

"When I leave here, I will visit Sir Dixon at the camp."

"As you wish, my lord."

"But I pay for three flame-and-death swordsmen, not just one doe-eyed boy. What sort of protection are you, mm?"

The doe eyes tried to look wild-boarish. "A Blade. Whoever they are, they must kill me to get to you."

"Wouldn't take much. Why isn't Commander Beaumont here?"

"I honestly do not know, my lord."

With that Wassail had to be content.

Seeing the conjurers moving to their places, about to begin, Arkell beat a hasty retreat out of the octogram, over to the wall, but that was still too close for him. Long before they rose to full chant, armies of goose bumps were racing up and down his skin as if he was buried in an anthill. He was sensitive to spirituality. At his binding he'd been twitching so hard that Wassail had almost missed his heart and killed him.

He wished the spirits of chance had given him an easier ward than the Weasel, and yet the old monster had some admirable qualities. Neither his fanatical loyalty to his King nor his courage in the face of pain and ill health ever wavered.

Where were the others? When Arkell had returned to the

embassy house at dawn—after a memorable and expensive night off—he had found Oak on watch. Oak had said Beau had discovered the most beautiful girl in Isilond in the kitchen and taken her for a stroll. Good chance to him!

But . . .

But the Weasel was on the King's business in a foreign city and his Blades were very green. Prudence would dictate that at least two of them, if not all three, should be in attendance on him whenever he was out of the house. If Prudence didn't, Grand Master certainly would. Arkell suspected the venerable Lord Roland would come close to mayhem if he knew what Beaumont was doing . . . or not doing, rather. Lord Weasel was obviously of the same opinion.

It wasn't Arkell's fault that he didn't look fierce! He was good by Ironhall standards, and that meant stupendous by anyone else's.

He shivered and shivered, wishing the conjuration would end.

When it did, Lord Wassail began bellowing for his boot. He then called Hagfield—who had brought the boot but no sock—every sort of idiot known to four languages and ordered him to give up a sock of his own. Leaving the man to pay for the cure, the Walrus stormed outside to be heaved up on a horse. Arkell barely had time to spring onto his own mount before they were off, just the two of them.

Wassail rarely went slower than full gallop, even in the sweaty congestion of a city like Laville. He had no interest in sightseeing, but Arkell was fascinated by the dramatic new government buildings and aristocratic mansions—stone edifices poking up through the old timber and thatch like a child's adult teeth growing in. Pigs and chickens still scavenged, of course, and the streets badly needed a good downpour to clean away the garbage, but Laville was a more

impressive city than Grandon. The poor had migrated outside the gates, and the poorest of all lived in hovels a full
league from the walls.

The meadow provided for the Chivian's camp lay beyond
even them. There Sir Dixon had set up a military-style camp
with the precious wagons in the center—no ambassador
traveled without sumptuous gifts to distribute. The banneret
was almost as old as the Walrus, but otherwise as different
as possible. A laconic strip of well-used leather, he had lost
an eye campaigning in Wylderland a generation ago. In the
Blades' opinion, which had not been solicited, he was long
past his best and chronically lacking in imagination.

Wassail dismounted to speak with him, which was a tac-
tical error, because a man with no manners was safer on
horseback. Although he was still not revealing his destination to anyone, he had realized that he was never going to
get there with teams of oxen. Yesterday he had ordered
Dixon to obtain horses and mount everyone and everything.
Apparently he expected to find this already done.

"Mounts hard to find, my lord, good ones." The old soldier was almost as laconic as Commander Vicious.

Wassail's setting-sun face always waxed larger and redder at
the least hint of defiance. "I wouldn't pay you if it was easy!"

"Lot of the men can't ride."

"They can learn!"

"Who can?" bellowed a crusty old man-at-arms behind
him. The camp had gathered around to listen. Shouts of
agreement began boiling into riot. Pikemen and archers had
not been hired to ride horses, and what about their women
and children? No one had mentioned the far ends of the
earth. Even the other knights protested the change, without
quite explaining why—possibly because riffraff were harder
to look down upon if they were mounted. Soon Arkell
thought it wise to draw his sword and step closer to his ward.

The sight of sunlight flashing on *Reason* calmed the babble and made the hecklers back away, like ripples on a pond. He realized that he was actually being a Blade, facing danger, doing what he had been training for all these years.

Ignoring the aborted protests, Wassail announced he would investigate nearby stud farms in person. He clambered back on his horse and set off at a gallop with Dixon, plus of course Arkell. As the banneret had implied, the only mounts offered for sale were hacks discarded by livery stables. Any decent stock belonged to the Conte de This or Chevalier de That.

Some hours later—tired, filthy, hot, and evil-tempered— King Athelgar's envoy returned to the embassy and learned that several visitors had come looking for him and not waited. Beau and Oak were still missing

Furious, the Walrus settled down in a small dining room to eat and drink. He was joined in both by Pursuivant Dinwiddie and in the drinking by their nominal host, Lord Ambassador Haywick. The Pursuivant was a gangly young man who wore eyeglasses all the time, even in public. They, and a total lack of chin, made him resemble an excitable cod. Haywick was as pasty as unrisen dough, too young for his responsibilities and too old for his permanent air of sulk. Lacking an invitation to sit, Arkell stood in a corner and salivated.

When a visitor arrived to see the Weasel, he ordered his companions out of the room. Haywick and Pursuivant went meekly. Arkell refused and had to endure a furious tirade from his ward; he still refused. The same thing happened repeatedly during the afternoon. A courier dressed as a merchant brought dispatches from Grandon, and two genuine merchants delivered items of jewelry fit for a queen. Two more callers were old personal friends, who cackled to his lordship in a north-Chivian dialect that totally defeated the

conjurers' gift of tongues. The most intriguing were anonymous characters who just delivered letters, which Wassail
read and stuffed in a pocket.

Neither Beau nor Oak had appeared when the time came
to prepare for the Regent's reception. Arkell was in a cold
sweat, Wassail a seething fury.

"This is not the service I was promised, boy! Special permission, the Ambassador negotiated—special permission
for me to bring three armed men into the Regent's presence.
That is no small honor, a sign of respect to our noble King.
I will turn up with only one, and a weedy stripling into the
bargain. What sort of insult is that? If I had my way I would
run you all off—after a good whipping apiece, I might
add—but I realize that I cannot. I certainly do not intend to
squander His Majesty's bullion on you so that you can go off
carousing or wenching when you ought to be on duty!"

"I cannot believe they are doing that, my lord," Arkell said
loyally. "I only hope that they have not fallen victim to foul
play." He kept thinking of the sinister de Roget, who had
been so shamed by Beau.

"If they did," the Walrus roared, "then they weren't much
good to start with, were they? We'll talk about pay again in
five years, boy."

With that he stomped off to his chamber. Arkell followed.
He grabbed his own kit on the way and changed in the same
room as his ward, who continued to growl and bark at him
without stop.

✦ 6 ✦

𝕿he narrow alley between the house and the mews was
crammed with horses and people. Sir Dixon and his knights

had arrived to escort the Walrus to the palace in style, and
the band was attempting to line up to lead the parade. Paulet
struggled to keep Lord Haywick vertical on a very miry,
slithery surface when all the horses seemed perversely intent
on backing into him. Hagfield trod at Wassail's heels, still
making adjustments to his lordship's attire, Pursuivant Dinwiddie in his tabard was flapping codlike as always, and
Percy and Kimberley were resplendent in their footman livery. Master Merrysock had come to see everyone off.

To Arkell's unbounded relief, Beau and Oak were there
also, both out of breath as if they had been running. He had
no chance to question them before Wassail let rip, making
horses twist their ears and hands widen their eyes.

When his ward paused for breath, Beau responded with a
look of dismay. "I am distressed that you are dissatisfied, my
lord. In what way did Sir Arkell fail in his duties?"

Wassail made incoherent noises, but he was not the first
man to be caught off-balance by Beaumont. He could neither complain that he had been murdered in his senior
guard's absence nor accuse him of not being available for
the audience, because he was obviously available now, if
somewhat sweaty and rumpled.

"You are the one who failed. In future you will not be absent
without my express permission or there will be a new leader! It
is time to go." He lumbered over to the waiting carriage.

Arkell said, "Where—"

Beau cut him off with a wink. "You ride behind his lordship. Oak will go in front." Then he disappeared into the
melee, and that was the last Arkell saw of him until the procession was under way, clattering along echoing streets so
narrow that pedestrians had to flatten themselves against the
walls, shouting protests.

Beau brought his horse alongside Arkell's and said,
"What trouble did you get into today?"

"Me? Trouble?" Arkell reported on the day's non-events.

Beau's eyes twinkled like silver spoons. "Good. Enjoy yourself at the palace. Oak has the sash."

"What? Where are you—"

Leader turned his horse into a side alley and was gone.

"Where is Commander Beaumont now?"

Arkell had read about men's faces turning purple but had never seen it happen before. Fortunately, the Walrus was Oak's problem now, not his. The parade had reached the palace right at sunset, as agreed. Heralds and trumpeters stood ready, the honor guard awaited. Among the pillars at the top of the steps lingered a dozen or so young men in the gold and purple livery of the Household Sabreurs, complete with flamboyant purple cloaks and gold-hilted swords.

Watching.

Even the imperturbable Oak seemed to wilt slightly in the sunshine of his ward's wrath. "Leader said to tell my . . . your lordship that he thought his presence might be con . . . con*stru*ed as provocation."

Wassail already had his mouth open. He closed it and then said, with a trace less belligerence, "Provocation? Of who? Why?"

"The King's Cup, Your Excellency. The Regent sent the champion of Isilond to compete—the Conte de Roget, a relative of his. He met Sir Beaumont in the qualifying round, my lord, and lost." Oak's honest, simple face registered unadulterated sincerity.

This time the Weasel's mouth opened and closed several times as if he were debating with himself the merits of various responses open to him. In the end he just pocketed his anger for later use; spinning around and charging up the steps without a word.

His Blades hastened after him. Flashing a sideways grin,

Arkell received no quiet smile of success in return. In fact, were it not an oxymoronic notion, he might have thought that Oak was worried—Oak, who had cracked jokes when his leg was bent like a dog's and only a tourniquet was keeping him from bleeding to death. Perhaps he was just overwhelmed at being acting leader for the first time.

They were in for a long night of boring pomp and protocol, but nothing worse than that. Except famine. Arkell had not eaten all day.

The royal palace was adequately spectacular and opulent. The pomp was everything he had feared. And yet . . . He could not put a finger on what bothered him.

The two peers followed the heralds, Wassail keeping a firm grip on Haywick's elbow. Arkell walked behind his ward's left shoulder with Oak's uneven tread going *dib-dab, dib-dab* on his right. The knights clanked along behind. By halls and stairs, gilt and marble, frescoes and mosaics, they paraded to an audience hall where flocks of butterfly and peacock courtiers flanked a center aisle running clear to the throne. Trumpets sounded again. Soft hands applauded the distinguished visitors.

Arkell's sense of wrongness clenched to a fist. This was all *froth,* he reminded himself. Everything of importance had been agreed months ago between Master Merrysock and some Isilondian flunky. Wassail had been promised safe conduct. Chivial and Isilond were on good terms at the moment, ganging up on Thergy in every way short of open war. Nothing could go wrong.

Yet something was not right.

The Duc de Brienne, Regent of Isilond, nested on the throne in a splendorous plumage of furs, silks, and jewels. Head thrust forward like a vulture's, scaly hands resting on the head of an ivory cane, he smiled amber teeth in a face of leather. De Brienne enjoyed a reputation for duplicity noteworthy even by the standards of wicked uncles. No one seriously expected the infant King ever to come into his inheritance.

A guard of a dozen Sabreurs stood around the throne, but in relaxed, informal stance to show their importance. Three were big men and two had scars; none had both. Possibly de Roget had been banished from court in disgrace, but Arkell assumed there were more Sabreurs in the offing. Determined not to gawk at the scenery like a hayseed, he risked one quick glance around and identified the wrongness: there was not one woman present. What sort of boy games did that portend?

Oak was chewing his lip, which was understandable. Arkell was fidgety, too, seeing so many swordsmen close to his ward.

To everyone's relief, His Excellency Ambassador Lord Haywick managed to carry off his part in the ceremony without disgracing himself or his King. He presented the visitor by the correct name. There was much bowing, advancing a few paces, bowing again. Credentials were offered and accepted. Wassail conveyed Athelgar's best wishes and a companionship in the White Star; in return he was inducted into the Order of the Silver Rose.

The nonsense ended with him two steps down from the throne and his Blades still at floor level, ignored. Even in Grandon, Blades were invisible at court functions. Dixon and his knights had halted much farther back and been submerged in the shifting tide of courtiers.

His Excellency was most welcome, said the Regent.

His Highness was exceedingly gracious, said the Ambassador-at-Large.

The Regent trusted that King Athelgar continued to be favored by the spirits?

The Ambassador was awed by the beauteous land of Isilond.

If there was anything at all that His Excellency needed . . .

Wassail needed a thousand first-class horses, both mounts and sumpters, with handlers and tack. He could probably get by on a couple of hundred if he must, but this was neither time nor place for real problems. This was froth and glitter time, sweet-talking time. That monstrous mass of fat and gristle, who normally seemed to lack the least idea of courtesy, could behave like a studied diplomat when he wished. Obsessed by rank, he was obsequious to his betters and rude as a hog to anyone else.

The small talk ended abruptly. The Regent changed tone. "And those are two of the celebrated King's Blades, are they?"

Arkell felt a cold draft on his neck. He thought the whole hall straightened up, as if every man had been waiting for this. The Sabreurs beside the throne adjusted the hang of their swords.

They also adjusted their smiles to convey maximum contempt. The widest possible gulf divided them from the King of Chivial's Blades, who were scofflaws and gutter trash. The Sabreurs were sons of great houses, whose forebears had borne arms for at least four generations.

Wassail's pudding face reddened. "They are but flunkies, Your Highness. Nimble and skillful, but not gentlemen."

"But unbeatable at the noble science? We heard that one of your own men claims to be champion of all Eurania." The vulture peered around in search of riper carrion. "Where is our cousin of Roget?"

A man emerged from the sidelines to make a leg and sweep the floor with his plumed hat. He wore the Sabreur gold and purple, bore a white scar across his right cheek, and was both larger and younger than Arkell had expected.

So the quarry was now in sight, and it was neither Lord Wassail nor his Blades, at least not yet. The hunt was hot on the trail of the Conte de Roget, who had disgraced himself, his Order, his country, his family, his uncle . . . What penalty must he pay? Why were there no women present?

"Ah, yes," the Regent said. "Which one of these two boys gave you lessons in Grandon, nephew?"

"A youth named Beaumont, Your Highness. He is not here."

"My Lord Ambassador?"

Where other men might have cowered in embarrassment, Wassail swelled like a bullfrog. "Highness, my King honored me with three Blades, but I brought only two this evening."

The Duc pouted as if some slight jape he had planned had gone astray. Had he wanted a rematch?

"Stay out," Oak whispered.

Arkell turned his head to say, "What?" and watched in horror as his companion lurched forward a couple of steps. His voice burst forth much louder than necessary.

"If the noble lord wants another lesson, I'll be happy to give it to him."

The constant insectile buzz of the court stopped. Arkell wished he could just faint, or wake up and find he was dreaming. To hear such words from Oak—gentle, good-humored Oak? What was the crazy man doing? This was lese majesty, sacrilege, casus belli . . . it would take years just to read the indictment. If the Regent didn't hang them, Athelgar would. Lord Wassail was purple again, about to have a heart attack. Before he could speak—

"So?" said the Regent. "Another Beaumont, are you?"

Oak thundered ahead. "As a Blade, I'm trash, Your Grace. I've got a game leg. But I could handle *him*."

De Roget's scar had disappeared in his pallor. His hand curled onto the hilt of his sword. "Your Highness will allow—"

"No!" The Regent was smiling again. "Peace, Lord Ambassador! You cannot, Cousin!—you cannot call him out. He
is not a gentleman. Commandant!"

"Your Highness?" The Sabreur nearest the throne advanced a pace. He was stocky and older than the others, but
still trim; he sported more gilt than they, plus an enormous
white mustache. He could be none but the legendary
D'Auberoche, who had turned back the Verouke rebels and
had once reached the finals of the King's Cup, the only non-
Chivian ever to advance so far.

"Your Highness!" Wassail did not know whether to cringe
or bluster. "I deeply regret this infamous behavior. King
Athelgar will certainly hear of it, and on his behalf . . . I wish
to offer . . . most humble . . ."

De Brienne was shaking his head. "No, no. We shall witness this celebrated Chivian style of fencing. D'Auberoche . . . What do you say we let the insolent yokel make
good on his offer, mm? To entertain this noble gathering. A
sparring bout, a few passes? You would officiate?"

Oak had ordered Arkell to stay out. Oak excelled only
with heavy metal—the man was a real dragon with
broadsword and buckler, for example. But de Roget had
made fish bait of Cedric, according to Hazard, and Cedric
had given Arkell some memorable bruises at Ironhall last
month. There was no question that the ranking was: Beau,
de Roget, Cedric, then a wide gap to Arkell, and Oak lower
yet. This was to be human sacrifice.

Beau must have ordered it, but why, for spirits' sake? The
humiliation he had inflicted on de Roget in that unexpected
qualifying-round defeat could not be undone by giving the
Sabreur a chance to thrash a cripple, however much the
spectators might enjoy such a performance. Beau would not
do that to a friend anyway.

The sneers on the rest of the Sabreurs needed no translation. They said that this was what happened if you gave swords to guttersnipes.

"I should be honored to officiate, Your Grace," D'Auberoche announced, predictably.

Whatever was going on, de Roget could not be faking his white-lipped fury. "As Your Highness observes, I cannot demand satisfaction from a hobbling churl. But Chivians hold a ward responsible for his Blade's actions. With your gracious permission, I will demand satisfaction of His Excellency, and accept his champion in his place."

"And I gladly waive diplomatic immunity, Your Highness," the Walrus barked. "No one will be happier than I to see the noble Sire administer a lesson to this buffoon who shames my colors."

All Arkell's Blade instincts screamed warnings. What were the rules here?

"Ingenious," the Regent admitted, "but we cannot sully our hospitality by allowing challenges to ambassadors."

"If Your Highness and my lord of Roget would consent," D'Auberoche suggested in tones as monumental as Grand Master's, "we could designate this encounter a prize fight, in which men of disparate estate may meet without respect to rank."

"Excellent, my dear Commandant! You agree, de Roget? A prize match. Set the terms, Commandant."

Arkell began to breathe a little easier.

D'Auberoche beckoned someone in the background, snapping his fingers. "With blunted swords, the first to score three hits shall win. No striking at the face or groin, upon pain of disqualification."

The lurking Sabreurs exchanged smiles, doubtless noting the lack of mention of masks or plastrons. Serious swordsmen usually trained without protective gear because nothing improved a man's defense faster than bruises and fractures, even when there were skilled conjurers available to heal them. Now de Roget could thrash the insolent yokel for his insolence, but he could win nothing. He was matched against the court jester with his uncle playing lord of misrule.

"Will Your Grace honor us by putting up the stake?" the Commandant asked.

The vulture smiled. "Indeed, we shall offer a prize—a side of bacon from the royal estates."

Recognizing their cue, the courtiers exploded in mirth and applause. De Roget flamed scarlet at this further insult. His matter of honor had been reduced to the level of a bout in a rural fair.

Typically, Oak was just standing in place. *Waiting until the wind drops,* was how the fisherman's son always put it. He barely seemed aware that he had been the cause of all the commotion.

• 7 •

Heralds cleared a space before the throne, footmen lowered chandeliers to provide more light, and a side of bacon from the kitchens was laid in the place of honor on the steps. The two fencers stripped down to their doublets and hose. Arkell took custody of Oak's *Sorrow,* taking the opportunity to move closer to his ward; the prospect of swordplay was making him uneasy. The big man twisted around to glare down at him.

"Do you know what that young blackguard is up to?"

"No, my lord." It certainly was nothing ever taught in Ironhall.

"Who's going to win?"

Being honest but feeling disloyal, Arkell said, "Not Oak."

"Certain?"

"Yes, my lord."

Wassail growled low in his throat. "Well, at least that's something! But His Majesty will have much to say on this!"

Doubtless.

The contestants seemed not ill-matched, being much the same age, and if de Roget was taller, Oak gave him nothing in shoulders. Oak might not be as fast, but he could exert incredible pressure when his blade was engaged. Both men were hefting the swords the Commandant had summoned, assessing them. They were narrow, with basket hilts to protect the hands—not as light as the rapier de Roget had been wearing, nor as massive as Oak's *Sorrow,* but obviously intended to represent cut-and-thrust weapons with both edge and point.

Fencing demonstrations in a throne room were a bizarre breach of normal protocol. The Regent had never been famed as a student of the science of self-defense. If his purpose was merely to humiliate de Roget, what in the world was Beau's?

The Commandant called the contestants together for a conference. They listened, nodding but looking only at each other. Then D'Auberoche made them step back five paces and Oak's slight limp was glaringly obvious. They raised swords in salute.

"My lords, you may begin!"

With remarkable rashness, they both rushed forward, Oak moving in a lurching run that Arkell knew from experience to be disconcerting. They were aiming their swords in line, like rapiers. *Clatter!* De Roget lunged and Oak parried with Butterfly, which led into a riposte at quinte—de Roget was forced to recover; Oak advanced with an appel almost too fast to see. *Clang! Clang!* The swords were blurs of light under the candles. Only Beau and Grand Master could analyze swordplay at this level. Still de Roget recovered, Oak in pursuit, giving him no respite. The spectators muttered surprise. *Clang!* Oak was not using Ironhall style, but de Roget tried Rainbow and failed. *How was Oak managing this?* The Isilondian should have sent him to the graveyard already.

Oak beat the Isilondian's blade aside, stepped inside his guard, and grabbed his wrist to yank him forward. Reversing his sword, Oak tapped de Roget on the side of the head with the pommel. The spectators howled in outrage.

"A hit!" He lowered his sword and released his opponent. Both turned to the Commandant.

De Roget was spluttering, almost beyond words. "The head was off-limits!"

"The face," Oak said stubbornly.

D'Auberoche rubbed his mustache thoughtfully. "I did say face. I allow the point."

Courtiers rumbled angrily, Sabreurs glared. The Regent smiled inscrutably on his perch above all others.

"That's allowed?" the Weasel muttered under his breath.

"Dead is dead," Arkell whispered. If Oak had been serious, de Roget would be leaking brains now. But Arkell had never seen Oak try that move before. It was almost as if he had known his opponent was going to offer the opening.

"Ha! A good Chivian can beat any Isilondian any day." Patriotism was winning out over a guest's courtesy.

For the second bout D'Auberoche let them start closer together. "You may begin . . ."

This time they began more cautiously, circling. They were both holding their swords higher, more ready to cut than thrust. Two feet came down in simultaneous appels. *Clang! Clang! Clang!* . . . The Isilondian had grasped the ricasso of his sword in his left hand, making it more responsive but losing his advantage of reach. *Clang! Clang!* He cried out in pain, dropping his sword.

"Monseigneur! I am truly sorry!" Oak cried. "I did not mean to hurt you." He both looked and sounded horrified. Arkell knew he meant it, but the audience might not believe.

Even clutching his elbow in the pose of a man with a broken collarbone, de Roget was a gentleman. "I accept that it was unintentional, Messire Oak." He ground his teeth. "My lord marshal, I must withdraw from the match."

The Chivian knights in the background began a cheer, then the Regent started to clap and the court joined in half-heartedly.

It made no sense! Arkell would have wagered the rest of his life to an hour that Oak was nowhere near de Roget's class. Isilond had no White Sisters, but it certainly had sniffers under some other name and they would be present here, at court. So however Oak had worked his miracle, it had not been by conjuration. Had de Roget deliberately thrown the match? Had Hazard been lying about the Isilondian's expertise? It made no sense at all.

D'Auberoche bowed to the Regent. "If you will graciously give the Conte de Roget leave to go in search of a healing, Your Highness? I declare Messire Oak to be the winner."

Oak looked confused, uncertain if he should march over and claim the bacon. The Regent beckoned, and he lurched forward and knelt.

"Your expertise amazes us all, Messire. Is every Blade so invincible?"

Oak actually blushed, perhaps the first man to do so in that palace since it was built. "Oh, no, Your Highness. And I'm not that good, not really. Not usually. Commander Beaumont is. He has been giving me some personal coaching." He pulled a woebegone expression. "I am sorry I hurt Lord Roget."

The vulture frowned, pondering, then said, "We see," as if the view distressed him. If anyone in the room had a mind devious enough to understand the real game, it would be the Regent de Brienne. Arkell certainly did not, although now he knew where his fellow Blades had been all day.

"We shall spare you the bacon, Chevalier," the Duc said acidly. "You have entertained us too much for that. Chamberlain, give this stout lad a purse of gold."

A state dinner followed. Arkell had been warned often enough at Ironhall that most of a Blade's working life was uttermost boredom, but no one had mentioned torture. He stood with Oak behind their ward, and their stomachs rumbled in duet. Beau would forget meals when he was doing something important.

The Regent's table was larger and set higher than Wassail's, but both were heavy laden—soups and roasts, fritters and fish, pots of savory-smelling purees, pastries and breads, enough to feed the entire court. The entire court stood and watched, while the host and guest of honor sat and ate. When the vast spread had grown cold, it was removed and replaced by a second course, as varied and excessive as the first.

The second course was removed and a third produced—roast piglet, a dish of lampreys, roast peacock with its tail replaced . . .

Wassail gorged. The Regent ate almost nothing. Their conversation was drivel. But, oh, the food . . . !

When the candles had burned low, long after midnight, Arkell found himself out in the soothing night air of the courtyard, under the stars. Amid the sparkle of lanterns, the familiar sounds and scents of horses, he watching the all-too-familiar sight of his ward's massive hindquarters heaving up into his carriage, with Oak assisting. Lord Haywick had been loaded aboard earlier.

"Chevalier?"

Arkell turned to face the grandiose white mustache and even grander attire of Commandant D'Auberoche. He had not seen the legendary Sabreur so close before, had not realized how sharp were the man's eyes, or dominating his presence.

"My lord Commandant?"

"Do you happen to know where Messire Beaumont is now?" The old warrior's voice was low but carried razor-sharp authority. Beside him stood the Conte de Roget, apparently healed of his injury. His face gave away nothing, either, although his scar stood out in bolder relief than earlier. There were more Sabreurs at his back.

"I regret that I do not, my lord." If he was wise, Arkell thought, Beau would be riding like a madman for the border. Alas, a Blade could not desert his ward.

The old man's voice sank even lower. "I very much want to meet him."

"And I am anxious to renew our too-brief acquaintance," de Roget added.

"I am sure he would be honored beyond words to meet all your lordships." One at a time, preferably, but that might not be what was intended.

"Will you tell him, when you see him, that the Conte de Roget and I, and a couple of friends, will wait upon him tomorrow at noon?"

Arkell's heart fell to the mire of the cobbles. "Of course I will so do, my lords."

D'Auberoche smiled. He and de Roget nodded the merest hint of bows to the guttertrash Blade, and withdrew into the darkness.

✦ 8 ✦

Wassail did not approve of Isilondians' sickly, bland cooking, nor their thin, insipid wines. A slab of roast boar and a horn of ale were a man's proper fare! Nor did he approve much of his coach companion, Haywick, who snored all the way home—the boy had no head for liquor, and an envoy needed that more than almost anything. The King must be told of his incompetence.

The Regent was impressive, though—a fine aristocrat with centuries of noble ancestors. The Silver Rose now adorning Wassail's cloak was a great joy. He had been secretly hoping for the Silver Rose *with Dewdrop,* but few of the oafs in Athelgar's court would know the difference.

In fact, the evening would have been a perfect success had it not been for that idiot young swordsman. Thank the eight that His Highness had been so forgiving! A pox on Athelgar for inflicting those pests on Wassail. The time had come to put those jackanapes in their place.

Back at the embassy, bleary-eyed flunkies helped him dismount and then turned their attention to unloading Haywick. Trailing his two Blades, Wassail stormed indoors intent on murder, mayhem, and high justice. He began with the doddering porter.

"Where is Commander Beaumont?"

He should not have shouted. The dodderer dithered in alarm.

"Er . . . Who? Oh, the young man with the sword? Er, I do think he's in the residence . . . yes, my lord. He said you was to go to him as soon as you returned, my lord."

"*Go* to him?" Wassail turned to the lanky Blade. "Find him and fetch him! Now! And you," he said to the one with the limp, "will explain to me why you made such a boar's nest of my audience this evening, disgracing me, your Order, and your King!"

The kid never flinched. "I was following Leader's instructions, my lord. I'm sure he will be glad to—"

"By 'Leader' you mean Beaumont? I tell you now he isn't 'Leader' any longer. There will be no stuck-up commanders in my guard. You will all take your orders directly from me."

The other one, Arkell, had queried the porter and gone racing upstairs. He now came racing back down again, four at a time. He had a strange expression on his face.

"Leader is waiting in your bedchamber, my lord. I think you had better go to him as he requested. There is a problem . . ."

Stairs were a problem, and having those nimble sword brats flitting around him like midges as he clambered up them only made it seem worse. Wheezing, Wassail trudged along the corridor to the room he had been assigned, which he did not really approve of. He'd accepted it only because it had tight casements and a good, stout lock on the door. He had double-locked that door when he left, but now it stood wide. Beaumont, beside it, greeted him with a smile and a small bow.

"How dare you pry in my room?" Wassail roared. "Where have you been? When I attend a royal function, I expect the leader of my guard to be at my side. From now on—" He stormed past the insolently smiling flunky, into his chamber where Master Merrysock sat in a chair, bound and gagged. Seeing Wassail, he began rolling his eyes, making urgent noises behind the gag, and straining at his bonds. The dispatch chest stood open at his feet, its contents arranged in tidy piles around it.

"I caught a spy, my lord," Beaumont said brightly. "He was making copies of your correspondence."

Totally winded, Wassail sat down. The other two Blades entered and closed the door but he dared not look at them. This was disaster. His Majesty had been insistent on secrecy. And the accursed Blade had to be the one to uncover the traitor . . . for a moment he wondered if the Secretary could be innocent and the Blade the traitor . . . but that was impossible. Absolute loyalty was what Blades were all about.

"How did he get in?" he said hoarsely.

Beaumont held up a knife, the sort of implement every man carried at his belt to use at table. "I presume he used this, my lord. He certainly used it to open your muniment chest. The handle is a conjurement—what the inquisitors call a 'golden key.' "

"But I have such a key!" Wassail's head was spinning. "Grand Inquisitor gave it to me at the King's express command. I know I used it on both those locks before I left."

"Then Merrysock's would appear to be stronger, my lord." Mockery lurked under the sunny smile, of course. "It probably came from the same source. He admits that His Majesty's Office of General Inquiry is one of his customers."

"He's an inquisitor?"

"Oh, not that bad, just a slimebucket spy. This amber rod—he rolled it over the originals to decipher them, copied out the plaintext, and then re-ciphered them again the same way. He admits that he was planning to make several copies of his copies and sell them—to the Dark Chamber, of course, but also to the Regent's Sewer, the Fitanish Embassy, the Gevilian Consulate, and a couple of others whose allegiance he hasn't remembered yet. I have promised him he will."

"Take off his gag. I want to hear his excuses."

"He will use a lot of language unsuited for your lordship's ears, and may waken the entire house. That's why I gagged him. I suggest we take him down to the cellars; there's a good soundproof room there we can use to question him in earnest. As I explained to Master Merrysock, Blades do not approve of inquisitors, so Ironhall teaches us our own fiendish means of extracting answers."

Arkell rolled his eyes in the background.

"So he's read all my private papers? And I suppose you have, too?"

"Oh, no, my lord. Certainly not. I did read his copies of them. They weren't secret then, were they?" Beaumont sighed at the wickedness of the world.

Floundering, Wassail demanded, "Why did you order Oak to throw challenges around in the palace tonight?"

The kid's smile brightened again. "He limps. If even a crippled Blade can beat the best of the Sabreurs, they will be less inclined to cause your lordship trouble, won't they? I have only my ward's best interests at heart. You know that."

Aware that he was losing this battle, Wassail heaved himself to his feet. "Well, from now on, *I* will decide what my interest are, do you hear? Spy-catcher or not, you are dismissed as commander, understand?"

"No."

"What'ju mean, *no?*"

"I mean," Beaumont said sadly, "that every guard must have a commander. That is a Blade rule. If Sir Oak and Sir Arkell conclude that one of them can do a better job as Leader than I am doing, then they can vote me out and I will accept that. But until they do, I am commander of your guard." He came a step closer. "Allow me to ask you this, my lord: Ironhall prepared us to handle almost every happenstance the Order has encountered in four centuries, but it never mentioned a ward who keeps secrets from his Blades. Why, my lord? Why are you not taking us into your confidence?"

"You'll be told everything you need to do your job!" Wassail thundered.

"With respect, not true, my lord. Why were we not informed that your ultimate destination is Kiensk, in Skyrria, your mission to escort Princess Tasha to Chivial? By the eight! Even this worm knows!" He pointed at the bug-eyed Merrysock. "He has known for months. He has told all his employers, every one of them! And you don't tell your Blades?"

Wassail sat down again. He put his face in his hands.

"Half a thousand wild leagues to Kiensk, my lord, and every petty prince and robber baron between here and there is counting the ransom money already. You say this does not concern your Blades? Furthermore," Beaumont added sweetly, "Master Merrysock accuses that boozer Haywick of being on more payrolls than he is."

It was too much, too late. Dawn could not be far off. "Tomorrow we shall look into this," Wassail mumbled.

"As you wish, my lord. Meanwhile, what to do with this offal? We can lock him in his room, or chain him in the cellars, or we can interrogate him thoroughly right away and tip the remains in the river."

Wassail did not look up. "Put him in his room."

The Blades gathered around the prisoner, freed him from the chair, and two of them hustled him away, still gagged.

"He will escape out the window, of course," said Beaumont's hatefully cheerful voice. "Is that agreeable to you? It does seem to be the simplest solution, unless you want him as witness at Haywick's treason trial."

"He should die a traitor's death!"

"Possibly," the boy agreed, "but how can you do it here in Isilond? I frightened him with tales of torture, but I was bluffing. I cannot break the law without jeopardizing my ward. You could summon inquisitors from Chivial, but they will lie to you if he truly is in the Dark Chamber's pay. Let him go."

Wassail was past caring. He needed a bucket of ale and his pillow. "He really confessed to all you say?"

"He spoke at length, graphically, biographically, and autobiographically. His handwriting is evidence."

Wassail shuddered. *A wise man is just a fool who has learned from his mistakes*—so his father had told him, long ago. If he were a wise man, he would have stayed home at Wasburgh to look after the lambing. "You are right, lad. This was good work, and I must learn to trust you."

"Thank you. We aim to please—Ironhall motto. Ah, Sir Oak! Did you get anything to eat at the palace? Tstk! How inhospitable of them! Well, if you will see his lordship safely into bed, Arkell and I will pay a quick visit to the kitchens and relieve you most soon. By your leave, my lord?"

As the two of them hurried along the corridor, Arkell said, "You saw Merrysock use the golden key on the document chest?"

"This is true."

"He then copied out several documents?"

"Still true."

"So where were you while he did all this?"

"Where do you think I was?"

"Behind the bed curtains, probably. You left a smear of mud on the windowsill where you came in."

Beau just chuckled.

Had he been there in his place, Arkell mused, he would have interrupted the thief before he read all the secrets. But then they would not have had the handwritten evidence. He was not thinking clearly—Blades could dispense with sleep, but not with rest, and he ached with weariness and hunger. He needed food and a few hours alone with a good book.

"Did you learn anything interesting?"

"Not much," Beau admitted. "It seems we're to cross the Skyrrian border at somewhere called Dvonograd, and the Czar's troops will escort us to Kiensk from there. Getting to and from Dvonograd safely is the problem. Wassail must have thought horses grow on trees . . . Oh, yes . . . Remember Grand Master wondered why Athelgar couldn't assign Wassail more Blades? Seems the Czar limited Wassail's train to ten armed men within the country and three in High Town, whatever that is."

"The Czar is reputed to be crazy."

"Aren't we all? How was the skirmish at the palace?"

"Bizarre. D'Auberoche and Sire de Roget plan to wait upon you here at noon. And I think the three lovelies standing beside them were included in their invitation."

"If they all want lessons, they'll have to take turns, won't they?" Beau said, unruffled. King Athelgar was not the only secrecy addict in the forest.

"Could you have beaten de Roget in the qualifying round if you hadn't watched him fight Cedric earlier?" They passed under a sconce then, and Arkell intercepted an amused glance from his companion.

"It would have been trickier. As it was, it was tricky enough."

In a reasonably even match, it helped to know your opponent's style. That was why the Guard coached the candidates whenever the King went to Ironhall—the inmates knew one another's quirks too well. But Arkell had never heard of a feat like this.

"You feigned de Roget's style for Oak? You spent all day being de Roget, remembering every ploy and gambit, every parry and riposte he used in those two matches, and imprinting Oak with the correct response in every case, over and over and over. You turned him into a de Roget expert. I didn't think that was possible."

"You never know until you try," Beau said cheerfully. But he had known. He had stage-managed the whole episode. For years he had been Ironhall's teacher of last resort. When a junior mangled his lunge or knotted his footwork, the masters would turn him over to Candidate Beaumont, because he had endless patience and an incredibly swift eye. Yet to recall every stroke of two fencing bouts that had been held weeks ago was pure miracle, even for him.

He reached for the handle of the kitchen door. "Watch your manners in here, brother." His voice lacked its usual banter.

Only one lantern burned in the steamy, airless, dark, and only one hearth glowed. In that patch of light, a girl was kneading bread. She heard the door, looked around, and for the merest instant her eyes lit up at the sight of Beau. Then she turned her face away and went on with her work. But that glimpse had been enough to give Arkell a pang of jealousy. Any man dreamed of having such a girl send him such a look.

The men wound their way to her, between tables, bins, and barrels.

"This is the Countess Isabelle," Beau said. "Your Grace, may I present my flunky, Messire Arkell the Insignificant?"

She shot an appraising glance at them both. Her eyes were black as coal, as was the hair tied behind her head, and both of them gleamed in the lantern light. "Go away! You will get me in trouble."

"Alas, Messire Arkell is in very poor health, my love."

The next flashing glance was directed at Arkell alone, but it held no interest. He was a pale moon next to Beau's sun.

"He looks sturdy enough."

"No. If he as much as smiles at you, he will die instantly. What do you think of my future wife, brother?"

For a moment her hands fell still, then resumed their work.

"Oak called her the most beautiful woman in Isilond," Arkell said. "He meant Eurania, didn't he?"

"Flattery will get you skewered," Beau said, but he looked pleased.

"Away with you both!" she shouted. "I know all about swordsmen and their sugary words. You will ruin me, get me in trouble!"

In the heat of the kitchen she was wearing only a thin cotton sheath, and as she lifted and stretched the dough, it both moved and clung, moved and clung, sketching the body within—teasing, maddening, intoxicating. She was not tall, but full-breasted, with strength in the round, smooth arms. Her face was flushed, her skin shone. Food? Rest? Who cared for those?

Beau pulled up his sleeves. "We are both famished, dearest. Truly, we have not eaten all day. Arkell, you know how to do this?" He edged Isabelle aside and took control of the dough.

"I used to watch my sisters, and I wield a spoon like a saber."

"Another omelette?" she asked.

"For me, certainly. Your omelettes are why I am going to marry you. Arkell?"

"Anything at all, mistress. Feed me or I will eat this dough raw."

"Stop giving me titles!" She clattered a pan angrily down on the hob. "You men all think I am just a slut you can take and enjoy and leave with the baby." She stalked off into the shadows.

"I haven't kissed her yet," Beau told Arkell, loud enough for her to hear. "I haven't even touched her hand. I promised not to until she asks. That's fair, wouldn't you say?"

"I'd say it demonstrates fantastic strength of will," Arkell agreed. Guard legend insisted that a bound Blade could take any woman he wanted, and Beau was no run-of-the-mill Blade. Nor was he a prude, for he had tied a longstanding record in the Guard's traditional rite-of-passage welcome to Grandon. Obviously he was just enjoying the sport, playing the fish on the line, knowing she was his whenever he wanted her.

◆ 9 ◆

Wassail was aware that his normal morning disposition would shame a constipated boar, and this morning he felt even worse than usual. The Merrysock traitor had vanished in the night. Beaumont deflected roars of complaint by saying blandly he thought his lordship had agreed that this would be for the best. Vague recollections of having given that consent brought no comfort.

"He should be hung in pieces around Chivial!"

"Granted, but how could we get him there? You lack power of high justice here, my lord. Would you ask His Highness to deliver him in chains to the quay? You would have to explain why."

Unthinkable.

But Haywick would not escape so easily. Even if he were not guilty of selling state secrets directly, he should have uncovered his secretary's treason long ago. The King must be advised. The Weasel must weasel again, it was his duty.

Which was why Wassail was wasting what was left of the morning vainly wrestling with the problem of writing a report. Quills were no more his weapons than battleaxes. Hoes, now, or pruning shears— He was too old for this mission, and giving in to the King's entreaties had been no true loyalty.

He could order Dinwiddie to write the report, but Dinwiddie had no discretion. He would also take three weeks and produce something in five colors with illuminated capitals.

It is with deepest regret that I must inform Your Grace . . .

The black-haired boy was on watch, standing near the window, sometimes peering down at whatever was creating that infuriating clatter in courtyard; sometimes just standing, smirking at nothing. There were times when the young oaf's vacuous good humor verged on the imbecilic.

"What is so flaming funny?" Wassail roared.

The Blade jumped and almost drew his sword in reflex. "My lord?"

"Why are you *smirking* like that?"

"Oh." He smirked again. "His Highness gave me a fortune in gold last night. I was spending it, as you might say. Dreaming."

"Spending it on what?" Wassail growled, realizing that a single purse of gold might be enough to change a man's life if it was the only one he had or was ever likely to.

"Buying a boat, my lord. I am of sailor stock. I can buy a boat and hire a lad or two. I'll be a rich man in the village."

"After I'm dead, of course."

The Blade's face turned bright red and then sickly pale. He licked his lips and did not reply. Feeling a curious mixture of sour satisfaction and outright shame, Wassail started on yet another sheet of parchment.

Clink . . . clink . . .

The accursed Blades were practicing again. They never missed a day. The weather was glorious and much too hot to order the casement closed. *I regret to announce that I have uncovered darkest treason in Your Majesty's . . .*

But he hadn't. Beaumont had. "Sporting false honors," his father would have called that. *Clink . . . clink . . . I sadly report to Your Clink . . .* With a bellow of frustrated fury, Wassail slammed a fist on the table. Ink leaped out of the inkwell, splattering the fine leather top and the stack of parchment.

Oak limped over to the bell rope to summon a servant. He paused, screwing up his face. "May I offer a suggestion, my lord?"

"What?" Wassail had ink on his fingers and his hose as well.

"Sir Arkell is very good at writing. He knows big lawyer words. He'd be happy to write for you."

"He would?" Wassail said incredulously. "*Happy* to?" The kid was no namby clerk. He'd sat for a sword through the heart.

"Well, you could *ask* him, my lord."

Not order. Ask.

"Call him, then."

The other Blades arrived all flushed and sweaty, Beaumont having come along to see what their ward wanted. Arkell beamed at the request.

"Glad to be of assistance, my lord." He promptly sat down at the table and set to work with the penknife, shaping quills.

The Commander raised no objection. "You want some sharpening now, brother?" he asked Oak.

"I pass. I can't move after yesterday."

"Softie. Leave you to it, then. By your leave, my lord." Beaumont departed.

"You wish to dictate to me or have me draft a text for your approval?" asked Arkell.

"Oh, write it. Tell everything that happened here last night. Exactly. Give Beaumont his due. Explain why we had to let the traitor run away. Recommend that Lord Haywick be recalled to answer questions before inquisitors."

"Then may I begin by writing a report to you from Sir

Beaumont, my lord, which he can sign and you notarize, so that His Majesty may depose it as evidence if he wishes? Then a covering letter from yourself?"

"Whatever you think best," Wassail said stiffly, aware that the other kid was smirking wider than ever.

Arkell muttered, "My lord," reaching for a sheet of parchment. He adjusted his sword so the hilt was out of the way of his arm and began. He wrote at high speed, quill racing across the page, depositing line after line in a clear, scholar's hand. Lots of big words, too. Once in a while he would chuckle to himself. It seemed but moments before he completed the first page and set it aside to dry. He took a fresh parchment and a fresh quill from the tray.

Wassail sifted sand on the finished sheet. He had just begun to read it when Arkell yelled an oath and leaped from his stool. He hurled the door open and disappeared along the corridor with his sword already drawn. Oak had dived for the window to see. Only then did Wassail register the familiar clatter.

Clink . . . clink . . .

Oak straightened up and gave his bewildered ward a sheepish smile. "False alarm."

"What? Who?"

"Some Sabreurs came to call on Leader. Call *on* not *out*. They're only playing."

A few minutes later Arkell returned, equally abashed. He sat down and carried on with his report as if nothing had happened. Down in the courtyard the racket continued intermittently.

By the time Wassail finished reading the three-page report—which was word-perfect and in fair copy on the first draft—Arkell had written half of another sheet. He sat back to massage his writing hand.

"Your letter to His Majesty, my lord . . . may I mention the Regent's remarks about Gevily?"

"What re— What about them?" Wassail vaguely recalled that country being mentioned during dinner.

"His Highness said he was concerned that Gevily is offering too much support to Thergy." Arkell waited for reaction, then hurriedly said, "If Gevily's traditional foe, Skyrria, were to rattle some sabers on the border, that would give the Thergians reason to distrust their Gevilian allies' support. Similarly, Skyrria can threaten Narthania, which will relieve its pressure on the Fitanish princes, so they can join in the Thergian partition, if it happens. He was implying that Isilond welcomes the new alliance between Chivial and Skyrria, my lord."

The devil he was! Wassail shrugged. "Might not hurt. Proves that the accursed spy has told them where we're bound."

What to say about his mission? That was the problem. He had grossly miscalculated the logistics. It would take him months to find enough horses, if he ever could, and the only alternative was to ask the Regent for help, a move that required Athelgar's permission. Add at least two weeks for that to arrive. Add a replacement for Master Merrysock to do the actual negotiating at the clerical level. Add the Skyrrian winter—

Beaumont's odious smile returned. He closed the door. "My lord, Commander D'Auberoche had to depart to meet a pressing engagement, but four of his finest Sabreurs are still here—the Marquis Vaanen, Lords Estienne, Ferniot, and Roget. They beg leave to pay their respects to your lordship."

"What for?" What was the insolent pest up to now?

"A courtesy, my lord!" He sounded hurt. He looked hurt. "They claim to have heard of your efforts yesterday to acquire horses, which is a reasonable excuse not to admit that they have always known your purpose and destination, or at least the Regent has. He must have given permission for this, although his name has not been mentioned. The four Sabreurs are all of the bluest possible blood, sons of great landowning families. They graciously offer to assemble whatever livestock you require, up to a thousand head, and put it at your disposal for the summer. They will also supply squires and custrels who can tend them and wield a lance should danger threaten. After all, they must protect their families' property! I believe this generous offer will solve your transportation problems at a stroke, my lord."

Wassail saw his own stunned disbelief reflected on the other two faces, so this was entirely Beaumont's plot. Whatever it was.

"It's impossible!"

"It's very generous, my lord." His eyes were wide with innocence, mother's milk wet on his chin. "There is no campaign planned this year, so the men and horses would in effect be idle, and this will be a valuable exercise to keep up their skills."

"At what cost?"

The Blade shook his head. "None at all."

On the surface it was the most perfect solution imaginable—the resources of the Isilondian crown put at his disposal without the need for any embarrassing official requests. But there had to be more to it than that.

"It's a trap! I don't trust free cheese in dark corners."

"My lord would question the honor of four of the most powerful and venerated families in Eurania? The Vaanens trace their descent from Varine the Bald, and de Roget's ancestors—"

Arkell's stool hit the floor with a startling crash. He was on his feet, white-faced and furious; and shouting. "Those four precious Sabreurs will accompany us, of course?"

"Of course."

"Traitor!"

Beaumont raised flaxen eyebrows in mock surprise. "Merely a higher loyalty, brother," he said softly.

◆ 10 ◆

"You insult me!" Isabelle said. "I hate you!"

She sat on the slopes of Montmoulin, gazing down at the evening shadows on Laville, the city sprawled around its winding river. It was an evening late in Fifthmoon, one of those breathless, perfect moments with wildflowers and butterflies and one evening star. The grass already bore the summer scent of hay; the only sounds were distant cows bellowing to be milked and sometimes sniggers from other couples nearby.

Beau was hugging his knees. He curled forward to rest his head on them, turning his face to study her. "Insult you, love? Never. How could I?" He knew perfectly well. Merriment gleamed in his eyes like quicksilver.

"For two weeks you say you love me and want to marry me and you have never even kissed me. Not so much as touched my hand!" It had been his idea to come up here. He must know why couples came to the woods on Montmoulin. If he didn't know before he must know now—you could see the grass waving where it was happening. She hadn't quite decided what she would do when he tried, but he hadn't tried, and she would have to go back to work soon.

"I promised I wouldn't until you asked me to."

"It is not for me to ask! It is the man's job to ask."

"It's a man's job to keep his promises. Say you'll marry me."

"No! I won't be bought by lies. You'll deceive me and then run away to find your Skyrrian princess, the Czar's sister."

"Who says so?"

"Everyone knows!"

He sighed and raised his head to study the city. Did he know what a perfect profile he had? He was trim, compact, barely taller than she—a terrier. His features seemed small for a man's and yet too bony to be effeminate. Even his ears were small, set close, no lobes. And those golden curls!

"Czar Igor doesn't have a sister. A sister-in-law, who is also his cousin, a princess of the blood. She is said to be stunningly beautiful. Maybe I will marry her instead. Tasha, such a pretty name."

Isabelle wanted to rip his eyes out, although she had spied on his fencing and knew he was far faster than she could ever be. If she attacked him, would he push her down in the grass and kiss her?

She was *not* going to ask first!

She could be just as stubborn as he could.

"The new Ambassador has arrived. The Conte d'Edgebury?"

"Hedgebury. An excellent man! A knight in my order. He was the most decorated Blade ever."

"You will be gone soon."

"Probably." He looked at her again, and now his eyes were leaden. "You think this is not agony for me, too, Belle? The moment I first saw you I went mad and swore that I would have you for my wife. I have told you that my ward must always come first, for I am bound by oath and by the eight, but you will ever be second, I swear. He is old and cannot live many years. Say yes and we can be married tonight with all the noble witnesses you want—peers of Chivial and Isilond lined up. You think my ward would ever let me break my word? He is a crusted statue of lithic honor. He is so honorable everybody hates him and he knows it. When we leave, you will stay behind in the Ambassador's house as my wife, not just the girl who makes the bread. On our way home we will come back through Laville, I am certain of that. And when I have seen my ward to his home in Chivial, he will never roam again—he swears it. He owns a fair castle, I'm told, and I will give you fine gowns and maybe some small jewels."

She dared not speak in case the wrong words came out. Beau was not boasting. Great nobles called on him every day and jumped to his bidding. Her mother would swoon to hear of such a wedding!

He sighed. "What I really want is not to have to eat in the kitchen."

Oh! *Monster!* He did that all the time—wove a spell and then snapped it.

Yet she was trembling. She ached all through. It would be so easy to whisper yes. Even Mistress Gontier, who had always seemed so fierce, had taken Isabelle aside and asked why she was snapping at everyone. And then—miracle!—she had laughed and said, "Don't ask him to kiss you—kiss him! Kiss him until steam blows from his ears. If he is any man at all, he will take care of the rest."

She put Mistress Gontier out of mind. "You don't even know if I'm a virgin!" If she wasn't, this would be much easier.

"I don't care whether you are or not. I'm not."

She sniggered and felt herself blush. "Men can't be virgins."

"Yes, they can, but not usually from choice."

"How long will you be gone?" She was wavering.

"Months."

"Ha! I would rather remember a lost lover than worry

about a missing husband. Suppose you never came back? Suppose Lord Wassail dies?"

His eyes turned steely. *"He will not!* We will bring our ward safely home to Chivial and the King himself will honor us."

She scrambled to her feet. "You insult me! Go find your queen, you stupid swordsman. If you still want me after seeing her, ask me then." She ran.

He caught up with her easily and jogged alongside. "Is that all? No promises? No understanding, even?"

"Nothing! Ask me again when you return. If you return."

She put her hands over her ears and ran on down the slope.

IV

The Sport of Czars

◆ 1 ◆

Klong-ng-ng! . . . The great bell tolled, the one they called Mother Tharik, mightiest of the High Town carillon. Its knell reverberated through ancient stonework and shivered in listeners' bones. Just as the clouds of panic-stricken doves began to settle on roofs and battlements, another stroke would send them thundering skyward again. Beyond the curtain wall, out in Great Market, a crowd was singing anthems. The Czar had returned! The Little Father had returned. *Klong-ng-ng!* All Kiensk rejoiced.

All Kiensk, that is, with the possible exception of Czarina Sophie, who was of two minds. Last night a razor-thin crescent in the sunset had signaled the start of Sixthmoon, meaning her husband had been gone nine weeks this time—and all those nine weeks she had languished in High Town, condemned to a life of excruciating stupid trivia. When he was in residence, she was wife, empress, royal hostess, but also permanently terrified. Hence her ambivalence.

Igor had returned last night, but he had sent her no word, no summons. Warned by her maids, she had lain awake for hours, waiting for the corner door to open. It had not moved.

Even now, standing at her window looking down on the open square of Great Market, she was keeping half an eye on that corner door. *Klong-ng-ng!* The tolling signified that the Czar was about to hold court, a royal audience. He was probably being dressed in his finery right now, behind those massive, soundproof timbers. Forewarned, Sophie was already clad in her state robes, ready to leave the moment he was. She had sent her ladies-in-waiting out to the Robing Room so there would be no witnesses to the imperial reunion.

She had known for several days that Igor would be returning because all the princes and boyars within two days' ride of Kiensk had been summoned to Court, and the Boyar Chamberlain of the palace had been ordered to prepare a feast. She relished the prospect of greeting family and friends.

The Czarina's floor-length state robes were as massive as the palace itself—layer upon layer of brocade and marten fur. Her ruby-studded hat weighed as much as a baby and its trailing lappets cut off her peripheral vision. Entombed in all these and armor-plated on top of them with jewels and cloth of gold until she was bell-shaped, Sophie felt like a national monument. In a sense that is what she was, a public demonstration of Skyrria's national wealth, the lion's share of which belonged to its autocrat, the Czar.

Klong-ng-ng! The singing crowd now filled Great Market to overflowing. Whips swung as coaches and parties of riders beat their way toward the gates like hares in long grass, terrified of being late for the audience. Kiensk stood on very level ground. High Town was merely the central complex of palaces and other state buildings—fortified, ancient, and labyrinthine. From the lofty viewpoint of her window, Sophie could see over the curtain wall to Great Market, then a rippling expanse of roofs that was the city itself, and finally fields flat as puddles spreading away into distant mist.

She wanted to pace, but the weight of her state robes dissuaded her. The Czarina's bedchamber was large enough to seem spacious although it contained numerous mismatched chests, chairs, tables, and a four-poster that would sleep a family of six. Ancient tapestries on the walls had been crudely cut to fit; under thick smoke stain they depicted strangely clad people in scenery that was certainly not Skyrrian. Sophie assumed they had been looted during some eastern campaign. Moth-eaten bearskins covered the floor.

Hinges squeaked . . . she jumped, but it was the other door, not the corner door. Every lintel in the palace was set so low that even a woman had to bend almost double to enter a room. One good swordsman could hold such a door against an army—and many had in the palace's long and gory history.

The woman who crept in and then straightened up was Eudoxia, Sophie's Mistress of the Wardrobe, childhood nurse, lifetime retainer. The hair under her head scarf had faded from gold to silver and her gait was a flatfooted waddle; she was stupid and ignorant, but devoted to Sophie. She also had courage, fighting constant battles to protect "her" girls from the predatory *streltsy* who garrisoned High Town.

She beamed. "The Princess!" Skyrria had many princesses, but Eudoxia would refer to only one of them that way.

"Send her in, grandmother!"

Sophie struggled forward as if wading through waist-deep snow and met her sister in the center of the room. Finery clattered and clinked. The door squealed closed as Eudoxia backed out.

"Tasha, dearest, how are you? Did you have a good journey? How is everybody? Yelena?"

The Temkins were all fair-colored, in varying degree. Bronze, gold, and silver their mother had called them—Dimitri being reddish, Sophie herself having hair like ripe wheat, and Tasha the palest of all, flaxen with eyes of midwinter sky. Today she wore layered robes of scarlet and royal blue, glittering with a thousand or so pearls. Tasha had always had flair, and had obviously learned how to choose a good dresser. At fifteen, going on sixteen, she was well aware of the overall effect she had achieved.

"Ugh!" Tasha pulled loose. "You are a fearsome collection of hardware, Your Imperial Majesty, like embracing an armory. Yelena's a week past term and *enormous*—it has to be triplets at least." She glanced inquiringly at the corner door.

Sophie nodded to confirm that the monster was probably in there.

"You look thin!" her sister said accusingly. "Are you well?"

"*Thin?* In all this? I am very well. And you?"

Tasha poked Sophie's midriff through the state armor. "Why no bulge yet?"

That was not a matter to be discussed with an unmarried maiden. "I realize I must seem ancient to you, dear, but I still have a few good years left in me. I'm only eighteen! And speaking of bulges—" she poked, too "—how much of *this* is real?"

Her sister sniggered. "Some of it."

"Not much, I bet! Your face is as thin as a sled runner. Isn't Dimitri feeding you?"

A faint smirk twitched the corners of Tasha's mouth. "We Temkins have never been big, Your Majesty!"

Sophie let the smirk go by, unsure of what it portended but certain it would return in due course. "Dimitri is well?"

"Solid as a castle. What does he *do* there? On and off all winter?" She meant Igor at Czaritsyn. "Other women?"

"He hunts," Sophie said vaguely. If Tasha had not heard the rumors about what the Czar hunted, then she should be left in ignorance. "I don't suppose he's chaste, dear, but if there's anyone special, I'll be the last to hear about her, won't I? And talking of being over the hill, my sweet, it's about time we found you a husband. You're older than I was."

Whispers about Tasha's future were creeping around High Town like slugs, but Sophie had not yet felt sure enough of them to mention them in her letters. Left to itself, court gossip would take years to reach the Temkin domain at Faritsov.

The smirk flashed back. Tasha's pale cheeks bloomed a trace of pink. "We do have someone in mind."

We? The little minx was probably leading Dimitri around by the nose now, while Yelena was preoccupied by her pregnancy. At the very least princesses of the blood needed imperial permission to marry, and in practice they were far more likely to be assigned husbands for reasons of state. In Sophie's case, her uncle had merely summoned her to Court and informed her than he was divorcing his third wife and she would be the next Czarina. He had taken her to bed that same night, as if to establish ownership, and had had sex with her again on their wedding night, a month later, and seven or eight times in the three years since. Her primary duty was to be seen at his side so other men might be jealous. Bedtime amusement he sought elsewhere, but Sophie must not say so even to Tasha.

Hiding alarm behind a smile, she eased her sister across to the window embrasure, dragging the state robes. "Has Dimitri talked to *him* yet?"

"He wants to ask your opinion, but if you agree, he's promised to ask the Czar today! Before we go home, anyway!"

"Who?"

"Vasili Ovtsyn!" Tasha was almost bouncing with excitement. The pearls danced. "Prince Grigori's heir! Do you know him? He's *so* handsome!"

"I don't know him well, but he's certainly a fine figure of a man." Now Sophie understood the earlier smirk, but it was an effort to imagine her diminutive sister beside the huge Vasili. The boy lacked obvious merit beyond his unquestioned beef, but he had no special vices that she knew of, and the Ovtsyn family was one of the wealthiest in all Skyrria. "Physically, dear, and financially, Vasili would be hard to beat, but politically . . ."

"What's wrong?"

"You know his sister Natalia has been one of my ladies-in-waiting for the last half year?"

Tasha shrugged, unconcerned. "So he said. I do not recall meeting her."

"You're not that innocent," Sophie said crossly. "You know who chooses my attendants and why. They're hostages for their families' good behavior, no more. So the Ovtsyns are out of favor, maybe even under suspicion. Whose idea was this match? Grigori's, I suppose?"

Prince Grigori was as sharp as his son was dull, far too clever and too rich ever to be trusted by the Czar. If he believed marrying Vasili into the imperial family would protect him from imperial spite, he could certainly offer an enormous price.

A good man on a horse, Dimitri was naive as a newt in politics.

"Suspicion of what?" Tasha demanded angrily.

"Treason, of course. Haven't you heard about Suzdena?"

"There was some unrest there?" Tasha avoided Sophie's eye.

"Quite a lot!"

Back in Fifthmoon, Prince Grigori had arrived in High

Town very agitated, seeking the Czar. Igor had been absent, officially residing at his private retreat, Czaritsyn. The story Sophie had later extracted from Natalia, between sobs, was that a band of brigands had attacked the Ovtsyns' outlying estate of Suzdena, striking in the night to loot and rape. By sheer chance—so Natalia had been told—Grigori and his son had been there, with their usual armed escort. They had beaten off the assault, but there had been casualties on both sides. Alas, dawn had revealed that the brigand corpses wore the wolf-head badge of the Czar's irregulars, the *streltsy*. Such harassment usually signaled that Igor had decided to move against a noble house—hence Grigori's rush to Kiensk to throw himself on the Little Father's mercy.

Worse news had followed. Just a week after the first attack, a much larger force had wiped Suzdena off the map, leaving a few dying survivors to tell the tale. The second assault had been led by a horseman directing a pack of giant dogs. No one would speculate who that might have been.

So Grigori thought he could hide behind Tasha, did he?

Repressing her anger, Sophie gave Tasha another hug. "Darling, how well do you know Vasili, really?"

"We have met several times. He offered me a ring with a ruby as big as this! Dimitri said I should not accept it yet . . ." She managed to fake a little smile. "You know, when he knelt to me, his eyes were still *this* high!"

So Tasha had set her heart on the biggest stallion on the greenest pasture, that was all. She was young. All would be well as long as she was not given time to convince herself that she was truly in love. Sophie said, "Dearest, I haven't dared mention . . . there are whispers."

"Whispers of what?"

"Of making you a queen."

The sapphire eyes widened in panic. "I won't leave Skyrria! You, Dimitri, Yelena . . . I won't go!"

"You'll do as the Czar says, darling! It is no small thing to be a queen. And if it really is Chivial he has in mind for—"

"Who?"

"Not who, *where,* dear." Few Skyrrians knew anything at all about the world outside the nation's borders. Few princes, even, were literate and most women's knowledge ended at their garden gate. At her mother's insistence, Sophie had been taught to read and write. She had learned how books would help pass the lonely hours in High Town, she spoke with foreigners, and she had access to palace gossip. "Chivial is a fine, civilized country, and King Athelgar is quite young, never married. It would be a wonderful match, believe me. Warn Dimitri not to mention this other match to the Czar."

"What match?" rasped a low voice.

It was not Igor's voice. Only Czarevich Fedor spoke in sepulchral tones like Mother Tharik's. (*Klong-ng-ng!*) Rising to his full height in his bulky fur robes he resembled a bear emerging from its den. He was not as huge as Vasili Ovtsyn, but larger than other men; not clever, but sly. In honor of the state occasion he was draped in gold and jewels from his conical leather cap to the spurs on his great boots; the sword and scabbard at his side glittered with emeralds. Fedor was the Czar's only surviving child and Sophie's stepson, one month older than she was. His straggly beard failed to conceal an ugly leer.

Tasha sank gracefully to her knees. Sophie offered Fedor a cold stare; he returned a loutish scowl. In public he had to kneel to her, but nothing would force him to do so in private. He had been with his father most of the winter, reputedly an eager partner in whatever secret horrors went on in the Czaritsyn dacha—and at places like Suzdena.

"Stand up!" he rumbled. "What match, cousin?"

Tasha arose pink-faced. "Your Highness, my noble brother has received an offer for my hand."

Fedor lumbered across to her, going so close that her nose was almost in his beard. *"Who?"*

To refuse him an answer would be insane, yet Tasha just glared up at him stubbornly until Sophie's heart rose into her throat. Then—

"Vasili Grigorievich Ovtsyn, Your Highness. But your royal father has not yet been—"

"Ovtsyn? *Ovtsyn?*" Fedor's thunderous laugh almost drowned out Mother Tharik's next great *Klong!* "That gang of traitors?" He shook his big head in disbelief and glanced at Sophie. "Go in. He wants you." Then down at Tasha again, with a leer that made Sophie wonder if she dared leave.

"You're certainly nubile enough," the Czarevich said. "Looks like you're growing a nice udder in there. *Go, Mother!* He's waiting."

Czar Igor had ruled Skyrria for thirty-three years, outliving two wives and four children. His third wife had been banished to internal exile for the sin of infertility. Since his fourth seemed equally unable to provide him with children, the court did not expect her to last much longer.

He was a bulky, bearish man with a nose like a moldboard plow and an apron of mud-colored beard now streaked with gray and frequently with spittle. However impassive the rest of him might appear, his eyes were never still. He would sit immobile and silent for long periods, slumped in his chair, watching everyone with the glittering scan of a bird of prey. He rarely bore arms, as such, preferring to carry a knout of pleated bull hide, with which he was said to have disarmed several alleged attackers, for one slash of its knotted thongs could shred a man's face.

Mindful of her towering hat, Sophie doubled over lower than usual to creep through into her husband's bedchamber.

She located him standing ahead of her and would have dropped straight into her obeisance had she not been attacked. Something roared and leaped forward. Screaming in terror, she slammed back against the masonry.

Chaos ensued, with the Czar roaring, "Iakov! Down, Iakov!" while heaving on the monster's chain and simultaneously thrashing it wildly with his knout. The contestants seemed equally matched in strength and ferocity, boots and claws sliding and slithering on the bear skins. Teeth flashed, the knout rose and fell. Only when the blows became so savage that they cut through the hairy hide did the snarling turn to howls; the brute rolled over to bare its throat in submission. Shaking as if she had an ague, Sophie looked down on what must be the largest hound in the world. Igor had always had a taste for such monsters, but she had never seen one this size before.

"That's better!" Igor slackened the chain to offer his left hand to the beast, keeping the knout raised and ready to strike in his right. Whimpering, the animal cautiously rolled over and raised its forequarters until it could lick his fingers. "Good, good! Good boy!" He fondled its ears. Whining in pleasure, it nuzzled his leg. Its tail thumped.

"How do you like my little pet, wife?"

"It is magnificent, Your Majesty—worthy of its master." Her heart was still careering wildly around inside her chest. "It would eat wolves for appetizers."

He smiled at that, but Igor's smiles were never welcome. "You know why I love my pets, wife?"

"Because they are brave defenders, sire?"

"Because I can trust them!" Eyes and teeth glittered. "I have enemies, hundreds of enemies plotting and conspiring, and I can trust no one, no one at all—except my dogs. I can thrash them and maltreat them and they still love me. Even Iakov, here. You see how I beat him and yet, look! He kisses my hand. People are not so loving. One word from me and he would kill you—you believe me?"

"Yes, I do believe Your Majesty!"

"Or anyone." He shuddered. "So many traitors! Witches, poisoners! They killed Ludmilla, my beloved. I loved her, loved her!"

"Yes, sire." Sophie braced herself for one of his mad, foaming harangues.

"And Avramia, my little rose. And Melania. Igor, my heir! Alexis—" His gaze darkened. "Well?"

The Czarina hastily remembered her manners and sank to her knees. More cautiously, she touched her face to the hairy rugs, for this move put her dangerously near Iakov's slobbering jaws. There was something unnatural about the way the hound's eyes watched her. It wrinkled its nose in a snarl, but made no sound.

"Your Majesty is most welcome back."

He grunted and bent to fondle the hound as it licked its wounds. "Me and Iakov? Up, then!"

Sophie rose. Her husband did not offer to kiss her.

"Shut the door."

Still shaking, she obeyed. Fedor must have heard the ruckus. Igor had staged the attack for his own and Fedor's amusement, setting the brute on her and then beating it off.

"No child yet?" He was petting the dog, yet watching her too.

"Alas no. I long to bear a child for Your Majesty." That was what a czarina was *for*. Motherhood would be an interest as well as a defense.

He did not comment. "Why was Fedor laughing?"

"My sister . . . mentioned Vasili Ovtsyn as a potential husband, sire."

He glared—face flushing, eyes glittering with fury. "By the stars! They would *dare?*"

"I am sure Dimitri means no offense, sire! If the notion offends you, then he will surely withdraw from any . . . discussion has been very preliminary. It can be canceled."

"Indeed it can. Follow!" Pausing only to unleash Iakov, the Czar headed for the door with the giant hound pacing at his heel.

* 2 *

The only thing worse than being first in line to the throne was being second in line—so the Czarevna Katrina had often told her son, and she must have known, because she had been either first or second all her life, as her brother's various offspring had been born, sickened, and died. The heir apparent had only to grovel and obey, she had said, but the next in line must always be suspected of plotting against both Czar and Czarevich. Twice a child's malady had raised charges of witchcraft against her, with threats of the stake. Innocence was a poor defense, for Igor saw conspiracies everywhere.

From her Dimitri had inherited a hatred of politics, which were bloody anywhere and especially so in Skyrria. With a wife and soon a child to cherish, he regarded ambition as pure folly. He had been sixteen when his parents died, probably from witchcraft, leaving him to care for his sisters and defend the Temkin lands from predatory neighbors and relatives, of whom his Uncle Igor was never the least rapacious. In the dozen years since then, Dimitri had stood second in line behind Czarevich Fedor. His most fervent wish had always been to find some means of shedding that grim honor, some way to renounce his kinship entirely and devote his life to being a simple landowner, husband, and father. Above all, he wished his sister the Czarina would start producing sons—healthy and many of them—for her sake and his.

Up on the dais, Sophie was so bundled inside her vestments that he could not have told if she were as near to term as Yelena. Only her face was visible, a lost waif peering out under a hat like a bejeweled kettledrum. Where was the merry child the Czar had married three years ago?

Igor himself dominated the hall on the ancient ivory throne of Kiensk. The Hall of Columns was very long and wide, but low-roofed and marred by the hundred pillars that gave it its name and ruined its sight lines. Clad in all their greatest finery—brocade robes, jewels, and towering fur hats—the nobility of Skyrria cowered on benches in humble silence, waiting for the Czar to explain his purpose. He was in no haste to do so, preferring to sit and finger the blood-blackened thongs of his knout while his eyes scanned the hall. A monstrous hound lay panting at his feet and black-clad *streltsy* guards prowled through the forest of columns, *streltsy* swordsmen guarded every door.

The throne was flanked, one step down, by two plain wooden chairs, one bearing his wife and the other the hulking Czarevich. Fedor was smirking, enjoying himself. Where Igor was mad but clever, his son was just a brute. It was not true, Dimitri's mother had insisted, that all the Tharik males were crazy, for Igor had been a good Czar until the death of Melania, his first Czarina. Convinced that her fever was caused by witchcraft, since then he had attributed every misfortune to treason—the death of his second wife, Ludmilla, and all his children except one. It was sad chance that Fedor had been the only survivor of the five. Fedor was Tharik male at its worst.

As senior among the princes, Dimitri occupied the center of the front row of benches, facing the throne. He had agreed that Grigori Ovtsyn might sit beside him today, but ever since Tasha had returned from greeting Sophie, he knew that he had been tricked. Fedor was sneering in his direction a little too obviously.

In his long rule, Igor had not extended the boundaries of his empire much, despite many bloody wars. He had met with more success in clipping the powers of the princes and boyars. One by one he cut them out of the pack and cut their throats—sometimes figuratively, sometimes not. If he felt merciful he would merely reduce a victim to poverty. They never dared try to unite against him, for his spies were everywhere—*The third man in a plot is the Czar,* said the proverb. The survivors were gathered there that morning, waiting to hear whose throat was next.

Experienced courtiers looked for clues: Igor himself showing more white in his beard but no obvious signs of ill-health, the Czarevich bigger than ever. Would he never stop growing? Had he been seated closer than usual to his father? Was the Czar about to proclaim him joint ruler? History offered precedents, but Igor was not the sort of man to share power with anyone. The Czarina's chair was farther from the throne than Fedor's, but not so distant as it would be if she were to be set aside. The senior officers in attendance nearby showed all the usual faces and no new ones—the brutal Viazemski, commander of the *streltsy,* aging Chief Boyar Skuratov, Chief Conjurer Ryazan in his somber robes, Imperial Astrologer Unkovskii—and the rest. Doubtless the Little Father would let his children know his purpose in his own good time.

"Eyes front!" Dimitri whispered, for the third or fourth time. Tasha was always a fidget, fingers working endlessly in her lap; today she kept stealing glances sideways along the row, past her brother, past Prince Grigori and his dumpy wife, to where young Vasili loomed like a mountain.

When Grigori had proposed the match, he had admitted he was out of favor and Dimitri would be taking a risk by agreeing, but the Ovtsyn lands were enormous, especially around Sprensk, where the family controlled possibly the largest single estate in Skyrria still in private hands. Young Vasili would have been an acceptable brother-in-law—not the brightest planet in the sky and handsome only in that he was young and virile, but solid and predictable. He had been enough for Tasha, who had not touched the ground since she learned of the proposal. She had seen herself as one of the richest women in the land, with twice as much husband as any other.

Now Sophie had said no, and Dimitri realized that he should have consulted her sooner, but it was hard for a man to seek advice from a woman, and she was not just his sister but his *younger* sister. He had reared her.

"Imperial Astrologer!" said the Czar.

Ancient Boyar Unkovskii rose from his seat on the sidelines, tottered forward, and prostrated himself unsteadily.

"What do the stars foretell for this day?"

With a long, wavering howl, the old man sat back on his heels, and raised his arms high. He could always be counted on for an impressive performance. "Most puissant Czar, whose greatness shines manifestly in the heavens themselves, hear what the planets declare!—Tidings, Your Majesty, great tidings! Tidings of evil unmasked, tidings of great joy to come, and tidings of our beloved Czar's mercy and love to all his children."

The hall buzzed as people tried to make sense of that. A few years ago Dimitri would have been concerned, too, but Sophie had disillusioned him since she came to Court. It wasn't his eyes on the heavens that made Unkovskii the Czar's favorite, she said, but his ear to the ground. Shocked,

Dimitri had taken note and seen that she was right; the old man's prophecies always gave Igor what he wanted.

"Dire evil may be exposed, Mighty Czar!" the astrologer bleated. "But also tidings of great rejoicing!"

He was dismissed; a herald helped him rise and stagger back to his seat.

Igor seemed to reflect, his face revealing nothing. After a few moments, he shook his head sadly and barked, "Prince Grigori!"

The prince rose and walked forward to kneel and touch his face to the floor. Then he sat back on his heels with gray head high and white beard thrust forward, waiting to hear his fate.

"Prince," said the Czar, "you have caused us grievous loss. Your men attacked a company of our noble *streltsy* near Suzdena and took a great toll of them. Why do you not keep your rabble under control?"

"Most Glorious Majesty, I have been misinformed on the events. Pray reveal to us the truth of the affair." That was as close as anyone dared come to calling the Czar an outright liar.

Igor's eyes narrowed. "My men were passing by. Your brigands ambushed them, overcame them by sheer weight of numbers, and slaughtered several. Then they ran amok, torching houses, murdering and raping. It is fortunate that my men were able to rally and restore order, or you might well be facing charges of high treason right now."

Ovtsyn must feel the chill touch of the executioner's ax measuring his neck, but his voice was still strong enough to carry throughout the hall. "Most lenient, loved, and merciful Czar, those responsible mistook your men for mere brigands. They have felt your just anger and paid for their error. How may I make recompense for my negligence in not keeping my serfs better supervised?" *How much will you take this time?*

Igor scowled as if he had hoped to play longer with his victim. "You have lands around Sprensk."

The prince flinched. A horrible wail from his wife suggested instant poverty. Big Vasili tried to hush her.

Ovtsyn blurted out: "Your Majesty—" Then sanity prevailed. Whatever pittance he was being left with would still be better than a grave. His shoulders slumped. Hoarsely he gabbled, "I gladly give them to Your Imperial Majesty as a token of my love and repentance." His wife wailed again.

"Chief Boyar Skuratov will assess them to see if they suffice."

"Your Imperial Majesty is the most merciful of rulers." Ovtsyn lowered his forehead to the floor in submission.

"Your daughter we return to you."

"Your Majesty is most gracious."

"But now we have questions for your son."

"My *heir?*"

"Let him come forward."

Big Vasili detached himself from his mother, and strode forth. He took his time kneeling down beside his father, and waited a deliberate moment before lowering his face to the tiles.

"Up! Right up! On your feet."

The boy rose. Like a pillar. He held the Czar's gaze, which was deliberate insolence; the assembly held its breath.

"You, too, Prince." The Czar scowled as Grigori scrambled up. His head did not reach his son's shoulder. "How is this? How does a pony like you sire a warhorse like that? Did your wife cuckold you with some serf, or is this *witchcraft?*"

The congregation moaned in horror.

"Oh, most merciful lord!" Grigori cried, his former confidence shattered. "Yes, there was witchcraft!" The audience gasped in unison and the archers raised their bows. "But it was long ago, Your Majesty, in your blessed grandfather's reign. It was directed against me. My forebears were all big men . . . my father, my uncles . . . I was a sickly infant, Your Majesty. My back is crooked, as you can see. The witches were caught and burned, but too late to save me. It has nothing to do with Vasili."

The Czar fingered his knout, as if considering whether to send one Ovtsyn to the stake, or both. "Very well. You may withdraw. Your freakish son may be of use."

Grigori backed away, bowing, until he could crumple down between his wife and Dimitri. He seemed a lot smaller than he had a few minutes earlier. The Czar sat scowling at the prince's son.

Vasili was swarthy, with heavy black tresses dangling under his fur cap down to his huge shoulders, but for a barely-bearded youth he was displaying remarkable courage. Dimitri was pleased to see his favorable judgment of the lad being vindicated. It no longer mattered, of course.

"What's your name, boy?"

"Vasili Ovtsyn, Your Majesty."

"That name is disgraced. From now on you will be just Vasili."

Vasili-the-serf balled enormous fists, but spoke calmly. "As Your Majesty commands."

"I heard tell of a giant leading the brigands at Suzdena."

There was a pause, as if the boy contemplated his future and decided he had nothing left to lose. "I was helping defend my father's people from a barbarous and unprovoked assault, sire."

Igor glared. After a moment he said, "So?" disbelievingly.

And then nothing for a while. In the silence, the Princess

Ovtsyn could be heard sobbing. Tasha's fingers were digging into Dimitri's arm.

"*Voevode* Viazemski?"

The one-armed man stepped out from the group at the side of the royal dais, came around to the front—but not too close to the hound—and went down on one knee. Viazemski was a convicted brigand, murderer, and rapist. It was said that Igor had stayed his death sentence and appointed him commander of the terrorists on the understanding that he would be hanged if he ever showed mercy to anyone.

"Your Majesty?"

"Here we have a bold defender who needs someone better to defend. Can you find a place for this lad, *Voevode?*"

"Sire, I'm sure I can make room if I move three or four out of the way." Viazemski was the only man in Skyrria who dared make jokes near the Czar.

"Then, boy, you will be privileged to serve us and expunge your shame." Igor gestured to the dais before him. "Sit there."

Vasili walked forward to perch on the edge of the platform, carefully not turning his back on the autocrat, but still not visibly cowed.

"Closer," said the Czar.

Vasili slid closer.

The dog's ruff rose. It bared its teeth and seemed to gather himself to spring, but the Czar snapped a command and it subsided again, snarling.

"What, are you afraid, little Vasili? Closer!"

The boy's next move left him almost touching the hound. Its snarl grew louder, its whole body seeming to vibrate with fury.

Igor seemed satisfied. "Now we have two staunch defenders, do we not? Can you still see, wife?"

Sophie said quickly, "Very well, thank you, Your Majesty."

Igor surveyed the assembly again. Everyone waited to hear who was next on his list of enemies.

"Prince Griaznoi!"

Igor toyed with his new victim for a while, but settled for appointing Griaznoi's daughter a lady-in-waiting to the Czarina. The terrified girl was directed to sit beside Vasili on the edge of the dais, fortunately on the far side of him from Iakov. Another prince lost his young wife in the same way, and then the Czar took Maliuta Seisse, Prince Seisse's eldest son, to be a gentleman usher. The youth looked even more frightened than the girls as he took his place beside them.

"Noble princes and boyars of Skyrria!" Igor abruptly changed the subject. "Our realm has prospered much in recent years from the trade we have fostered with the distant land of Chivial, thanks to our wisdom in granting Chivian ships access to our port of Treiden. We have now agreed to grant an oft-repeated petition from King Athelgar that we give him the hand of our fair cousin Tasha in marriage. You should consider what gifts you will offer us to celebrate this joyous occasion."

Dimitri heard Tasha gasp before he realized what Igor was saying.

"Smile!" he whispered, turning to her with a big grin of his own, as if he had been waiting for this moment. He kissed her ear. "Even if he's marrying you to that hound, keep smiling." He helped her rise and they walked forward together while cheers and applause echoed through the hall. He was careful not to look at Vasili.

Sophie came sweeping forward to meet them, hands outstretched, and her glowing smile seemed genuine. She gave her sister a hug and Dimitri a quick kiss, then turned to lead them to the base of the throne. Igor was actually smiling into his greasy beard. Usually when he smiled someone was either suffering or about to, but perhaps this time was different.

Tasha prostrated herself. Dimitri made a speech of gratitude for the honor being bestowed upon his sister.

"Princess, you must stay here in the High Town and help the Czarina plan your wedding." Amusement faded into threat. "Your wife, Prince? She was summoned." His fingers started playing with the knout again.

Dimitri said, "She is already past her term, sire. Much as she wanted—"

"Kiensk has the best midwives in Skyrria. Send for her."

"As Your Majesty commands." A very old messenger on a slow horse, Dimitri thought; better that Yelena give birth before leaving Faritsov than in some hedge by the roadside.

"We shall see she is well cared for while you are gone."

"Gone, sire?"

"The Chivian envoys are on their way here to hail their future queen. It is fitting that you meet them and escort them to Kiensk."

Dimitri bowed again as he expressed delight he did not feel. Yet Igor was honoring both Tasha and the Chivians by sending a prince of the blood as his delegate. To Treiden, he assumed. How far away was Treiden? Somewhere up north.

He told himself sternly that the Czar was not being unreasonable in making Tasha come to live in High Town, now she was a dynastic bride. It was even understandable that he would hold Yelena and her baby hostage while Dimitri was near the coast. Igor grew very irate when even the lowliest of his subjects fled abroad. He regarded that as treason and rank ingratitude.

♦ 3 ♦

Two men rode over a stony plain under a sky astonishingly huge. The greatest heat of summer was passed, but wind and sun together could still flay a man, and the horses' hooves hammered on scanty grass, too scorched to make decent grazing. A pitiless glare rippled up from the landscape; sinister whirligig dust wraiths swirled over it like lost demons.

For almost three months the Wassail expedition had trekked eastward, through more types of scenery than a man ever dreamed possible—rich meadows and vineyards in Isilond, then Fitain's craggy hills topped by fabled castles, forests of elm, beech, oak, maple, and linden, and now the sorrowful dry steppes of Dolorth. Life had dwindled steadily. From Laville's splendor they had come at last to charred skeletons of villages, pathetic reminders that war was as common as weather on these grasslands. Even in such seeming emptiness, Monseigneur D'Estienne never let down his guard. Always he kept outriders scouting on every side. These two were returning after reconnoitering to the south.

"The Czar is crazy!" the Marquis said. "He makes war on his own people. He's an autocrat who can do anything and frequently does. You would be insane to trust your ward to the whims of such a maniac. Why are you laughing?"

"Just thinking we should get along well together."

"Who should?"

"Me and the Czar," Oak said. "If we're both crazy, I mean."

"I am serious! Do you doubt that I have only your best interests at heart, my good friend?"

Oak had no doubt that his good friend Orson—His Grace the Marquis Vaanen—was sincere, although perhaps not being completely honest. The strangest of all the strange things that had happened in the last few months was that a fisherman's son from a shack on the rocky coast of Chivial had become fast friends with one of the grandest nobles of Isilond, heir to a name almost as ancient as Wassail's.

Why they so enjoyed each other's company was a mystery. They were the same age, but seemed to have nothing else in common except a love of fencing and a preference for brawny women. Orson was lean and impetuous, a ferret to Oak's badger. His daily income must exceed what a fisherman would earn in a lifetime. He owned several counties, was lord of the high justice and hereditary champion of the queen of Isilond, except there wasn't one of those at the moment. Whereas Oak never regarded himself as more than the junior member of Beau's tiny team, the Marquis's exalted rank automatically made him commander of the entire Isilondian contingent. In practice he was content to let the more experienced D'Estienne attend to tactics and logistics, and the diplomatic de Ferniot handle cranky Lord Wassail. He also acknowledged de Roget as master of fencing, which was the expedition's primary purpose so far as the Isilondians were concerned. Perhaps that very willingness to let the winds of chance blow as they willed was what he and Oak most shared.

As the horses reached the crest of the rise, Oak saw the expedition snaked out across the plain far ahead of them, four hundred men and almost a thousand horses. Orson was still ranting about the Czar.

"He hunts with monstrous, unnatural dogs—dogs that make wolves look like kittens. He sets them on *people,* to tear them apart."

Oak made noncommittal noises. These lurid tales of a murderous Czar riding to supernatural hounds through the icy rigors of a Skyrrian night seemed to him just a little too, um, lurid.

"And what of the depravities in his retreat at Czaritsyn?" Orson persisted. "Foul orgies, fiendish tortures, gruesome conjurations!"

"You think I'll get invited?"

"To what?"

"The orgies."

The Marquis exploded in laughter. "You really are crazy!"

"Those tales come from Basmanov," Oak said complacently, "who is biased. He admits that the Czar would hang him if he ever went home."

Beau had discovered Basmanov serving beer in a fleabite Fitanish tavern and hired him to be their guide and their instructor in Skyrrian language, history, and customs. He might be either more or less than he claimed to be.

"Basmanov should know," Orson protested. "He was a boyar."

"So he says."

"When he fled into exile the Czar had his wife raped to death by the *streltsy* and then fed his children to hounds!"

"So he says. For all we know, he's a spy or an escaped convict."

He also bragged about vast estates and innumerable mistresses.

"He uses a sword like a gentleman!" Orson announced, forgetting that a certain fisherman's son could do far better. "And others have told us similar stories."

"Basmanov's a thief. The night we stayed in the margrave's castle, he went prowling, pocketing things."

"What!" Orson was aghast at such a breach of hospitality. "Why did you not tell me?"

"Because I made him put them back," Oak said complacently. At sword point. He had told Beau.

Oak's experiences now included lodging as guest of high nobility in palaces, bivouacking in leech-rich swamps during thunderstorms, and everything imaginable in between. Wassail's safe-conducts, the Marquis's letters of introduction, D'Estienne's field craft, and de Ferniot's glib tongue had brought the wayfarers safely across Eurania to the Skyrrian border. They had been fortunate that this year—for once—nobody was at war with anybody else. If you believed in mad Czars, things might now start to get interesting. If you didn't, you could look forward to a gaudy state betrothal ceremony and a long ride home again with the princess and her entourage of silken ladies.

Soft, scented ladies were an intriguing thought. It was a long time since Oak had dallied in the velvet brothels of Isilond, and he found no pleasure among starving peasants who would sell their children outright for a crust. Dust swirled in his eyes, making him curse. His teeth gritted with the stuff. Arkell claimed you could drop all Chivial on these steppes and never find it again.

"Something is happening," Orson said, rising in his stirrups to peer ahead. "D'Estienne is shortening the column."

"Perhaps they have sighted a tree?"

Grin. "Improbable. More likely Dvonograd. Basmanov says it will be soon. And then we must part, my friend!"

"I hope we will meet again."

The Marquis smirked. "At the King's Cup?"

Oak smiled uneasily. Preferably not. "Our ward swears if we ever get him home he will never leave Wasburgh again."

Orson was perceptive enough to spot the evasion. Amused, he asked the question nobody had yet put into words. "What are your Blade friends going to say if we win?"

"*When* you win. Beau promised, didn't he?" Beau's pledge that the Sabreurs would sweep the quarter finals and take the top four spots did not seem crazy now. Any one of the four could beat Oak or Arkell without drawing breath. Orson and de Roget were the equals of Beau himself.

"He is an incredible instructor. But won't the others call you traitors?"

"Not once they get used to the idea," Oak said stoutly. "Wards must come first, so any of them would have done the same." If they had seen the possibility, that was. Beau had offered Ironhall expertise and his teaching skill as the price of Isilondian support—Oak remembered watching the Regent work it out, on the night of the de Roget match, which now seemed so long ago.

"I am assured that decapitation is painless after the first few minutes." Orson squinted into the wind. "The vanguard has returned. They must have sighted Dvonograd, or the river, at least. It is farewell, friend."

"I am sorry. We are all grateful. We could never have come here without your help."

The Marquis's dark stare rested on him for a moment. "But how will you make your way home? You think Sir Dixon's gallants will be escort enough? Returns are always more dangerous, because the evildoers have had time to prepare—assuming Skyrria does not swallow you whole so you are never seen again. Friend Oak, will you not at least try to convince Beau to turn back while there is still time?"

This was what he had been leading up to. His concern was flattering, but Oak shook his head.

"He is Leader. He decides."

Orson sighed. "Are all Chivians mad?"

"Just us Blades."

"I tried to convince Estienne we should wait here for you, but he convinced me we cannot. The days are growing short, the weather will soon turn, and the grazing is bad now. This is Eighthmoon already! We must hurry if we would be home before winter sets in. How long will your business in Skyrria take?"

"Don't know. Banquets and state weddings don't get dashed off in an afternoon."

Arkell claimed another week or ten days should see them in Kiensk, but return would take longer; a queen and her train would travel slowly—and it was a long way back to Laville.

"You will have to stay in Kiensk until spring."

"It would seem so," Oak said imperturbably. If he didn't see Chivial again for another year, did that matter? His life belonged to his ward. "The Czar will see us safely on our way home."

"But how far? If he sends troops into Dolorth or Narthania he will be breaking treaties. He may provoke a war he certainly does not want. He may abandon you here at Dvonograd!"

"Is he mad enough to abandon his sister-in-law?"

"Perhaps. So, listen," Orson said, as if coming to a decision. "Remember Gneizow?"

"Could I forget a place named after a sneeze?"

"The landgrave seemed an honest man. I will leave some men and horses for you at Gneizow—Sergeant Narenne's troop. If you can send word ahead, he will meet you here at Dvonograd. If you can't, he will be waiting there. Should you decide to return home by sea, please send him word."

"That's incredibly generous of you!" Oak had never anticipated such an offer. "I am sure my ward will insist on reimbursing you!"

"No. It is for friendship." Orson's eyes twinkled. "The least I can do for a lover!"

Oak laughed. Yes, he could laugh now, but he had been appalled the first time he realized what other men thought of their friendship. Orson, man of the world, had an aristocrat's disdain for anyone else's opinion. His fellow Sabreurs had pretended not to notice, Beau and Arkell knew Oak too well, and lesser men dared not jeer openly at a Blade. It was old Lord Walrus—the ultimate prude, who disapproved of a man even smiling at a woman other than his wife—who had considered himself entitled to ask.

Furious, Oak had snarled, "If we're happy, why does it matter?"

His ward had turned an immediate deep puce.

Fortunately, Beau had been present. "We had some friends so inclined at Ironhall, my lord. They tended to pester me more than most, and I can assure you that Oak was not one of them. Nor Arkell. And I always declined. Your Blades' lusts, while outrageous in intensity, are all orthodox in direction."

His lordship had grunted furiously and changed the subject.

Now Oak could joke about it. "It's still very sweet of you, darling."

By the time they reached the column, the Dvono was in sight as a distant glimmer of silver. The smudge on the far bank must be Dvonograd, which had sounded like a grand city three months ago and was now known to be some sod-roofed cabins inside a stockade. It belonged to Czar Igor, who had forbidden the Ambassador to bring more than ten armed guards across his borders.

Orson rode off to confer with D'Estienne. Oak went to join Beau, Arkell, and their ward, who traveled in a litter slung between two horses. The custrel riding ahead, leading the litter horses, was young Wilf, who rarely spoke to people much.

The trek had taken a great toll of Lord Wassail. He blamed gout, but gout would not explain his constant exhaustion, the once-bloated face sagging in loose folds, the former high color faded to the hue of stewed liver. Upright he seemed stooped and shrunken, and even prone and bundled in marten skins he could find no rest. He rarely roared or tried to bully now, as if he was afraid bad temper might seem weakness. His ward's courage left Oak breathless.

He had seemed to rally after a healing in a swampy hole of a town called Radomcla, ten days back across the plains. Dvonograd would have an elementary, although Basmanov claimed that Skyrrian conjurers were ignoramuses, little better than shamans. The exile could not find one good word to say about his native land.

"Good chance, Sir Oak," Wassail said. His lungs sounded like a cat.

"And to you, my lord. The Marquis has just promised to leave some men and horses for us at Gneizow. I told him that was very generous."

Wassail mumbled agreement, but the news did not produce the joy Oak had expected. The mood was somber.

"Over there," Beau said, waving at the river, "is Skyrria. Our Isilondian friends can take us no farther. The Czar's troops should be waiting to escort us. If they don't murder us instead, we shall be entering a land where law as we know it isn't even an idea. You've heard the tales of Igor being his own chief brigand. Since the fortune in gifts we carry is destined for him, he probably won't try to rob us, but others may, if news of our coming has spread. Blade regulations and our bindings require us to keep our ward away from peril whenever possible."

Oak shrugged and said, "Yes, Leader."

"Well?" Beau's eyebrows were silver streaks on a face weathered ruddy by the wind and sun. Constant dust had painted red rims around his eyes, but they kept their steely glint. He always seemed more dapper than anyone else, his chin better shaved, his livery cleaner and less faded. That was largely because Lord Wassail's servants—Hagfield, Kimberley, and Percy—tended him as enthusiastically as they did their master. Beau had that effect on people. He was also mounted on the best horse in the company, Triplets, a magnificent bay he had won off D'Estienne's aide-de-camp in an all-night dice game. "We all want to turn around and run away. All we need is a good excuse. We're hoping you can suggest one."

There were times when Beau's humor seemed strained. Arkell was frowning and the sick old man in the litter did not smile either.

"Blades do not overrule their wards lightly, Leader," Oak said. "I assume Lord Wassail wishes to continue his mission?"

Wassail scowled the best scowl he had produced in a week. "I am worried, Oak. Very little news comes out of Skyrria. I suspect His Majesty would never have sent us here if he had heard these wild stories about the Czar. We knew he bargained faithlessly with merchants, but not that he broke his word to other princes, as he apparently does. What will I do if the beautiful child princess turns out to be a waddling hag? What if he demands new concessions? I feel responsible for all of you and Sir Dixon's men also. I have ordered Commander Beaumont not to proceed if he feels the risks are too high." He closed his eyes as if this speech had exhausted him.

That was not the tune the bird had whistled back at Ironhall. Was the Weasel trying to weasel out and blame his Blades? Startled, Oak looked to the others and found no help. Were they seriously expecting an opinion from *him?* He saw himself as the rearguard in the chase scenes, never the strategist.

"You can reasonably plead ill health, my lord, so why not stay in Dvonograd and ask that the princess be brought to you there?"

Without opening his eyes, the Walrus growled, "No!" He rattled, then started to cough, screwing up his face in agony at every spasm and making Oak writhe in sympathy.

"The trouble with that notion, brother," Beau explained,

"is that the Czar has probably dispatched a substantial force to escort us. Remembering Boyar Basmanov's stories, if Igor had sent you on such a mission, how would you feel about returning empty-handed?"

"Suicidal."

"Exactly. If we set foot in Skyrria we will go on to Kiensk, like it or not."

Wassail choked and gasped into silence, his face streaming sweat.

If Beau really wanted Oak's opinion, that meant that he and Arkell disagreed. As Leader he could overrule the other two, but Beau would not want to do that. Arkell was a finder-of-problems; obviously he was the one wanting to play safe and turn back. To let Beau make the choice, Oak must vote to continue.

"I think we should go on, Leader."

"Why?" Beau snapped, sounding like Grand Master in a strategy class.

Um. Well, the most obvious reason was that this journey was killing their ward. To head home now would finish him. He would never make it back to Radomcla, whereas the elementary in the town over there could restore him; the next section of the journey was to be by boat down the Dvono, which should be restful enough. Old Walrus would be deeply offended if Oak said all that, though.

"Matter of honor, Leader. Our duty."

Beau just sighed and rode on in silence.

Suddenly everything *flipped* as if someone had cracked Oak on the head with a beam. Beau had *not* been joking. He agreed with Arkell. They really did want a good excuse to turn back and run, but their ward needed enchantment in Dvonograd and could not stand the journey back to Radomcla. Somewhere in the last few days, without realizing it, the Blades had passed a point of no return.

"Unless my old eyes deceive me," Beau said, "a sizable contingent is fording the river. Coming to intercept us."

✦ 4 ✦

Arkell estimated that the Skyrrians were about two hundred strong, so the two sides were roughly equal in fighting strength. They approached each other circumspectly over the swampy flood plain of the Dvono, like dogs sniffing the air for the scent of treachery. Why so big an honor guard? Did the Czar's guests really need this much protection, or was he just wary of any foreign force near his borders?

They seemed a ragtag mix of archers, lancers, and swordsmen riding in no sort of order. Already Arkell could make out swarthy little men on shaggy ponies, red-haired giants like Baels riding high chargers. Some wore helmets and cuirasses or even antique chain-mail shirts, others not much at all in the summer glare. They followed two standards, but with the wind at his back he could not discern the emblems.

The leaders cried halt just out of bowshot. Pursuivant Dinwiddie and the Isilondian heralds rode forward to parley with their Skyrrian counterparts.

"If you trust yourself to that mob, Chivians, you are crazy!" shouted Basmanov, riding toward Wassail's litter.

Arkell intercepted. He distrusted the Skyrrian turncoat. "Why so?"

"That is the demon Viazemski himself!" Basmanov's pocked face was twisted in anger, or fear. He was an ungainly, humorless man with a highly unpleasant odor.

"You have remarkable eyesight."

"I know his banner. When he cuts your throats, remember

my warning!" The exile spurred his horse savagely and rode away to the rear. Charming fellow!

The colloquy went surprisingly fast. Cantering back to report to Lord Wassail, Pursuivant began shouting the moment he was within earshot.

"Joyous, tidings, Your Excellency! Their leader is Prince Dimitri Temkin, the Czar's nephew!"

To a herald, that was clear proof of royal favor and honorable intentions. Arkell wondered how a mad Czar defined honor.

"Who else?" Wassail demanded.

Pursuivant reined in, flushed and blinking through dust-coated glasses. "General Viazemski, aide-de-camp to His Highness. They would have speech with you and His Grace of Vaanen."

"You didn't forget us, I hope?" said Oak.

Offended, Dinwiddie tried to look down his nose, a posture that merely emphasized his lack of chin. "Of course not. The Prince will bring three guards also. Your Excellency, there was a Master Hakluyt present. They introduced him as Chivian ambassador, but I assured them that His Majesty has not yet accredited an ambassador to Skyrria. That is correct, is it not?" he queried nervously. Poor Pursuivant would not sleep for months if he had unwittingly insulted an ambassador.

"He's just a consul," Wassail growled. "Hubert Hakluyt of Brimiarde, a merchant authorized to speak for the others. What's he doing here?"

"They brought him along to interpret. His services were not required, of course."

"Did he not carry some dispatches between the two courts last year, my lord?" Arkell asked. He handled all Wassail's correspondence now, and had seen the name. "The Skyrrians may be flattering both him and themselves by granting him diplomatic rank."

"Well, now he can go back to peddling fish," Wassail said. "Pursuivant, see if His Grace of Vaanen is ready to meet with the Prince."

A few minutes later, riding out with the leaders, Arkell was furious to note that the Blades' counterparts on the Skyrrian team were archers—short, ugly men on even uglier ponies, armed with deadly recurved bows. He made a note to dismember Pursuivant at the earliest possible opportunity, if Beau did not do so first.

The Skyrrians were led by a lardy young man with a streaming sandy beard. In himself he was not impressive, and his clothes were fine but not exceptional—linen breeches, an embroidered shirt, and a three-quarter-length coat of silk with silver buttons. What made Arkell whistle was the glitter of jewels on him, everywhere from his red leather boots to his fur-trimmed cap; his sword and horse trappings alone were worth a fortune. This was Dimitri, Athelgar's brother-in-law-to-be.

At his side rode a soldier in black cuirass and helmet. He had lost his left arm at the elbow and his beard was streaked with gray, but he still looked a man to be reckoned with. This must be the notorious Viazemski, whom Basmanov described as more dangerous than a bedroll full of vipers. More than half the Skyrrian contingent wore *streltsy* black and the wolf-head emblem; the others must be the Prince's retainers. The unarmed, scraggy man whose trimmed beard marked him as a foreigner would be Master Hakluyt, and he should be a useful source of information.

The delegations met in no man's land. They exchanged elaborate, wordy courtesies and began correcting certain misapprehensions, starting by excluding Hakluyt from the discussion.

Fortunately, nobody asked Arkell's opinion of Prince

Dimitri, who soon showed himself both ignorant and stupid—he was amazed that foreigners could be enchanted to understand Skyrrian, thereby confirming Basmanov's opinion of national conjuring standards; he was also confused about the relationship between Chivial and Isilond—although King Athelgar would never win medals in geography either. He did agree that his sister was the Czar's niece, not cousin as she had been represented. Yes, his other sister was Czarina. Lord Wassail did not say that Chivians disapproved of such matches, but he scowled mightily and forgot to fawn at the Prince for several minutes.

Viazemski was harder to judge. He sat impassively, studying the Isilondian troop, seemingly ignoring the delegates' talk around him. His reins were tied to his stump, leaving his sword hand free, yet he had his horse under perfect control.

"I was told a week!" Wassail roared, snapping Arkell's attention back to the palaver. The Weasel was sick and in pain, trying to negotiate from a litter, staring up at faces against the sky. His diplomatic manners had slipped under the strain.

Voevode Viazemski dropped his pose of inattention and sent the Prince warning glances.

"Your Excellency's sources may have been misinformed," Dimitri retorted stiffly. "From here to Kiensk will take at least a month."

"Sir Arkell?"

As geographer for the expedition, Arkell had rummaged through all the libraries in Laville for information on Skyrria. Since then he had cross-examined every traveler they'd met on the road who claimed to know anything relevant, including some Narthanian soldiers who'd marched almost to the gates of Kiensk in the last war. He probably knew as much about western Skyrria as anyone could who had never been there, but he could hardly argue its geography with a member of the royal family, no matter how furious his ward was.

He turned to the merchant sulking in the background. "How long would you estimate, Master Hakluyt?" He spoke in Chivian.

The consul glanced nervously at the *streltsi* and replied in Skyrrian. "Speed depends on who is traveling, Sir Blade. A courier hastening to report the glad news of your arrival to His Majesty will undoubtedly cover the ground faster than a large party such as His Excellency's."

"Such a courier," Lord Wassail growled, "might mention our urgent need to return to Dvonograd before winter sets in."

The Prince grew flustered. "I was not planning to—"

"This is a vast land," Viazemski said harshly, demonstrating who was really in charge here. "Forage and shelter are grave concerns for large parties. Expect to reach the capital no sooner than the end of Eighthmoon."

Dimitri rallied. "You can be no more impatient to reach Kiensk than I am, Excellency. I have a daughter there I have never seen. I have endured two months here, waiting for you, and Dvonograd is nobody's favorite place. We can leave," he added with a wary glance at his one-armed companion, "first thing tomorrow, if the stars are favorable."

"That can be arranged," the *Voevode* conceded.

Skyrrian messengers galloped back to the town to summon porters and more wagons, but separating the Chivians from the Isilondians was a complex task that seemed likely to take up most of the day. Wordy farewells turned almost tearful. In two months their baggage had become hopelessly mixed. An Isilondian courier was ready to leave, so Arkell had to close Wassail's latest report. As he was kneeling on the pebbly grass, trying to write legibly on the lid of the dispatch box despite the romping wind's playful interference, it occurred to him that Lord Wassail would never have arrived at Dvonograd at all without Beau's masterstroke in enlisting the Sabreurs' aid. Was it possible for a Blade to be *too* good for his ward's well-being? About a dozen men came shuffling over to ask if he would write letters home for them.

He had just finished the last hasty scrawl when Beau himself arrived, beaming cheerfully atop a wall-eyed, spavined nag.

"Time to go, brother! The nefarious Viazemski reports that the town elementary is ready to perform a healing. We'll head down to the ford and leave minions to bring the baggage."

"Find me someone to take charge of this accursed box!" Arkell eyed the dog-food horse. "What happened to Triplets?"

"He has been reunited with his previous owner. With every indication of approval, I point out—ungrateful brute!"

"You sold him back, you mean? I trust you profited?"

"I collected a handsome ransom," Beau conceded smugly.

As the litter and its escort moved off, who should reappear but Master Hakluyt on his palfrey, easing himself into the Ambassador's party and obviously heading for the litter. He looked around in alarm as two swordsmen closed in on him.

One of them brandished a smile that would have disarmed a shipload of Baels. "Consul, I am Beaumont, my friend is Sir Arkell, and the Blade up ahead is Sir Oak."

The consul scowled. "I need to speak with His Excellency."

"That can be arranged. May I ask your business?"

Obviously Hakluyt dearly wanted to say, "No." Discretion prevailed. "I intend to petition him for redress."

Beau's sigh conveyed immense sympathy. "Believe me,

this is not the best day to try it, master. What is your griev-
ance?"

"I had barely reached Kiensk this summer before I was
dispatched here, to Dvonograd, to interpret for the Ambassador. Buried alive!"

"We do not need interpreters."

"I explained that, but the Czar had decreed otherwise."

"I am sorry we have inconvenienced you."

"So am I!" The scrawny merchant was almost shouting. "I
have lost a whole season's trading. If my ship has sailed
without me, I may have to overwinter in Kiensk, which is a
fate to dread. The King should compensate me for my
losses!"

"I do counsel patience," Beau said soothingly. "As the
Skyrrians would say, the stars are unfavorable for financial
dealings today. You are well acquainted with Skyrria?"

"This is my eighth summer here," the merchant conceded
sullenly. "If I am not to be allowed to speak with the Ambassador—"

"Are you married, master?"

Arkell wondered what that had to do with anything.

So, clearly, did Hakluyt. "Yes. Why?"

"Your dear wife is at home, minding all your fair children
in Brimiarde?"

"Yes."

"How would she like to be *Lady* Hakluyt?"

The trader's sudden flush was answer enough. If the present Mistress Hakluyt was at all typical, she would have an
attack of the vapors at the prospect of being catapulted to the
social summit of her poky provincial town. "That is . . . ? His
Majesty has . . . ?"

"His Majesty will naturally reward those who assist in ar-
ranging his marriage. That is traditional. His Excellency has
brought letters patent conferring knighthood in the Order of

Ranulf on you, in recognition of your services to the Crown."

Arkell wrestled down a grin. Wassail's dispatch box did contain several such documents, signed, sealed, and awaiting names—honors cost the King nothing—but the Walrus would have apoplexy at the idea of knighting a mere merchant. On the other hand, he never argued with Beau now.

"This is indeed an honor."

"It merely needs his signature. I have a few questions about local customs that may concern His Excellency's safety."

The trader's face, weathered and furrowed like tree bark, twisted into a surprisingly convincing smile as he saw the deal being offered. "How may I assist, Sir Beaumont?"

"I expected to see border guards around here."

"The Border Patrol has gone underground," the merchant said with a sneer, "because Viazemski and his *streltsy* are better bullies than even they are. I am sure they will be back. They are known as the White Hats for some reason. Their headgear is usually a muddy gray color."

Beau nodded. "And this conjuration. Is it safe?"

"I would not risk it for myself, but the *Voevode* arranged it, did you see? The witches will never risk angering the *streltsy*."

"So it won't do harm. Will it heal our ward's maladies?" Arkell demanded. "Is their conjuration any good?"

"It differs from what we know in Chivial, certainly." Hakluyt spoke like Oak, with the soft vowels of Lomouth and the West. "They are skilled at curses and some of their transformations are incredible. The Czar is rumored to employ a stable of skilled enchanters and to dabble in very nasty witchcraft experiments at Czaritsyn. But the tales of what he does or does not do at Czaritsyn—"

"Witches?" Beau said. "Witchcraft? Why 'witches'?"

"Skyrrians distrust and fear enchantment. They tolerate it

for healing—as a last resort—but they blame all unexpected misfortune on malicious witchcraft. No one ever dies of natural causes, only from witchcraft."

"We were told they are superstitious. They believe in astrology?"

"I fear so." Hakluyt shook his head. "All of them, even the nobility, who should know better. Nothing will be done on a day the stars have named unfavorable."

"But chance is elemental!" Arkell protested. "Stars are fire and air; they cannot influence other elements."

"You and I know this, Sir Arkell, but the Skyrrians do not. May I ask, noble sirs, how things are back home in Chivial?" A trader expected tit for tat.

Beau's smile flashed in acknowledgment. "We have had very little news in the last three months, and none of consequence. We left in Fourthmoon. When did you sail?"

"In Thirdmoon. From Brimiarde."

"Arriving in Skyrria?" Arkell demanded.

"Third week of Fifthmoon. That is fast passage."

Arkell said, "Why another month from here to Kiensk? When the explorer Delamare came through here a hundred years ago, he needed only three days to sail down the Dvono to Morkuta. From there three more on a horse saw him to Kiensk."

"The river is low just now. When was this man here?"

"Eighthmoon, like now."

The trader eyed him thoughtfully. "You are well informed, Sir Arkell."

"That is my business." Did the man think Blades were only trained killers?

"Well, much has changed in a hundred years. The recent wars devastated western Skyrria. A lot of it is just desert. The Czar . . ." Hakluyt frowned at their smiles. "I said something humorous, Sir Beaumont?"

"A private joke, master. Pray forgive us and continue. Your information is extremely valuable to us and our ward."

"You will mention to his lordship—"

"He will hear of your contribution, I promise. Now—the journey?"

The procession was nearing the river, so the interrogation would have to be set aside.

"The Czar is determined that strangers shall not learn how much Skyrria has been weakened. Most foreign traders are forbidden to wander outside the walls of Treiden. Even those with permits, like myself, are escorted to and from Kiensk by a roundabout route. Once there we must dwell in the foreigners' enclave and stray no farther than a day's march from the city walls. You will go by the route the Czar has decreed or not at all."

The Blades exchanged sad frowns. They would certainly have to overwinter in Skyrria now.

Beau said, "Thank you, master. We must converse again. Brother, you go and reconnoiter the elementary. Oak and I will see his lordship across the river."

Hakluyt chose to go with Arkell, and as they coaxed their mounts into the water side by side, Arkell said, "If the Czar is insane, master, explain to me why the people do not rise and depose him."

"I wish I could, Sir Arkell." The consul was eager to earn his knighthood. "He may be crazy, but he is not stupid. Never underestimate his cunning! He has clung to his throne a very long time."

"But hunting down men with dogs? Hounds that rip people to pieces?" The water had risen almost to Arkell's stirrups.

"Czar Igor has not done well in warfare with his neighbors," the trader said. "But he had some cause to blame his failure—at least in his early days—on opposition from his princes. Everything he tried to do, in war or peace, was blocked by the princes or the boyars or both. He is also convinced that they murdered his children and his first two wives with witchcraft."

If the uncouth Basmanov was a typical boyar, the Czar's attitude might be quite reasonable.

"That is why he makes war on his own people?" They were past the midpoint and the water was dropping. The litter should be able to cross without wetting its occupant.

"Just say that he has tamed the nobility. His hold on the country has never been tighter, and in that sense his reign has been a success. His successors should have an easier time."

As his horse reached the bank, Arkell looked back and saw the Ambassador's litter advancing slowly toward him, floating above the silver water like a boat reluctant to get wet. A dozen would-be helpers were creating waves as they milled around, all shouting at the same time. He carried on with Hakluyt toward the stockade.

Cities were all disgusting, Arkell had decided, but Dvonograd was the worst yet. If a thousand or so log shacks had been dropped from a great height into a cesspool, they would have made something better than Dvonograd. True, pigs rooted in the streets of Grandon or Laville also, but here they wallowed, for the sewage in the streets was hock-deep on the horses. The air was thick enough to stand on and yet there seemed to be no people anywhere. Pigs, dogs, and evil-looking black birds, but no people.

"Where?" he inquired. "Is everybody? Not that I wouldn't live somewhere else myself if I lived here."

"We have *streltsy* with us. The locals hide from them."

"Are *streltsy* really as bad as we've been told?"

The merchant pulled a face. "I don't know what you've been told. Can you imagine anything *worse* than that?"

"No."

"Then they are as bad as you heard."

"Fire?" They were riding through an empty space floored with cinders; stark stone chimneys stood in bleak memorial to lost homes.

"Of course. Happens a lot in winter."

"But this looks old!"

"I told you—people have gone. There is no need to rebuild. Many towns have been abandoned completely."

Thinking of fair Chivial and even fairer Isilond, Arkell could admit that Igor might have problems other rulers did not. But soon he and his guide reached an open bog, evidently the town center. Many of the buildings flanking it were larger and in better shape than the hovels they had been passing, and the merchant identified one on the far side as the elementary.

Arkell looked down as his horse swerved to avoid a buzzing heap lying in the mud. "What is *that?*" he demanded, his voice an octave higher than he had planned. He pointed. *"And is that another?"*

"Bodies." The trader shrugged. "You will see them in Kiensk, also. You get used to them. Skyrria won't change, Sir Blade. You had best let it change you as quickly as possible."

It was about to change Arkell by making him lose his last dozen meals.

"No one is allowed to touch them," Hakluyt added. "They must be left for the dogs and maggots."

"But who? What were their crimes?"

"These just annoyed *streltsy.* Some of Viazemski's men have been billeted here for two months. Rapes, robberies, beatings go on all the time. What else is there to do?"

Lord Wassail was lifted from his litter and carried inside the elementary. It was only a one-room log shed with an octogram outlined in white stones on a dirt floor, but it was tidy enough, and if the lighting was too dim to reveal what was rustling up in the rafters, that might be just as well.

The conjurers were another matter. There were three of them, instead of the standard eight. One appeared to be female, but all were hairy, near-naked savages—painted, bedecked in beads, bones, and disgusting fragments of animals. Arkell would have objected to letting his ward be exposed to their hocus-pocus if he had expected them to achieve anything at all. Confident that no self-respecting elemental would answer a summons from such freaks, he leaned against the wall beside Beau and waited to see.

For the first few minutes, the conjuration was as farcical as he had expected. The enchanters leaped around in the octogram, howling, screeching, and rattling things. He was studying the building, wondering what sort of trees produced such enormous logs, when a blast of spirituality almost knocked him over. All the hairs on his body stood on end, his hands twitched, his teeth began to chatter wildly. Beau gave him a surprised look and gestured at the door.

Arkell fled. His extreme sensitivity was well known and nothing to be ashamed of. He *could* stand conjurations if he had to. It was embarrassing, all the same. He'd had to run out of Ironhall bindings more than once.

He emerged into blinding sunlight and paused to wipe his brow and gag at Dvonograd's version of fresh air. He could still hear and feel what was going on inside, but at this range it was bearable. It might or might not be useful. Just because Skyrrian-style conjuration could summon spirits did not necessarily mean they would do as they were told.

"Sensitive?"

He was being studied by a dozen or so assorted *streltsy* guarding the horses. The man who had spoken was Viazemski himself. Dismounted, he was unexpectedly big.

"Very."

"Me too." An unpleasant sneer showed through his tangled beard; the mangled nose was better ignored.

His henchmen chuckled. One said, "Sensitive as a babe on a tit, he is."

"Never heard that sensitive meant soft," Arkell remarked, but he assumed such ruffians would cut their own throats before they admitted being sensitive to razors.

"You're one of the Blade things," Viazemski said. "Conjured loyalty?"

"Correct."

"You wanna show us some fancy swordwork?"

"No. I'm not a fairground tumbler."

Viazemski contemplated him for a few minutes with apparent disdain and all his men smiled, waiting for the devilry to start. Arkell wished he could grow a monster black beard like Oak's so everyone wouldn't pick on him, the kid who'd hung his sword on the wrong side.

"Suppose I order Sasha, there, to cut you up a bit?"

The man indicated grinned obediently. He was a lanky youngster in a cuirass and helmet, wearing a curved cavalry saber on his left hip.

"I told you I won't play games. If he draws on me I'll maim him or kill him." Arkell had no trouble making that pledge and meaning it, because it obviously defined his duty to his ward in these circumstances. His defiance provoked jeers and catcalls, of course.

Viazemski did not join in. "Sasha?"

"Yes, *Voevode?*" Sasha took hold of his sword and his neighbors stepped clear.

"The horses are thirsty. You and the boys take them down to the river. The foreigner and me'll stand watch."

The *streltsy* scowled but did not argue. Without a word they unhitched reins, tightened girths, and mounted. Arkell watched them drive the herd out of the square and was suddenly furious. Perhaps he had been more frightened than he knew, or perhaps the skin-prickling, gut-churning spirituality was getting to him.

He was alone with the infamous Viazemski. The man's nose had not been cut away; it had rotted. He was hard to look in the eye and knew it.

"You have your men well trained, *Voevode*. When they murder and rape is it because you have told them to?"

The monster seemed more amused than offended. "Sometimes, but mostly it's just high spirits. I'll make a deal with you, Blade."

"I doubt it, but you can ask."

"Hakluyt's told me about your binding conjuration. We don't have that in Skyrria. I want you to keep your trap shut about it—your trap and all the others', including the fat old man you're guarding."

Arkell laughed. "You don't want the Czar poking swords in your heart to see how it's done?"

The terrorist chief smiled nastily. "Got it first time, smart little sweetie that you are. 'Tis all I ask. In return, I can be a good friend."

"I told you I don't do party tricks, *Voevode,* and we don't go around bragging about our prowess either." In Chivial Blades did not have to, but here they had no established reputation.

"Not what I said. I don't care how good you are with those fancy swords because I've got a thousand men to each one of you, so that don't matter. It's your binding I don't want mentioned."

Arkell calculated quickly and decided he would be giving up nothing if he agreed. In fact, the man's request was so trivial that it was probably just an opening for something bigger to follow. "If Hakluyt has already told you, then don't bet your horse that the Czar doesn't know already. All the knights and heralds and servants we have with us know how a Blade is bound. Keeping all those mouths laced up would be tricky, especially if we have to hang around Kiensk until spring. I might promise to try for a very good friend."

"You want to leave here tomorrow?"

"Ah. If the stars are favorable?"

If a pig could smile it would look like Viazemski. "We all like to play safe, sonny. An astrologer tells you the omens are good and you meet ill chance, then he's in trouble. If he tells you they're bad so you stay home, then nothing happens. Understand? I can make the whole of next month inauspicious."

So not all Skyrrians were equally superstitious and the Chivians could stay in Dvonograd until they rotted like the corpses in the mud.

"I'm sure you can be persuasive, *Voevode*. I'll do the best I can to make our binding a state secret. The sooner we complete our business in Kiensk and depart the better, understand?"

"Yes. Deal, then." The *Voevode* held out a large, calloused, and dirty hand. Arkell shook it with a shudder of disgust. Horror though he was, the man might be sincere in this case. Surely the Chief Deputy Monster would welcome any friends he could find, and what he was asking was very little . . . so far.

Busy day—Beau handing out knighthoods and he making treaties with mass murderers.

The shamans' wailing in the elementary wound down in a rumble of drums, and the sun had slid close to thatch roofs. The shaggy pony that came splattering across the square was slung about with many weapons and ridden by a slit-eyed, straggly-whiskered little man wearing only a hide around his loins. Beaming broadly, he reined in close and handed the *Voevode* a bloodstained sack.

Viazemski hauled out the contents to look at. He nodded. "So I was right? Well done, Kraka! Anyone see you?"

"No, *Voevode.*"

"Good work. The Little Father will be pleased."

As the pony trotted off, Viazemski replaced the gruesome relic in its bag, dropped it at his feet, and turned to Arkell with a look of innocence incarnate. "What else do we need to talk about, Blade?"

Dry-mouthed, Arkell said, "Nothing. Nothing at all."

The malodorous exile had come home to stay. The thing in the sack was Basmanov's head.

◆ 5 ◆

The best part of a day was the end of it, after all the disrobing ceremonies required to prepare a Czarina for bed. Then Sophie could send her ladies away, settle on her favorite chair with a thick wool rug over her knees, and read by candlelight until the words swam off the page. Only thus could she stop worrying—worrying about anarchy in the streets, about servants and ladies-in-waiting being insulted or assaulted, about Tasha's interminable wedding preparations—and especially worrying about when Igor would return this time.

A rusty groan from the door tore the silence like a fanfare. The massive book slid off her lap and thundered on the rug hard enough to stun the bear had the bear still been wearing it. But the person who crept in was not Igor.

"Eudoxia! You startled me. Why aren't you asleep? . . ."

The old woman displayed her stumps in something be-tween a smile and a grimace. "Letter for you, Majesty."

At this time of night? There was no writing on the outside. Sophie broke the wax and unfolded the paper.

Must see you! Please please please come!—T.

The writing was smudged and barely recognizable as Tasha's.

"Who brought this?" Sophie's throat would barely release the words.

"*Voevode* Afanasii," Eudoxia mumbled. "Says he don't know what's wrong, but he's lying."

"My robe . . . boots . . ." Hindered by her flustering old nurse's efforts to help, Sophie whirled herself into outer gar-ments, pulling them over her night attire while her mind skittered around like a drunken bat. Dimitri had decided, no doubt wisely, that Tasha would be safest staying in the Temkin Palace with Yelena, but the Temkins' household troops had been stretched to futility guarding both it and Faritsov while providing an escort for the Prince himself at Dvonograd. Old Afanasii had been dragged out of retire-ment to help, but he had less than a dozen men.

"Who has the guard tonight?" Sophie demanded as she headed for the door and just heard Eudoxia answer, "Both," before she ducked through into the anteroom. That was bad news. Igor had formed the *streltsy* irregulars for many rea-sons, but foremost had been his distrust of the Household Regiment, which had traditionally garrisoned Kiensk. It was, he said, "crawling with boyars' sons." Given responsi-bility for maintaining law and order, the *streltsy* had enthu-siastically promoted anarchy. Lately the Czar had started dividing the watch between the two forces—not because he disapproved of mayhem, but because he was starting to dis-

trust the *streltsy* too. The result had been worse chaos, sometimes including pitched battles.

Voevode Afanasii was waiting out in the Robing Room,
majestic in flowing brocade robes and towering fur hat,
sporting an avalanche of white beard and a gold-headed
staff. It was beneath his dignity to carry a sword and he was
long past being able to wield one. He bowed stiffly to the
Czarina, who had known him all her life and trusted him as
she trusted Eudoxia. Two young swordsmen behind him
held lanterns, and some trick of the light on their eyes and
cheekbones made them look terrified. They had probably
been plowmen until four months ago.

"It was good of you to come, old grandfather." Without
breaking step, Sophie headed across to the stair. "What in
the world is happening?"

He limped after her, thumping his staff. "Her Highness
wanted that message delivered to you at once and without
fail, Your Majesty. I thought it safest to bring it myself."

He wasn't going to elaborate, obviously. "Shall I summon
a coach, Your Majesty?" He wheezed with the effort of
keeping up with her.

"It will be quicker to walk." She wondered what Igor
would say if he heard his wife was out in the streets at this
hour, virtually unattended. She should have taken time to
waken some of her ladies and bring them.

Stairs in the Imperial Palace were almost as awkward as
the doorways, all narrow and tightly spiraled. One of the
swordsmen went first and she followed the light of his
lantern down.

She might be chasing the wildest of wild geese.
Princesses were still innocent children at an age when peasant women were mothers, and Tasha was as jumpy as a
dozen grasshoppers at the prospect of being shipped
halfway round the world to a country she had first heard of

only four months ago. Yelena, who should have been a steadying influence, was being no help at all. After her harrowing experience of giving birth in a peasant's hovel at the roadside, and still deprived of her husband, she had withdrawn into a sort of permanent trance, obsessed with her baby.

But the geese did not feel wild. And what could Sophie do instead—ignore the note and go to bed? She stopped at the bottom of the stair.

"Who has the watch tonight?"

"It's shared, Your Majesty," her guard said. "Wolf-heads here."

Afanasii arrived. Sophie went on, under low lintels into the Assembly Room, and then the Hall of Columns. A solitary puddle of candlelight revealed a dozen men in black at one of the long tables, with wine and dice, and it was a wonder they didn't have women there as well. Their leader scrambled to his feet and stepped forth to block her, putting his fists on his hips without a thought of bowing or saluting. He was an ape who had been in trouble so often that she knew his name.

"I have to go out, Sergeant Suvorov. I shall want an—"

"Got a pass, girlie?" He leered.

His men clustered around menacingly. Sophie's heart thumped in her throat, but she had faced this scene often enough in nightmares and had always known it would become real sooner or later—facing down the *streltsy*. Now she had no choice; Tasha needed her.

"*A pass?* Sergeant, you know who I am! Stand aside and detail some men to escort me."

His hesitation told her that there was no standing order about obeying or disobeying the Czarina, no rule that said she could not leave the palace at will.

"By the stars!" she roared. "My husband will hear of

this!" She spread her glare around the others. Even the youngest of them had several years on her. "You *dare* defy your Czarina? You shall dance with the knout in the Market, I swear! All of you! Two hundred strokes for you, Suvorov, and fifty for each of the rest."

That sort of argument they understood. Suvorov glowered, but clearly saw no honor in winning the argument and total disaster in losing it. He stepped aside with a mocking bow to save face.

"Aleksei, Posnik, escort Her Majesty."

The men designated crowded in at her back, jostling Afanasii and the Temkin guards aside, but Sophie did not argue priority. The instant she knew she had won, reaction set in and she could barely keep her teeth from chattering. She stalked out without a word.

She had a lesser tussle at the outer gate, which was held by men-at-arms of the Household Regiment. Playing on the blood feud between the forces, she demanded a larger escort and was granted four pikemen; she quashed a brewing battle over precedence by putting the *streltsy* in single file on the right and the others on the left. With all factions now represented, she should win past any other checkpoints.

Out into windy streets under icy stars. High Town alone would rank as the largest city in Skyrria, without counting the rest of Kiensk. Within its crenellated walls stood the sprawling Imperial Palace, the national treasury and mint, barracks of both *streltsy* and Household Regiment, court houses, state armory, government offices, and many palaces of princely families, some now fallen into ruin. There were also stables, prisons, bathhouses, elementaries, a hospital, and other buildings of obscure purpose.

The Temkins had been a minor clan before Sophie's father married the Czarevna Katrina. Their palace was one of the smallest, but also one of the newest, having been designed for Sophie's grandfather by imported Ritizzian architects. Lights showed in the windows. Sophie hauled on the bell rope herself; the door swung open at once.

The entrance hall was a glittering marvel of marble and gilt, of frescoes and candles in crystal lanterns, and there the entire staff seemed to be gathered, all ashen-faced and taut as bowstrings with terror, from the tiniest scullery drudge up to Majordomo Lokurov, who had been acclaimed a national hero in the Narthanian wars. They were packed back against the walls, in doorways, some on the staircase, and all except Lokurov knelt as she entered. He bowed. There was no sign of Tasha or Yelena, and the noose of fear drew tighter around Sophie's throat.

"Where is my sister? Where is Princess Yelena?"

Lokurov was a portly, ponderous man, whose beard was just starting to show gray. "Their Highnesses are in their chambers, Your Majesty. They are . . . unharmed." The hesitation implied *not seriously*.

"You," Sophie told her escort, "wait here. And behave yourselves!" She headed for the wide staircase, aware that she was leaving armed men from three different commands mixed in with a herd of panic-stricken civilians. That was like waving a flaming torch in a hay barn, but even the *streltsy* had caught the scent of fear now. Whatever had happened here would draw the Czar's personal attention.

Raising her skirts, she started up the stair and Lokurov came shambling behind her. "Explain!" she commanded.

He began puffing out words of explanation, but one name would have been enough—Fedor. *Fedor!* Sophie trod on a hem and very nearly fell headlong up the steps. That explained the universal terror and the reluctance to talk. Fedor had been showing a very dangerous interest in Tasha ever since that day her betrothal was announced.

If the Czarevich was back in High Town, then Igor probably was, too.

"Did he—" she began, realized she must not ask. Oh, not that, spirits! "Go *on,* man!"

"The Princesses were holding a salon, Majesty . . . some highborn ladies . . . the string quartet from Ritizzia . . . just taking their leave . . ."

Arriving at Tasha's room, Sophie hammered on the panels with both fists. The Temkin Palace was not a fortress like the Imperial Palace; its doors were enameled, not iron-studded, but they were stout enough. "Tasha! It's me, Sophie! Open up." And to Lokurov: "Keep talking! Then what happened?"

It was a tale far too familiar. Czarevich Fedor, drunk, had come calling on a girl he fancied in the company of some equally brutish friends. The servants had not dared deny him entrance. He had found Tasha, abused her, insulted her, and forced his attentions on her. In all other cases Sophie had heard tell of, he went on to rape his victim and his friends either found victims of their own or took turns with his. Lokurov was trying to convince her that in this instance it had not gone so far.

"He, er, did tear her gown, Majesty. She scratched his face. He struck her, knocking her down, and then . . . well, I think he realized . . . she ran . . ."

"Others saw this?"

"Oh, yes, Majesty. Many witnesses. Princess Yelena, the ladies, and many servants. I had been summoned, but had not arrived. Her Highness fled past me, screaming. She ran up to her room and locked herself in. Princess Yelena ran upstairs also." Of course Yelena would head straight for baby Bebaia. "The Czarevich's companions persuaded him to leave then."

Any lesser man than Fedor would be hanged for this.

"She slid the note underneath the door, Your Majesty."

Tasha was clattering the bolt inside.

"Very well. Inform Princess Yelena that I am here and ask her to join us." Sophie slipped in through the opening and Tasha hit her like a runaway wagon, hurling her back against the jamb.

Screaming and weeping . . . It took several minutes of hugging and soothing before the Czarina was able to look for damage by the light of the solitary candle. The right side of her sister's face was puffed and red. She would have a black eye by morning, and it was too late to prevent it swelling. Her gown had been ripped open to the waist. All in all, it was not too bad, considering what usually happened, but Tasha was still shivering with an ague, racked by hysteria, hardly able to breathe.

Sophie hugged her again. "Now listen, darling. I must know. Whatever you will tell everyone else, you *must* give *me* the truth now. Did he rape you?"

Gasp. Gulp. Tears trickling down the Czarina's neck . . . "No."

"You're certain? I mean, this *is* the truth?"

"Yes." More gasps, very loud in Sophie's ear. "He forced a kiss on me, pawed me . . . I struggled. Then he tore my dress. I clawed his face. He hit me. There were people there, all screaming. I ran up here and bolted the door. No one came . . . until Lokurov . . ."

Sophie hugged her even tighter. "Good. I wish you'd torn his eyes out. But there's no permanent harm done."

"Doesn't matter!" her sister sobbed. "Everyone will say it happened. They'll all think he . . . did . . . did it."

Tasha was inexperienced, not stupid, and she had had time to brood. Certainly no king would ever accept a rape victim as his queen. Royal majesty would not allow it. Tonight's scandal was quite enough to terminate the Chivian betrothal.

Coverup! Ship all the staff out of Kiensk, back to Far-itsov . . . No. Impossible. The boyars' wives had already fled home with the story. The secret was out.

Nevertheless, Sophie said, "Nonsense! You'll come with me now, sleep with me tonight, and we'll deal with Fedor tomorrow."

"I want to stay here, and you with me!"

That made more sense, except that if Fedor had returned to Kiensk, his father was probably around also. "No. Find a cloak."

"Must change," Tasha mumbled, looking at the remains of her gown. It was a spectacular ruin. Fedor had ripped the heavy brocade open to her waist, but he had also rent three more layers, including a lace shift—which might look flimsy but was tough as iron—and torn all the grommets out of the linen petticoat below. Had he been disappointed to find how little of Tasha there was inside?

"Leave it. Did he just . . ." Sophie mimed two hands grabbing and pulling apart. "All at once?"

Tasha nodded. Her teeth were still shattering.

The brute must have the strength of horses. "Wrap up well, dear. We'll go and tell Yelena where you've gone."

◆ 6 ◆

Tasha whimpered at the sight of the armed men waiting downstairs, but the ensuing quick walk in the dark seemed to steady her. By the time they reached the Imperial Palace, she was breathing more easily and clinging less tightly. So-phie felt better, too, in that every step made her rage burn hotter. She had crossed a bridge when she faced down the *streltsy* and she was never going to go back. Igor must be made to see his son for the lunatic sot he was and bring him to heel. If no one else in the empire would tell him so, then it was his wife's duty.

The guards had changed. There were *streltsy* on the main door and others had replaced Suvorov's troop in the hall. None spoke, but they all stared at her, some leering, most glaring with a rage that plainly said their predecessors were in trouble. So Igor was back and she would have it out with him now, tonight, while her fury was hot. By tomorrow her mad courage might have faded back to timid sanity.

She hurried up the stair in the dark, one hand trailing on the rail, letting Tasha follow. They stooped through into the Robing Room, lit by a single twinkle of candle but empty of people. A whiff of dog confirmed that Igor was home.

Another single candle lit the anteroom where Eudoxia slept. She was not present, although her bedclothes lay rumpled on the couch. Sophie closed and locked the outer door. The inner door was slightly ajar, with light showing beyond.

"I'll go first. We have company."

Tasha squeaked. *"Who?"*

"The one man who can bring that brute to justice. If you feel like having screaming hysterics again, darling, just let yourself go." The hinges groaned. A dog growled. Two dogs.

"Quiet!" said the Czar. "Iakov, quiet!"

Sophie blinked at the brightness of a hundred candles. Igor hated shadows, always insisting on abundant light. He sat facing the door, huge in his bulky robes, glaring, toying with the thongs of his knout. He frowned when he saw Tasha as well. Sophie curtseyed, but did not kneel. He noticed. Tasha sank down on the rugs and touched her face to the floor.

Yes, two dogs. One was the enormous Iakov, but the other was even larger, a pitch-black monster as big as a pony. They crouched on either side of his chair, baring teeth like daggers at the intruders.

"What does this mean, wife? Have you no shame?" His voice was low and controlled. Rage was not an emotion, it was a weapon. He would rage later. "The entire court will hear how the Czarina walks the streets by night!"

"I expect it will, sire. But the shame is not mine."

She had done it! She had spoken up at last.

He noticed and sneered through his beard. "Convince me."

"I was summoned to an emergency, sire. Tasha . . ." Sophie hauled her reluctant sister to her feet. "No, let him see your face. There, Your Majesty! When will the Chivian Ambassador arrive, do you know?" Dimitri's last letter had promised it would be soon. State wedding and the bride with a black eye?

Igor said nothing, still toying with the knout. That was another of his tricks, for no one could long endure a silent stare from the Emperor of Skyrria, but his eyes' angry glitter acknowledged that there was more to this affair than a wilful wife in need of a beating.

Tasha moaned but did not resist as Sophie lifted away her cloak. She stood in silence, shaking violently, her delicate little breasts exposed to the Czar's furious gaze. After a moment, Sophie covered her up again and put an arm around her.

Still he waited.

"This is *your* niece, *my* sister, a royal princess. I demand that the man who did this be brought to justice, Your Majesty!"

He scowled. "I expect she led him on."

"No, sire. Tasha, tell His Majesty how it happened."

With many pauses, mumblings, and gasps for breath, Tasha repeated her story, looking all the while at the floor. She did not mention the criminal's name, but Igor had worked that out for himself. The tale was damning—witnesses of quality, no provocation, no room for misunderstanding. The way Tasha described it, Fedor had just walked in the door and ripped her dress off. No doubt that was how she remembered it.

When she finished, Sophie said, "Were she the humblest of your subjects, the penalty for such a crime would be death, would it not?"

The Czar of Skyrria scowled without quite meeting her eye. "Bah! Youthful high spirits. He had a cup of wine too many. She's probably been teasing and taunting him for months."

"And the Chivian Ambassador will undoubtedly hear—"

"Will hear *nothing!*" Igor roared, jumping to his feet. The dogs tensed, hackles rising again.

Sophie's knees turned to soup and her heart to stone. It took more courage than she had known she had, but she stood her ground. "You would let no other man off with this . . ." Not true. "Except the *streltsy,* of course."

"Yes, the *streltsy!*" the Czar repeated, stepping forward and putting his great nose close to hers. "The *streltsy!*" His breath reeked of wine. "And do you know why I favor the *streltsy,* wife? Do you know why I encourage them to rape and loot and do anything they want? And never punish them?"

"No, sire, I have often wondered." She was past caring now. Any minute he would strike her.

"Because it keeps them *loyal!* Loyal to *me!* Without my arm defending them, they would be torn to pieces, all of them. What can the princes and boyars and all the other traitors offer them to match that?" He was spraying her, but she was sure his rage was faked. "Only my dogs are more loyal than my Wolf-heads."

Fedor ought to be beheaded and she really did not care how the charge sheet read. "There were *streltsy* with Fedor tonight."

Igor reared back as if she had hit him with a mace. "No!"

"So say the witnesses!"

He roared at Tasha: *"You're lying!"*

Sophie held her sister in place when she might have fled or fallen. "No, sire. Three *streltsy.*"

"Who? What were their names?" He sank back on his chair, mumbling. "Never mind, I can find out. I will find out."

Sophie twisted the knife. "Sire, do be careful!"

Igor looked up, aghast. He was blind to rape or murder, but conspiracy was his demon.

"No," he mumbled. "Not Fedor. He wouldn't." Subvert the *streltsy?*

"Why wouldn't he? What else does he stop at? Murder? He revels in it. Torture. Rape? Certainly. This is not the first time, Your Majesty! The Czarevich has molested even my ladies-in-waiting. Princess Agnia, Princess Ketevan—he *raped* them, right here in the Imperial—"

She realized with dismay that she had raised her voice to the Czar. She was standing over him, practically shaking her fist at him, and now his scarlet glare of rage was genuine. She remembered hints that Wife Number Three had shouted and that was why She Who Must Not Be Named had disappeared so abruptly.

"Ketevan?" Igor sneered. "Bulat's girl? Yes, we laughed over that. It will teach that slimy traitor what happens to those who conspire against me. I hope Fedor bred a child on her. I'll make her father rear it, by the stars!"

"That's what they say, isn't it? No girl is safe from the Czarevich and—"

Sophie felt the palace collapse beneath her feet.

"And what?" the Czar asked in a very soft, feline snarl.

And no boy safe from the Czar. That was another of his weapons against the princes, like the midnight attacks on the villages or letting Fedor abuse their daughters. If they displeased him, the Czar might abuse their sons. They all knew it, and yet it was the one unspeakable thing. Call him tyrant, murderer, sadist, or rapist and he would smile—the people even seemed to admire his atrocities, as if those showed strength in an autocrat. But to lust after men was feminine and weakness and the merest hint that he did so would bring instant death to the speaker. It had taken Sophie long enough to learn who were her rivals for her husband's bed.

And now she had almost said the unspeakable.

"And what?" he repeated, rising.

"And that is wrong, sire! Fedor shames you. But now, I beg you, my sister is exhausted. Let me put her to bed here, where she can feel safe—and then you can show me how much you have missed me, for I have most certainly missed you."

The issue hung in the balance for a dozen heartbeats before the Czar actually smiled. She could not read what lay behind that smile. He might be admiring her courage or planning to strangle her.

"Very well. Sleep well, Princess. Come in when you are ready, wife. But hurry, for my desire burns hot."

He walked over to the corner door and then turned. "Ah, my pets! Come, Iakov. Come, Vasili." The monsters leaped up and ran after him, wagging their tails. The one he called Vasili almost filled the doorway.

With her heart pounding like heels on a dance floor, Sophie went in to him, closing and locking the door. His chamber was smaller than hers and stank of animal, but the dogs had been banished to the anteroom. His clothes lay in a heap on the floor. He sat upright in bed, bare-chested, drinking from a wine bottle by the light of a hundred candles, which would burn until day. He watched her as she dropped her robe and climbed in beside him. Then he tossed the empty bottle away, lay down, and rolled around to face her.

"So you want a baby, do you?"

"Very much, Your Majesty."

"You're a fool. You produce another czarevich or a czarevna, and what'll happen to it the moment I'm dead? Or even before? Fedor will twist its head around till it comes off, that's what. But if whelping's what you want and just in case you have any crazy ideas that I'm not capable of doing what is necessary . . ."

He did what was necessary.

Afterward she lay in silence staring up at the canopy, waiting to be dismissed. Other women enjoyed what had just happened, and there had been times at first when she thought she might learn to. She lacked practice.

"The Chivians will be here by noon tomorrow," Igor said. "That sister of yours must be gone at dawn and the Temkin woman with her."

"To Faritsov?"

"Of course. We will apologize for her absence and send for her. She can come back when her face is healed."

Then it would be too late in the year to travel to Chivial. Sophie was suddenly too exhausted to care. She was drifting off to sleep when Igor's voice made her jump.

"You disgust me."

She shivered. "How I have displeased Your Majesty?"

"Nothing you have done. You behave well. You just are." He was much drunker than she had realized. "I forgive your behavior tonight. You did well under the circumstances. The guards who let you out will be punished, so don't try it again."

"Is that fair?"

"Yes. They had to displease me or you and they chose wrong."

"And Fedor?"

"He will teach my *streltsy* not to befriend him."

After a while he said, "A Czar should make lots of babies so the people do not doubt him."

"I am willing."

"But what I said about Fedor . . . He really will kill any child of yours."

She believed him.

Igor grunted. "Unless."

"Unless what, sire?"

"Unless he is its father."

She sat up. "You are joking!"

"Lie down!" he grumbled. "There's a draft."

She lay down and he pulled the covers snug around himself.

He chuckled. "No. We'll let Fedor give you the baby. He's more inclined to it than I am. You'd rather bed with a lusty young lad your own age, anyway. The brat will be safer if it's his."

"*Your Majesty!* You cannot—"

"Now go! I want to sleep."

She obeyed, sliding out of the bed, donning her robe, and returning to her own room. As she was climbing in beside Tasha, she heard the bolt click.

◆ 7 ◆

"Good chance to you, Sir Arkell," Lord Wassail declaimed cheerily. It was a fine morning. Cane tapping, he walked briskly along the paved path to the river. "Today we arrive in Kiensk, I understand." Percy, Kimberley, and Hagfield trailed after him, well laden.

"Good chance to you, my lord. Let us hope so. We have been this close to Kiensk at least three times before."

"Ah, so you say. But rivers twist and roads wind. Some of the forests were thick enough to hide the sun. How can you be so certain, mm?"

"I have a memory for maps and a knack for direction." The boy was confidence personified. "Kiensk lies that way. Sprensk, where we were two weeks ago, is a couple of days over there, Dvonograd about ten days' ride that way . . . We've been led in circles."

Wassail chuckled as he accepted the lad's steadying hand to descend the slimy steps. "Just teasing. You haven't been wrong yet, any of you." This prolonged trip had not been all bad, for his health was much improved. Leisurely boat trips and short treks were restful—he had not needed a healing since Dvonograd. Food and accommodation had been superb, all the way, and the countryside enviable. He approved of Skyrria, so far. "If His Majesty said circles, obviously circles it has to be. I hope I can talk him out of circles for the return trip, though."

Fine morning or not, summer had gone. Tomorrow would be Ninthmoon.

Beaumont aided him down into the big river boat. "Even if you do so, the timing will be tight, my lord. We must cross the border no later than the middle of this month if we're to make Fitain before really bad weather strikes. We'd avoid a *Skyrrian* winter, then, but we can't expect easy roads anywhere. We cannot remain more than four or five days in Kiensk."

Wassail settled on the thick cushion provided for an honored guest; he scanned the heaps of baggage amidships and the dozen or so brawny rowers, many of them already stripped to the waist for their exertions to come. A few of them he recognized as *streltsy* and others had been rowers on the Dvono. He did not need Arkell to tell him that most of their journey had been unnecessary.

There were six boats in the convoy. Prince Dimitri was in the one directly ahead—scion of an incredible royal lineage all the way back to Tharik; pleasant enough lad, if not the brightest jewel in the crown. Pursuivant Dinwiddie was with him, Sir Dixon in the craft directly behind. The boorish Viazemski usually traveled in the last boat, keeping watch for strays.

Arkell and the servants moved to the bow, Beau settled on a thwart nearby as if he had something to discuss. While the boatswain began beating stroke and the boat pulled away from the steps, Wassail took another approving look around. The left bank was meadowland, although he could see far too many herds of black cattle for the available pasture. It had been stocked up just to impress him. Opposite, of course, stood the palace where he had spent a very comfortable night.

He caught Beau's sharp eye on him. "Fruit rotting on the branches," he said triumphantly. "Trees need pruning."

"Nests in the chimney pots," Beau countered.

"Fumets all over the orchard!"

Beau challenged that one with a frown. "Surely it is normal for beasts of the chase to enter into such a demesne at night to feed?"

"Never so many," Wassail insisted.

"In that case—the windows. There's dirt in the corners of every pane."

"You'll see that anywhere!"

"No, this is always the same, meaning a uniform layer of dirt and a single cleaning."

"Now you're reaching!" Wassail said, and they chuckled.

Every night a fine palace was offered for the travelers'

rest, but no host or hostess ever appeared. Elaborate stories would be offered to explain their absence, but Sir Hubert—the former Master Hakluyt—was convinced that the owners were all dead. The visitors had made a game out of finding evidence that the palaces had been specially refurbished for their visit.

"It troubles me, my lord," Beau said, suddenly serious. "It's so *stupid!* Does he think we don't know the sun rises in the east? That we can't see water damage that would have any sane homeowner re-leading his roof in no time? Empty houses *smell* empty."

"Autocracy is stupid by nature, son. It assumes that one man can always be right. If some of my ancestors hadn't made that mistake, I might be—" Wassail abandoned the notion as treasonous. "Not all kings of Chivial have been as brilliant as our own beloved Athelgar, but they all must heed the Lords and Commons, and that's healthier." If Athelgar had paid more heed to his Privy Council, Wassail might never have become involved in this present madness. That idea felt treasonous too.

Any Chivian-speaking spies Viazemski had planted among the rowers would understand nothing of this conversation, which was being conducted in a random mixture of Chivian, Fitanish, Isilondian, and Dolorish words, a language named "Beauish" after its inventor.

Oars creaked in rowlocks. A white heron flapped across the stream above its own reflection, and Beaumont stared absently after it, looking very young—young enough to be the grandson the spirits had not granted to carry on the Wassail name.

After a moment he said, "It was a stupid thing to try, and it was done so badly! I have this feeling that the emperor-whose-name-I-won't-mention may be clever himself, but he has morons carrying out his orders. You suppose that's true of all autocrats, my lord? That they surround themselves with stupid people?"

"It's true of most. They won't tolerate criticism. They distrust clever subordinates."

"Ah!" Beau was smiling again. "Reminds me. Is our one-armed friend clever, would you say?"

"Like a wild boar, but more dangerous."

"He is still very anxious that our binding conjuration remain a state secret, my lord."

"It's safe with me." Wassail knew that his aging memory had just been given a tactful jog. Personally he thought there would be little harm done if the Czar tried sticking swords through all his *streltsy*'s hearts, assuming they had any.

"He has a request."

Wassail distrusted that babyish innocence. "Namely?"

"He has a paper he wants signed and sealed by you, testifying that the bearer—whose name is fictitious and immaterial—is an honest, worthy gentleman, in whom you have every confidence."

"I'd sooner sign my own death warrant!" Wassail studied Beau's hurt expression for a moment, wondering what was being brewed this time, then said, "You want me to perjure myself?"

"Oh, don't call it *that,* my lord!" The silver eyes twinkled. "That's so *crude!* A momentary lapse of exactitude! Ever since Dvonograd, I have been working to convince that scum that I am his truest friend in all the world and you are his next best and he can trust us to save him no matter what."

"I didn't know he needed saving."

The Blade grinned happily. "Being what he is and working for whom he does? Oh, he is certain to need saving from somebody someday, and sooner rather than later—as I have explained to him. He hadn't known about gift-of-tongues conjuration until we came. I explained that, too. I have assured him in your name that if he wishes to accompany us when we leave Skyrria, we shall be delighted to take him with us and help find him a new life somewhere, to live in luxury on all his ill-gotten loot."

"Spirits preserve me," Wassail muttered. Back in Chivial, the prospect of letting that Viazemski horror loose on Eurania would have appalled him. Out here in the wilderness, he had to consider survival—not just his own, but of all those dependant on him. Values changed. If saving a monster's hide was a necessary price, then he would have to pay it and hope nobody ever found out.

Beaumont was gleeful. "We had difficulty setting out mutually acceptable terms and warranties, my lord. I described those bankers' drafts you carry, but his simple soul cannot believe a piece of paper will change into bags of gold on demand. Naturally he won't accept anything with his own name on it, either. Much too incriminating! In the end we agreed that he would write a testimonial for your signature, as a token of good faith. If I may say so, it is a masterpiece of romantic fiction."

"You trust him?"

"*Trust* him, my lord? You are joking, aren't you? He doesn't trust me either, so that's fair. But if all else fails us, perhaps he won't. Who knows? He *may* be useful, that's all."

Just as Sir Huckster Hakluyt had turned out to be a fountain of information about Skyrria, and might be of more use in future. Considering his youth, Beau had an astonishing eye for the terrain.

"Very well, I'll sign it."

The Blade produced a roll of parchment from his cloak. "Conveniently, Sir Arkell has already attached your seal, my lord."

✦ 8 ✦

Kiensk at last! After so long, any destination would have been welcome, but this one looked much better than Arkell had expected—so good, in fact, that he decided the river-bank had been specially cleaned up for the Chivians' arrival. Boats were tied up along the stone quay at suspiciously regular intervals; lumber, grain sacks, and other cargo were tidily stacked against the stockade that served as city wall; there were more horses in view than horse droppings.

The lead boat had gone on ahead to carry warning, so the reception party was waiting when Wassail stepped ashore around noon. Bands played hobnail Skyrrian music like cats quarreling in a thunderstorm, peacock Pursuivant preened amid an exaltation of Skyrrian heralds, and a dozen hairy grandees glittered welcome in the sunshine. Why would men deck themselves up in so much jewelry and gold brocade, and then hide behind such jungles? Even the liveried pike-bearing men-at-arms had whiskers down to their belts. Strike a spark and they would all go up like dry hay.

Igor was not present, of course, because monarchs did not skulk on docks. The Senior Beard was presented as Chief Boyar Skuratov, who must correspond roughly to Lord Chancellor, and he had brought other important hair-balls to support him—astrologers, conjurers, hereditary boyars of This and That, every one leaning on a staff of office. Prince Dimitri was there, too, looking as if he had an imminent appointment with the Imperial Tormentor. Curious!—last night he'd been bellowing out bawdy songs at the prospect of being reunited with his wife. Arkell caught Beau's eye and confirmed that he had noticed the change.

The three Blades crowded in around their ward. The scene had an uncomfortable stench of unreality about it, as if even the participants were taking this staged pomp seriously. The line of black-clad men on the rampart showed no weapons, but could be *streltsy* archers.

The reason for Dimitri's unhappiness was revealed when Chief Beard Skuratov announced, with deep regret, that, contrary to all previous reports, Princess Tasha was not currently resident in Kiensk; she was home with her sister-in-law at Faritsov. She would be summoned immediately, of course. Dear Dimitri had been sending his darling Yelena letters for the last month and receiving replies almost daily—how odd that he had not known where she was!

So died any chance of leaving Kiensk and Skyrria before spring.

Arkell made a mental note to buy some fur underwear as soon as possible.

The open carriage provided for His Excellency's triumphal entry into Kiensk resembled a converted hay wagon, but it was drawn by eight spectacular white horses. Wassail and three Best Beards climbed aboard. The heralds expected the Blades to ride with the mounted escort; Beau insisted that he and Arkell cling like footman to the back of the carriage, and Oak ride right behind them. Then Wassail, in turn, became uncooperative. By the terms agreed, Sir Dixon and his men would not enter High Town, but old Walrus insisted on seeing and approving their quarters before going to his, so the parade route was adjusted to pass through the Foreigners' Quarter. By this time the Beards were looking testy.

Eventually the band struck up again and the parade lurched forward. Once through the gates, Arkell was astonished by the width of the streets and the open gardens everywhere. Most of the buildings were built of stout logs, but none looked like hovels and some were mansions fit to hold up their roofs proudly in Grandon or even Laville. Over everything loomed the towers and domes and massive walls of High Town, a city within a city.

The house provided for the Chivians in the Foreigners' Quarter was humbler and dirtier, but could not be faulted. Sir Dixon declared himself well pleased, so Ambassador-at-Large Wassail shed his knights and most of his lesser followers. The parade proceeded on to Great Market, into High Town, and thus to the gates of the Imperial Palace itself, where he would be accommodated. This was, according to the Chief Boyar, a great honor.

The guests' quarters were a separate wing with a score of rooms on three levels, all cold and gloomy, with furniture to match. This was certainly adequate for a mere eight men—one earl, three Blades, one herald, and three servants—but it still felt like a jail. Windows were barred, staircases narrow spirals, and doorways never higher than chest-height. Smelly skins covered the floors and no tapestries or paneling masked the ashlar walls. Beau made a quick exploration and came back down to report.

"It's defensible enough, my lord, yet it would be a deathtrap in a fire. There's only one way in or out." He frowned. "That feels wrong!"

"Obviously I can't help," Arkell muttered. "Why don't I go back to Chivial?" Then he had to explain to his ward that the stairs had been curved and the doors hinged to favor right-handed defenders.

Wassail snorted at the idea of three Blades holding off the Skyrrian Empire. "They'd starve us out."

"I'm almost there now, my lord," Beau said.

"Spirits! So am I, lad. Where's that chamberlain?"

So Percy was sent off to find food and returned leading an army of Skyrrian footmen and pages bearing silver dishes. The fare was familiar—rich and heavy, roast meats, chickens, stodgy pies, rice, fish, cabbage soup. Wassail set to with verve, heedless of his imminent dinner with the Czar. Although this was to be a relatively informal event, Hakluyt had warned it would still be a major bloat-and-drunk. Having learned to eat when they had the chance, the Blades accepted their ward's invitation to join him.

"I am hopeful that I will soon regain the weight I lost on the journey," Lord Wassail declared as he beckoned for Kimberley to bring him another helping of dessert.

Autocrats, if Czar Igor was typical, looked much as other men. He wore jewels and gold cloth in abundance, but so did every noble in the hall. He was paunchy and hairy, but that also was the norm. His eyes were perhaps shiftier than most, his nose larger, his mouth unpleasantly sensual. Indeed, the most surprising thing about him was that such an ugly old man had managed to produce so beautiful a grandchild. Then Arkell realized that the golden-haired beauty sitting beside him must be the Czarina Sophie.

The surly lout was Czarevich Fedor, not the state hangman.

The Czar had no Blades, but he did have hounds, one seated on either side of his throne. The brown one was larger than any dog Arkell had ever seen, yet the black one was even bigger, probably outweighing most men in the hall. Suddenly the wild stories about Igor's hunt seemed credible. Every Blade knew about Chivial's infamous Night of Dogs a generation ago, but the monsters that invaded Greymere Palace then had been mindless killers. These two were impeccably trained; their eyes followed the action with human-seeming awareness.

Ambassador Wassail presented his letter of credence. Flowery words were spoken and gifts exchanged. The gruff old man could turn a fair phrase when he wanted and he had been well rehearsed by Pursuivant. Presenting a sapphire necklace to the Czarina, he declaimed that if her sister were a tenth as lovely, then King Athelgar would be the second most envied monarch in Eurania. The girl blushed crimson. Igor looked pleased, perhaps at hearing his country included in Eurania, which was a matter of opinion. Fedor just sneered. He barely managed civil thanks when presented with a jewel-encrusted hunting horn.

After fifty or so boyars and wives had met the Ambassador, the company adjourned to a pillared hall for some refreshments. The courtiers sat at a single long table. At one end, two smaller tables stood at an angle to each other, forming an arrowhead—the highest for the royal family and Wassail's slightly lower, but higher than the boyars'. Everyone ate off gold plate. The toasts began.

Igor's hounds crouched at his feet, staring fixedly at the visitors. Arkell resigned himself to standing behind his ward's left elbow until dawn.

Czarina Sophie ate and drank little and spoke only to answer questions. Her husband made no effort to include her in the conversation and the betrothal that had provoked the gathering was barely mentioned. No one inquired about the groom's teeth or the bride's breath.

Oak had shaved off his beard sometime during the afternoon.

It was apparently acceptable for guests to nod off and take up feasting again when they awoke. Most of them were built like carthorses and also grossly overdressed, in layer upon layer of silks and brocade. The women did not drink as much as their menfolk, but they ate more.

*   *   *

The hounds' teeth were daggers and their lolling tongues as long as insoles. Surely it was unnatural for dogs to stay awake for hours on end? Once during the evening the huge black one rose, walked over to a pillar, and relieved itself. When it came back to its place, the other did the same. The Czar spoke and a nervous footman brought buckets of water for them to drink.

More toasts, more food, an army of fresh servants . . .

The Czar volunteered almost no information. He asked a lot of questions.

The Walrus turned lobster-red but held his liquor well. He minded his manners, fawned as expected, and talked as required—about his journey, his ancestors, modern farming (a subject that did seem to interest the Czar a little), and also about the Chivian form of government, which made him sneer. Fedor had been sneering all night, except when he looked at the Czarina.

There was something between those two, but Arkell could not guess what. Fedor stared a lot at the lovely Sophie, yet Sophie never looked at him. Arkell made a mental note to ask Beau's opinion. Beau's instincts for people were rarely wrong.

Along toward morning, when the candles were winking out in the chandeliers, when the servants had stopped bringing food, when most of the guests were asleep in their chairs or stretched out on the floor, and the Czarevich snored with his head among the dishes, the Czar suddenly said, "So those are Blades, are they?"

Arkell snapped alert.

Wassail said, "Hmm?" He glanced over his shoulder as if he had forgotten them, his eyes sadly blurred. "Yes, sire. Three of them."

Not six, just three.

The Czar had drunk far more than Wassail had, yet did not show it. "Present them."

Wassail started mumbling about Blades never being presented, then remembered he was addressing an autocrat. *"Voyvode* Beaumont . . ."

Beau nodded respectfully, an acknowledgment that raised the Czar's eyebrows.

"Sir Oak . . . Sir Arkell . . ." Two more nods.

"So," said the Emperor of the Skyrrians. "Beaumont, was it?"

Beau spoke for the first time in hours. "Yes, Your Majesty."

"What noble house bred you?"

"I am baseborn, sire."

The Czarina's blue eyes widened in surprise. The Czar frowned.

"Tell us about Ironhall."

A coldness like steel touched Arkell's spine. He had a bizarre hunch that Igor had been waiting all night to ask that question, possibly waiting for months. He might even have arranged his niece's wedding just to . . . No, that was ridiculous! But clearly *Voevode* Viazemski's little plot to keep his imperial master ignorant about the Blades' bindings had been doomed from the start. Monarchs asked questions in public only when the matter was utterly trivial or they already had a very good idea of the answers.

No one else except the Czarina was paying attention. The few remaining servants would not care; the guests were either unconscious or too drunk to understand.

"Ironhall is a school where unwanted boys are trained as swordsmen, Your Majesty."

Silence.

The Czar said, "Continue talking about it until we tell you to stop."

Beau talked: history, setting, architecture, climate, inhabitants, curriculum, diet.

When he came to the wildflowers, Igor said, "Stop. You would die to save your ward? You are bound to absolute loyalty?"

Again, the Czar knew the answer. The only reason he had allowed Wassail to bring three Blades into High Town was because Blades could not be parted from their ward. Arkell wanted to kick Beau's ankle.

But Beau had seen the trap. "We swore an oath. Many of our Order have given their lives for their wards."

"More than an oath. Describe how you were bound to your ward."

Only Arkell and Oak could have seen Beau's finger jab into his ward's back. Wassail was having great difficulty holding his head up, but at that he roused himself.

"Don't answer, Beau. Sorry, Shire. Bindinsh a shtate shecret."

Igor's eyes narrowed. He spoke to Beaumont. "And you cannot refuse an order from your ward, yes?"

"Not so, sire. Absolute loyalty, not absolute obedience. I will refuse an order if I think it puts him in danger."

"So!" The Czar disapproved of that. "And when your ward dies you go insane and slaughter innocent bystanders."

"That can happen, if our ward dies by violence. This prospect is another layer of defense, of course."

The Czar smiled his approval of that. "Master Hakluyt insists that the conjuration involves a sword driven through your heart."

Jab! again.

Wassail sighed and seemed to swallow a yawn. "Thash correct, Majesty. Common knowledge."

"Does it leave a scar, Beaumont?"

"Yes, it does, sire."

"On your back as well? The sword went right through you?"

"So I am told."

"Show us this wonder."

"Sire?" Even Beau could be surprised sometimes.

"Bashful?" Igor smiled. "Reluctant to uncover your manly chest in public?"

Like a reflecting pool, the scene rippled and changed. The Czarina blushed madly and dropped her gaze. The Czar's contempt became lechery. The unspoken word *autocrat* slammed down like a broadsword. Arkell looked in horror at Beau. Oak, beyond him, was aghast.

Beau's smile never flickered. "It hardly seems proper in these surroundings, if Your Majesty will forgive my saying so."

The Czar said, "Vasili! Iakov!"

The hounds were on their feet in an instant, teeth bared, hackles rising. Arkell's hand reached for *Reason*.

"But you would satisfy our curiosity in private, Beaumont?"

Surely this was a nightmare! If the Czar reported back to Chivial that the Ambassador had never reached Kiensk, that brigands had ambushed and slaughtered his whole train, there would be *nothing Athelgar could do!* Except cut off trade, and small compensation that would be.

Incredibly, Beau was still smiling. "I should be honored to satisfy Your Majesty's curiosity."

"We so wish," the Czar said.

"Eh?" Wassail said, reacting at last. "What? Now, look here—" He moved as if to rise and Beau's hand on his shoulder pushed him down.

Beau unfastened his baldric and handed *Just Desert* to Arkell, scabbard and all. "You have the sash," he said softly.

Arkell opened his mouth to protest and the steel in Beau's

eyes cut him off. Beau stepped around him and bowed to the Czar. The dogs curled their lips but did nothing more.

Igor rose. The Czarina rose, keeping her face lowered. Czarevich Fedor snored on. A few guests lurched to their feet and tried to bow. The Emperor of the Skyrrians walked unsteadily from the hall with his arm around Beau's shoulders, leaning on him, followed by Vasili, Iakov, and then the Czarina.

✦ 9 ✦

It was almost morning. Dawn would soon be slipping poniards of light between the bed curtains, but Sophie could not sleep. It was not Igor's shameless behavior that kept her staring at the darkness with eyes sore from weeping—not that in itself, at least, although his actions were becoming more and more blatant. Many people who might overlook his degradation of upstart princes would draw the line at baseborn foreign soldiers. The whispers would grow louder, and there *were* whispers, whether he admitted it or not. What worried her was that such gossip would make him even more anxious to prove his virility. The need for another czarevich would grow more urgent, and that meant Fedor.

Fedor knew. Oh, yes, Fedor had been told the plan. If he had not said anything to her last night it was only because he had not been able to catch her alone. His sneers had been message enough. Fedor would love to father a brother for himself on his stepmother.

Sometime today she *must* have a private word with Igor, although how she would arrange that she could not imagine. She *must* explain to him that his plan to safeguard her child would not work unless Fedor was absolutely certain that it was his. Since Igor had lain with her last night, she might be bearing already. Igor must hold Fedor back for at least another month. That would buy her some time.

Time for what she could not imagine.

Light? Morning? Had she slept without knowing it?

The chinks of light grew brighter, dimmed, brightened again, and then faded away altogether, as if Igor had opened and closed the corner door. On the rare nights he wanted her, he threw it wide and shouted for her. He would not enter a dark room.

So it was not Igor.

She rose on one elbow to peer through a gap. She made out the blur of a face, pale hair. Even his hands. He was standing by the connecting door, waiting for his eyes to adjust to the dark.

Strangely, she was not afraid. Not at all. Sorry for him, yes. Afraid for him, if he was about to try what she thought he was.

Minutes dragged by like hours, but eventually the Chivian began to move, very slowly, toward the outer door. He would know that the direct exit from Igor's room was guarded by the dogs.

"You'd better not open that one either."

He turned. "Your pardon, Majesty. I mean no harm."

"My maid sleeps out there. She is old, but not deaf, and sleeps very lightly. Even if she does not waken, you cannot leave the royal suite without running into *streltsy*."

He sighed. "Then I beg you to forgive my intrusion. I will go back and wait until His Majesty awakens and dismisses me."

"Wait!" she said. She did not know why. A strange man in her room and she had no clothes on—it would be his death warrant, hers as well, and the nastiest sort of deaths. "Pass me that robe. On that chest."

He handed it in through the drapes. When she emerged, he had moved over to the window, where he was more visible. She walked across to him—barefoot, her hair unbound. She was being very foolish and did not care. How long before Igor wakened and came looking for his new friend?

"There is another way out."

"Ah!" The foreigner's eyes caught the light of the sky and shone silver.

"But of course that won't work, will it?" What had she been thinking of? The swordsman was clever, as he had shown under Igor's questioning. "You weren't trying to leave." He had been snooping. Looking for something to steal, no doubt.

"I was bored, my lady. But you are right—I cannot use the secret way without incriminating you. Unless the access is from your husband's room?"

"You know what I am talking about?"

"I knew there must be hidden exits when I examined our quarters in the West Wing. Whoever designed those doors and stairs would never tolerate dead-ends. There must be bolt-holes. I planned to look for them tomorrow. Today, I mean."

"Look for trapdoors next to the outer wall. Here." Between window and fireplace— "Help me move this chest."

"Let me, please!" He wrestled the chest aside without her help, although she had seen porters twice his size strain to move that one. She knelt and pulled back the bearskin rug. "You can't see it, but there is a finger hole, looks like a knothole . . . here. A section lifts out."

He was kneeling close beside her. Their hands touched. She took hers away.

"Found it," he said softly. He tilted the slab, then closed it. "Where does it lead?"

"Down to the cellars. They all lead there. I don't know if

there is a shaft under the Czar's room or not, but there are certainly others in the palace." She assumed Igor knew, although he had never mentioned them. Dimitri had shown her the secret when she was a child, one time they had come to Kiensk with their parents. He had learned it years before from Czarevna Avramia, who had been about his age and had died when Sophie was very small.

"I am deeply in your debt, Your Grace."

"I think Skyrria owes you something." She was very conscious of the man's nearness. Her heart was flapping like a chicken coop with a fox in it. "The shafts are narrow, like chimneys. My husband could not get through them. Or Boyar Wassail. They are exits only, not entrances. It would be very hard for a man to come in this way, even if he knew where to look. He would need to climb on something to reach the—" She hesitated. "The hatch in the cellar roof."

"But a small, nimble man could?" There was mirth in his voice.

"I did not mean that!" Hurriedly—"Please, will you tell me something?" She must send him away. Igor might waken.

"Anything, Your Grace."

"What sort of a man is King Athelgar? Really, I mean? My sister—"

"He is a good man! I have met him and the Blades know all about him. Thirty years old. Slim, taller than me—about the same build as Sir Arkell, who stood on my left tonight. He is abstemious, restless, active; has no serious vices. Tell your sister not to worry."

"I shall. Thank you."

"He is also a very lonely man, I think."

"A king lonely?" She tried to make the question sound flippant, and it did not. It seemed to echo: *a queen lonely?*

"I have heard that ruling is a lonely business."

Their shoulders were touching. She did not pull away.

Nor did he. "Athelgar was born and raised in a distant land. Many of the friends he brought with him to Chivial shamed him, and he had to send them away. If he starts favoring a lady, he upsets the political balance of the country. He has learned to be a solitary, self-contained man, but it does not suit him. He needs a soul mate."

"We all do."

He slid his arm around her. She did not protest. This was madness! Considering the risks he was taking by just being here, he ought to be trembling like jelly. She was, but he was steady as the palace. Igor was a coward, with his dogs and his fear of the dark. This man was not.

"I also have a question. Why did your sister leave Kiensk so hurriedly?"

"What makes you think she did?"

"All the time we were being led around in circles, your brother was writing to his wife here in Kiensk and she was replying."

"Will you keep it a secret?"

"If I can. A Blade's loyalty to his ward is absolute, my lady. I have no choice in that."

"She fell and bruised her face. The Czar thought it would be inappropriate for her to—"

"Fell?"

"Princesses can fall like lesser folk."

His grip around her shoulders tightened. "Not without reason, Your Grace."

"Her horse shied, and—"

"Your brother said she is a keen and skilled horsewoman and was unhappy because she had no chance to ride here in Kiensk."

She was silent.

"Sophie?" —very softly.

"Fedor struck her. He was drunk."

"I can believe that of Fedor."

"That was all, I swear! There were many witnesses, and she came to no harm but that."

"Then I will tell no one. I also swear. Thank you for trusting me."

She had thought that all kisses tasted of stale wine, but his did not. It was a surprise. It was sweet. She did not know how it had happened. Or how to end it.

He ended it. "I must go," he whispered.

"Yes."

Yet still they knelt there with their arms around each other.

"Tomorrow I will see if our quarters have access to the cellars," he said. "Are all the cellars connected?"

"Yes."

"How could I know this shaft?"

He did not ask her if she had explored it, but of course she had, the first time Igor had gone off to Czaritsyn and left her. "By smell. The vinegar store. The ceiling tiles are patterned. Circles mark the hatches."

"May I come and see you tomorrow?"

"You are insane even to think of it!"

"Beauty does that to men, and women more beautiful than you do not exist." He kissed her again, for longer, and ended with a sigh. "I think you are in need of a little tenderness. Am I right?"

" . . . Maybe."

"I am. It is many months since I bade farewell to the woman I will marry. Sharing tenderness is all that gives us strength to face the cruelty of the world. But you decide. Hang a cord through that finger hole so I can see it from below. That will be the signal. No cord, no caller."

He did not ask if she would be alone. He could guess how little interest Igor had in her now.

"You must go!" she whispered, and added, "Another night would be safer." There!

"And better. I am not looking for revenge, Sophie."

"I am." She said it without knowing she was going to, or even that it was true. But it was.

He kissed her a third time, his hand wandering inside her robe. When she began to shiver with joy, he pulled away. "Not revenge," he whispered. "We must make love to take joy in each other, not just to get back at him. That would spoil it."

"It would make it sweeter, far sweeter. Don't stop now."

He laughed softly. "Lady, you have flattering faith in my power of concentration."

"You could. Are you not aroused?"

"Very much so. But I need an entire night to make love to you as you deserve. I will begin by kissing you all over and carry on from there."

She heard the amusement in his voice and smiled gratefully into the darkness. "Promises! You know the risks."

"I will risk the risks gladly, Sophie. Will you?"

"Eagerly."

He rose, lifting her. He replaced the chest. "Tomorrow, or the night after."

"I will be waiting."

He led over to the bed. "Pretend to be asleep, just in case." As he prepared to close the curtains on her, he said, "Remember that life is like a diary, Sophie."

"What do you mean?"

"The front and back covers are provided, but we have to write the pages ourselves." He chuckled and was gone.

She did not hear the bolt click, but soon light flared up. There was no roar of fury from an outraged Czar. The chamber went dark.

She lay and stared up at the canopy, daring to hope that she had acquired a lover.

◆ 10 ◆

The cramped little dining room that Beau had designated the Great Hall contained eight battered chairs and a table on which Acting Commander Arkell had just lost over two million crowns at dice to Pursuivant Dinwiddie. As he could usually win the equivalent of a small county an hour off the herald, this showed how distracted he was. It was almost noon. *Just Desert* in her scabbard lay in full view beside them, still unclaimed by her owner.

Oak came in and held the door for Wassail, followed by Hagfield carrying his lordship's cloak and Kimberley with a tray. His Excellency's glare would melt plate armor. He sat down gingerly. The footman poured him a tankard of breakfast. No one spoke.

After a long draft, he wiped the foam off his mustache and opened his eyes again to scowl furiously at Arkell. "No word?"

"None, my lord."

"Barbaric! Pursuivant? How do I go about reclaiming my stolen servant?"

Dinwiddie opened and closed his mouth in panic, making Arkell imagine gills flapping.

"Well?" roared His Excellency. He thumped a fist on the table and winced. "How do I get my Blade back?"

"You could try whistling for him," Beau said cheerily, walking in. "Good chance, my lord." He took up his sword and slung the baldric around him. Then he sat down and smiled at four angry stares around the table and the two happy smiles on the servants.

"Kim, I've asked Percy to run a small errand for me. Would you go and keep an eye on the skivvies, please? If they're not spies they're thieves. And send in something for me to eat?"

Kimberley hurried out. Beau was certainly showing no ill effects from whatever had happened. He looked sparkling new—freshly shaved and ironed.

"They have wonderful bathhouses here, my lord. I was advised that the Palace facilities are substandard, and I should try an excellent place two chancellories east of here. There are more out in Kiensk, just off Great Market. They steam you like fish and beat you black and blue with their fists and tip ice-water over you. It's very . . . very cleansing. I recommend it. Much favored for hangovers, I understand."

Wassail's blood-pudding face darkened several shades. "Is the Blades' binding truly a state secret? Or did that scoundrel Viazemski just trick us into saying it was?"

Had he tricked *Arkell,* was the problem. It was Arkell who'd agreed to keep the damned thing secret. He was grateful that Beau did not look in his direction.

"It's certainly an Ironhall monopoly within Chivial, my lord. The King does not want robber barons setting up private orders of Blades. As to what would happen if the Czar asked his future brother-in-law for a copy of the ritual, I don't know. Arkell? Precedents?"

"None that I know of."

"I told dear Igor," Beau said, speaking more deliberately, "that I could not help him even if I were allowed to do so, and I was sure that was true of all of us. In my five years at Ironhall I witnessed bindings maybe two dozen times. But—as I explained to His Majesty—the rituals are written in incomprehensible Old Chivian, hundred of years old. The prospective ward and his Blade have to be inside the octogram with another six people. Most of them have very little to say or do, admittedly, but three of them have very long conjurations to chant. Some parts are mumbled while the spectators are singing, some of them vary depending on how many men are to be bound. There are a couple of tests involved that I certainly do not understand, and the octogram in Ironhall may have special properties all its own. In short, even if we wished to instruct His Majesty's Grand Wizard, or whatever his title is here, we could not possibly do so."

Again everyone looked at Arkell. "I agree. We might recall four fifths of the ritual between us, but that's as useful as four fifths of a bowstring."

The Walrus snorted. "Did he believe you, Beau?"

Beau sighed. "I don't suppose so, my lord. I doubt if he believes anyone."

"The man wants his own Blades. He *trusts* no one, that's his problem."

"Would you, if you had his record?" Beau grinned at his ward's apoplectic glare.

An hour or so later, after Wassail and Pursuivant had settled down to inventory the baggage and learn how many of their precious baubles had disappeared en route, Beau put Oak on watch and took his leave, with a nod at Arkell to follow. Carrying the sack Percy had brought him, he trotted up the first staircase, then strode along to Wassail's bedchamber. Although gloomy and oppressive, it was large enough not to be crowded by the four-poster and other chunky furniture; if the fireplace would not handle a whole ox, a sheep should fit nicely.

Beau locked the door behind them. All pretense of humor had vanished, leaving his face as bleak as Starkmoor in Firstmoon.

Arkell said, "Well?"

"Very unwell, brother." Beau's voice was incongruously soft. "I will tell you this once. I will tell Oak—once. Forget it and you will die. Remember it and you may still die. *The Czar is a mad dog.* He kills people. He kills people for any reason he fancies or no reason at all or just because he enjoys killing people. He cannot tolerate anything that blocks his current whim. He may strike at any moment and without any warning and *he is bound by no law at all.* Do you understand this?"

Arkell nodded, trying not to shiver. "Yes, Leader."

Beau's smile flashed back. "Then I wish you good chance." He glanced around the room. "If the *streltsy* attack us en masse, where will you make your last stand?"

"Here, probably. The upper floor would be too accessible to men cutting in through the roof." To show that he could keep up sometimes, Arkell added, "You still think there's secret passages?"

Beau's eyes twinkled silver. "How would you start looking for them?"

"Measure the thickness of the walls," Arkell said, "and the height of the ceilings and count the steps in the stairs."

"And what did you discover when you did all that?" It was impossible to deceive him.

"The floors are very thick; a man could crawl along between the beams. The walls are solid, but only the outside ones could contain passages."

"All the walls are bare stone with mortared joints," Beau said. Testing.

"But moth-eaten hides on the floors? They may be warm in winter, but they're filthy and they stink. I went looking for trapdoors close to the outer walls. There's one here, between the window and the fireplace, and one in your room, too." Arkell lifted back the edge of the rug, stuck his finger in the knothole provided for the purpose, and raised the slab until he could get a proper grip and lift it free. "That's as far as I got."

Beau thumped his shoulder. "It's farther than I ever would." He studied the manhole doubtfully. "I think we'd have to put our ward down that in sections."

"He'll never go around the corners otherwise."

"My belief is that it leads down to the cellars. You found it, so you should have the honor of exploring it."

"No, I'm the brains of the team. And I'm bigger—might get stuck."

Smirk. "I just had a bath."

Arkell sighed and started to strip. From his sack, Beau produced a coil of rope, a tinderbox, and a lantern.

Wearing only his smallclothes and the coil of rope, Arkell slithered headfirst into a coffin-sized gap below the floorboards. He waited, legs still in the room and shoulders almost touching the beams on either side, until his eyes adjusted to the lantern's faint gleam. His guess had been correct. The gap tunneled into the masonry of the wall, to a shaft leading downward. Rusty iron staples provided an awkward ladder.

Shivering already, he squirmed back to where he had started and began again, this time going feetfirst and banging his head on the roof every time he tried to see where he was going. When his feet reached the shaft, he had to roll over to contort himself into it and begin his descent. The need to keep one hand free for his lantern forced him to brace himself against the opposite wall whenever he needed to change his grip, and the stones were cold, rough, and undoubtedly filthy. Old Wassail could not come this way and his Blades would never go without him, so as an escape it was hypothetical. It might prove to have other uses, though.

A score of rungs brought him to the bottom of the shaft and another tunnel between two massive beams, just like the one upstairs. The gymnastics became even more complicated, but eventually he managed to squirm in on his back. Working out the geometry as he went, he decided that he must be under the kitchen. He could see the trap, but he was quite unable to lift it, and something was blocking the finger-hole—probably a chest or dresser.

By that time his feet had found solid timber blocking the tunnel. This secret passage seemed utterly useless except as a source of illicit midnight snacks. He lay and shivered until he worked out the design and realized something was poking him in the back. He rolled over, finding hinges and a metal ring set in the floor.

As usual, then, Beau had been right. The passage did lead to a cellar, and it might just be possible for the Walrus to squeeze through from the kitchen, going straight down. The hatch was gruntin' heavy, and had to be lifted at an angle designed to give him a double hernia and crushed fingers, but eventually he was able to raise one side a fraction and prop it open with the coil of rope. The space below was dark. He detected a strong smell of apples.

When he poked his head up through the bedchamber floor, the first thing he saw was his leader relaxing on the bed, reading a book.

"Nice cobwebs!" Beau said. "Make you look quite Skyrrian."

Arkell spat out a few choice words in Fitanish, which had a brutal, bone-grinding sound to it when necessary.

Beau tutted. "Shame! You're disgusting, a disgrace to the Order. Why don't you have a good roll on the rugs? What did you find?"

Arkell scrambled out. "I won't spoil your fun by telling you."

"Your shoulders are bleeding."

"Surprise me." Shivering with cold and grubby as he had ever been in his life, he went over to the washstand. "It goes down to the cellars, a crypt full of apples. Baskets of them, packed to the roof. You can't get out of the shaft without making them into cider." He tipped water into the basin from the ewer.

Beau put down the book and stood up. "Wait before you dirty the water. The shaft in my room may have a better exit.

You can't possibly pass up an exciting opportunity to explore it too."

Arkell regarded his leader with resentment. "Who, me?"

"Why not? I'm not just thinking about escape. I'm planning to go exploring. Tonight I'll take a look around the cellars. I have a thing about spiders, though; I'm running you through first to clean out the cobwebs."

Arkell sighed and took up the rope and lantern again. "You're going to owe me one after this."

"Possibly." Beau held the door for him. "How about an hour or two off? You need a bath even more than usual. The house I went to was segregated, but I was told of one that isn't. Very steamy, I understand."

Arkell was seriously overdue for some of that sort of relaxation. "Leader, you are forgiven. Lead on."

✦ 11 ✦

All day Czarina Sophie had been telling herself that last night's bizarre encounter had been nothing but a dream. All day her conscience had been growling that it wasn't. The touch of his lips, his hand on her breast . . . even his scent seemed to haunt her.

She must have drunk far too much wine at the reception. It was extremely fortunate that terrible consequences had not ensued.

Nevertheless, she did spend the afternoon rearranging the furniture in her chamber, amusing her ladies-in-waiting and working two unfortunate porters like mules. After a dozen variations, she settled on much the same pattern as before, except that her favorite chair now stood between the window and the fireplace. In winter a candelabra on the mantel shelf would shed good light on her book, she explained, and she would have daylight in summer. The chair she could lift.

Kiss you all over—Those foolish words had been echoing in her head all day. Just a joke. Very vulgar humor.

She had found a length of white tape left over from some dress fitting. She had no intention of using it as the swordsman had suggested, of course, but it might come in handy for something.

So she had been telling herself all day, but when the moment came, when she was left alone with her book at last, she quickly moved the chair aside, pulled up the edge of the rug, and fed some of the tape down the hole. Then she replaced the rug, leaving the chair where it was. She held on to the other end of the tape, ready to pull it clear of the hatch if Igor opened the door.

The classic love story that had been so engrossing two nights ago was now gibberish, meaningless marks on paper. Her heart was racing. She started at every tiny sound. This was the stupidest thing she had ever done in her life. And for what reason? If revenge for neglect and loneliness was her only purpose, then she was risking her life and the Chivian's for a wickedly petty cause. Blocking Fedor would be a better excuse, but to treat Beaumont as a stud animal would demean him horribly. And if she had merely succumbed to his good looks, then she was no better than a cat in heat.

To share tenderness, he had said; to take joy in each other. Were men capable of tenderness? Was love ever more than a poet's conceit?

And what was in it for him, that he should risk his life? With his looks he should have no trouble taking pretty girls to bed, girls with rounder curves than hers. Not revenge, he said, but he might be a spy, hoping to learn state secrets, or a thief after her jewels. He might strangle her and no one would know who the intruder had been.

She started at a sound, not having realized she was asleep. The candle was almost gone; she was stiff and frozen. The rug behind her chair was stirring. She pulled the edge back and helped him lift the slab of timber aside. He scrambled out of the trap.

"Wait!" he said quietly. "I'm filthy!" He was almost invisible in dark clothes, the sort of peasant shirt and trousers found on half the stalls in Great Market, plus a head cloth like a woman's. When he stripped them off, she was relieved to see that he wore other garments underneath—an absurd reaction under the circumstances. Then, with finger and thumb, he snuffed the candle and plunged the room into darkness.

"Now!" He kissed her, and his kiss was as sweet as she had remembered. "This has been the longest day of my life!" he said as he led her over to the bed.

"Why?" she whispered as he removed her robe. "Why are you taking this awful risk?"

He chuckled softly. "I cannot tell you why, Sophie. All the poets who ever lived could never put it into words. I can only try to show you."

"Do you know what he will do to you?"

"Do you know what I am going to do to you?"

"Kiss me all over?"

"That will be a good beginning, but only a beginning."

And so it was. Yes, some men could be tender.

◆ 12 ◆

The roosters' dawn fanfares came much too late to waken Tasha. She had been staring at the darkness for hours, listening to the rain on the roof, thinking of the past, which was sad, and the future, which was both exciting and terrifying.

Her face had healed. Today she would leave Faritsov and never see it again. She must say farewell to all the places and people that had made up her life.

In two days she would be back in Kiensk, meeting the Chivian Ambassador, preparing for her wedding—her *first* wedding. Dimitri joked that she was going to be married in two halves. Imperial Astrologer Unkovskii had not chosen the date yet and the Czar would still have to approve it, but she hoped it would be soon, because after that she would receive royal honors.

First the wedding, then preparations for departure in spring. She was going to need a thousand camels to transport all the *absolutely essential* baggage she was collecting. And who would go with her? There had been endless discussion while she was in Kiensk and would certainly be more.

Olga Yurievna, of course, her lifelong friend and near neighbor—she would be Mistress of the Queen's Robes in Chivial. The betrothal treaty said Tasha could take twelve attendants, and she had expected half of those to be servants, but it was heartrending to see so many noble families clamoring to send a daughter or two off in the future queen's train, all thinking their children would be safer and happier out of Skyrria and yet terrified that the Czar might suspect that they thought that way. Negotiations had been confusing, to say the least. After all, she could acquire mere maids in Chivial.

Sophie's letters said that King Athelgar sounded like a very good match, a good person. She had not added, "Better than Igor," but that went without saying.

V

The Road to Morkuta

◆ 1 ◆

Darling, be careful! ...

Winter was almost here; specks of snow danced under leaden clouds, or scuttled into corners. Oak was in a hurry, almost running as he zigzagged between the stalls and crowds in Great Market.

Normally he liked to linger, for this was the throbbing heart of Kiensk, a roaring all-day, every-day fair. Its multi-colored booths and tents displayed an infinite variety of wares—banal vegetables to exotic weapons from lands he had never heard of. Here, too, were barbers and for-tunetellers, masseurs, tattooers, and spirits knew who else. He enjoyed watching the jugglers, buskers, and acrobats; he liked hearing the minstrels and the cries of the hawkers. He cared less for the screams of criminals being knouted and the public executions. Bear-baiting he enjoyed once in a while, although he cheered for the bear.

The imposing buildings enclosing the square held no interest for him. Behind them lay streets of more modest dwellings, one- or two-room cabins built of thick logs. Their doors opened on the road, but they all had carefully tended yards in the back, usually with a pig and a few chickens. One of these houses was his destination, today and most days.

He was late. Afternoons were when he could enjoy some free time and attend to his personal assignment, which was to explore the outer city. Beau took night hours, usually, when the cavernous cellars under the Imperial Palace were deserted. He had explored them from one end to the other and could tell where he was by smell alone, or so he claimed. Morning belonged to Arkell, who had already mapped out the Imperial Palace very thoroughly and was now working on the rest of High Town.

Their personal lives had adjusted to fit. Arkell played the field at the Treasury bathhouse. Whoever Beau's close friend was—and Beau never discussed women—she must live in the Palace itself, because the *streltsy* patrolled the streets of High Town at night. Most afternoons Oak came and tapped on this door here . . .

And it flew open and Bassa said, "Darling! You're late. I was so worried. I was afraid you weren't coming."

By then the door was closed and he was kissing her. Bassa was gorgeous—dark-eyed and voluptuous. She had a sickly boy child who sat on the rug all the time, sucking on a chicken bone and paying no heed as his mother and the man hauled off each other's clothes in frantic haste, leaving a trail of garments from the door all the way across to the bed. Bassa was young and big, and randy as a cat. Oak had never known a woman so everlastingly eager, so inexhaustibly energetic. His friend Orson would have raved about her.

Bassa's husband Mikhail, who was sometimes a farrier

and sometimes a cobbler, might be around the house before noon, but not between then and curfew. Oak had never met the man whose wife's breasts he was so eagerly kissing and fondling, but he could do Mikhail no permanent damage as he rolled on the bed in joyful struggle with Bassa, because she was already carrying a second child. Although it was early days yet, those glorious breasts were swelling splendidly.

Strong as Oak was, she always gave him a good workout. Eventually, inevitably, he conquered and pinned her; she wrapped her legs around him and they coupled. She cried out, clawing and biting, driving him on. He exploded into her. *Oh, Bassa, Bassa, Bassa!*

In the quiet times, as he lay listening to the slow, satisfied beat of his heart, Oak often wondered if there really was a Mikhail, and who enjoyed her mornings. The first time she had brought him home, she had insisted she was not a slut, selling her favors for money—but of course Mikhail earned so little and the child pined, needing witchcraft. Sob, sob. Oak had left a kopek on the table. One day, feeling especially mellow, he had left two, which had turned out to be an excellent idea. He couldn't afford three, and was not at all sure he would survive the results anyway.

She nuzzled even closer: *Again?*

Again of course.

Again? Had he inadvertently paid her twice yesterday?

"No, not again! It's late. I must go."

"But *darling!* . . . Let me try this . . ."

Oh yes! He let himself be persuaded.

The curfew was tolling. He leaped off the bed, dragged on his shirt and doublet, then hose, boots. Dusk showed through the window. The watch set up street barriers after curfew, the gates of High Town would be closed. Boots, jerkin, hat. He fumbled with his purse and laid three kopeks on the table, made sure of the baby's location so he wouldn't step on it, said, "Bye, love, do it again tomorrow," and headed for the door.

"Darling, be careful."

What!? It was only a whisper and she had her back turned, seeming asleep.

Oh, it was like that, was it? He sighed. For a moment he thought of taking back the coins, but she had certainly earned them, no matter what They might have promised her, and more likely They had used threats instead. Would make more sense to leave her the whole purse, since he wasn't likely to have more need of it; but he didn't.

The bell had stopped. That alone was serious trouble. He wrapped his cloak around his arm as he had been taught— two turns as padding, the rest hanging loose, available to distract or blind an opponent, or entangle his sword if it was light enough. He drew *Sorrow* and kissed her. "Dance with me," he whispered.

The door opened outward, so he hurled it wide and leaped out, swinging his long sword like a scythe in case They were waiting there, but there was no one. The dusk was full of fog and whirling snow. The flakes seemed dark instead of white, tickling eyelashes, dancing in front of him, bewildering him so he wanted to swat them away. He could barely see across the street. He wouldn't see Them coming, but equally They might not find him again if he could once break free. All he need do was make it to the Foreigners' Quarter and the knights' house. Indeed, he could bang on any door, beg shelter, pay for lodging, but he would not do that before he had escaped from Them, or They would burn the house down on top of him and his innocent hosts.

He went left instead of right. That might throw Them off

for a moment and it also kept his sword arm free of the wall, but They would know Bassa had warned him; he hoped she would not be in trouble.

He carried his long sword at high guard, which meant almost overhead. *Sorrow* had a point, but even he could not flicker her around like a rapier, or poke her through a man with a twitch of his wrist. She was not even especially sharp, lest she chip and break in engagement; to do harm she must be swung like an ax, but one hit would always be enough.

The silence was creepy, as if the snow had shut down the city, but he had never been out after curfew before, so he couldn't judge. His feet made no sound. He reached the corner, glanced around it, and ran along the rail fence to the next house.

They would be behind him, almost certainly, expecting him to take the shortest way home. He found he was walking crabwise, trying to look in all directions at once. He came to the second corner and peered around, straight into a man's eyes. The man yelled and tried to draw; Ironhall reflexes brought *Sorrow* slamming down on the base of his neck. Oak cried out in dismay and pulled her free from the corpse. Voices rose behind him, a sudden thud of hooves.

He ran. He had been a fair sprinter before he mashed his leg on Starkmoor, but that old fall might be going to kill him after all. A horse thudded past him on the far side of the road, accompanied by two other shapes than ran in silence, things like bears. A voice spoke and those two turned on him, snarling and growling. He fell back against the house wall, lowering *Sorrow* to outside guard and raising his cloak-wrapped arm to protect his throat.

The voice called again. The monsters wheeled and were gone into the snowstorm, but the damage was done. The men had arrived. He was hemmed in.

Two of them edged closer, emerging from the fog as black

shapes almost invisible. They separated, came at him slowly, blurs in the night. Two-on-one was safe enough if the one was a Blade. Seniors trained against juniors in pairs.

"Don't do it!" he said. "I don't want to hurt you."

"Don't worry, you won't!" said the one on his right.

"I know you," he said. "Sasha!" They had played dice on the journey, gone drinking together.

Sasha favored a curved saber. The man on Oak's left was holding his weapon point-on, so it was either a rapier or a light blade intended more for thrusting than cutting. They ought to change sides, but Oak was not about to suggest it to them.

For long, cold moments nothing much happened. The rapier man tried a few feints, which Oak ignored. Then Sasha yelled, "Now!"

The *streltsy* leaped. Oak deflected the rapier with the loose folds of his cloak, weighing it down. He beat Sasha's stroke aside with *Sorrow* and stepped past him, slashing him across the kidney as he went. Then he pivoted to deal with the other man. Rapiers were deadly at arm's length and useless as pudding at close quarters. Oak closed and slashed low, feeling *Sorrow* thud into flesh, also feeling a searing pain run up his sword arm. In the darkness he had failed to see the man's dagger.

Two down, although both were writhing and crying out, certainly not dead. There were many more people out there. The high black shape across the road was the man on horseback, and the two bear-things were his dogs, all watching.

"Come and help!" Oak shouted. "Get them to healers, quickly!"

"Three!" said the man on horseback.

Swine!

Three snow-caked shapes solidified out of the murk. Wishing he dared hunt for the dropped dagger, Oak moved farther along the wall to give himself foot room. His right forearm ran blood, pulsing with beats of pain, but it seemed to be working properly, which was all that mattered at the moment. The *Litany* at Ironhall told of several three-on-one battles and mostly the hero died. It also told of Grand Master's famous exploit, half a century ago, besting four on open ground, but Oak was not Durendal. Nobody was. Face it, three was not possible.

But he did have the wall at his back and they had just lost two men. Sasha was still screaming. Sasha had been their best, so seeing him cut down so fast ought to make them pause. While Oak could strike anywhere, they must watch out for one another.

They came slowly. He twitched with eagerness to jump one of them, but dared not leave the protection of his wall.

"Cowards!" he taunted them. "There's only two balls among the four of us. Better on women and children, aren't you?"

They continued their measured approach in silence—rapier in the middle, cutting swords raised on either side. This time no one made the mistake of shouting warnings, but that helped him as much as them, because when the one in the center lunged, the others were a fraction later. Life became a blur of clashing steel and leaping feet, parry, beat, slash, and even one desperate lunge, shapes dancing in the murk, heaving breath and a terrible fire in his ribs, then stumbling back against the wall and screaming.

Wasn't him screaming, though. He was leaning against the wall with hot water scalding his side. Two bodies and an abandoned sword lay nearby, and one man was staggering away, bent double as he held his guts in, leaving a black trail on the snow.

They'd told him wounds didn't hurt until later, but that wasn't true. His arm was nothing compared to the chest wound . . . bleeding like a stuck pig, blood hot on his belly, cold on his legs. It hurt, it hurt! He forced himself upright and leaned against the wall, panting and gritting his teeth.

"Now four!" said the horseman.

Oak charged him. It was hopeless, but he was as good as dead anyway. The dogs leaped forward. The small one was as big as he was and the other much bigger. He swung *Sorrow* and felt her bite. The dog screamed, very humanlike. The big one went for his throat but he raised his arm in time to catch its teeth. The impact hurled him flat, and the monster jaws were big enough to close over his cloak wrapping. He felt bones crack. Then the hound shook him, tearing his arm from its socket. He screamed and tried to strike at it, but he had lost his sword. It shook him again, lifting him off the ground and flapping him like a rug. He was past screaming.

"Vasili! Back!" A whip cracked. The dog yelped.

Oak lay in the snow, feeling it cold against his head, feeling the cold of blood on his side. Pain. Choking. Dying.

Something was howling most horribly.

Shouts: "The dog! Look at the dog! It's changing! Witchcraft!"

"Cover it, *Voevode!*" barked a familiar voice. "Quiet, fools! It's dead, that's all."

Hooves thumped close to Oak's ear and he sensed the horseman looking down at him. "He killed Iakov! How much is he hurt?"

A shape knelt over him. "Chest wound. Looks bad, sire." Viazemski's voice.

"Stars! How long has he got?"

"Three or four minutes. No more."

"He killed my dog! Get him to a healer! He must suffer longer than that."

"No hope, sire. He'd never make it. Chest wounds, you know."

"Fire and death! Then strip him and make sure he dies there in the gutter. Leave the body for the rats. Get our wounded to the healers and remove the other corpses."

"Yes, sire."

Hooves receded and were gone.

"I'd say he's as good as dead."

"Yes, *Voevode*."

"Look after the wounded, then. Report to me when it's done."

"Yes, *Voevode*."

The world was fading in and out, mostly out. The pain had gone. Oak could barely feel his chest, darkness . . . He saw the flash of a dagger as the man knelt down beside him. Didn't matter. He was going to die soon and then it wouldn't hurt any more.

"Easy, easy!" the man said. "Just cut this away, see how bad . . ." He faded away and came back. Light flared painfully as someone held a lantern down. "He's not bubbling." The dagger man was peering at Oak's chest. "Took a slice of meat off him, broke a few ribs, but didn't get inside . . . can staunch the bleeding . . . healers . . ."

"But," Oak said . . .

"Quiet!" the man snapped. "You're hallucinating. None of this is happening, understand?"

And it wasn't. Nothing was.

◆ 2 ◆

Something was very wrong tonight.

Sophie assembled with her ladies-in-waiting in the Robing Room. She usually had a long wait there for her notoriously unpunctual husband, but this evening his anteroom door stood open and his guards were nowhere in sight, meaning he was not in his bedchamber. Proper procedure would be for her to ask one of her ladies to ring a bell to summon a page to send to find out where the Czar was. Instead, being daring, she announced that they would go on down to the Assembly Room. She led the way, with her be-gowned entourage rustling and twittering along behind her.

Tonight's reception was an important one, the first giving of gifts, starring the most senior princes and their wives. Sophie would have expected Igor to be there in person, noting who had been too stingy (and therefore deserved to be taxed more) and who too ostentatious (and therefore could afford to be taxed more), and also calculating how much of the treasure he could carve out for himself.

Tasha and her ladies were already there, all young, gorgeous, and frosted with jewels. Tasha had blossomed amazingly since her return to court, glowing with excitement at her forthcoming adventure. The Queen Elect of Chivial did not correct anyone who addressed her as "Your Majesty." She could even ignore sour-faced Fedor, who had been forced by his father to flog his three *streltsi* accomplices to death in Great Market and also write Tasha a letter of apology, which had bothered him a lot more.

Lord Wassail and his Blades were not there. He had never been late before. Sophie dispatched a herald to his quarters, making Fedor frown at her presumption. The man returned with word that His Excellency was indisposed. She knew enough diplomatic gabble to know that this meant absolutely nothing and enough of Lord Wassail to guess that the matter was serious.

"Then we shall proceed without them. Son, your arm."

"You can't do this!" Fedor bellowed.

"Oh? You know where His Majesty is?"

"Whether I do or not, you can't go ahead without him!"

So he did not know. Unusual! "Possibly he and Lord Wassail are in conference. We shall proceed."

Sophie was much less frightened of Fedor now, and even of Igor himself. She had not told him her news yet, because she was not absolutely certain, but she felt *odd* in a way she never had before, and there were times when thoughts of banquets brought her out in a cold perspiration. Nor had she told Beau.

"If you want to stay away, that is your right, *Son*. Come, Tasha, we'll go in together."

Fedor strode forward furiously to escort his stepmother.

Free of the Czar's brooding shadow, the reception was a stupendous success. Tasha and her ladies went into ecstasies over the gifts. Sophie enjoyed the chance to mingle with the guests. She chatted at length with Chief Boyar Skuratov, who survived in his post by virtue of outstanding senile incompetence. He could not select a pastry from a tray without specific instructions from the Czar.

She flirted mildly with Prince Sanin, recently appointed Marshal of the Army. Any sign of ability or ambition was especially dangerous in that post, but young Ivan Sanin's only qualification was a spectacular profile. He was probably craftier than Igor realized, but still vain enough to expect the Czarina to be equally charmed by his looks, which he played like a harp as he tried to wheedle Igor's current whereabouts out of her. She enjoyed the battle of wits.

"You must miss your husband frightfully when he is away!" Sanin's sigh was accompanied by an arpeggio of eyelashes and shining ivory to explain how fortunate she was that he was available instead.

That was going too far! "But it will not be for long this time. As His Majesty told us . . . Oh!" She clasped her hands in distress. "But you aren't a member, are you?"

"Member? Member of what?"

"The Regency Council, of course. I wonder why? You should be, since you carry such awesome responsibilities."

Having never even heard of this imaginary council, Sanin could only stammer in alarm.

"I will urge His Majesty to include you from now on!" Sophie said firmly.

"I should be most frightfully grateful." His restored smile implied that he would be hers to command, body and soul.

She fancied neither.

Eventually she homed in on the raucous laughter of Imperial Astrologer Unkovskii, wild-eyed and scrawny in his cabalistic robes, paying tribute to the Czar's fine wine.

"Have you found an auspicious date for the wedding?"

He leered cautiously. "Ah, we are working very hard on this, Your Majesty. So many calculations needed at this time of year!"

"We all hope it will be soon. We are eager to see the matter closed."

He eyed her with suspicion. "Even Czars cannot rule the stars."

But they could rule stargazers. It was Sophie who wanted to see Tasha safely married. Igor's instincts were usually to procrastinate, and Unkovskii was too shrewd to back the wrong horse.

The party grew louder and merrier. She was almost reluctant to withdraw and head upstairs for the endless ritual of being put to bed, but it was a relief to shed her finery. When the door was closed at last, she hurried across to the trap to put the signal in place.

She lay awake a long time, but this night Beau did not come calling. There was something wrong.

✦ 3 ✦

Wassail had learned of the problem while draped in a sheet, waiting to be shaved. Percy was laying out his decorations and jeweled orders while Dinwiddie rehearsed him in the names of the nobility he would meet tonight. The Blades considered him secure there, so for once they were not hovering over him. But just as Hagfield removed the first hot towel, Beaumont crouched in and straightened, frowning.

"My lord . . . by your leave . . ." He addressed the servants. "I have told Kim to send all the Skyrrians away and guard the door himself. Would you two please search the entire wing for intruders and then join him?"

They hurried out. Arkell came in, looking even grimmer than the Commander.

"Well?" Wassail barked.

"Oak is missing, my lord. He did not return before curfew."

"Tarried too long in some brothel?"

Beau shrugged, but his eyes were daggers. "Possible. Even Blades are not infallible. If that is all, I shall ask him to name his punishment and probably impose about a quarter of what he suggests. This is not like him."

Wassail tore away the sheet and said, "Pass me that shirt. No, it isn't." He realized that he was not surprised, as if he had been waiting for something like this to happen. "You think he's met with foul play?"

"I fear it. Obviously the Czar wants Blades of his own. Taking Oak alive would not be impossible—men with clubs and nets."

Then the maniac would try to torture the words of the ritual out of him, no doubt.

"The reception, er . . . ?" Dinwiddie was glancing from one face to another in panic.

"No reception," Wassail snapped, before his swordsmen could give him orders.

"My lord, is that not overreaction? There may be a very innocent explanation."

"Even if there is, Pursuivant," Beaumont's voice was steely, "His Excellency will have shown that he takes the matter seriously. If an inquiry comes, return a noncommittal reply."

Dinwiddie moaned. "Diplomatic indisposition?"

"Diplomatic buboes!" Wassail roared. "Tell the Czar to bugger himself and Kimberley to bring me some supper."

Pursuivant went scurrying out, leaving him with the Blades. Wassail felt trapped as he had never felt trapped in his life—besieged in a castle inside a fortress wrapped in a vast frozen wilderness. His last dispatch had gone with Hakluyt two weeks ago and no ship would return for half a year. Fury was sending waves of pain through his chest.

"Understand this," he said, "loyalty is a two-headed coin. I have always stood by my people. I will not change now."

There was no mirth in Beaumont's smile. "Your principles do you honor, my lord. Ironically, I fear that you would be safer here if you had not brought Blades with you."

"You are the ones in danger, not me."

Arkell looked even grimmer. "No, my lord. Bringing Blades to Skyrria has put you in more danger, not less. If Igor can lock you up in his torture chamber, he can force us to do anything."

"I'll have no suicidal volunteering!" Wassail barked.

Neither Blade replied.

✦ 4 ✦

By morning the whole Court knew that the Czar had left town. His normal reaction to anything that displeased him was to ride off to Czaritsyn and vent his rage on some innocent victims. His timing had been bad, for the evening's snow had grown to a howling blizzard, and Sophie was amused at the thought of Igor and a hundred or so *streltsy* trying to shelter in some peasant's hovel, although she was sorry for the evicted peasant. She had still not discovered what the bad news had been.

She received a maundering memorandum from Imperial Astrologer Unkovskii to the effect that the fifteenth of Tenthmoon would be an extremely auspicious day for a royal wedding. Typically, the old scoundrel had covered himself by naming a date almost impossibly soon. If Igor wanted to delay, he had an excuse to demand a later day.

But Igor was not there. Triumphantly, Sophie ordered Boyar Chamberlain to proceed with the arrangements, notifying Tasha and Ambassador Wassail. No one dared tell her she had no authority to do this. If Igor raged, she could explain that she very much wanted to attend her sister's wedding and by tradition a Czarina never appeared in public when she was known to be with child. *That* argument should stop even him.

Seemingly recovered from his indisposition, Lord Wassail turned up that afternoon for a discussion of preparations. The sly old man was capable of faking his good humor, but Sir Arkell was not and seemed equally happy. Oak was not present and she had a rule never to look at Beau. That was the cruelest law in the world, but if she ever caught his eye in public she would turn scarlet from her scalp to her elbows.

*   *   *

Even when they were alone she did not see her lover, because he always put out the light the moment he arrived. Blades never took unnecessary risks, as he would explain while climbing into bed with the autocrat's wife.

Tonight would be different. After two interminable days apart, the lovemaking should be even sweeter than usual and Igor was not available to interrupt, although he never had. Tonight, moreover, a fire crackled on the hearth in honor of the storm still howling outside the casement. She would see her lover.

He arrived early. They embraced—kissing, fondling, and mumbling endearments. She tried to undress him.

"Make love to me here," she whispered, "in front of the fire."

"No. You may be warm enough, my little Skyrrian she-bear, but I'm frozen. Into bed with you!"

The feather mattress engulfed them like a snowdrift. Serious talk could wait. They were both experts now, knowing the touches of lips or tongue or fingers that aroused the other soonest and prolonged the joy longest.

The bolt on the corner door clattered. Light showed around the drapes. If they had been sporting on the hearthrug they would have been in full view. Beau rolled and was gone. As always, he had been careful to tuck his clothes under the bed and to lie on the side farthest from the door. He passed under the curtains and dropped silently to the rug. Sophie dragged the quilts up to her chin.

The candlelight was dimmer than she expected and Igor's harsh voice did not call her. Instead the drapes were hauled open. A giant shadow leaned over her and said, "Hello, Mother!" in a growling bass.

"*Go away!* I shall scream!"

"Scream all you want." He closed a paw on her covers. "Wait a month, Czar said. This is a new month." He was drunk, predictably. "Time for a little brother."

"No! I am already with child, you fool! Go!"

Fedor chuckled, hauling the quilts to him and dragging her with them. "Should have said so sooner." His eyes flashed red in the firelight. He was naked.

"It's *true!*" Sophie was screaming now, but Eudoxia would not hear her through the massive timber door, which was bolted anyway.

"Then we'll make it twins!" He wrenched the covers from her grip. In doing so he straightened up. There was a noise like an ax striking a stump. Fedor fell to his knees, toppled, rolled over, and ended flat on his back, mouth open.

Beau was standing there holding a chair.

"Oh, stars! Death and fire!" she gasped. "Have you killed him?"

But Beau dashed for the secret hatch and in a moment was back with a sword.

"I need your help. Lift up his wrist. Quickly!"

The urgency in his voice steadied her. She slid off the bed and did what he said without asking why.

"Hold his hand over his face . . . a little higher . . . now let go."

Not understanding, she did so. Beau sighed and lowered his sword.

"Good! And he's still breathing. I suppose that's a good idea?" He clasped arms around her and let her indulge in a small display of hysteria.

"All right!" he said. "All right! Everything's going to be fine. But we should hurry. Hold this." He gave her the sword. "If he starts to wake up, I'll need that very quickly, understand? The moment he gets those hands on me, I'm borscht." Gripping Fedor's ankles, Beau began backing across the floor, a small naked man towing a huge one.

She followed, horrified at what her madness had caused, for Fedor would certainly remember unbolting the door and stripping her. He would know she could not have moved him back to Igor's room unaided. He would know he had not just passed out. Beau could save himself now by killing Fedor, but that would be cold-blooded murder and it would not help her. She was ruined. They were both dead.

Yet Beau seemed unworried. He arranged Fedor just beyond the doorway, rolling him over, face down. Then he closed the great door.

"Just a moment, love!" He ran around the bed to where he left his clothes and returned in a moment to tap the door with something he held in his hand. "There! Done."

She thought he had gone mad, but when she tried the door it was immovable. "How . . . ? I did not hear the bolt!"

"A conjuration I picked up in Isilond. Thought it might come in handy some day." He shivered. "Back to bed! Excuse the interruption . . . where was I?" He pushed her in, rolling in beside her and pulling the quilts over them both.

She fought him off. "Stop! You're crazy. Fedor will wake up any minute and raise the roof."

"No, he won't." Kiss. "He won't be feeling at all amorous when he does wake up." Stroke. "He probably won't remember coming in here at all, and even if he does it can't be true, because the door's bolted on his side." Nuzzle. "He banged his head on the frame."

"What are you going to do if he does come back?"

"Kill him and stuff his corpse down the shaft. He deserves it for interrupting me. Now stop talking and concentrate . . ." A few moments later he muttered, "I've earned this," and did not speak again for quite a while.

A log collapsed in the fireplace; the room brightened. The lovers lay at peace.

"What was that dropping Fedor's hand on his face thing for?"

"Mm?" Beau said sleepily. "It's a test. He might have been faking, but people can't hit themselves in the face. Try it some time—it's impossible. When you told him you were carrying a child . . . ?"

"It may be Igor's, that's all that matters."

He sighed. "I'm a scullion's bantling. My son will be a prince?"

Until Fedor got his hands on him. "Igor's child. Never doubt that."

"Oh, you wonder!" He kissed her, a very long, expressive kiss. "Why would Fedor dare try to rape his stepmother?"

Reluctantly, she told him what Igor had planned.

"Will he believe you are carrying his child now?"

"Yes! He'll believe."

"Until he returns, my darling, you had better sleep in Eudoxia's room with the doors locked."

She had been thinking the same. It might be a long time until they could meet again like this. "Why did you stay away last night?"

"Emergency. Oak disappeared."

She felt alarm like a splash of icy water in a steam bath. "What happened?"

"He was ambushed by a troop of *streltsy*. He got six of them—four dead and two mortally wounded but saved by a healing. And the dog, Iakov, too. Yes, Igor was there, watching the sport. When his other dog brought Oak down, Igor gave orders that he was to be left to die there in the snow."

So that was why he had ridden away in a fury—because he had lost a dog.

"I'm sorry," she whispered. "Oh, Beau, I am so sorry!"

"Fortunately, Oak survived. But it would please me to think that's my child you are carrying. That would help a little."

"I hope so, too, but we'll never know. Why didn't Oak die?"

"We may never know that, either. They carried him to an elementary in the Foreigners' Quarter. This morning, after curfew, he went to the knights'. He's resting there."

"You saying *streltsy* disobeyed the Czar?"

"Definitely."

"But why?"

"Probably because Oak is just so damned *nice!*" Beau said with anger. "They were some of the men who escorted us in from Dvonograd. They knew him. Or because he fought so well, maybe. Igor wouldn't expect that. Even *streltsy* can have secret decencies."

Igor would massacre them when he heard that, she thought.

"We're going to keep Oak out of sight for a while. Some of his rescuers may want to find other employment." He kissed her again, but there was still too much to discuss. "Darling, what do you know about those dogs? Oak had some strange idea that the one he killed . . . changed . . . He was in bad shape and may have imagined things."

She shivered and clung tighter. "There are rumors of witchcraft at Czaritsyn. Igor often takes noble sons as hostages and sometimes they vanish without explanation. That huge black hound he calls Vasili appeared soon after a very big young man named Vasili Ovtsyn disappeared."

"Spirits!" Beau said. "That's horrible."

"Why would Igor set the *streltsy* on Oak?"

"Because Blades are the ultimate bodyguards and he wants Blades of his own. I hope I convinced him that we can't reveal the binding ritual, but he wanted to see how good our swordsmanship really is. It's lucky Oak didn't guess that, or he might have thrown his sword away and let them kill him."

"The swordsmanship isn't conjured?"

"No, it's taught and learned."

She shivered. "You're in danger! Terrible danger! He'll stop at nothing."

"We must live while we can." His kisses were growing more urgent.

"Wait! You must go, leave Skyrria! You and your ward." The thought of losing him was agony, but thinking of what Igor might do to him was worse.

Beau made a surprised noise. "Huh! How can we? In winter? It's possible?"

"Of course it is. I will help you." Help her lover go out of her life forever? How could the spirits be so cruel?

"I don't want you to help me. It would feel like *using* you, using your love."

"Don't be absurd! Who else could you trust? Right after the wedding . . . Oh, make love to me again and I'll explain later."

✦ 5 ✦

"Your Majesty!" Thecla shouted. "Stop wriggling!"

"You're tickling!" responded the Queen Apparent. "It's a capital offense to tickle a reigning queen!"

"Unless you're a reigning king," said Neonilla.

Everybody laughed uproariously. Tasha's ladies were helping her undress—all slightly tipsy, some more than slightly.

"It was a marvelous wedding!" Olga said.

"The music! The singing!"

"The dancing!"

"The food!"

"The wine!"

"The *men!*" said Neonilla. "Do you suppose all Chivian men are as beautiful as that *Voevode* Beaumont?"

She would never find out! After the way she had been flirting at the ball tonight, Neonilla had been struck off Tasha's list. With dozens of princesses to choose from, Tasha could afford to be ruthless and her own reputation would suffer if her ladies misbehaved, here or in Chivial.

"The other one's a bit nondescript," Ketevan remarked judiciously. "But one out of two's not bad odds."

"And the blond one's stupendous! Did you notice how the Queen blushed when he went over and asked her to dance?"

"Did you see how furious the Czar was when she accepted? He's not even a boyar! A lowborn swordsman!"

Tasha knew, as they did not, that Sophie had little to fear from Igor at the moment. Her joyful news would be made public in a couple of days. Igor was extremely pleased. He had already showered a fortune in jewels on Sophie.

"I heard somebody say a Skyrrian would have had his head chopped off, but he's a diplomat and the Czar can't touch him."

"Whatever happened to the third one? There used to be three, weren't there?—three swordsmen?"

"You're lucky! I had to dance with the Czarevich. He dances like a bull with the staggers."

This was Tasha's wedding night and she would be sleeping alone, but there would be another wedding, next year, with a handsome bridegroom instead of a fat old stand-in. And now she was a queen, a slightly tipsy sixteen-year-old queen. Until the roads dried in the spring she was going to have her own, small establishment in the Temkin Palace, here in High Town.

"Heard a *very* interesting story 'bout Fedor," Ketevan said in a hoarse whisper. "Remember when the Czar left town, couple weeks ago? Seems that the guards found Fedor in the Czar's bedroom, unconscious. He'd knocked himself out trying to get into the Czarina's—"

"How dare you!" Tasha roared, wheeling on her, dragging two helpers around with her. "You *dare* insult my sister? Never let me see your face again!" She swung a slap at the offending face and missed.

Ketevan gasped and fled. As she reached the door, it swung open and Sophie herself walked in, followed by a pack of her own ladies-in-waiting. Suddenly the bedchamber was a duck pond of bobbing heads as everyone tried to curtsey at once, to one queen or the other.

Remembering in time that she did not have to curtsey now, Tasha nodded regally and said, "Good chance, Sister!", spoiling the effect with a slight hiccough. "Did you enjoy my wedding?"

"I see you did! Yes, it was wonderful. And you were wonderful! You made every male heart in the room turn cartwheels." Sophie hugged her . . . then held her a moment while subjecting her to a studied look. "I just came to say so and wish you good night."

"That's all?"

"I think it had better be all. Come and see me first thing in the morning." Sophie spread her smile around the princesses. "You were all wonderful—storybook beauties, all of you!"

With that she took her leave, but Tasha was just sober enough to know that whatever lay behind the cryptic summons was probably not good news.

◆ 6 ◆

Horse-drawn sleighs swept along the streets of Kiensk with bells jingling and whips cracking. Low morning sun and ice haze turned the sky to milk; the air felt like icicles up his nose. Muffled in his own weight of furs, Oak hurried along a trench that pedestrians had tramped through the drifts. Four or five months of this and a month or two of mud and mosquitoes, and then the Chivians could load up and leave—unless the Czar decided to enlist three Blades in his *streltsy.*

Oak now shared the late Boyar Basmanov's low opinion of Skyrrian healers. They had repaired his sword arm and most of the damage to his chest, but the bout of wound fever that followed would never have happened in Chivial. They had fallen short of healing the shoulder the dog had wrecked, and he doubted he would ever have much use of it in future. Still, one arm was better than none and it was a huge relief to be heading back to his ward at last.

Wearing *Sorrow,* he was challenged at the gate to High Town and again at the Imperial Palace. Both times he was allowed through when he showed his pass and no one seemed surprised that a dead man had returned. He marched along high corridors, ducked through doorways, and arrived at West Wing.

Percy let him in and beamed with delight at seeing the lost sheep. Apparently the sheep was late—Wassail was perched on a stool in the entrance hall, although more of him hung over than fitted. Beau and Arkell and Dinwiddie were standing around. All the faces lit up.

"Sir Oak!" Wassail rumbled. "You are welcome back, my lad! We have all missed you."

Oak bowed as well as his furs allowed. "It is pleasure to be back, my lord!"

"You have recovered your health, I understand?"

"Indeed I have, my lord." He did not like the look of his ward's health, though—color too high and face too puffy—and he could hear his lungs bubbling like brewers' vats. "You were a handsome bridegroom yesterday, I understand."

The Walrus chortled. "Wish I had been! His Majesty will be rapturously pleased when he meets his charming young bride. Yes, the ceremony was a great success. Let us be on our way, Commander." He heaved himself upright and lumbered in the direction of the door, leaning on his cane.

Arkell followed, glowering, and then Pursuivant, who looked like a fish with sea sickness.

Beau, of course, was smiling cheerily. "His Excellency has requested an audience. We are about to beard the wolf in his den."

"Wolves don't have beards," Oak protested. He was letting his grow in again.

"This one does. Understand—the only levers we have are that the Czar values Chivian trade and is flattered to see his niece be a Queen. He wants Skyrria recognized as a part of Eurania and himself honored as a great and civilized monarch."

"So?"

"So you are evidence that he's a monster criminal barbarian. Try and stay invisible until you're needed. Don't be surprised at anything the Walrus says." Smiling angelically, Beau stooped into the doorway.

Being invisible was no great trick when everyone was muffled to the eyes against the cold, even indoors. Oak just hung back a little as the Ambassador and his delegation entered the Hall of Columns by a side door; heralds escorted them toward the center aisle. A hundred great pillars, no two alike, were doubtless of artistic merit, but they ruined the sight lines. Oak caught brief glimpses of the Czar enthroned at one end with the giant dog called Vasili at his feet, some wretch who was currently the focus of imperial attention kneeling before the throne, and various high officials lurking nearby. The shadowy outer reaches of the hall were crawling with *streltsy* cockroaches. When the Chivians were halted to await their turn, these ominous figures began drifting inward.

The Ambassador was not kept waiting long. Heralds proclaimed him and the old man trudged forward with Pursuivant, Beau, and Arkell. Oak leaned against the nearest column, folding his arms because that made his shoulder hurt less. He couldn't see the Czar from there, or even Wassail, but he could hear perfectly well, and he could watch Beau.

Streltsy emerged from behind nearby pillars to scowl suspiciously at him. Soon more joined them, and he supposed he ought to feel flattered that his demonstration of fencing had scared the Czar into mustering such an army.

Igor terminated the formalities abruptly. "And what is so urgent or secret that you will not reveal it except to us personally?" His voice was harsh.

Wassail's sounded deceptively jovial. "Yesterday's felicitous nuptials having brought my primary mission to fruition, sire, all that remains for me now to complete my charge is to escort Queen Tasha and her train and baggage to Chivial. I came to request—"

"You are not proposing to drag all those highborn ladies all across Eurania at this time of year, I hope?"

"Of course not, Your Majesty. But I wish to consolidate my mission under one roof. The quarters you so generously put at our disposal in the town will be more than adequate for all of us."

"You spurn our house?" The Czar's anger crackled.

Wassail's voice remained calm, but it was easy to imagine his pudding face set in stubborn folds. "I have certain reservations about security and will feel happier with an independent establishment. Her Majesty will expect all the fine treasures recently presented to her to be transported to the—"

If that was a diplomatic way of calling the Czar a thief, it was not diplomatic enough.

"*Security!?*" he bellowed. "*Reservations?* What reservations?"

Oak did not need Beau's nod to recognize his cue. He walked out from behind his column and took up position behind his ward.

Igor's tirade choked off in a gurgle of fear. The hound leaped to its feet, bristling. Then it bayed. Shuddering, Oak reached for his sword. The Czar yelled at the brute to sit, but he was unable to drag his eyes away from the newcomer. Had it occurred to Beau that Skyrrians were superstitious, that Igor might denounce Oak as a walking corpse and order him buried or burned at the stake?

Courtiers stared in puzzled surprise at the Czar's dismay. The Czarina and Czarevich were certainly absent. *Voevode* Viazemski seemed to be, but might be lurking in the shadows.

"Need I go into detail, Your Majesty?" Wassail demanded.

"*Get out!* Go!" The Czar did not enjoy being threatened in his own throne room.

"May we first discuss the inventory of wedding gifts and make arrangements for them to be packed and delivered to—"

"Go *away!*" Igor roared, jumping up. Vasili bayed again.

The boyars were aghast. Wassail, normally so obsequious to monarchs, was sneering as if he dealt with a surly churl.

"Am I to infer from Your Majesty's remarks that I am now *persona non grata?* If so, will Your Majesty kindly instruct Chief Boyar Skuratov to issue me my passport, so that I may make plans—"

"*Get him out of my sight!*"

The guards advanced. Wassail shrugged. Without as much as a nod, he turned his back on the Emperor of the Skyrrians and trudged away. Oak brought up the rear.

✦ 7 ✦

𝒩ot a word was spoken until they reached West Wing, although Oak thought he heard Dinwiddie moaning to himself a few times. Wassail headed straight for Great Hall and slumped down on the oversized stool he favored. For a moment he was an exhausted old man, then he replaced his mask to leer at Pursuivant.

"Enjoyed that!"

Dinwiddie shuddered. "Your lordship set the Skyrrians a strange example of chivalric deportment."

Curiously, the big table was piled with clothes, documents, and other personal possessions. Oak recognized some of his own among them.

"You were magnificent, my lord," Beau said. "If his mother had taken that tone with him more often, he might be better behaved now."

"Well, Pursuivant? Have I royal leave to go home?"

"*Home,* Excellency?" Dinwiddie howled. "In midwinter?"

"Tell him, Commander."

Beau was enjoying himself, as always. "It is not midwinter yet, Pursuivant. This is an excellent time to travel if you want speed. Those horse sleighs go like lightning. The question is, has the Czar dismissed his lordship?"

The herald looked as flustered as a wet rooster. "Well . . . no . . . Leaving Skyrria without permission is a capital offence. Foreigners' movements are strictly controlled. Despite the Czar's peremptory words, you still need your passport, Excellency."

The Ambassador and his chief Blade exchanged glances.

Oak felt sick. "Why?" he demanded. "You cannot expect Queen Tasha and her ladies to travel in winter, surely? And all her baggage?" It was impossible to imagine the obdurate old Wassail giving in so easily, terminating his mission, abandoning the new Queen and her riches.

"No one could expect that," Beau said, "which is— Enter!"

Kimberley crouched in. "A messenger, Commander. He insists on delivering a letter to you personally."

"Send him."

A moment later a page entered. He bowed to the Ambassador, but then went to Beau to hand him a paper.

Beau broke the seal and read it, frowning. "There may be an answer shortly. Wait outside, lad, please."

"Thank you, sir." He bowed again and turned to the door.

"Boy!" Wassail barked.

"My lord?"

"What's your name?"

"Timofei, Your Excellency."

"Your mistress trained you well."

The kid smiled. "She will be pleased to hear that, my lord." He went out, still grinning.

"So, where were we?" Beau said. "Ah, yes. No one will expect his lordship to leave now, without the ladies. But he did twist the Czar's nose, and when Igor is upset by anything—the loss of a dog, for example—then he usually goes off to his lair at Czaritsyn to cheer himself up by massacring a few peasants or torturing somebody. We are hoping that he will do that now."

"We're leaving?" Arkell said incredulously. "When?"

"Today. We're officially off to the knights' house, but most of us won't be stopping there. You've got to find Morkuta for us. Then we head upstream, on the ice. I've been told we will make Dvonograd in three days if the weather holds."

Dinwiddie was green again. "But Her Majesty! Queen Tasha!"

Beau and his ward exchanged more glances.

"You didn't look very hard at Timofei, Pursuivant," Wassail said, with a notably carnivorous smirk.

Oak sat down. The herald made a strangled noise. Arkell turned stark white; his hand groped for his sword.

"I'll explain later," Beau said softly. After a quick glance at Oak he went back to watching Arkell. "Perhaps you should change for the journey now, my lord? Take this watch, please, brother. Oak, look over this gear and pick out anything you absolutely cannot part with. We'll be traveling light."

"Me too?" Pursuivant wailed.

"You stay in Kiensk," Wassail said, heaving himself off the chair. "As chargé d'affaires. You and Sir Dixon will be escorting Her Majesty's ladies next spring."

Oak stayed seated until everyone except Beau had left. Neither spoke while Beau pulled up a chair in front of Oak. Only then did he meet his eye.

"It'll kill him," Oak said.

Beau sighed and nodded. "Yes, Oak, my good friend. *But he's dying anyway!* Can't you see? He's never going home. He won't breathe the scents of spring, here or anywhere."

"Who are you to say that?" Was there *any* way to stop this madness?

"I'm his Blade," Beau said sadly. "And I'm encouraging him in something that's going to kill him. No, I'm not a healer or a medico, but I don't have to be, do I? Brother, if his heart doesn't give out on its own, the Czar will kill him! Igor is obsessed with learning the secrets of the King's Blades. He'll never let us three leave Skyrria. Even if he doesn't lock up our ward to coerce us, Wassail wouldn't leave without us! He's just as stubborn."

Oak rubbed his shoulder. It hurt more when he did that. He wanted to scream.

"I'm breaking my oath, I suppose," Beau said, "but it doesn't feel like it. My binding isn't stopping me. I don't expect him to survive the journey, no. That's why I didn't consult you or Arkell—when he dies, you'll need someone to blame, and you'll have me. I'm ordering you to obey, Oak."

"What about the wedding gifts?"

"His lordship says they aren't worth a man's life. Not many people would agree with him, but that's what he says."

"And that *girl* is coming with us?"

Beau's eyes shone like old, smooth silver coins. "The boy, you mean? That's why the Walrus is doing it, of course. He's escorting his Queen home to Chivial, as he set out to do. He'll die doing his duty, not drowning in phlegm in a foreign bed or screaming in Igor's dungeons."

"And what's in it for her?"

"Freedom."

To hear Leader pleading for his approval made Oak squirm.

"She's terrified of Igor," Beau said, "and that brute son of his. And work it out—if Igor locks up three of Athelgar's Blades and murders his ambassador, is he likely to let his niece go strutting around Athelgar's court telling tales? Or part with that hill of goodies the princes gave her for wedding presents? You should have seen him drooling over them. Tasha's young, but she knows enough to go while the going is good."

Oak sat for a while. How in the world had Beau ever organized this? "No," he said. "You're not ordering me. I insist you do it. I won't let you have all the guilt."

Beau grinned. "Oh, good man! Good *friend!* And the old rascal may surprise us yet. He's tough as flint and he dearly wants to parade into Greymere Palace with Queen Tasha on his arm. Look over that heap and tell me if there's anything you need."

"There isn't."

"Then go and relieve Arkell. Send him down here so I can twist his ear next."

❖ 8 ❖

"I am to wait for a reply," Timofei announced.

"Well, you won't wait here," the footman retorted, "snooping around, pocketing valuables. Kitchen for you, my lad. You can wash dishes while you wait, and I know how many silver spoons we got."

Tasha swallowed a grin and said, "Yes, sir."

Playing dress-up had always been a favorite winter pastime in the Temkin family, so she had no doubts that she could pass for a boy. The problem was remembering that this was *real,* that a mistake could bring huge trouble. She knew that, but even before Sophie had finished proposing the plan to her, she had known that it was the right thing to do. Lord Wassail was a wonderfully grandfatherly old boyar, very trustworthy. All the Chivians were trustworthy, Sophie had insisted—without, come to think of it, explaining how she knew that.

It was true that Tasha might never see all her wonderful wedding presents again, but there would be jewels aplenty in Chivial. Her hair would grow back. Escape was more important—escape from the prison of High Town, from hateful Igor and even more horrible Fedor. Escape to a throne and a handsome, royal husband! Especially escape from Fedor. He hadn't forgiven her for the apology yet; he still looked at her as if he were plotting evil.

Of course no lady could go traipsing off across a continent without at least one female companion, and again Tasha had not hesitated. Olga was the only possible choice. It was not very long since they had played dress-up together, and she had the same slim, boyish figure as Tasha.

Dark and smelly, the kitchen was a nasty yank back to reality. She stared in horror at the bucket. Wash dishes? She had no idea how to wash dishes.

Fortunately, Timofei was rescued from the kitchen before his ineptitude aroused suspicion; he was led out to be tucked into a sled beside Lord Wassail. One of the swordsmen went on the front seat with the driver, two more sprang onto waiting horses, and off they all went—out through the gates into Great Market, with its gaudy awnings like flocks of parrots nesting in valleys between hillocks of snow, and on to the Foreigners' Quarter. Having never been there before, Tasha-Timofei wanted to explore, but she was smuggled indoors and hustled away into a private room. The window was so caked with frost that she could see nothing and her new freedom was starting to feel suspiciously like imprisonment when the door opened to admit one of the Ambassador's swordsmen, the burly one with the limp.

He grinned shyly. "Been told to guard you, Your, um . . . Timofei. Mustn't give you titles."

"By all means call me Timofei and I shall call you Oak!"

"If we're going to be realistic, Your, um . . . I mean, a boy like you would address me as 'sir' because I'm wearing a sword. In fact, you'd call almost any man that way."

"I don't mind calling you 'sir' if you'll stop calling me your um," she said. "How many of us are going?"

"Um . . ."

"You're doing it again!" Tasha snapped, just to see him blush.

He didn't. "Shuddup, boy!" He had a nice smile.

"That's better, sir."

"Not sure how many. You and another um?"

"Princess Olga. Sergei, I mean—sir."

"Timofei, Sergei, Lord Wassail, and three Blades. That's six. Sir Cuthbert—he's a knight, quite handy with a sword—and Wilf, his custler. He's not exactly king's counselor material, if you follow me, but horses will turn somersaults for him."

That did not sound very helpful, but she understood. "Makes eight. No Skyrrians?" she added suspiciously.

"Seems not. They'd never be able to come back, see?"

"Not just two sleds, I hope?"

"No, Beau said we'd take three." Oak looked doubtful. "How hard are those troikas to drive?"

"Easy enough." Nobility traveling around Kiensk or their estates liked having the center horse trot and the two outside horses gallop in different styles. That needed a professional driver, but Tasha had driven a standard "unicorn" team often enough.

A rather *chesty* boy swept in and said, "Darling! You look wonderful!"

"I don't think you should call me that, Sergei, dear! It isn't manly."

They hugged, sniggering nervously. The swordsman looked shocked.

Time slipped by faster with Olga there. A swordsman entered, carrying a load of furs, and was followed in by Lord Wassail, leaning on his cane. He bowed to each of them.

"Your Majesty, Your Highness. This is the last time I shall give you titles until we have left Skyrria. And this is your last chance to change your mind—Timofei."

"We do not change our mind!"

"Spoken like a queen born to the purple." He smiled horribly. How could a man so ugly be so likeable?

She did not feel brave. "I have questions, Your Excellency. I fear my uncle the Czar, but I fear winter more. Have we heated bricks to keep our feet warm? You have packed food, but no liquids that will freeze? What provision have you made for watering the horses and what tools and implements do you carry for emergencies?"

"Beau?" He turned to his companion, the handsome, insolent one who had danced with Sophie.

The man's eyes gleamed like silver buttons over the bundle he carried. "Hot bricks, yes. A week's supply of food, leather canteens, no bottles. For water: axes, buckets, and rope. Oats for the horses. Shovels, lantern and tinderbox, a few pots and spoons, basic farrier equipment, and straps for repairing tack . . . we did take advice from Skyrrians." He was amused at her!

"I am relieved to hear it. I shall inspect the rigs."

"I was going to ask you to do so."

Three sleds and nine horses completely filled the yard behind the house. Tasha walked all around them with Beaumont at her heels and was peeved that she could find no fault with anything. The third swordsman and a vacant-faced youth were already settling into the front sled, a large man was helping Olga into the third, and the rear seats of both those were high-piled with baggage, so clearly she and Lord Wassail and two swordsmen were to ride in the second. He was large enough in indoor clothing; in furs he took up almost all the passenger bench. She scrambled up on the front seat.

Smartalecky Beaumont joined her and adjusted robes around them both.

"I'll drive!" she said, prepared to argue.

His smile almost blew her out of the sled. "That's an excellent idea!" He glanced around to see if everyone was ready, and then called, "Arkell?" to the swordsman in the front sled.

"Leader?"

"Go. Stop when you reach the sea."

As she steered the team out into the street, Tasha realized that she was trembling, but not from cold. "This is exciting!"

"Let us hope it stays at exciting," the Chivian said, "and does not mature into fine vintage terror. The best news is that a party of *streltsy* rode out North Gate a little while ago, following a pack of gigantic dogs."

"The Czar!"

"Certainly. He can't disguise that nose of his. Seems no one dares make decisions when he's not around, so when the boyars finally realize that the Ambassador has absconded, they probably won't do more than send Igor a message, and that may take days to find him."

"I hope so." Managing a unicorn team in a crowded city was a little harder than she had expected.

"How long before you're missed, do you think?"

"Two days at least." That had been Sophie's estimate. "After that, the stars will decide."

"The boyars may think we've kidnapped you. That'll be more serious. They'll send the army after us."

Unless Sophie could distract them. Even Dimitri and Yelena did not know yet that Tasha had left. She would never see them again. She had not said good-bye and she mustn't think about that or her cheeks would be covered with icicles.

Three troikas rushed unchallenged out the West Gate of Kiensk and nobody noticed that the heavily muffled driver of the second one was the Queen of Chivial. The towers and walls of the city soon blurred and shrank away. With them went servants to prepare beds, dress hair, lay out clothes, empty chamber pots. Neither Tasha nor Olga had ever had to fend for herself before.

Skyrria was a marble corpse asleep in a shroud of ice haze, dreaming of a distant spring. Only overhead did a sickly blue show through, and the only wind was the rush of their own speed, which snatched breath away and peppered faces with gritty snow. Snow muffled the beat of hooves and the hiss of runners, so there was little sound as the three sleds hurtled westward over the frozen land. Traffic on the trail was light. Stark trees and cottages were black scribbles on the whiteness.

Home lay to the east, so Tasha would be seeing country new to her. "Who's our guide?"

"Arkell. He's got an infallible sense of direction and an incredible memory for maps. We took advice from some locals, though."

"And where will we stay tonight?"

"Anywhere we can find," the swordsman said cheerfully. "The moon is just past the full, so it all depends on the horses."

"It all depends on the weather! And on not getting lost. Who were these experts who helped you with so much good advice?"

Beaumont tried his woman-killing smile again, but most of his face was covered, so it lacked impact. "I swore not to reveal names, Timofei."

"I remind you that I am your Queen, Sir Beaumont!"

"Only if I can get you safely to Chivial, Your Majesty."

Insolence! A lowborn insolent mercenary refusing to answer her questions?

"I am curious to know. I certainly will not repeat their names. Now tell me."

He smiled and went back to studying the landscape.

✦ 9 ✦

Ᏸn Skyrria, by custom, on the day after a wedding the female guests gathered again to display their second-best gowns and dissect the proceedings. These nuptial wakes were almost the only occasions on which women might drink wine in the absence of their husbands, and a state wedding without a bridegroom was especially noteworthy. It was no surprise, therefore, that the assembly of princesses and boyars' wives over which Czarina Sophie presided soon became raucous, even boisterous, requiring no hostessing efforts from her. This was fortunate, because she was torn between nerve-racking anxiety and a numbing need to close her eyes and sleep for a week. She would have heard by now if Tasha had been caught while leaving the city, but the days of peril had only just begun.

She was the only person in Kiensk who knew the full extent of the conspiracy. The remaining Chivians would mask Lord Wassail's departure by staying busy and visible—buying food in the market, lighting up windows at dusk—but few of them knew that their new queen had gone with him. None had been told about the Pickled Fish, a curious Chivian term Beau used to refer to a special little chicanery he had devised.

Sophie must cover for her sister as best she could without implicating herself. Today Tasha was supposedly in the process of moving her household back to the Temkin Palace, so half her abandoned ladies-in-waiting now thought she had gone there and they would follow as soon as the rooms were ready. The rest had gone ahead and expected her to follow. Tomorrow the Czarina could reasonably be indisposed. By the day after, Igor would almost certainly have come

roaring back to High Town and Sophie must just hope that
his rage would be aimed entirely at the missing Chivians.

The only aid she had given Beau that might incriminate
her had been travel directions to the Dvono, dictated by *Voevode* Afanasii. The old man would never betray her and had
now vanished back into his retirement at Faritsov. The Chivians themselves had done almost everything else, even sup-
plying garments for the fake Timofei. It was only because
Sophie had managed to convince Beau that she would not be
in danger that he had agreed to take Tasha along; his loyalty
was to his ward. It was only because she feared for his life
if he remained in Kiensk that she had helped him plan the
flight.

Life was cruel when love itself forced lovers to contrive
their own separation. Last night she had wept in his arms.

They had found no time for sleep, certainly, and thus
today she sat on her chair of state and struggled to stay conscious while exchanging pleasantries with the noble ladies
drifting by. Two hundred others stood around, drinking,
munching, and shouting over the din. She was seriously considering the merits of staging a diplomatic swoon, which
would be a dramatic announcement of her happy condition
and would certainly result in her being carried off to bed. On
the other hand, healers would start fussing over her and
someone might start a hunt for Tasha.

Suddenly a worried herald was bowing before her and
awareness of danger blew thoughts of swooning right out of
her mind.

Out in the corridor Chief Boyar Skuratov fussed in such a
state of agitation that his silver beard almost stood on end.
He had brought his usual knot of attendants, but he shooed
them all away like chickens so he could be alone with the

Czarina under a window. The paper he held out to her shook violently, as did his reedy old voice.

"Your Majesty! I beg of you—is this the Czarevich's hand?"

It was the Pickled Fish. Neither Beau or Sophie had dreamed it might trap her instead of its intended victims—the dithery old man had never tried to shift his problems onto her shoulders before. Perhaps Igor had returned already and his evil mind already sought to implicate her in the conspiracy. She held the evidence to the light and struggled to think while pretending to read its illiterate scrawl. If she were truly innocent, how would she react, what would she say?

"Oh, this is frightful! Wicked! This is high treason!"

Skuratov's eyes were bulging with terror. "Yes, yes! But is it genuine?"

"I cannot . . . I mean, I have rarely seen anything written by the Czarevich. How in the world did you come by this? It is a joke in very bad taste, surely?"

"No. It cannot be. But is the writing genuine? Oh, spirits! What can I do?" He was close to gibbering.

"You must inform the Czar immediately. Where is he?"

"I don't know," Chief Boyar wailed. "He has left the city."

"He did not tell me he was going." She folded up the damning evidence and firmly handed it back. "Send messengers to every place he may have gone—Czaritsyn, of course, but any others you can think of, a dozen if necessary. You will have to spell out the problem very clearly in your letters, lest he suspect a trap. And best write them yourself, so he can know your writing."

"Yes, yes, of course!" The old man was melting with relief at having someone give him orders.

"That way as few people as possible learn of the problem." And the process would take as long as possible.

"That is exactly why I consulted you, Your Majesty."

"I am happy that you did. You have the Chivian house under surveillance?"

"Just one watcher in the building across the street, plus the usual delivery people and minor servants."

"I would suggest you put all your best men there, Chief Boyar—but discreetly, of course."

He nodded vigorously, flapping his beard. "Of course!"

"And perhaps—with the greatest prudence—you should have Czarevich Fedor's movements noted also?"

"Oh, that is standard procedure, Czarina."

She was not surprised. Several of her ladies-in-waiting were spies, and Igor had more reason to distrust his heir than his wife. He probably spied on his dogs.

"And *Voevode* Viazemski?"

"Him too, naturally."

"Then I think you have the matter under complete control, Chief Boyar. Personally, I find it beyond belief. Remember that your office is not the only branch of government keeping watch on others. This paper may have been planted in . . . planted wherever it was found, I mean, by some of His Majesty's other loyal servants, possibly even on his orders."

Skuratov brightened considerably. "That is indeed true, Your Majesty."

"A more probable explanation than treason by Czarevich Fedor."

"Certainly!" He beamed toothlessly.

She could not resist adding, "It may even be a test of your own loyalty and efficiency?"

He blanched and said, "Oh!" very faintly.

"Unlikely, I'm sure. But you will take those precautions I suggested?"

"Oh, of course! Thank you, Czarina, thank you!"

✦ 10 ✦

Again and again Arkell had warned them that vague talk of heading west to the Dvono and then south to Dvonograd was very different from finding a passable route across unfamiliar country, but neither Beau nor the Walrus had been willing to listen.

Admittedly, the first day went quite well. Beau would not say who had given him directions, but only a soldier and probably a man experienced in command would have provided such detail: "West by north for two-thirds of an hour to the ruined fort; west-northwest veering southwest by west for one quarter hour to the ford with a jetty on the near bank." And so on. Alas, to a foreigner's eye the landmarks were all too similar—how many trees made a clump, and was that a village or a large farm? Arkell was forbidden to stop and ask, even if the peasants would have stayed to tell him instead of just running for cover.

A couple of hours into the journey the directions themselves became vague, as if now they were based on hearsay, but Arkell already knew he was lost. All he could do was keep heading west. Villages became rarer and traffic nonexistent, until roads were indistinguishable. Fortunately, there were few fences or hedges. Even in Chivial, major highways were usually more visible on maps than on the ground, and it was no rarity to see a dozen muddy tracks braided, with a coach or wagon struggling to add another. Here the ground was marble-smooth and marble-white. So long as the horses could find footing, the sleds would run. Runners were tougher than wheels and axles, too.

They were making good time. He would know the Dvono when he saw it tomorrow.

At least he was not distracted by chatter from his companion. To call the taciturn Wilf a halfwit would have been unkind, a three-quarter wit generous, but the man had an incredible affinity for horses. Whenever there was space, the other drivers would pull alongside, so the custler could watch over all three teams. He seemed to know each animal's worries by instinct and he called a halt the moment a hoof became plugged with ice.

By the time the west burned scarlet, the horses were worn out and Arkell was half blind from staring into the light. Ice-flat grassland had given way to slightly rolling country patched with scrub that made hard going for both horses and sleds. He had seen no houses for a long time, so when a settlement showed to the north, he headed straight for it. It had once been the home of some boyar or minor prince, a grand building surrounded by barns and cottages, but it had been sacked and abandoned years ago. There were no human tracks in the snow.

They found a one-room cottage that had kept most of the weather out, located the well, built a fire, and set the women and the Walrus to tending it. Then everyone else went to help Wilf with the horses until he was satisfied that they were faring as well as possible. It was then Arkell thought he heard a faint wail in the distance—a long, bloodcurdling howl in the dusk. Wolf? He caught Beau's eye but no one said anything and the call was not repeated.

Sir Cuthbert of Canbridge was a large and physically powerful man. His speech was almost as laconic as his custrel's, but he was probably the brightest of Sir Dixon's knights, and certainly the best swordsman among them. An experienced campaigner, he organized the camp, demonstrating how to thaw out hunks of sausage in ashes and build makeshift bedding of scrub. The two women did nothing to help, either from habit or because they were in shock at the primitive conditions. Wassail seemed to be in pain, for he ate almost nothing and spoke little. His spirits were high, though. He chuckled a lot at having outwitted the detestable Czar.

Five slept around the fire. Three kept watch, usually huddled together to keep warm, but also fetching firewood under the cold moon, heating the bricks that would keep feet warm for a few hours in the morning, waiting through an endless winter night.

They did not stay for daylight. The fire began smoking more than before. A rising wind was stirring the snow, and Beau became worried enough to waken the sleepers. Queen Tasha agreed that the weather was changing and the expedition should find better shelter while it still could. The moon was bright enough, so they struck camp and moved out before first light.

Even when dawn came, the going was much harder than before. This was the country Hakluyt had named for Beau's sword—*Just Desert*. Depopulated and abandoned, it had reverted to scrub that hid thorns, stumps, and hazards of all sorts. Soon the wind cut like a sword, so Arkell perforce turned south to put their backs to it. Then he was no longer leading his ward to the border, but there was a fifty-fifty chance—and his bump of direction said more than fifty-fifty—that he would soon intersect the road from Kiensk to Morkuta. Morkuta was inhabited. They would find shelter there and perhaps danger also, but without shelter they were going to die.

A perverse trick of memory kept tormenting him with visions of that brave day back in Fourthmoon when three proud new Blades had ridden the lanes of Isilond to Laville, escorting their ward. They had not expected their mission to end in this ignominious flight.

Snow streamed past horizontally, coating sleds and horses

and people, turning everything into a white fog until sky and earth merged and even the other teams were hard to see. The cold grew more deadly by the minute. They had gambled and lost, and Tasha would be the first queen of Chivial to freeze to death.

"Bad for the horses," Wilf complained.

"If they freeze solid we'll have to carry them."

Wilf never understood jokes and that one wasn't very funny anyway.

The cold and endless travail had thrown Arkell into a sort of trance, and it took repeated shouts from the rear to jerk him out of it. He looked back to see Beau waving frantically. When his signal was acknowledged, he turned his sled around, so Arkell copied and followed. Beau had seen a gap in the scrub, which Arkell had missed completely in the white hell, but a few moments sufficed to confirm that it was indeed a trail, a track worn through the bush by traffic. The drivers urged their teams into a trot and life began to seem possible again.

The going was still not exactly easy, for the snow had drifted unevenly, making the horses stumble. Once or twice Arkell thought he saw traces of hoofprints, which were a reminder that the government must not be counted out yet. A courier who knew the way could have reached Morkuta already and alerted the garrison. Still, even a jail would be better than this.

The right horse stumbled, the others whinnied in alarm, and the rig came to a shuddering halt, tilted to the left. The second sled emerged from the blizzard.

"What's wrong?" Beau yelled. One lame horse could kill them now.

The trouble was a high drift across their path, and the obstruction blocking the wind was just visible through the swirling white murk. Arkell pointed a snow-caked arm at it.

"Morkuta," he said.

* 11 *

Oak doubted that. It was a stockade, too new-looking to be what he expected of Morkuta. The gate stood half open, lodged in place by drifts, not wide enough for three horses abreast.

Beau, an anonymous snowman, twisted around to him. "Any port in a storm. Go bend a hawser on a binnacle or whatever you sailor types do."

Oak climbed out of the sled where he had spent two days crammed in beside his ward, powerless to help as the cold and buffeting drained the old man's life away. Wassail desperately needed rest and shelter, and so did Oak himself. He was sick from the throb of pain in his shoulder.

Just inside the gate he found tracks not yet obliterated and horse droppings that steamed when he kicked them. The timber buildings looked new, built after the wars, and the chimney on the largest was smoking. He floundered across to it. Finding the door unlocked, he let himself in, taking the storm with him.

The squinty little windows were caked over, so most of what light there was came from a blaze in the fieldstone fireplace occupying much of the far wall. Oak forced the door shut, then turned to face the occupants as they scrambled to their feet and drew swords. There were eight of them, all hairy, scruffy, and unprepossessing. The leader who stalked forward was a big man missing an arm, and the sight of him raised Oak's heartbeat to fighting speed.

"Declare yourself!" Then Viazemski's eyes widened at the sight of the cat's-eye sword. He laughed and sheathed his own. "By the stars, I feel outnumbered already. Welcome to Mezersk, Sir Oak." He offered his hand.

Oak ignored it. "Travelers seeking shelter, eight of us."

"We are the Czar's men and this is a royal hunting lodge. His Majesty would never refuse hospitality to wellborn travelers on such a day, let alone the honored Chivian Ambassador."

Mezersk seemed more like a fort than a lodge. Heaps of baggage and a stink of wet fur suggested that the *streltsy* had arrived very recently. Now the sheep had followed the wolves into their lair, but they had no choice. Shelter first and fight later.

"We need assistance with the horses."

"Gladly. Fyodor, Andrei—all of you—go help our guests. I am happy to see you in good health, Sir Oak."

"I was in better health when we met the last time."

"But not when I had to leave so hurriedly." The smirking scoundrel thought he could call in a debt—*I saved your life.* His henchmen might not know that story, or they might be friends of the men Oak had slain, with debts of their own to repay.

"Your companion on that occasion was surprised to see me yesterday."

"Wasn't he!" The *streltsi*'s pig face was particularly horrible when he smiled.

"You were present?"

"I heard."

Either the scoundrel had just come from Kiensk or some of his men had. Had Viazemski been sent to hunt down the fugitives? Or had his actions in saving Oak turned him into a fugitive also? Oak did not think this meeting could be pure chance.

"We can reminisce later." He went back out. The others had unharnessed the outside horses of Wassail's sled and brought it right to the door. They were about to unload their ward.

"Viazemski and seven other *streltsy*," he announced. "They just got here."

"I don't mind killing *streltsy*," Beau said. "Was he surprised to see you?"

"Yes."

"Good. Remember your bedroll, Timofei."

"Don't you speak to me like that!"

Beau caught her arm as she tried to go past. "Listen! Viazemski himself will certainly recognize you but his men may not. It's possible the *Voevode* can be bought, but *streltsy* turn brigand whenever the fancy takes them. Rape first and ransom second? Stay in character!"

The girl screamed at him, close to hysterics with fear. "You incompetent idiot, you've ruined everything! You couldn't find a way out of Skyrria in ten thousand years. You'll run around in circles until you freeze to death or the Border Patrol drags you back to Kiensk. You think the Czar will honor my marriage treaty after this insult? I don't! And if he does, I swear I'll have your head on a post for a wedding present."

But Queen Tasha did grab up a bundle to take in with her, and so did the Yurievna woman. Beau and Oak carried their ward inside and set him on a bench by the hearth.

Beau glanced around the hall. "Help the men unload, boys."

The Queen glared. "Come, Sergei!" She led the way outside again.

Two long benches stood by the fireplace and two more flanked a plank table in the center of the hall. There was no other furniture, but the floor was littered with heaps of clothes, blankets, and tack. Bags, baskets, pots, buckets, and a skinned sheep's carcase on the table showed that it would serve as a kitchen. The *streltsy* were camping, not resident.

The Blades could not leave their ward, who huddled on his seat, head down, breathing loudly. Viazemski sat at the table in the middle, showing no special interest in Queen Tasha. A couple of the *streltsy* helped bring in the baggage. Everyone else had gone to see to the horses.

When Timofei and Sergei had finished, they shed furs and came to kneel before the hearth. Throwing another log on the blaze, Beau leaned over them. "That's good! You really look like boys sitting there. If there's trouble, get under the bench—fast!"

Oak expected another blast from Tasha, but Wassail spoke first.

"Timofei?"

"My lord?"

His face was a sickly gray, his mouth loose, eyes half closed. He spoke in a hoarse whisper. "I am sorry. We nearly died out there."

"No one can predict weather in Skyrria, my lord. Not your fault."

"Yes, it was my fault. I want you to know. I suggested this and overruled my Blades' objections. The fault is mine."

"There may be no fault, grandfather. One storm does not make a winter."

Oak upgraded his opinion of Queen Tasha from Spoiled Brat to Spoiled Brat with Promise.

The *streltsy* began drifting back in ones and twos. Eight were not bad odds for three Blades and a knight, and if the Viazemski snake changed its skin there might be no fight at all. Weeks ago he had accepted a testimonial from Lord Wassail. Since then he had defied the Czar by sending Oak to the healers—why, if not to curry Chivian favor? Nor would he overlook this opportunity to gain merit by aiding a king's bride.

"Timofei?" Beau said again.

She grimaced at him. "Sir Beaumont, sir?"

"Bring a grub bag. I'm hungry."

Queen Tasha rose and walked the length of the hall, to the baggage heap. She brought back a heavy pack, deliberately walking in front of the *Voevode*.

He studied her progress with interest, then sneered across at Beau. "A promising lad you have there, Commander. I know his sister."

Door and shutters rattled, fireplace puffed smoke. The hall grew warmer, water began dripping somewhere. The newcomers held the fireplace, the *streltsy* the table, and time crawled by. The two factions snacked, conversed in whispers, each watching the other. It was an absurd standoff and Viazemski was the key—he knew that and found the situation amusing. Oak could not decide what to make of the man, unwilling to believe so despicable a reputation could hide a heart of gold, yet aware that the ruffian's brazen lack of conscience gave him an odd sort of charm.

A couple of hours passed. Wassail seemed somewhat restored, sitting between Beau and Arkell. The women had moved to the opposite bench, beside Cuthbert and Wilf. Oak stood behind his ward, brooding on the accursed misfortune of the storm that had delayed their escape. Without that, they would have been well on their way up the Dvono by now.

Apparently Wassail was thinking much the same. Suddenly he said, *"Voevode?"*

The *streltsy* leader rose and walked closer, but not too near the unblinking Blades. "My lord?"

"Spirits of air and chance rule the weather," the Ambassador rasped, "and certainly it was prankish chance made us meet in this lodge. But Skyrria is very big and there must be a reason why we are both in the Morkuta area at this time. Will you tell what business brings you here?"

That awful smile again—"You left Kiensk without leave, my lord. I was sent to catch you and bring you back."

"Nonsense. Even ignoring Sir Cuthbert, you know that eight men cannot arrest three Blades."

"I was separated from my main strength by the blizzard, but they will come in time. Meanwhile, you will not be leaving." He was lying, of course . . . wasn't he?

"Then I should ask Sir Beaumont to kill you all now."

That did not seem such a bad idea to Oak. The *streltsy* would dislike it, though, and they were listening intently.

The one-armed man shrugged. "It would be an act of war. Your retainers back in Kiensk are hostage."

When it came to deceit and perfidy, Wassail was out of his class dealing with a thug like Viazemski. He coughed a few times and tried again. "You still have that paper I signed for you once?"

The brigand lowered his voice. "It may be around somewhere."

"We lost our way. I'm thinking of hiring some local guides. Guards, even. I could pay well."

"How fortunate some people are!" A grin twisted Viazemski's beard. "Wouldn't mention that happy situation too loudly around here, Your Honor. If I were you, I mean. I have my suspicions not all those lads of mine are perfectly honest."

"Just you, then?"

"I'm certainly not."

The Walrus glared. His lungs bubbled.

Arkell came to his rescue. "You told me once that you could be a good friend."

"I tell 'em all that, sonny. Have you heard what I did to my mother?"

Oak decided it must be his turn. "Did you talk to the Czar yesterday?"

Viazemski chuckled. "Mostly I *listened* to the Czar yesterday."

"How did you explain my resurrection?"

"Told him I was sure you were dead when I left. Your binding makes you very hard to kill, see?"

"Thanks for that." And that was all the thanks Oak would ever give him.

"You're welcome. Next?" He leered.

"Me." Beau's smile was brilliant and Viazemski's grew more cautious.

"How may I help you, Commander?"

"No, how may *we* help *you?*" The Blade chuckled. "My lord, the *Voevode*'s tale smells of fish. I doubt he would ever lose his way, yet he arrived just before we did. One asks oneself why any honest man would leave Kiensk in the middle of the night during a blizzard and take the shortest road to the border."

"Suggest a reason," Wassail growled.

"Because he has spies within the Imperial Chancellery, perhaps? Could he have learned that Chief Boyar Skuratov had sent word to the Czar denouncing the notorious Viazemski as a traitor?"

The *streltsi*'s furious pallor was confirmation enough. "What are you implying?" He spoke through clenched teeth. "What do you know?"

"I know that you are a wonderful trader, *Voevode*." Beau seemed barely able to contain outright laughter. "Igor's dogs are snapping at your backside and yet you pretend indifference when His Lordship offers you the chance to escape from Skyrria with us. What terms shall we offer? You want to hear our fees for killing off those ruffians behind you before they decide to sell you to the Czar? How much will you pay us not to tell them the truth?"

"You did this?" Viazemski was white with rage. His hand toyed with his sword. "You chose a strange way to reward me for saving your man's life, Commander."

Behind the inevitable smile, Beau's eyes were cold as steel. "I was rewarding you for not warning us that Oak was in danger. The saving came a little late. We may credit it to your account, if you and your pack wish to discuss cooperation."

"In return for what?"

"Guide us to the border, help us past the White Hats, escort us across Dolorth."

For himself, Oak would sooner share a bed with a pack of hungry wolves, but his ward needed all the help he could get.

The *streltsi* glanced around to confirm that his men were listening. "Make us an offer."

"My lord," Beau said, "buy me these brutes."

"A thousand Hyrian ducats apiece." Wassail gasped for breath and then continued. "That's about fifteen hundred rubles. Three times that for you. I have the money in bankers' drafts, so warn your shifty friends they can't . . ." *Gasp!* ". . . earn it with a knife in my kidneys. I can . . . turn it into gold when we reach Konigsfen, in Fitain."

"Four times for me."

"No. Take . . . it or leave it."

Viazemski scowled. "I'll have to consult my boys. If we have dissenters, can we divide their share among the survivors?"

Wassail tried to laugh and grimaced in pain. "Beau?" he gasped.

"Why not? Make it ten thousand for the gang of them, my lord, and may the worst man win."

The *streltsi* went off to confer with his accomplices. They removed to a far corner, but whispers soon grew into argument. Trust was in very short supply.

"Beau?" Wassail croaked.

"My lord?"

"What have you been up to now?"

That was something Oak wanted to know also, and Arkell was almost gnashing his teeth.

"Me?"

"Don't deny it, just tell me."

Beau sighed. "When we moved from West Wing to the Foreigners' Quarter yesterday, my lord, your red silk hat box was inadvertently left behind."

"Didn't know I had a red silk hat box."

"It is of no matter in itself. It was empty, except for the secret compartment, which the Chief Boyar's spies would find very easily as soon as we had gone. Of course VoevodeViazemski has his own spies inside the Imperial Chancellery, so he heard the news and decided to leave town before the Tsar was summoned back. Certain papers discovered in that secret compartment were written by Czarevich Fedor himself, clearly showing that he has been conspiring with a foreign power, namely you, to overthrow his father. Shocking! One of the notes implicates His Turpitude over there as a fellow conspirator. Czar Igor will certainly want to get to the bottom of the matter."

Wassail gagged and turned almost purple before he caught his breath. "You made me a spy? Spirits! Igor will be after us with his entire army."

Even Arkell was horrified. "You implicated your ward in sedition and high treason? Why?"

"Why?" Beau looked as innocent as spring flowers. "Isn't

that obvious, brother? No one plants documents that incriminate himself, so these must be genuine—simple, yes? But the *Czarevich?* I'll guarantee Skuratov and the rest of those geriatric boyars went into such a tail-chasing spin that they won't think to look for us for days."

"But what of Sir Dixon and all the others we left behind? They'll be arrested and tortured. Beau, that's terrible!"

"Rubbish!" Beau said impatiently. "Igor will see through the whole thing the moment he returns. He knows Fedor wouldn't write letters to a man he's been seeing practically every night for months. He can barely write at all. My imitation of his hand was very crude."

"But Viazemski must know he's innocent!"

"Innocent?" Beau echoed incredulously. "That horror isn't innocent of any crime ever invented. Obviously he panicked and ran when he heard he was under suspicion—why? The chance that dropped us together here may have been good luck."

"I doubt it," Oak muttered.

"What of Fedor?" Arkell said. "Will he learn of this?"

"Sure to," Beau said cheerily. "He's the heir and there's always lickspittles slobbering around the heir. Someone will tip him off."

"You certainly left them something to think about," Arkell conceded.

Surprisingly, he laughed. Then Wassail chuckled.

If they were happy, Oak supposed he should be. Night was falling, the hall almost dark, and the stack of firewood would have to be replenished soon. Who would dare leave the standoff to do that—one Blade and three *streltsy* perhaps?

The door crashed back against the wall, admitting a blast of snow and fog, a troop of men, and a chorus of obscene complaint. They stamped their boots and shouted, then slammed the door shut. Their insignia were too caked with snow to be discernible, but clearly they were not *streltsy*. There were about a score of them, enough to make the hall crowded and tip the odds drastically. Even before they uncovered their faces, Oak recognized the sepulchral growl of Czarevich Fedor.

VI

Journey's End

⋆ 1 ⋆

Convinced that Fedor had come to take her back, Tasha clutched Olga's hand and shrank down low on the bench behind her, cowering against the chimney stonework. Lord Wassail rose and his Blades closed in around him. Viazemski and his men drew off to one side; the newcomers to the other, and there was a three-way confrontation.

"Death and blood! What have we?" The giant Czarevich was shedding fur in all directions—hats, robes, boots. He was looking at the *streltsy*, though, not at Tasha. "The traitor himself!" He took his sword back from a helper and slung the baldric around his great bulk.

"No traitor, Your Highness," Viazemski retorted, bowing low. "Your royal father's most loyal servant."

"We'll let him decide that."

"I have caught fatter fish for you, Highness. Look there!"

Fedor's emotions were never a secret and the sight of Lord Wassail clearly astonished him. He frowned uncertainly when he saw Tasha—she tried to look away, but his eye held hers like a snake freezing a bird. He laughed and came strolling over with his men trailing after him. One caught his arm and muttered a warning, pointing at the Blades.

He brushed the hand off impatiently. "I was told yesterday that you were indisposed, Cousin."

Tasha shook her head and clung even tighter to Olga.

He chuckled and turned his sneer on Lord Wassail. "You have some explaining to do, old man."

"I am completing my mission, Your Highness, escorting Her Majesty to Chivial."

"Show me your passport. No one leaves Skyrria without my father's permission."

Tasha hoped Lord Wassail would produce a paper, any paper, because the Czarevich was a notoriously poor reader. Instead he just said calmly, "I interpreted his final remarks as dismissal."

"Not enough. Good chance, Cousin!" Fedor smirked at Tasha.

She nodded, not trusting herself to speak. Her fear amused him. Why couldn't she be brave, like Sophie?

"Two birds with a single shot! This has been a profitable trip. Hand over your weapons, all of you. Viazemski, your lot first."

The *streltsy* bristled like cornered wolves, showing teeth. Their leader smiled unctuously. "That would not be advisable, Your Highness. You need our support. Those Blades are deadly."

Tasha saw the explosion coming. Cousin Fedor would never tolerate argument.

"Disarm!" he bellowed. "You are coming back to Kiensk with me—in chains! I don't know what you've been up to, but you've dragged me into something nasty, and I won't stand for it."

Viazemski looked as if he were weighing odds, choosing sides. "My men and I will be happy to lay down our arms if the Chivians do so first." Which would be never, of course.

"If I may make a suggestion, Czarevich?" said a new voice. Everyone turned to scowl at Beaumont's dazzling smile. "Why cart him all the way back to High Town? Why not just torture the truth out of him here? It will help pass the time."

"What do you know about this?" Viazemski demanded. "I know someone's lying about me. How did the Czarevich get involved?"

"Truth is always so elusive!" Beau said sadly. "Don't worry—you'll think of something convincing when they start on your fingernails. If not, there's always toenails. Until they go too, I mean."

Fedor chewed his beard as he tried to work this out, while Beaumont seemed to be having the time of his life. Tasha had never seen anyone stand up to Fedor before. Could the Blade really be as confident as he sounded?

"Tell us, Viazemski," he said, "have you decided to accept His Lordship's offer of employment? I can testify that he is a generous and honorable master. He believes strongly in the two-edged nature of loyalty and takes very seriously his duty to stand by his servants. Right now, for instance, should you feel the need of armed support, I am certain he would direct us to aid you in your righteous struggle against imperialism."

"Have you been slandering me?" Viazemski roared.

"*Voevode,* I wouldn't know how to start. But I do think you had better choose sides, once and for all. Big Lumpkin, there, has a round score of beards behind him, but most of them are aristocratic trash. You have seven, plus your formidable self, and Lord Wassail has four. The odds are acceptable. I'll hamstring His Nibs for you, if you have scruples about shedding royal blood, but I think the rest had better die, don't you? Tidier that way."

The listeners had been shifting, dividing into two factions. Viazemski's men clearly preferred him to the prince who had beaten three of their fellows to death in Great Market.

The Czarevich seemed uncertain how to proceed, but then his gaze fell on Tasha again and he beckoned. "Come here, Cousin. You're not safe there."

She shook her head.

"Come *here,* Cousin! You don't want to make me *angry,* do you?"

He moved forward with bovine obstinacy. She cowered back against the stonework at the end of the bench.

"Tasha, I'm warning you. You won't like it if I have to get rough."

She did not try to stand; her legs would not hold her if she did. She could not breathe . . .

Lord Wassail stepped between them. "Czarevich, you are addressing the Queen of Chivial. I ask you to be more respectful."

"Stand aside, you festering old fool!"

With no more warning than that, the world went mad. Fedor raised a fist to swipe the old man out of his way. Sir Arkell's sword flashed out to block the giant, who was a good head taller than the Blade. Fedor reached for his own hilt and Arkell's wrist moved. That was all . . . Tasha saw his wrist move . . . no more than a gesture . . . but the point of his sword jabbed through the Czarevich's beard. Fedor dropped to his knees and pitched forward. Lord Wassail uttered a strangled cry and toppled back into Sir Beaumont's arms. Swords flashed out all over the hall and voices roared.

Tasha had hit the floor and rolled under the bench before her mind made sense of it all. Where was Olga?

"Stop! Stop! All of you!" Viazemski shouted. "Wait!"

Tasha stared into the astonished eyes of Czarevich Fedor, level with hers as she cowered in her refuge. A river of blood spurted out of his beard, a torrent, an ocean, more blood than any mortal frame could possibly contain. She had seen pigs' throats cut often enough. They bled into a bucket, but not this much. He raised a hand to his neck as if he would plug the leak with his fingers.

"You're dying!" she said. Strangely, she laughed, although it should not be funny. Why was she laughing? He was Igor's heir. He mustn't die!

Fedor blew a string of red bubbles. Beyond him, Lord Wassail lay on the floor with his Blades kneeling around him. His face was blotched and screwed up in agony; his breath came in irregular rasps. He pawed at his chest.

"Wait!" Viazemski yelled again. "Your leader is dead! Do you think the Czar will forgive you? Not Igor! He'll have every man in this hall ripped and roasted and fed alive to his dogs."

The listeners growled like angry wolves, but for a moment nobody moved.

Fedor had stopped bleeding. His eyes were not moving and his face was a sickly paper color. She could not mourn him, Tasha decided. Skyrria would do better without him. Dimitri was now heir to the throne. No . . . the baby that Sophie carried . . .

The old man was dying too. The hall had stilled to watch, fallen silent in the presence of death. His rattling breath stopped, started, stopped.

After a moment, Beaumont closed the staring eyes.

The three Blades rose as one and drew their swords. They leaped forward. The screaming started. Sir Cuthbert followed them into the melee of blood and clashing steel, stamping boots, shrieks of rage, and howls of terror. Tasha squeezed her eyes tight shut and clapped her hands over her ears. Mostly there were no words, just sounds of animal fury or terror, and heavy thumps, but rarely someone would curse or beg for mercy. Something warmly wet splashed over her hand. The door thundered against the wall again, an icy gale swept around her. The yells and stamping grew rarer, meaning fewer fighters. The door boomed again, blown shut, and the hall fell silent, almost silent, just someone, somewhere, whimpering in agony. Cautiously she opened her eyes. She was splattered with blood, but not her own.

The world had gone mad.

There were bodies everywhere: Fedor, Wassail, the young custler—who had found a sword somewhere and been run through—and Viazemski, face down. It was his gore that had splashed her.

"Olga!" she yelled, scrambling to her feet. *"Olga?"*

She found Olga near the door, dead. She could not find Beaumont, or Arkell, and there seemed to be others missing, too. There had been no time for anyone to don outdoor clothing, and no one would survive very long outside without it. She found Sir Oak cut to pieces, surrounded by bodies. If no one came back soon, she would have to assume that she was the only survivor.

When she began counting the corpses, she realized one of the *streltsy* was watching her. He lay on his side, hugging his knees. She forced herself to crouch beside him and clasp his red hand. His face was lined, his beard streaked gray, and his robes were a gory mess.

"Can I help?"

He nodded.

"How? Bandages?"

"Dying . . ." He gasped a few times. "Don' wan' . . . take three days doing it."

"I don't know what you mean."

"Drink, then?"

"Yes." She scrambled up. "I can get you a drink."

She picked her way between bodies to the water buckets and brought the dipper to the dying man. Most of it spilled, but he seemed to get some. He closed his eyes. She waited, but he did not speak again.

Shivering, she hurried over to the fire. It was hot enough, yet she was still cold. She could see no more firewood and what would she do when it went out? She was confused, not thinking very clearly, much as she remembered from the night Fedor hit her. Shock.

The door flew open to admit the snowy arctic blast and a man carrying another over his shoulder. He picked his way between the bodies, over to the fire; she moved away from him and eventually thought to go and close the door. When she dared creep back to the hearth, she barely recognized Sir Beaumont's face under a mask of dried blood. He was kneeling beside the man he had brought in.

"Is he dead?" she asked.

He looked up at her as if he had trouble remembering who she was. "I'm all right now. Don't be afraid." He was weeping, tears turning scarlet as they ran down his cheeks.

"I'm not." Should she be? Hard to think. "Is Arkell dead?"

"Can't find any wounds. He had a bang on the head."

She jumped back as the swordsman rose, but he ignored her and went wandering around, talking to the corpses. "You picked a poor moment to die, my lord. Skyrria's better off without you, Fedor, but your daddy won't be pleased. Oak, Oak! What do I tell them when I take *Sorrow* back to the Hall? Cuthbert, ah, you fought in knightly fashion. And Wilf? Wilf wouldn't have hurt a bug. Sergei?" He turned his dread mask to Tasha. "Your friend. Why did she run?"

"If you hadn't played your stupid games with forged letters, none of this would have happened!"

He shrugged, then rubbed his face as if he had just realized how it looked. "Anyone else alive in here?"

She pointed. He went to see. She heard a murmur of voices back and forth. Then Beaumont came back, sheathing his sword.

"Your Majesty . . ." A grotesque smile flickered under the bloodstains. "You don't look very majestic. Your Grace, how long will the storm last?"

"How should I know?"

"You're more familiar with the weather here than I am. I don't know how many got away—three or four, and they weren't dressed warmly. How far to Morkuta? Will they come back with help? We must leave before the snow stops, so we don't leave tracks."

"We are going back to Kiensk, aren't we? I insist we go back!"

"And tell the Czar what, exactly?" He flopped down on the bench and stared bleakly at the body of his ward. "I must go and see to the horses. Fedor's men just left their mounts out there, still saddled. Brutes! How long do we have to stay here?"

"There's no more firewood."

"If it's just for one night, we can put up with it here. If it's more, we should move to a smaller place. There's other chimneys."

"But then we have to go back to Kiensk." Faritsov would be even better. She wanted Sophie, Dimitri, family . . . Not this blundering monster.

"Horses first." Beaumont heaved himself off the bench and shuffled over to the door, where the furs were. Dressed, he disappeared in another cloud of fog and a slam.

"Shame, shame."

She jumped. Sir Arkell's eyes were open. She knelt beside him.

"Would you like a drink?"

He gaped a bizarrely unseeing smile at her. "Shame, shame shame shame shame . . ."

"Stop that!"

"Pity pity pity pity pity . . ."

"Stop!"

But he didn't. He kept repeating, "Pity." On and on and on.

Shouting at him helped her but not him. His wits had gone. She found hers coming back, bringing horror with them. Thirty people dead! The Czarevich among them. What if Sophie failed to bring her baby to term? Dimitri was next in line. How long would gentle Dimitri hold the throne?

"Pity pity pity . . ."

What was to become of her, locked up here with two murderers? She must pretend to trust the Chivians for now. Perhaps other travelers would arrive. Someone must come looking for Fedor soon, surely?

The fire was collapsing into embers. She poked them together to make a blaze, and remembered what Sir Beaumont had said about finding a smaller place—no bodies, easier to heat. She could collect the baggage, maybe. She started to do that. Her pack and some food. Her outdoor robes. She couldn't recognize Beaumont's. Chilled, she went back to the fire.

Arkell was sitting up. It was "Shame!" again: "Shame, shame shame shame shame . . ."

"Stop it!" she screamed. He grinned his open-mouth leer at her and spoke louder.

She yelled, "Idiot! Moron! Madman!" She struck him. "Lackwit!"

He blinked. "By the light of legal reason the right is discerned."

"What?"

"Certainty is the mother of quietness and repose, and uncertainty the cause of variance and contentions." He laughed like a child pleased with himself. "Here is good counsel and advice given—"

He went on gabbling steadily until Beaumont returned. Retaining his furs, he came to huddle and shiver by the fire.

"Arkell's gone crazy!" she said, but he could see that and hear that.

"It hath been anciently said, that the heriot shall be paid before the mortuary."

Beaumont listened to the babble for a while, then shrugged. "He needs time. I've found a place easier to heat."

"We are going back to Kiensk, aren't we?"

He sighed. "Not me, thank you. Or Arkell. Your Majesty, I am a King's Blade and you are the King's wife. I have no ward now. I pledge that I will do everything humanly possible to escort you in safety and honor to your new country and your throne and the husband who awaits you."

"You? You couldn't find water if you fell through the ice."

"It's not quite hopeless, Your Grace. We must be very close to Morkuta and the Dvono."

"And the White Hats! And if you get past them, then what? Dolorth! Fitain! Isilond! Months! Brigands! Outlaws!"

"True, but . . . Well, let's talk about that when we're settled in. I haven't found the woodpile or the well yet. I hope there's a woodpile."

He had chosen a tiny office off one of the stables. The horses' heat had warmed it a little already and by the time he took her there, he had a blaze going in the fireplace. He found lanterns and some oil; he brought all the baggage they would need, plus several days' food; he located the well and watered all the thirsty horses. He dressed Arkell in furs for the move and undressed him again in the new quarters. The hall was allowed to freeze and become the mortuary. Beaumont even dragged to it all the stiffened corpses of the men who had died outside. He brought more firewood, laid out bedding, offered to cook a meal.

Tasha refused food. Fully dressed, she lay on straw under piles of furs. She did not truly feel cold, and yet she shivered and shivered and shivered. Flame-danced shadows filled the night with images of dead bodies and blood until she did not know which were dreams and which madness.

Horses fretted and fidgeted, storm wailed in the rafters, and Arkell babbled endlessly. "He said it that knew it best, and had by nature himself no advantage in that he commended . . ."

"What?" she said. Someone had spoken her name. "Who's there?"

"Just me, Beaumont. You were screaming."

"No, I wasn't! I couldn't have been. I wasn't asleep."

"Well, someone was," he said resignedly. He sounded alarmingly near.

"How's Arkell?"

"Asleep. Sleep may help. I had to hit him pretty hard. There's no predicting how a Blade will take his ward's death."

"I thought you went mad."

"We did."

"Oh."

"Some of us recover quickly. Some need longer. Some never do. Are you warm enough?"

"No." She had no idea what part of the night it was, early or late.

"Arkell helps keep me warm."

"What is that meant to mean?"

"If you want to join us, I will not take advantage of you."

"That is a highly improper suggestion!"

"It's a sensible one under the circumstances," he said wryly. "His Majesty will not be pleased if I deliver a frozen wife."

She lay and shivered, listening to the storm and the clink of horseshoes, the clatter of her own teeth. "You swear?" she whispered.

"I swear," came the response at once.

She scrambled in under the robes beside him. He was fully dressed, too, of course, and the bed was warm. It was not proper, but rules of protocol and demeanor hardly applied here.

Last night she had bedded down with Olga. Olga, frozen solid now, her head almost cut off . . . Suddenly Tasha was sobbing, sobbing hysterically—shaking, fighting for breath. The swordsman wrapped strong arms around her and crushed her against him.

"Let it come. This will help. Weep all you can." He was warm and she was so cold. She wept. Every time she caught her breath he would say, "Weep more!" So she did. "Don't fight it. Weep for all those useless deaths. Weep for fatherless children and women bereft. Weep!"

"Boldness is a child of ignorance and baseness," Arkell muttered, on Beaumont's far side, "inferior to other parts."

◆ 2 ◆

Next day the sun came out a few times, but the wind continued to hurl snow around, and the cold seemed more intense. Beaumont fed and watered the horses, which was an epic task in itself. He dug out one of the sleds, pushed it into the stable, and began loading it. He chopped wood, heated water for washing, cooked a warm meal. Tasha knew she should offer to help, but she had no experience at doing any of those things and was afraid her ignorance would make her a hindrance.

Arkell showed no signs of improvement, babbling nonsense all the time and barely able to attend to his own toilet or feeding. Beaumont cared for him, too.

When darkness fell, he spread out the bedding again.

"The wind's dropping. I hope we can leave here at dawn."

"I will go to Morkuta, no farther!"

He did not answer. When he had the bedding ready, he removed Arkell's boots for him.

Arkell grinned, slack-jawed. "When any of the four pillars of government are mainly shaken or weakened, men had need to pray for fair weather."

"So say all of us, brother. Lie down there."

He had prepared only one bed, she noticed. She turned away from the fire so he would not see her blushes. He threw off his own boots and squirmed in beside his moronic friend.

" . . . the despising of them many times checks them best."

"So it does," Beaumont said. "Trust me, Tasha. I am the same man I was last night."

"I must trust you," she grumbled, wriggling in beside him. "But I will go to Morkuta, no farther."

After a moment he said, "I value my neck and Arkell's too much—and even yours, Your Grace. Your uncle is a madman and capable of anything. I can find the Dvono, and the Dvono will lead us to Dvonograd."

"Where the Border Patrol will catch you."

"Maybe. We came through Dvonograd, you know. Your noble brother had been waiting there for months for us. Did he by any chance make any friends there?"

"Are you insane? There aren't even boyars there, let alone anyone of princely rank."

"Pity. Consul Hakluyt was there, too. He made friends." He waited in vain for a comment from her. "He made friends among the White Hats, lots of them. That's just good business, you understand. He also made friends with the local smugglers—who are much the same people, or close relatives. The night I was there, he introduced me to both sorts."

"You are a trickster, aren't you? A schemer."

"I try to look ahead. I do have money, Your Grace. Lord Wassail made sure I had funds, in case something like this happened. My acquaintances in Dvonograd will see us on our way west, and hopefully send some strong lads with us. A few days' travel should bring us to Gneizow, and I have friends there, too, Isilondian knights. They will escort us after that. It really should not be that difficult . . . Your Majesty."

She sighed. "Very well. Whatever will my husband say?"

" 'Welcome!' I expect. And, 'Did you have a nice trip?' "

"You ought to be in line for a peerage if you can do this."

Beaumont rolled on his side, away from her. "I wouldn't want a peerage, begging Your Grace's pardon. It is my duty—to him, to you, and to my ward."

"By the civil law every man is bound to warrant the thing that he selleth or conveyeth, albeit there be no express warranty."

"Yes, brother. Go to sleep."

After a moment, Beaumont said, "Mostly duty to my ward. He knew he was dying. He was too old to go adventuring, but his king asked him, so it was his duty. He loved the King. Athelgar was like the son he never had. His dearest wish was to walk into the palace with you on his arm and watch Athelgar's face light up when he saw you and realized that you really are as gorgeous as the portrait the Czar sent. That was what he wanted. He signed most of the letters of credit over to me and taught me the code that validates them. I have enough money to *buy* a peerage, Your Grace."

"That was not what I meant!"

He did not answer.

The storm rattled and wailed. Arkell mumbled. The horses chomped and stamped and staled loudly.

"Did you really imitate Fedor's writing?" she asked.

"Mmph. Yes. Not well enough to fool his father, though."

"How did you know what his hand looks like?"

"I found something to copy."

"What? He wrote me a letter once and it was a horrible scrawl, like a small child's, wandering all over the page. Sophie . . . the Czarina said it was a unique document and ought to go into the state archives."

Whatever had happened to that? Maybe Sophie had kept it.

Beaumont was starting to snore.

He must have been busy for hours before he wakened her and the imbecile. He had prepared a simple meal, fed the horses, finished loading the sled, even put hot bricks in it. While she ate, he dealt with Arkell.

"We'll take the bedding with us," he said, "because it's warm. I'll need help with the sled."

Stars burned with barely a twinkle in the terrible cold. The evil wind had gone elsewhere, leaving drifts almost head-high in places, but eventually Beaumont wrestled the sled and six horses out of the stockade, with some help from Tasha and none from the babbling Arkell. He harnessed three and tethered the rest behind as spares. The last thing he did was put a torch to the hall, returning its grisly collection of bodies to the elements.

"No funeral service?" she asked when he came back out to the sled.

"No time. Mostly I want to confuse the issue—who died and who didn't. Make sure he stays covered up, will you please?"

"Until I go crazy," she said grumpily. He had seated her in the back with Arkell, who was admittedly a minor source of warmth, but a maddening traveling companion.

Off they went. Her last sight of ghastly Mezersk was flames leaping high in the night and spilling redness on the snow.

They made slow progress, winding between drifts too deep for horses and windswept gaps the sled could not cross. The sun rose reluctantly, giving light but no heat. They had lost the road by then, but that hardly mattered in a land so barren. Eventually they came to a gentle slope downward and Beaumont yelped in delight, gestured all around with his whip.

"The Dvono!"

That wide expanse of blank whiteness could be nothing else. The banks were patchy brown boundaries trailing off to north and south. Now the fugitives might make good time over the ice, provided they were not seen. If any of the men who had escaped the massacre had reached Morkuta, they would certainly have warned the White Hats or other troops in the area.

"Which way is Morkuta?" she shouted as they drove down onto the ice.

"Upstream or possibly downstream."

"The king judges by his judges and they are the speaking law!" Arkell struggled free of the rugs, letting in a torrent of icy air. He pointed to the north and leered witlessly at her.

Had she not been wearing a double layer of fur over her head, Tasha's hair might have stood on end. "Which way is Dvonograd?"

Out came his other arm, to point roughly southwest. "Faculties by which the foolish part of men's minds is taken are most potent."

"Let's get cosy again." She replaced the covers. Perhaps Arkell was starting to come out of his daze. She dearly wished he would stop babbling.

The sled whistled over the ice, drawn by the steaming horses, and eventually she realized that Arkell had been right—they had bypassed Morkuta. Had that been only a lucky guess?

Fine though they were, the horses could not run forever. By the time the short day faded they were exhausted, almost staggering. Tasha was frozen to the bone. Arkell wept all the time, not understanding; his stubbled beard was caked with frozen tears.

They had not met one living soul all day. Here and there blackened chimneys showed where houses had stood, and there were a few ruined jetties along the banks, but this part of Skyrria had died in the wars. The desolation was infinitely sad and she understood now why the Czar would not let foreigners see it.

"Where will we spend the night?" she asked.

Beaumont peered around at her. His eyes were red, slitted against the constant glare. "Somewhere near here there's some deserted cottages on the left bank. They're kept stocked, to be used by royal couriers and others. We should survive well enough overnight if they're not full of *streltsy*."

Somebody had coached the foreigners well, but perhaps not well enough to locate an unfamiliar landmark in this ice haze and universal whiteness.

"How will you find them?"

"By chance," he said without looking around again.

"What's it called, this place?"

"Nelsevo."

"Arkell, where's Nelsevo?"

The madman just scowled at her and snuggled down in the covers.

"Lackwit, where's Nelsevo?" she yelled.

Sulkily, Human Compass freed an arm and pointed back.

"Turn around, Beaumont!" Tasha shouted. "You've gone past it."

• 3 •

There were no *streltsy* lying in wait at Nelsevo. The following evening the fugitives reached Dvonograd and Beaumont made good on his promise, finding men there who remembered him and were willing to help. For a price, of course, but he had money and a sword to guard it. Tasha dared not start to hope, not yet.

The day after that, she crossed the Dvono and thus left Skyrria. Their sled was escorted by six others bearing villainous-looking men who would doubtless sell her to a higher bidder, or rape her if they discovered she was a woman. The bitter wind that blew all that day would help cover their tracks, as Beau cheerfully pointed out. No White Hats came racing in pursuit and when she commented on that, he just laughed and gestured to the escort. "Why should they? They're here already."

Every night she slept at his side and gradually the nightmares of Mezersk began to fade. The ruffian guards never seemed to notice that the "boy," unlike themselves, did not treat the whole world as one gigantic urinal.

Four or five days after that, Beau paid them off at a rough little fortified settlement named Gneizow, for there he had more trustworthy men waiting, a troop of Isilondians led by a gruff, stolid-seeming Sergeant Narenne. Tasha did not know their language or they hers, but their loyalty was to their lord, not just to gold, and she found that knowledge comforting. Although they paid very little attention to her, she soon realized that they had guessed who, or at least *what,* she was. They usually remembered to turn their backs when they made yellow patches on the snow—and also when she had to, which mattered more.

Not everything went smoothly. Winter could be deadly in Dolorth and Fitain, too, and the terrain harder. They boarded in peasants' sheds, mostly, or wayside hostelries when there were any. In those the Isilondians set watches all night. Three times Beau had to push her under the table and draw his sword—the fights were never about her, just drunken brawls over gambling or foreigners making eyes at local women, but blood was spilled and once a young man died.

Sometimes wolves, two-legged or four-legged, left tracks around their path, but none dared show teeth. Midwinter came and went. Days grew longer and the countryside more settled.

Like all travelers, they were plagued by vermin and the flux. Tasha succumbed to sickness no more than the toughest of them, even Beau, but when she did, he halted the expedition and patiently nursed her back to health.

Eventually the going became impossible for sleds, so they switched to horseback. That slowed them a lot. Lackwit had to be carried in a litter or a cart, for he fell off at any pace above a walk and screamed hysterically if Beau tried lashing him to the saddle. Spring came early by Skyrrian standards; rivers flooded, roads turned to quagmire, insects swarmed. But one fine day at a guardhouse beside a bridge, Beau paid off some officials and escorted Tasha across the river into Isilond.

"There should be a decent elementary here," he told her, riding at her side. "Your husband gave my ward strict instructions that only Chivian conjurers are competent to enchant you in Chivian, but I can't see that it would hurt to provide you with Isilondian. Then you'll have someone else to talk to besides me."

He was enough, but she did not say so. She pointed at the little town ahead. "What quaint buildings!"

"Your Grace?"

"You should call me Timofei—sir." She grinned and stuck her tongue out at him.

He remained solemn. Hooves drummed a dirge on the timbers. "We cannot be overheard at the moment, Your Grace. If I may presume to advise Your Majesty . . . Another day or so will bring us to Vaanen. Even if Orson himself isn't home, his mother the Dowager Marquise will be. So Narenne says. Blue blood doesn't come any bluer than theirs. I do believe it would be safe now for you to bury Timofei and become Queen Tasha."

"No!" she cried. She didn't want that. She had not admitted it before, even to herself, but thoughts of Chivial and a throne and a strange man's bed terrified her.

"Why ever not, Your Grace?" he asked, frowning.

"Oh . . . Riding sidesaddle, or in a coach with Lackwit? I'd never realized how much more sheer freedom men have. They don't have to worry all the time about . . . well, about other men. I'll feel safer if we just carry on the way we are." Being a boy. Being anonymous. When she became Queen of Chivial, she would have to stop sleeping with Beau.

◆ 4 ◆

$\mathfrak{T}$here was something magical about Laville in the spring, unfortunately. It magically attracted pests, and Chivian pests in particular. At the crack of Thirdmoon the Chivian rich and fatuous flocked south to Laville, and it seemed the worst of them were those who brought letters of introduction to the Chivian Ambassador. This was why Lord and Lady Hedgebury were currently entertaining Baron and Baroness Gallmouth.

Their name was actually Gelmouth, but Hedgebury had to think about something while they talked. If he let that *Gallmouth* slip out, Agnes would turn purple and never forgive him.

The Galemouths talked in shifts. Before lunch, the Baron had described his new mews down to the last bird dropping and then given a long dissertation on the finer points of cockfighting. During lunch he was too busy stuffing himself with the free food to say a word but his scraggy wife took over the monologue, recounting the exploits of their excessively cute grandchildren in lethal detail. Agnes, who had not seen her own brood of cute grandchildren for almost a year, listened with a waxy smile. By the second course, the increasingly loud Baroness had progressed into palace gossip, slandering people the Hedgeburys neither knew nor wished to know.

Apart from ringing mental changes on his guests' name, the Ambassador just nibbled and sipped and thought of all the more interesting things he might be doing. He could be riding his new roan gelding on Montmoulin, for example. He could be strumming on that fascinating antique Ritizzian lute he'd acquired last week, or just ambling the alleys of Laville listening to troubadours and watching flowers and people blossom in spring.

A footman filled the Baroness's goblet yet again. *(Gillmouth—drinks like a fish.)* She was thin and hard and turning redder by the minute, looking and sounding like a rusty saw.

"Of course," she rasped, "you have heard about His Majesty's friendship with Lady Gwendolyn?" She wiggled threadbare lashes over the rim of her goblet.

"We prefer not to heed scandal." Anyone who knew Agnes would have fled in screaming terror from that smile.

"Oh, but this isn't really *scandal!* I mean, there's no doubt about it, so that makes it *news,* wouldn't you say?" The harpy's laugh was even harsher than her voice. "The man is bewitched! He follows her like a lap dog! And she . . . *well!* Let me tell you about the night of—"

"Have you tried these eels in ginger?" Agnes snarled sweetly.

Almost certainly, the Baroness was working the conversation around to the King's betrothal. That was general knowledge now. Without it the sordid little story of his infatuation with the slinky Lady Gwendolyn would hardly merit a single sideways glance—monarchs had more opportunity for dalliance than other men and a lot less privacy. Athelgar had been more restrained than most, at least since the Thencaster Plot, but the outlandish bride in the wings added zest to this latest indiscretion. The Hedgeburys were not about to discuss state business with a drunken, tattling baroness.

Like a death-cell reprieve, Lindsay stepped inside the doorway and looked meaningfully over at his employer. Lindsay was First Secretary, an excellent lad—a lad of thirty-six, Sir Lindsay, late of the Royal Guard, who must have been born about the time young Wat Hedgebury was admitted to Ironhall. Receiving a nod of consent, he glided forward to murmur in the ambassadorial ear.

"Forgive the intrusion, Your Excellency. A Master Starkmoor is here to see you. I do believe his business is urgent."

There was no Master Starkmoor; there were a thousand of him, and if this one wanted nothing more than to pass on a bad joke, he would be a welcome distraction. Carefully avoiding Agnes's eye, Hedgebury muttered an apology, rose, and led the way to the door.

"Who?" he demanded as he strode across the entrance hall to the library. He knew hundreds of Blades, but by no means all of them.

"Beaumont, my lord."

Returning without his ward? Bad, *bad* news!

Lindsay knocked before opening the door to the dark-paneled, leather-scented chamber. Hedgebury had furnished the library with a set of massive Cumber chairs and used it as a reception room. With a spasm of shock, he saw that one of those chairs had become a throne. A flaxen-haired boy sat on it, flanked by the equally blond Beaumont, and a heavily bearded Arkell. All three wore travelers' garments, shabby but not shameful.

"Fetch my wife! And get rid of those Gelmouth pests any way you can. Think of an excuse."

"Bad family news." Lindsay closed the door on him.

Turning to the youth, Beaumont spoke in an unfamiliar, guttural tongue. Even had he not caught his own name, Hedgebury would have known who was being presented, who was receiving. He doubled over in a full court bow, advanced, and then knelt to his Queen.

She smiled stiffly and offered fingers to be kissed. "I am very happy to meet you, Lord Hedgebury. I have yet to meet a Chivian I did not like." She spoke Isilondian with what Lavillians would disparagingly call a *pays d'en haut* accent.

"And you will never meet one you do not enchant at first glance, Your Majesty. My house is graced by your presence—technically this embassy is part of Chivial, so it is my great honor to welcome you to your new homeland."

She was just a child, but perhaps the combination of male

costume and smooth face exaggerated her youth. The King favored nymphs.

As Hedgebury rose and stepped back, he took a second look at Beaumont and blurted out, "Death, man! What happened?" In less than a year he had aged ten. Then— *"Brother Arkell?"* That gaping, vacant grin was even worse.

Arkell said, "Whatsoever was at the common law and is not ousted or taken away by any statute remains."

Death and perdition! Understandably, the dullard was not wearing a sword. Hedgebury shuddered, looked at Beaumont and again saw more than he wanted to see. Obviously Wassail was dead. There had been a third Blade . . . Beech? Oak. And what of Sir Dixon and all the rest? What of Lady Gwendolyn, swooping around Grandon as the King's mistress? He thrust that thought aside.

He wished Agnes would hurry. It would be more proper to have another lady present. Belatedly he registered the significance of the male clothing. Who had chaperoned the King's wife all the way across Eurania? Why not send for Baroness Gelmouth to start spreading the scandal right away?

"Your Majesty has had a difficult journey, I fear."

"I would never have made it without Sir Beaumont." She smiled at the man in question.

Even an ambassador could be at a loss for words. Hedgebury wanted to scream, *Don't look at him like that!* Incognito, starry-eyed, juvenile queens were not mentioned in the protocol manual he had studied before taking up his posting. The child was brittle as crystal, understandably, shimmering with nervousness.

Beaumont seemed at ease. "Her Majesty has agreed that a few days' rest in Laville would be restorative and also tactful." He flashed a glint of the boyish amusement Hedgebury recalled from last year's brief acquaintance. Then he had been considerably impressed by Beaumont, even prepared to believe his reputation might not be too much exaggerated. But Grand Master's glowing predictions would carry no weight in the face of this disaster.

"Of course my wife and I would be deeply honored if Her Grace would deign to make this house her home while we await word from Grandon. His Majesty will wish to . . . finalize preparations for Her Grace's reception." Dump Lady Gwendolyn, for instance. Oh, spirits! *why* did Athelgar have to indulge in a stupid infatuation *now?* Also get Beaumont out of sight so the bride did not simper adoringly at him all the time. *Brother, what have you done?*

"Your kindness is overwhelming, Your Excellency." The Queen's childish enjoyment of royal honors was endearing. The Court would fall at her feet—and rip her to shreds the moment she turned her back.

Agnes swept in. She appraised the situation at a glance and performed all the necessary court folderol without a moment's hesitation. Then she threw away the rule book.

"How absolutely appalling! Your Grace must be just dying for a proper toilette . . . your poor hands . . . garments . . . coiffeur . . . my daughter and I will be so happy to assist . . ."

Agnes could be fierce as the pard or gentle as turtledoves and now she was turtling. The terrified child queen melted visibly. Her lip trembled. Tears sprang into the cornflower-blue eyes. In moments she was swept away to feminine care and gentle company.

Two Blades bowed the women out and a third babbled nonsense. The door closed. In the serene silence, Hedgebury drew a deep breath.

Beaumont's smile was deadly as a rapier. "Do you sense a burden being dumped, brother?"

"I sense a lot of work and woe. Pray be seated, both of you."

Beau sat and pointed at the nearest chair. "Sit, Lackwit."

"They which are for the direction speak fearfully and tenderly," Arkell told a bookshelf.

"Oh, spirits!" Hedgebury said. "Your ward died?"

"Completely. *Lackwit, sit!*"

The imbecile flopped down on the floor.

"How can you call him that?" Hedgebury snapped, more strongly than he had intended.

"I have to call it something and it is not Arkell."

Hedgebury had met bereaved Blades before. Most either recovered in an hour or never did, although there were always exceptions. Some lived out their days in chains; others turned into toadstools.

"Does he have any flashes of rationality?"

"A few," Beaumont said. "He has a party trick that saved our necks a few times. Lackwit, which way is Trienne?"

The halfwit pointed at the fireplace, but his eyes stayed dull. He was drooling.

"He asks about his sword sometimes. He called her *Reason.*" There was no reaction. "He lost her in his frenzy. He was using another when he came at me and I never found his. I brought Oak's *Sorrow,* though."

"When *Sorrow* goes home to Ironhall," Hedgebury said, "see that Arkell goes with it. Master of Rituals can sometimes find a way through the grief. A replica of *Reason,* for example." Was that a momentary flicker of life in the dead eyes? "Can I offer you refreshments, brother?"

"Kind of you. May we attend to business first?"

"Gladly. What do I tell the King?"

Beaumont produced papers. "This is a list of people we left behind, and a partial list of the wedding gifts, although I doubt if those will ever reappear. And my report. I respectfully suggest you seal it as soon as you have read it. It is combustible."

"There is no need for me to read it at all." Much safer not to know.

"You are a member of the Privy Council, brother," his visitor said softly, "as I recall. I do wish you would read it."

"*That* bad?"

"Worse."

"If you feel it will help," Hedgebury said resignedly. He was in a swamp and sinking.

"You have heard no recent news from Skyrria?"

"None." He felt he should add, *Should I have?* "The Regent is unaware of Queen Tasha's presence in Isilond?" That was certainly an ambassadorial problem.

Beau smiled thinly. "As far as I am aware, he is unaware. The only persons who knew who the boy Timofei was are she and me. Lackwit doesn't speak. Even Czar Igor cannot be certain she still lives."

"But why did you not wait in Kiensk until spring? I was informed that this was your ward's intention."

"There were problems." Beaumont's eyes implied much more than he was saying. "Right after the proxy marriage, we made a dash for the border, eight of us. Complications ensued. A massacre, to be specific. We three were the only survivors."

"It takes two to massacre. Who were the other team?"

"As I mention in my report, the light was very poor, but one of them bore a strong resemblance to the Czarevich Fedor. I expect the Czar will inform us when he writes."

"Spirits of mercy!" The Ambassador wondered why the odious report did not just burst into flames in his hand. If the Czar's response included a declaration of war, the fragile diplomacy Hedgebury and the Regent had been working on all winter would collapse instantly. Eurania would burst into flames. "Was this crazy flight your idea or your ward's?"

Beau shrugged. "No matter now."

Everything mattered now, from war drums down to the slimiest gutter scandal. Apparently the future Queen of Chivial had been traveling unchaperoned in the company of two *Blades,* men with the worst possible reputation as debauchers of women.

"What sort of person is she?" Hedgebury asked. "I mean how will she stand up . . . ?"

"She's a child. Skyrrians wrap their women in lamb's wool and store them in jewel cases, princesses especially. Her brother did let her ride horses and drive sleds, which most men would regard as scandalous. Of course," Beaumont added with a gleam of mockery, "recent experience has broadened her mind considerably. She's tough, but still very immature."

Hiding his anger, His Excellency rose and stalked over to the bell rope. The potential for disaster was sickening. Would Athelgar accept a bride whose reputation was so tattered? He would be a laughingstock.

Lindsay answered the summons, raising an eyebrow at the sight of Arkell on the floor.

Hedgebury said, "Sir Beaumont, you will eat something?"

"Are the hens laying here yet?"

"I have no idea. Have we any eggs, Sir Footman?"

Lindsay smiled politely. "I think we do."

"Then I should love an omelette, and Lackwit eats anything you put in his mouth. But first . . . My lord, is Isabelle still here?" He looked at his host with childlike appeal.

Hedgebury chuckled. "The fair Isabelle? We promoted her to pastry cook soon after you left—not immediately, of course, but soon. And, oh, those flans!"

"The *tartes!*" Lindsay sighed.

"Then my wife took her on as ladies' maid."

"Criminal! Unforgivable!"

"But apparently she works equal miracles with needles and lace and curling irons. She is probably upstairs right now, assisting Her Majesty. As far as I am aware, you were not replaced in her affections."

Lindsay made a diplomatic throat-clearing noise. He had discovered the inestimable Isabelle for himself a few days after his arrival last spring and had been so badly bitten that Hedgebury had explained the Beaumont connection to him.

"Today is her day off, my lord. She goes to visit her mother. Somewhere east of here, I think."

"Deuflamme!" Beaumont spoke the name like an oath. "The stage came through there this morning. If I'd known . . . ! Pray hold the eggs, my lord, and lend me a horse."

"She will be back here tomorrow evening."

"Too late. Two horses?"

Reluctantly Lindsay said, "We'll look after Sir Arkell for you."

"Would you, brother? That would be a great favor." Beaumont's smile showed that he knew what the others were thinking. "You must remember to take him to the privy and remind him what to do there, but he does it. And spoonfeed him. I will be back by dark, I promise."

"We'll mother him," Hedgebury said. "Choose a mount. The hostler will honor that sword."

"You are most kind, brothers. By your leave, my lord . . . I must to Deuflamme." Beaumont hastened from the room.

The thump of the door was followed by a heavy silence.

Lindsay stared in disgust at the halfwit on the rug.

"Suppose we'll ever see him again?"

The Ambassador sighed. "Not if he has any sense." Beaumont had done his duty by his ward and even by Arkell. He must have acquired at least some of Wassail's considerable expense funds. Whether he still wanted the girl or not, she provided a wonderful excuse to liberate a good horse and vanish off the face of the earth. "He would be utterly crazy to stay within the King's grasp. Give Arkell to Jacques and tip him well." Hedgebury sat down to read the dread report.

◆ 5 ◆

Deuflamme was not so much a wide place in the road as a shallow place in the river—a gravel ford for vehicles, stepping stones for people. Road and river together divided the village into four, and the red-tiled, white-walled cottages faded away at the edges into hedges and vineyards. The wine shop also sold bread and some other essentials—salt, oil, and spices—and even a few luxuries like candles. Wagons and coaches went through Deuflamme several times a day. Add the usual dogs, cats, children, and chickens, and it was a pleasant enough place to be *from*. It might even be an adequate habitation if you found slug racing a thrill, but Isabelle came home now only to see her mother and rarely a visiting brother or sister. All her childhood friends had vanished into Laville or matrimony or both.

Their parents, regrettably, were mostly still present. Walking across to the wine shop for a bottle of the ordinary, she was accosted by Madame Despreaux and Madame Duchâtel. Madame Despreaux was less fat than Madame Duchâtel, but had more mustache. They greeted Isabelle warmly so they could recount all the magnificent husbands and wives Alice and Maude and Blanche and Louis had acquired—one each, and of opposite sex in every case. Maitre This, a tailor's apprentice and Maitre That, senior assistant gamekeeper to the Minister of Fisheries! The good ladies rhapsodized over the numerous grandchildren produced already.

They wanted to know why Isabelle was not married and if she were a kept woman in the wicked city and what her prospects were and the torturers of the Sewer could not have improved on their interrogation. She tried in vain to insert a retort beginning, "Madame the Contesse was saying just yesterday . . ." although she knew her mother must have worn the Contesse Hedgebury threadbare by now.

A man on a white horse came galloping by, heading for the ford.

He swept past, then clattered to a halt so suddenly that his horse reared, clawing the sky with its hooves, and the ladies turned to stare in astonishment.

A voice shouted from on high, "Isabelle! Are you married?"

"Beau!"

His boots hit the dirt almost at her toes. *"Are you married?"*

The horse snorted.

"No!" Oh, Beau, Beau returned at last . . .

"Are you betrothed?"

The worthy old hags were watching openmouthed. A gentleman! On a white stallion!! With a sword!!!

"No."

"You are now!" Beau embraced her, and kissed her. And kissed her. And kissed, kissed, kissed her, on and on, hard and passionately, deep and sweet and hot, squeezing all the breath out of her, kiss, kiss, kiss. It was a totally shocking, shameful thing to do in public in the middle of the highway in the middle of the afternoon, but to resist in front of Madame Duchâtel and Madame Despreaux was not to be considered. Besides, after the first petrifying shock Isabelle had no desire to struggle at all, only to return the kiss with a worthy passion of her own.

"Oh!" she said faintly when he moved his lips back a finger-width. "I won. I didn't have to ask!" If he let go she would collapse in a heap.

"Ask now!" His eyes shone like stars right in front of hers.

"In a moment."

He removed one arm. "I did promise you jewels, didn't I? I left the ring back in Laville. It is of gold, although I think not very good gold, and it has a stone, a jade, so big. But I did bring this." He lifted a rope of pink beads from his pocket, like a very long, shimmering earthworm. "I bought this for you in Kiensk, but it comes from much farther away, from the farthest ends of the world. It is coral."

He had to take his other arm away so he could fasten the necklace around her neck. She did not fall down, but she did not feel so happy as she had done while he held her.

"It is gorgeous!" she said, although she could barely see it now. "I dreamed of you every night you were gone. Kiss me again!"

That one was even more shameful. He practically made love to her standing in the road, right there in front of the outraged mesdames, and she did not care one olive pit.

"We shall be married tomorrow," he said.

"Before witnesses of quality?"

"The Conte and Contesse of Hedgebury, Messires Lindsay and Arkell. And royalty, but royalty prefers to remain incognito." He knew why she had asked. He knew she would accept a stuffed duck as a witness now.

She was about to ask about Lord Wassail and stopped in time. Behind the silver eyes lurked shadow, and she sensed that this was not the Beau she had known last year. This one had a sharper edge. This one would not have waited for an invitation to kiss her; this one would have slid her into bed the first night they met.

"You promise I will be married before royalty?"

"I swear it! Tomorrow."

"Oh, Beau! What am I thinking of? I must present these good ladies . . . Madame Despreaux . . . Messire Beaumont, a Sabreur of the King of Chivial . . ." He bowed low to each of them. They were crushed. How sweet! How inexpressibly sweet!

"If the good ladies will excuse us, we must go and discuss the arrangements with your mother."

"Yes," she sighed, "that would be wise."

Half Deuflamme had emerged to watch them walk to her mother's cottage, leading the horse. Best of all, she had never told her mother about him.

"Didn't fool me," her mother said with a sniff, reaching for her cane. "I knew there was someone! Tomorrow in Laville? I see you do not believe in long betrothals, monseigneur de Beaumont. I will go and see if Louis can take me there in his cart."

Beau opened his mouth and Isabelle kicked his ankle.

He did not say one more word until the door of the cottage closed.

"How long will she be?" he murmured, untying Isabelle's head scarf.

"All day. She has to tell *everybody*." She fumbled with his cloak. "I am not practiced at this."

He loosed her laces. "Then you are doing well." He kissed her again. It took a dozen kisses, or one kiss with eleven brief interruptions, to remove all her clothes and enough of his, but the entire process from head scarf to naked on the bed was the most enjoyable experience she had known until what happened after that, which was astonishing and beyond words, beyond thought, almost beyond enduring. She very nearly cried out in the intensity of her joy, and that would have been shameful. Or so she thought, until suddenly he muttered, "My turn now," in a choked sort of voice, and his lovemaking went from slow and tender to abundantly vigorous for a few moments and then he moaned loudly and collapsed. Extraordinary! But now she knew that making odd noises was all right after all, and when next she felt the need to do so, she did. Every time.

"You are a very quick learner," he told her later.

"I think I have a very good teacher," she murmured happily.

◆ 6 ◆

Every garment in Deuflamme that had ever been near a wedding was offered to Isabelle and her mother. Every woman able to wield a needle spent half the night with them in the cottage, preparing for the great occasion, but when the carriage arrived the following morning, as Beau had promised it would, it brought the skilled Jeanne, Madame the Contesse's dressmaker, armed with a wondrous selection of lace, frills, beads, and other flourishes. In a twinkling she transformed the merely impressive into the spellbinding, and she continued to nip, tuck, hem, and adjust all the way to Laville, until the very moment the carriage rolled up to the embassy steps and the Conte-Ambassador himself came forth to welcome the bride and her mother. Which was a dream.

The entire staff had been invited to the wedding and many of them had forsaken their beds all night to make the celebration as splendid as possible. Which it was. The only sour note was sounded by Queen Tasha, who was indisposed and sent her regrets—so Isabelle was informed then, but she heard later that Her Grace had thrown a fearful tantrum, categorically refusing to attend the wedding of "a mere pot-carrying chambermaid."

The following day, the Contesse offered to present the new Lady Beaumont to Her Majesty and the Queen turned her back.

This was a trivial regret amid the sudden wonders of married life, the thrill of going from servant to honored guest, the glories of new gowns and new status, but it was one that a woman must address. Isabelle chose a moment on the fourth afternoon of her marriage, when she and Beau were sitting in the flower-scented rose bower, holding hands and just being rapturously happy together. She could speak Chivian now, having been conjured. That morning she had walked in the grounds of the royal palace on the arm of a handsome swordsman and watched a hundred other women grind teeth in jealousy. Was not life perfection?

Not quite.

"Why does Queen Tasha hate me?"

Beau laughed. "Don't worry about her. She's jealous because she only gets a king and you got me."

Which was true, possibly too true. "She may cause trouble?"

"She cannot. I am more worried by that mole on your thigh."

"What mole?" his wife demanded indignantly. "And stop changing the subject. Were you lovers?"

"It is in a place hard for you to see. But exceptionally beautiful. I think it needs to be looked at more closely, in daylight."

She avoided his kiss. "Beau, did you lie with the Queen on your journey?"

"Come with me. I will examine—"

"Why will you not tell me?"

"Aha! Was that our first angry word?" His smile would break a million hearts. "Because, my dearest, a question that should not be asked must not be answered. The mole?"

She should not have asked—he had not asked her. She knew how stubborn he was.

"Let us go upstairs immediately," he said. "The problem becomes more urgent by the minute."

"No. You are too greedy. It is shocking to jump into bed in the middle of the day."

"You didn't say that yesterday, or the day before, or . . . Your Excellency?"

They rose to offer bow and curtsey respectively.

The Count of Hedgebury returned a worried nod. He was a compact, fair-haired man, stockier than Beau because of his age, but still trim. He would never have been so handsome, of course, but this might not be far from how Beau would look when he was fifty. "Forgive me, I am but a crow croaking at two love birds. May I have a word with you, Sir Beaumont? I promise it will be brief."

"Join us and welcome," Beau said, waving at the other bench. "Whatever you wish to say you may say before my wife."

"And perhaps should." The Ambassador perched as if not intending to stay. "I suspect she has all the brains in your marriage. Brother, you must leave."

Beau raised flaxen eyebrows. "I just arrived."

"Don't play stupid with me, boy! You know what I mean. I will gladly give you two horses, any two you wish from my stable. Take them and the money and begone forever. Isilond is a fabulous land. You are young and in love and free to live as you please. Why throw all that away?"

"Because I have duties, of course. I have not yet escorted Her Majesty to Court. I have—"

"Her Majesty refuses to have anything more to do with you! She screams if you are mentioned."

"She is under strain," Beau said smoothly. "I brought some of my late ward's personal effects, which I shall return to Lady Wassail. I must testify to her husband's death, for legal reasons. I have monetary instruments to restore to the Royal Exchequer, and Oak's sword to Return to Ironhall. I must see poor Arkell settled somewhere. Now I have fulfilled my duties to my ward, His Majesty will formally dub me knight, according to custom. After that—" he flashed his glorious smile at Isabelle. "*Then* life and love and youth and fine wine. But duty first."

"Duty?" The Ambassador was growing irate. "You did your best. I'm sure you achieved more than other men would regard as humanly possible. No one could have asked more of you. Go!"

Beau sighed, turned to Isabelle. "One day, dearest, I must tell you the tale of a stalwart young Blade who leaped off a cliff because he thought it was his duty to his ward."

His Lordship's face flamed scarlet. "That was necessary! This isn't. What do you expect the King to say when he reads that his wife spent months traveling like a vagabond, *unchaperoned,* in the company of a *Blade* and a halfwit?"

"I didn't tell him that exactly," Beau said cheerfully, "and surely a king will not be so crass as to ask for details? He can establish discreetly what really happened and then turn the tale into high romance. Bards will sing, strong men weep, and ladies cry out in terror. All Eurania will thrill to the adventures of the young queen hastening to her bridegroom's side through snow and storm and—"

"That is one alternative!" the Ambassador barked. "The other is to bounce your head across the grass for high treason. Already, here in my house, the Queen has done and said enough to damn you. Rumors fester in the Regent's Court that the Czar's son has been murdered and he is blaming certain foreigners. That could mean war, man!"

For the first time, Beau's sunny smile seemed a little forced. "Believe me, brother, Fedor wasn't worth a cats' spat, let alone a war. I know your advice is well meant, but to take it would be to confirm the sneers of the nasty-minded. It would damn the Queen. I am shocked that you would ever doubt her virtue. I expect to be questioned before inquisitors, of course. I shall tell the truth. They will so testify. If the King then offers me a peerage, I shall respectfully decline. A bag of gold and a manly handshake will suffice. Meanwhile I refuse to let your croaking spoil my love song, Master Crow."

The days passed in bliss, the nights in rapture. A good horseman could ride from Laville to Grandon and back between dawn and dusk, Beau said, were it not for the Straits. The crossing depended entirely on the winds. It was a week after the Ambassador's warning that the summons came. By coincidence—the spot must be cursed—the lovers were sitting in that same gazebo, amid the same flowers and the same sunshine, when Sir Lindsay came strolling along the path, escorting two young swordsmen in blue and silver livery.

Beau said, "Ah!" and stood up. "My dear, may I present— Sir Rivers . . . Sir Clovis . . . companions in my Order. The monkey suits mean that they serve in the Royal Guard. My wife, brothers."

As the guardsmen paid their respects, she noticed how similar all four Blades were, almost as alike as the cat's-eye jewels on the pommels of their swords. The newcomers were dusty, wind-burned, and sweat-stained; they stank powerfully of horse. Their brief and cheerless smiles implied no joy.

"Sir Beaumont," Rivers said, "the Pirate's Son has sent us to convey you into his presence."

"I shall be happy to wait upon His Majesty."

Their grimness eased a little on hearing that. Isabelle knew their authority ended at the embassy wall, which happened to be almost at Beau's back. Were he to vault over it, he would be a free man. She wished she could throw him over it.

"Arkell also," Lindsay remarked from the background. "Can he ride?"

"No. He bounces on tender parts and gets upset and weeps. Besides, my wife would prefer a coach."

Clovis looked quizzically at Rivers, who reluctantly nodded.

"His Excellency will be happy to lend you his carriage, brothers," Lindsay said. "If you leave at dawn, you can be in Boileau by dusk."

"If we leave now, we can sail at dawn," Rivers retorted. "We have a ship standing by."

"As you wish. The Queen will not be accompanying you?"

Clovis shook his head, Rivers shrugged—*what queen?* The Queen did not officially exist yet.

"We have been starved for news," Beau said brightly. "Who won the King's Cup this year, brothers?"

They reacted as if he had kicked their shins.

"Some Isilondian!" Clovis snapped, "whose name I forget. There was a whole gang of the horrors. Had you anything to do with that, brother?"

"Nothing whatsoever," Beau assured him. "Unless you mean the Conte de Ferniot, the Conte de Roget, the Marquis Vaanen, and the Conte D'Estienne?"

Rivers said, *"Traitor!"*

Sir Lindsay made an unhappy-diplomat noise. "You are being a little extreme, brother."

"I don't think he is," Clovis said grimly.

The carriage ride to Boileau was an experience even the joy of Beau's company could not rescue. Arkell bounced on the opposite bench until he became nauseated, after which it was worse. Clovis and Rivers had wisely chosen to ride and insisted on pushing on when darkness fell, crawling through the night. They reached Boileau not long before dawn, going straight to the docks and a shabby little cog tied up at the quay.

The guardsmen wanted to embark immediately, and were repelled at the gangplank by the master, Captain Bird, who would have been termed buxom had he been a woman. He flourished thick white eyebrows on a florid, baggy face, and was abrasively unimpressed by King's Blades.

"High tide isn't till noon and the wind's contrary anyway. Go find yourself lodging and I'll send the boy for you when we're ready. Maybe tomorrow."

"We hired your boat and we will live in it until you've fulfilled your contract!" Rivers announced haughtily.

"It ain't a *boat*, sonny, and no jack-a-napes, wood-chopping man-at-arms gives me orders."

"Excuse them, Captain," Beau said soothingly. "The innkeepers won't let them in—because of the fleas, you know."

Bird surveyed Beau from plumed hat down to cat's-eye pommel and back again. He thawed a fraction. "Or they're just too cheap to spend the money, more like?"

Beau sighed. "There is that. They squandered all their expense allowance on Isilondian fencing lessons. And all they know about wind is too personal to mention."

Rivers and Clovis were not amused, but they chose to conserve the rest of their dignity by going in search of accommodation. Beau parted from the Captain like an old friend. After all—as he tried to explain to Isabelle later—any sailor who named his ship the *Unexpected Tern* had to be one of nature's gentlemen.

* * *

Boileau was a dull runt of a port, the inn had abundant fleas of its own, and Isabelle was happy when the wind changed the following day and *Tern* stood out to sea. Greatly excited, she leaned on the rail with Beau's strong arm around her— and her arm around him—watching the homes and fields of Isilond fade back into haze. Ahead lay the snow-capped foam of the bar and the cold gray-green hills of ocean beyond. Hours, days, or weeks ahead lay Chival, a new life, and the scent of adventure in the salt air was intoxicating.

Suddenly Rivers and Clovis were there in menace.

"It is my sad duty, Sir Beaumont," Rivers announced— looking triumphant, not sad—"to require of you your sword."

Beau had not expected that. Isabelle felt his shock through their body contact; the watchers could not have known of it. There, on the restlessly swaying deck, he looked from one sneer to the other. He could almost certainly take those two men on together and defeat them both, but what good would that do now? In silence he unbuckled his baldric and handed *Just Desert* to Rivers. Then he turned his back and stared out at the heaving water. It may have been only a caprice of the wind, but Isabelle was certain she saw tears in his eyes. His arm around her tightened almost to hurting.

"Petty men!" he said bitterly. "No Blade deprives another of his sword."

"You should have listened to Hedgebury."

"Or obeyed the instructions written on her blade."

◆ 7 ◆

A day at sea and another all-night carriage ride brought them to Grandon and its Bastion, a fortress whose grim reputation had reached even backwoods Deuflamme. In the dank light of dawn, the rumble of wheels on the drawbridge seemed as ominous as the slimy green moat below and rusty portcullis above.

Beau remained unruffled. "Yes, its dungeons are celebrated, my love, and its torture chamber is the toast of connoisseurs everywhere, but it is also a fortress and even a palace. Not a few monarchs have fled here with the Grandon mob baying at their heels."

Isabelle was exhausted. "I suppose you're going to lodge in the royal suite? Where am I to sleep?"

"In nobody's bed but mine! I am charged with no crime. I am a royal guest and you will share my quarters."

She distrusted his eternal good cheer. To look at him, no one would know he had not slept all night, but she had never felt frowstier in her life. Poor Arkell was a whimpering heap of confused misery, unable to understand why the world kept bouncing him, bruising him, and making him giddy.

The Bastion was almost a town in its own right, a wide bailey cluttered with sheds and tents within a coronet of forts, towers, and battlements. Even at that early hour it bustled like a market. The moment the coach halted, Beau jumped out and she heard him hail someone in pleased tones. Then he handed her down and she guessed at once, even before she saw the cat's-eye sword, that the dapper man in the elaborate livery was yet another Blade.

"Love, it is a true honor to present you to Baron Bandale, Constable of the Bastion. In all my years at Ironhall, his was the only Durendal Night speech that did not put me to sleep."

The Constable bowed over her hand. "The honor is entirely mine, Lady Beaumont. I wish the circumstances were happier." He was much older than Lord Hedgebury, but he had the same gracious smile and supreme self-confidence— gold-plated steel.

His bushy salt-and-pepper eyebrows made his frown a serious matter. "Your sword, Sir Beaumont?"

"It has fallen into bad company, my lord," Beau said, with a nod at Clovis and Rivers, who had dismounted and stood scowling on the sidelines. "And here is a greater sadness—brother Arkell."

Bandale grimaced as he watched the shambling invalid descend from the carriage. "No charges have been brought against him or you, but His Majesty requires that you tarry here during his pleasure, which is his right as head of our Order. If you will give me your parole, brother Beaumont, I will lead you and your gracious lady to suitable quarters. What care does Arkell need?"

"Much. He would be happiest boarding with us. Certainly you have my parole, Constable. My wife is free to come and go as she pleases, of course?"

"Of course. May I escort you?" Bandale offered Isabelle his arm. "I will inform my wife of your arrival, Lady Beaumont. She will provide suitable attendants and whatever else you need for your stay here."

Isabelle felt better already and the rooms to which the Baron escorted her were a delight—not large, but bright, sweet-smelling, and by no means dungeons. Their unbarred windows commanded a fine view of the river. Promising to send servants with hot water, refreshments, and a cot for Arkell, the Constable withdrew, leaving the door ajar.

"A splendid gentleman," Beau said, satisfied. "And a legendary Blade! He was Leader during the Monster War. Had it not been for him, Ambrose's reign would have ended twenty years sooner." He peered out at the scenery. "His wife was a friend of Queen Malinda's."

Isabelle flopped down on the bed and sank almost out of sight. "Do Blades run everything in Chivial?"

"Quite a lot of things," Beau said thoughtfully, as if that

idle query was portentous. "Ever since the Thencaster Affair, Athelgar has been much inclined to trust members of my Order and appoint them to weighty posts. The Blades have acquired great influence, these last few years. Of course bound companions must serve their wards without question and some knights fade into obscurity, but enough of them acquire enough influence that even the King might hesitate to antagonize the Order now."

"And how would one go about antagonizing it?"

"Ah!" He turned to her with eyes glinting mischief. "Bartering the King's Cup away to foreigners might be a good way to start."

"The King cares about that?"

"Oh, no. Athelgar regards fencing as a sweaty indignity." Beau's mood darkened. "But losing one's ward is another way, and bringing back a Lackwit is a third, for that is every Blade's nightmare."

"This is a wonderfully soft mattress. It would be good for sleeping on, too." She squirmed luxuriously.

"Don't get comfortable just yet. Athelgar is not known for patience, and he's been waiting many days to question me. We may be summoned before the Council sooner more than later."

"*We?*" she squealed, struggling to sit up.

"Of course," Beau said. "I keep telling you—I am not under arrest! I am the King's servant reporting to him on the death of the faithful friend he charged me with defending. Naturally he will receive you, although I expect you will be allowed to withdraw before we get down to business."

For once Beau was only half right. Isabelle had not even completed her toilet before word came that His Majesty was on his way to the Bastion.

The hall was lofty and dim; dust motes silvered the shafts of light angling down from high windows. A great crackling fire smoked as if recently lit, adding to the centuries of soot stain on masonry walls and the many tattered banners hung among the rafters. At least two dozen Blades in the livery of the Royal Guard stood watch around the walls.

Isabelle entered on Beau's arm, following Constable Bandale, with Arkell and more Blades behind her. The King, made conspicuous by his crimson robes and the heavy gold chain across his chest, stood to the right of the great fireplace, alongside a swarthy-faced Blade wearing an official-looking baldric. Two men in black robes and birettas stood on the left. Athelgar was surprisingly short and plump—a pompous, middle-aged cock robin, not at all as she had imagined him. Then she realized that the procession was not heading in his direction. The young man pacing back and forth was the King.

This genuine Athelgar was slender and restless, with a narrow, bony face spoiled by a foolish tuft of ruddy beard. His attire was subdued but faultless, repeating the exact same shade of green from plumed hat to pearl-embroidered boots. She had not decided if his fidgetiness was a sign of anger before she was too close to stare and must lower her eyes. Baron Bandale made the presentations.

"Pray rise, Lady Beaumont," the King said. "I see your husband stayed true to Blade tradition by winning the fairest damsel, even if he fell short in other ways. Constable, you have our leave to withdraw."

Startled, Isabelle glanced around and confirmed that no one was waiting to escort her out; seemingly she was expected to stay. She found that situation worrisome and edged closer to Beau.

The King inspected Arkell with distaste and tried speaking to him. Winning no response, he turned abruptly to the Blade by the fireplace. "Commander Vicious?"

"Ward bereavement, sire. Correct, Beaumont?"

"Plus a hefty bang on the head, Leader."

"How did that happen?" the King snapped.

"It was him or me, sire."

"Your counsel, Commander?"

"Ironhall, Your Grace. Let Master of Rituals see what he can do."

The King nodded. The Commander nodded. Two Blades came forward and led Arkell away. He went without demur, smiling vaguely, as if he recognized the liveries.

Isabelle, unable to stare at the King, glanced around at the cordon of Blades. They stood too far back to overhear the conversation, but Arkell's performance had left them understandably bleak.

The two motionless inquisitors by the fireplace were nondescript men of middle years, yet somehow they seemed more sinister than their black vestments and glassy stare justified. The red-robed, red-faced man on the other side must be an important official. There was not a seat in sight and she was bone weary.

"Now, Sir Beaumont!" Athelgar resumed his pacing. "Grand Master praised you as a Blade worthy of your Order's ancient glories, and we entrusted our dearest friend to your care."

"I was proud to serve him, Your Grace. I wish it could have been for longer."

"We have read your report and find it incomprehensible. You expect us to believe all that scurrility about the Czar?"

"I stand by what I wrote, sire. I do not presume to judge a crowned monarch and certainly not an absolute autocrat, but by commoners' standards he would be deemed a homicidal maniac. He slaughters his own subjects without any pretense of a trial, he—"

"You have witnessed this behavior?"

"Not personally, sire, no. But Sir Oak testified—"

"That is still hearsay!"

Beau remained silent.

"Well?" snapped the King, spinning around at the end of his beat.

"With respect, sire, Oak was reporting to me, his leader, on a matter relevant to the safety of our ward. His binding would not have let him lie."

"Commander?"

"Correct, sire." Sir Vicious was as impassive as ancient timber and seemingly little more talkative.

The pert little man in the red robes spoke up for the first time. That he did so without being bidden indicated that he must stand high in the King's esteem. "But he could have been mistaken. Blades are not infallible. It was night. The man was seriously, even mortally, injured. Yet he thought to identify his assailants by their voices alone." His own voice was distinctively squeaky.

"He also knew the dogs, Your Excellency," Beau said. "Only the Czar courses hounds the size of horses."

"Rubbish!" the King snarled, still pacing. "Dogs have ancestors and siblings. Granted that the Czar may be strict or even brutal by our standards; granted that his power is absolute, you have no personal knowledge that he abuses it, have you?"

"No, sire."

"The witness is lying."

The voice came from the two inquisitors. Isabelle had not seen which spoke, and now she realized that they were identical twins. Somehow it was that bizarre equivalence that made them seem so sinister.

Athelgar stopped in his tracks to stare at Beau. "Well?"

Beau spoke carefully. "I did not witness any of the crimes I mentioned in my report, sire."

The fire crackled merrily in the silence.

"I see," the King said uncertainly. "Then let us discuss his son, Czarevich Fedor. Another homicidal maniac?"

"An extremely violent man, Your Grace. It was public knowledge, confirmed to me by many people—"

"More scandal? Is it relevant?"

"Very relevant, sire."

"Go ahead then."

"Not long before we arrived in Kiensk, the Czar took exception to three of his son's friends and ordered Fedor to flog them to death in the market square. Which he did."

The King spun around to the inquisitors, as if daring them to support this appalling tale. They remained silent and yet somehow it continued to defy belief. Here in sane and civilized Chivial, princes did not perform as public hangmen.

"There may be more to that tale than you heard. You saw the Czarevich die?"

Beau hesitated, as if hoping one of the listeners would object to the question or the King would withdraw it. Eventually he said, "I did, Your Grace."

"Who killed him?"

"Sir Arkell."

He had never told Isabelle that. He was in far greater danger than she had realized. Athelgar was out for blood and the Czar would soon be demanding Beau's head, if he had not done so already.

"Describe what happened."

"There was a fireplace much like— If Your Majesty would permit me to stage this, it would be easier to describe. If you would face this way, Your Grace, and be the Czarevich. Commander Vicious, stand here, please and be Sir Arkell. Lord Chancellor, you will stand in for Lord Wassail?"

"I fear I am a poor substitute." The tubby man in the gold chain came waddling forward. That beak-nosed little pigeon was First Minister of Chivial?

Beau gestured Isabelle forward. "My wife will be Queen Tasha."

"Princess Tasha," Athelgar said coldly.

"I crave pardon," Beau said.

Poor Tasha! Would she not win even the consolation prize?

"She sat about here, with her lady-in-waiting. And I, here, am myself. Now, sire, remembering that you are a much larger man even than Lord Wassail—and younger, my age almost exactly—you strike at him. Arkell blocks your arm with the flat of his sword. Now you go to draw . . ."

The King made him run through the events three times, then said, "Well, Lord Chancellor?"

"Drawing against a Blade defending his ward? In Chivial it would be classed as suicide, sire."

Isabelle approved of the cocky little redbreast. The King glared. No one dared smile.

"How do I explain that to the Czar?" Athelgar demanded, obviously not expecting an answer. He began pacing again and the others scuttled back to their previous positions, Isabelle moving even closer to Beau. "In his last dispatch, Lord Wassail indicated he would remain in Kiensk until late spring or early summer. Now you tell us he changed his mind. He deserted most of his followers and set off on a mad dash through the Skyrrian winter. That does not sound like my old friend! Whose idea was this change of plan?"

"Mostly mine, sire," Beau said.

"The witness is lying." That was the left-hand inquisitor.

Beau tried again. "It emerged in discussions between my ward and myself, and I cannot recall exactly who first suggested—"

"The witness is lying." Now the other. How did they choose?

"Sir Beaumont!" the King roared. "Loyalty to your ward

is commendable, but your ward is *dead!* Your sovereign lives. Answer!"

The watching Blades must have heard that.

Beau sighed. "His idea, sire. I agreed that it would be possible."

"Yet it was obviously dangerous. Why did you encourage him in such folly?"

"Because I believed he would be in greater danger if he remained in the Czar's realm."

"Danger from this mad, homicidal sovereign?"

Athelgar continued firing questions. The tale that unfolded was new to Isabelle, because Beau had refused to speak of his ward's death. Soon anger drove away her weariness. Obviously the King was going to make Beau the scapegoat for the disaster, yet Beau seemed absurdly reluctant to clear himself. Any fool could see that the escape had gone so horribly wrong only through an absurd combination of chances: the change of weather, the bizarre meeting with the Czarevich, Lord Wassail's apoplexy, but no one said so. She decided Beau was too proud to make excuses, shouldering blame needlessly, yet when he finally balked, it was only to make matters worse.

By then Athelgar was almost shouting. "You arranged it, you said. You must have had help, Skyrrian help. Who were your fellow conspirators in devising this midwinter madness? Who were the traitors?"

"I humbly beg Your Grace's leave not to answer that question."

The King stopped pacing to glare. "Permission denied! Answer!"

"I am honor bound not to reveal names, sire."

"Your loyalty is to me, your sovereign lord."

The fire crackled.

A question that should not be asked must not be answered.

Athelgar turned scarlet. The silence continued.

"This is lese majesty, Sir Beaumont!"

"I deeply regret the offense, Your Grace."

"I can force an answer, you know!"

Beau knelt and bowed his head. "I humbly beg forgiveness."

The King began pacing again. "The Princess had brought a lady attendant. What happened to her?"

"She, too, was slain in the massacre."

"Who did that?"

"I did not see, sire."

"How many people did you kill personally?"

"I do not know. My memory of that time is very blurred."

"Sir Vicious?"

The Commander nodded. "Standard symptoms, sire."

"Grand Inquisitor?"

"He speaks the truth," said Left.

"So who survived?" the King demanded.

"Her Highness," Beau said, "Sir Arkell, and myself. A few Skyrrians escaped on horseback, but they likely died in the blizzard."

"You then proceeded to the next town?"

"Not the nearest. We reached Dvonograd two days later."

Athelgar swung his attention to Isabelle. "And that was where you joined this itinerant disaster?"

She gaped, bewildered. "Me, sire? No, sire? . . ."

"My wife was still at home in Isilond, Your Majesty," Beau said. "My future wife, then."

"I thought—" The King scowled at having been caught out in error. "You mean you obtained no substitute attendants for Her Highness? You brought her all this way without any female companionship at all?"

"We dared not reveal her identity. She was masquerading as a boy."

Athelgar stared at him in disbelief. "You have destroyed her reputation utterly."

"Such was never my intention, sire."

Isabelle wanted to scream. What else could Beau have done? Abandon her in the forest? Why did he not ask the King that? Why did he not comment on Tasha's courage and endurance, lead the man to the romantic idyll?

"I trust that you always obtained separate accommodation for her?"

"I could not do that either, not without betraying the deception."

"You mean you shared rooms!?" The King was chalky white with rage.

"When necessary, sire."

"And beds?" demanded one of the inquisitors.

Beau gave him a look of intense dislike. "When necessary—and when there were beds to share. Often there was only straw, or rushes."

Athelgar seemed to be speechless.

Into the silence crept the soft voice of the pert little Chancellor. "This is not unusual, Your Majesty." Kings' experience of hostelries must be limited. "Travelers often sleep five or six to a bed, and quite often men and women are bunked together."

Athelgar continued to glare down at the kneeling Beau. "You give us your word, to be verified by Grand Inquisitor, that nothing improper happened between you and her Highness?"

Beau sighed. "May I ask Your Majesty to define 'improper'?"

"I thought any man of honor would understand plain Chivian. Let us start with words of endearment, then."

More silence, much more.

"So?" said the King. "Will you answer if I send your wife away?"

Beau sighed again. "No, sire."

"I do not have to be Czar Igor to find such insolence intolerable. We have devices here in the Bastion that will make brass statues talk."

Beau remained silent.

Again the little Chancellor showed his mettle. "Torture and the Question are reserved for cases of treason, Your Grace, and the Council should first consider whether there is a prima facie—"

"Grand Inquisitor?" Athelgar snapped.

The right-hand twin said, "During the first session the witness will be encouraged to make confession of treason and thereafter the point is moot."

"Commander, inform us of the procedures for expelling a man from the Blades."

"As Head of the Order, Your Majesty may expel any man, without recourse or appeal."

"Prepare the deed for our signature. Charge Beaumont with high treason and chain him in the lowest dungeon in the Bastion." King Athelgar headed for the door.

* 8 *

Chivians had no idea what food should be. Although Isabelle appreciated the Bandales' kindness in treating her as a houseguest, she found their table disappointing, while the muck thrown to prisoners was unfit for pigs. It made even the rats sick, Beau said. Most inmates were fed by visiting friends or relatives and Isabelle carried meals down to her husband twice a day—he would not let her come to see him more often, or stay very long. It wasn't healthy there, he insisted, in grotesque understatement. He had endured two weeks of it so far, but he was losing weight and he coughed a lot.

Table scraps were not good enough. The Baroness allowed Isabelle to cook him special treats in her kitchen. That was why, this sunny spring afternoon, she was haggling at one of the stalls in the bailey for fresh eggs. Eggs were expensive now that the laying season was over, and Beau's money had been confiscated by the inquisitors, who claimed it belonged to the King or Lady Wassail and muttered darkly of an audit and embezzlement. Isabelle's own purse was almost empty, so she was haggling hard. She had nothing better to do with her day.

"Lady Beaumont?" The speaker was a dandily-clad man of middle years, sporting a neat red-and-silver beard. A very large mouth and a button nose made his smile both comical and winsome. She need not look at the pommel of his sword to guess that here was yet another of the ubiquitous Blades.

"I am."

"My name is Sir Intrepid. I'm Master of Rituals for the Order. I brought a friend of yours to see you. Or, to be exact, he brought me, for otherwise I'd never have found you in this mob."

She looked past him, at Lackwit's dead gaze.

"He is no better?"

Intrepid's smile waned. "Only very slightly, perhaps. He asks for Beau once in a while and even for yourself. Arkell, here's Belle."

Nothing. Hawkers and hucksters shouted all around; customers shouted right back. Arkell heeded none of it.

"Lackwit?" she tried.

His eyes turned to stare over her head. "Common law itself is nothing else but reason, gotten by long study, observation, and experience, and not of every man's natural reason."

"Well done, brother!" Intrepid said cheerily, thumping him on the shoulder. "That's good. Keep trying. Now, where's Beaumont?"

Arkell pointed, mostly downward.

"I can take you to him, Sir Intrepid." Isabelle welcomed any excuse for an extra visit.

The guards at the top of the stairs knew her, saluted Intrepid's sword, and dismissed Lackwit as unimportant at first glance. But the stairs were long and steep, twisting down from sunlight into foul, stygian dark. About halfway, Intrepid began coughing violently.

"Does it always smell this bad?" he gasped.

"You get used to it," she said bitterly. "We should wait here a moment to let our eyes adjust."

"You mean they'll stop watering?"

"You're going to get your boots wet, too, sir. The tide's in."

He muttered under his breath.

"The water isn't so bad, Beau says, it's what floats in it."

"I'm going to—" Intrepid chuckled. "I was about to say I was going to raise a stink over this, but I'll need to find a better metaphor."

She decided she approved of Sir Intrepid. He must know he would never get the prison stench out of that expensive outfit.

The rusty gate at the bottom stood open. This, the lowermost dungeon, was a windowless cave lit by a single candle, and although it had space enough to hold a dozen inmates chained to its stout bronze staples, there was barely air for one. At the moment it contained only Beau, sitting crosslegged on his bed above the ankle-deep tidal seepage. He must have heard the voices on the stair and his eyes were very well adjusted.

"Welcome, brother," he said. "I suggest you stay where you are."

Isabelle didn't. She went splashing over to him, and the two newcomers followed her. Beau kissed her with heavily stubbled lips. She sat on the bed and cuddled close to him. He stank like overripe pig dung. The links of his chain rattled as he put an arm around her.

"Can I offer you some refreshment, Master?" he inquired. "Fresh slugs on wet toast? Ah, brother Arkell?"

Lackwit just stood, did not look down at him.

"Hopeless?"

"Well . . ." Sir Intrepid sighed. "Not quite. I think he's still inside there somewhere. That gibberish he spouts is all real stuff—he's quoting books from the library. We almost had him once. Master Armorer had made a replica of his sword and he recognized it. His face lit up—then he seemed to realize it wasn't the real thing and faded away again."

"You didn't try a reversion ritual on him?"

"Faugh! That thing does more harm than good."

"Oh? That isn't what you teach the seniors, brother."

"Seniors have enough to worry about," Intrepid said breezily. "If we told 'em the whole truth, they'd never sleep at all." He sat on a corner of the bed. "The last reversion ritual to work perfectly was almost fifty years ago. Also, it needs the original sword. Even the King releasing a guardsman must use the actual sword that bound him. Until we recover the real *Reason,* we're stymied."

"It's somewhere in Skyrria," Beau said, in a not-joking voice. "The King could ask for it back as part of the settlement."

"Settlement?" Intrepid snorted. "Horse-trading! What you should be worrying about is what's going to be sold in the opposite direction. The Guard scuttlebutt is that the Czar wants your head, with you still attached so he can arrange the separation personally."

Beau shrugged. "I'd heard that."

Isabelle had not. The Baron visited his prisoner regularly and Intrepid would certainly have called on Lord Bandale before seeking her out.

Typically, Beau diverted the talk away from himself. "How do you explain that Human Compass trick Arkell does?"

"Now, that is *fascinating!*" Intrepid said with professional enthusiasm. "If we could reproduce that effect, every sailor on the seven seas would give his left arm for it. Ask him the way to anywhere and he'll point. He doesn't even need to have been there! It's spiritual, no doubt about it. It even works on people. I came into the bailey and asked him where Belle was and he pointed. What did you make of it? You used to ask the most sensible questions in conjuration class."

"That's very meager flattery, brother, but since our binding involves every one of the eight elements, I assume that when it was broken by his ward's death, some of the elementals failed to escape and he was left with relict conjuration?"

Intrepid made a grumpy noise. "I was hoping to write a monograph on that. Yes, you're right. There's residual spirituality there. If we could banish it, we might cure him. If we ever do cure him, he'll lose the knack. The problem is knowing what elementals could produce the effect! Earth and fire, maybe? I'm going to take him over to the College and let the—"

Lackwit said, "No."

"Death and fire!" Intrepid exclaimed.

"What did you say, brother Arkell?" Beau asked, but received no answer. "Seems like you're right, Master," he said excitedly. "He *is* still in there somewhere! And if your precious conjurers of the College want to examine him, they can flapping well come here, to the Bastion. You want to stay with us, Lackwit?"

No reply.

"I'll look after him," Isabelle said.

Beau conveyed his thanks with a squeeze, rattling chain. "I have another question for a brilliant conjurer, brother Intrepid. The Czar has some truly gigantic dogs. Superstitious Skyrrians believe these beasts are men transformed by witchcraft. Since Skyrrian conjuration is reputed to be primitive compared to ours, I didn't believe that tale at first. But Igor set a couple of them on Oak, who managed to kill one; apparently it started to change back as it was dying. Possible?"

Master of Rituals pondered for a moment. "It would be very hard to assemble a transformation as complicated as that and make it stable. Witchcraft is a primitive form of conjuration, lacking the subtle layering of spirituality. I'd guess they cut corners in balancing diametric complements and failed to differentiate applications." He piled on more long words. Isabelle rapidly lost track, but Beau continued to nod.

"So you wouldn't dare try it?"

"You mean apart from the ethics, I hope?" the conjurer muttered. "It would be an interesting challenge, but it would be very vulnerable to counter-spelling. I'll think about it. Just a theoretical problem, I hope?"

"You imagine I intend to return to Skyrria voluntarily?"

"No, nor otherwise!" Intrepid stood up. "First, I am going to go and have another chat with brother Bandale. I hear you refuse to answer any questions at all now?"

"While they keep me down here I do."

"Even so, this is no way to treat a brother Blade, no matter how mad he made his sovereign lord the king."

Yes, Isabelle definitely approved of Master of Rituals—

clever, fastidious, self-assured. If he was as influential as he seemed to think he was, better things might start to happen.

"Bandale's done as much as he could," Beau protested. "He had to obey the royal commands, but he provided a bed to keep me off the damp spot on the floor, he supplies candles, and my tether is ten times the length it need be. I could be much less comfortable."

His visitor used a vulgar expression and apologized to Isabelle for it. "Well, I assure you this talk of handing you over to the Czar is mere marsh bubbles. When Grand Master hears about that, he'll rattle Ironhall to the foundations. You've made a lot of enemies and you may never see your sword again, lad, but the Order will not stand for one of its own being served up to some foreign tyrant as a sacrificial lamb."

Beau said, "Thank you. And if I sign the statement they want me to sign, naming the man who did kill the Czarevich, will the Order stand behind brother Arkell as staunchly?"

Intrepid glanced at Lackwit. "Even more so."

"Thank you again."

Yet Intrepid had hesitated and Beau sounded skeptical. They spoke bravely, but the Czar had a son to avenge and three dozen Chivian hostages to bargain with.

Either Beau's stubbornness or Intrepid's influence worked a fast miracle. The following day the prisoner was moved to better quarters, above ground. He was locked in there, but let out to exercise. Isabelle was allowed to visit him and, better still, allowed to sleep with him. Prison was rarely as good as that, Beau said, as if speaking from experience. She was excluded when inquisitors came to interview him. He would never say later what they had discussed, merely pointing out with his invariant good cheer that he still had all his teeth.

Rumors flowed to and fro. Princess Tasha had arrived in Grandon. The King, it was whispered, was very taken with his bride. Plans for the royal wedding were being rushed ahead. Less certainly, Lady Gwendolyn *might* have left court, and a special ambassador had *perhaps* been sent by fast ship to Skyrria to negotiate return of hostages and delivery of wedding presents.

✦ 9 ✦

The end, when it came, was surprisingly sudden. A week after Sir Intrepid's visit, early on a sunny-showery Fourthmoon morning, Isabelle headed across the bailey to her own quarters in the Sable Tower, having just been released from Beau's cell. The hucksters were erecting their stalls with all the usual territorial squabbling; clangs from the armory and the thumping of dies in the mint showed that the Bastion itself was already at work on the King's business. She saw two men-at-arms with their tall pikes approaching, then Baron Bandale, whose escort they were.

He greeted her with a flourish of hat and a brilliant smile. "I am on my way to discharge a prisoner. Would you care to accompany me, Lady Beaumont?"

Of course she would. She almost jumped in the air. "He's free to go?"

"Not merely free to go. He's to get out of town and stay out. All charges are stayed."

It was the thirty-fifth day of her marriage and now their life could begin. She headed back toward the River Tower with Bandale.

"The news is not all good, I'm afraid. Beau is expelled from the Blades. That is least he could expect, after his insolence to the King."

"I suppose so." But it would break his heart.

The Constable lowered his voice so his escort would not hear. "The rumors are that Princess Tasha's testimony before the inquisitors cleared him of all suspicion."

"Well, I should hope so! Do you imagine I ever doubted him?" Isabelle had, of course, just a little. The Skyrrian minx was a very beautiful child and had very much been available. Eager, in fact. Tail up and nose twitching.

"Others did doubt, mistress, but the midwives have certified that she is a virgin—I merely repeat unseemly rumor, of course."

"And she is not expected to remain one for long?"

Bandale chuckled. "Not if I know my sovereign lord. He is rarely patient. Nor forgiving. I am to give you money to leave Grandon. Beau will remain out of sight from now on, if he is wise."

Her husband was clever but possibly not always wise, she thought. "You and Lady Dian have been extremely kind, my lord. I don't think Beau realizes all you have done for both of us. He will never accept open charity. May I ask—since I know he will—where this money came from?"

"It was provided with my instructions. I think it must be his own, wages due to him."

"Then it comes from Lady Wassail?"

"Lady Wassail," Bandale said with obvious amusement, "has applied for royal permission to marry one of her knights, a lad about a third of her former husband's age. Rumor—my, but those tongues work hard!—rumor suggests the matter is fairly urgent. I don't think Beau need worry about Lady Wassail."

A moment later, as they climbed the stairs to the cell, Bandale added gently, "If I may offer some friendly advice, Lady Beaumont, the wind sets fair for Isilond. He has friends there who will offer him honorable employment."

And few friends in Chivial.

*   *   *

Less than an hour later, Isabelle found herself strolling on her husband's arm along the alleyways of Grandon, following close on the heels of the shambling Lackwit and a boy pushing a barrow. The barrow bore all their worldly possessions, most of which were the gowns Beau had bought for her in Laville. He owned almost nothing, not even a sword.

"Pick a country," she said. "Anywhere but Skyrria."

He sighed. "Not yet, love. I still have some unfinished business."

"Not Lady Wassail, I hope?"

He shook his head impatiently. "The friends I left behind in Kiensk."

"You had no choice! Others may call it betrayal, but your ward—"

"I call it betrayal. At least it feels like betrayal. I want to be sure they will be safely returned. If Igor offers Athelgar a choice of Tasha's wedding treasure or his own people back, which will he choose?"

The alley was crowded. "Beau, you shouldn't talk like that!"

"It is folly," he agreed. "Igor will never dream of giving up the treasure. But if the wolf can track the dog back to the sheepfold, can the dog just curl up and sleep at the shepherd's fireside?"

"What *are* you talking about?"

He banished the topic with one of his damsel-destroying smiles. "I hoped if I couldn't be a swordsman I might make a poet. Love, I promised you fine gowns and some small jewels. I still do, but you will need to be patient. Don't worry! A Blade, even a disgraced Blade, can always find employment. I can be some noble lord's castellan, or I can teach fencing. You will never starve."

"So we are not going to leap on a stagecoach and race for

the nearest port?" She had many sisters who ought to be shown such a husband.

"Not yet. See here? This is Gossips' Corner, well named. We'll take a room while I look around for employment. Ears here hear everything worth hearing."

Isabelle was overwhelmingly unimpressed by the sight of the tavern and repelled by its smell, but she could stand anything for a day or two. "As long as it won't be for long," she said.

VII

𝕿𝖍𝖊 𝕾𝖙𝖔𝖑𝖊𝖓 𝕭𝖑𝖆𝖉𝖊

◆ 1 ◆

"*What!?*" Isabelle cried. "Don't give me shocks like that! It's bad for the baby."

"I said I know who 'Osric' is," Beau repeated, "and so does Lord Roland. The problem will be catching him in time. The warrant was dated the third. Assume Osric rode posthaste from Grandon to Ironhall—"

"How do you know he was ever in Grandon?"

Beau grinned approvingly. "He was, but what I mean is that the date had to seem reasonable to Grand Master. The warrant is addressed to him, but it's a royal command to the bearer, too—if the King gives you a commission like that, you do not drop it in a drawer and forget about it! You move. You act! So Osric probably arrived at Ironhall late on the fourth or on the fifth. The ritual begins with a daylong fast, so the actual binding could not have been done before midnight on the fifth or sixth. He and Swithin left early on the sixth or seventh; Valiant and Hazard arrived later, probably around noon. Today's the ninth, so old Durendal did very well to get here in just two days. Well for his age, I mean. But where are Osric and Swithin?"

She was lost in this labyrinth. "What are you going to do?"

Beau's laugh showed all his teeth. "I'm not going to do anything. You are."

"Me? You are out of your mind."

"No, love." He slid *Just Desert* back in her scabbard. "You are going to put on your best bonnet and head over to the palace. I wonder if the King is back from Avonglade yet?"

She sat down. "Beau, what *are* you raving about?"

"The Queen, my dearest. Tasha is, as even you must know, very high in royal favor now. She is with prince, or perchance with princess, and several months farther along than you are. You may compare symptoms with her and reminisce about the old days in Laville. The need for haste is manifest."

"Beaumont! If you do not explain this instant what—"

Beau opened the door to display Mistress Snider, eavesdropping *flagrante delicto*.

Unabashed, the old hag snapped, "There you are! Lolling about when I need that sauce made! Ned, you get your lazy carcass out to the stable this instant. The stage is in and all those horses—"

"Look after the horses yourself, mistress." Beau offered Isabelle a hand. "Broiled with a light strawberry glaze would be best, I'd think. My wife and I just left your service. We shall also quit your rat-ridden attic by tomorrow at the latest. Come, darling."

"Oh no, you don't!" the old hag screeched. "There's notice owing."

"You just received it. Begone and cause no trouble."

"You can't threaten me!" She was turning heads in the taproom, audible even over the carpenters' hammering.

"You are the easiest person in Grandon to threaten," Beau said cheerfully. "If Belle and I turn king's evidence about what goes on in Gossips' Corner, the Watch will triple its price for turning blind eyes. I'll thank you for a sheet of paper, ink, a decent quill, and some wax right away. Run upstairs, darling, and put on your best gown. I'll be there in a jiffy."

Isabelle's most favorite gown was one of blue and green velvet. She had worn it only once, on the day she had arrived in Grandon, the day she was presented to His Majesty in the Bastion. Since then it had lain in lavender at the bottom of the chest. Could she fit into it now?

Just. Breathing was going to be a problem. She had barely sat down to brush her hair when she heard Beau coming. Swordsmen needed good legs and he could run up all five flights without puffing. He took the brush from her hand and replaced it with a sealed letter addressed in a bizarre script.

Then he began brushing her hair with the long, powerful strokes he knew she enjoyed. "In the cause of righteousness and justice, my love, you go to Greymere and hand that to the Queen. If the guards will not admit you, you insist the matter is urgent and you will wait for an answer. Not a woman in a million has hair as thick as this."

"How do you know? And if she sends a lady-in-waiting?"

"She won't, I'm sure. The Czar sent none of her Skyrrian friends to join her, so she's the only person in the palace who can speak the language. She will send for you."

"Then I scratch her eyes out or she scratches mine?"

"Neither. But you must be very careful not to seem to threaten her or imply that she is involved in any wrongdoing."

"And why," Isabelle demanded through clenched teeth, "would I do that?"

"Because of what Durendal said, of course!" Beau could be the world's most maddening tease sometimes. "Think back, dear. Lord Roland told us Valiant and Hazard arrived at Ironhall soon after the fake Osric and his Blade rode away. He was hinting that they passed on the road—that's a safe guess on Starkmoor. Now Hazard is the biggest blabbermouth in the Royal Guard, which says a lot, so he would most certainly have commented to Grand Master. 'I thought he sailed home a week ago,' is what Hazard would have said, and, 'What's the Pirate's Son doing giving that one a Blade?' Now do you see the need for haste? Valiant and Hazard had a job to do in Nythia, but it won't take them much more than a week or two. The instant Hazard draws breath here in Grandon, the story will be everywhere, trumpeted from rooftops."

"*Who* did Hazard recognize?"

"Think back a couple of months. Remember when the Skyrrian hostages disembarked? You must! There was a parade." Beau tossed the brush on the bed and began dividing her hair into bundles.

She said, "I remember reminding you that you had told me over a year ago you would stay around in Gossips' Corner just to keep track of what was being done to secure their release, so now they were safely home we could get out of this awful place."

"And I begged you for just a little longer, because the man who brought them home . . . Remember?"

"Whatsisname, the Queen's brother?"

"Prince Dimitri. He came on a state visit as part of the renewed accord. Dimitri's chin sprouts a sandy-colored floor broom, although he did keep it trimmed to a respectable length while he was here. Remember what Durendal said about Osric?"

"Oh," she said. "Oh, dear!"

Beau chuckled, weaving the ropes of her hair as expertly as he wielded a sword. "It is common knowledge around Grandon, and certainly in the Guard, that Igor's original price for releasing Sir Dixon and the rest included a selection of King's Blades he could take apart to see what made them quack. Athelgar refused. He must have been tempted to send me in a barrel, but either the Order pressured him, or he just had the sense to see that he mustn't do that. Now along comes Grand Master himself claiming that a Blade has been stolen and Osric's warrant was forged. He said the seal was genuine, remember? The form had to be."

"Why?"

"Because it was printed." Beau must find her excessively slow sometimes—he must find everyone slow, but impatience never showed in his voice. "Even the Sniders' sleazy jobbers would balk at setting a royal warrant, and if you have an original to copy, why not use that? So, beloved, name three people who might reasonably find a chance to filch a piece of stationery from the King's desk. Name two who would want to. Name one who might pick up his signet ring if he left it on the dressing table overnight."

"*What!? You're saying Tasha forged that warrant?*"

"Sh! Even Grand Master dared not say that aloud. It would be quite a feat for her. Tasha is visible only in pitch darkness and Dimitri does not burn much brighter. If I had to, I'd cast him as the forger and her as cat's-paw, but *don't* say even that much. Concentrate on the appalling scandal this will cause if it comes out. Spirits! Nobody in Chivial had ever heard of Czar Igor until he locked up Dixon and that rest, but that made him a national monster overnight. Now Swithin? There's Blades in the Privy Council, Blades in the Commons, Blades in the Lords, Blades being sheriffs and wardens and spirits-know what else. They will all scream about a loyal Chivian lad betrayed into the tyrant's torture chambers. Mobs will burn the Queen in effigy. Pass me the combs."

"What's in the letter?" she asked with a shiver.

"Hints, nothing treasonous. If heads must roll over this, I'd rather that yours wasn't one of them." He finished setting the combs in place. "I'd hate to waste all this work."

"I will kill you with bare fingernails!"

"Doubtless. Some of the lads have promised to look after Lackwit while we're gone. I'll see you to the Palace gate."

"You'll wait there for me?"

He held out her cloak for her. "No. I have to rush around the back and visit with Grand Wizard."

"Who?"

"Your old friend Sir Intrepid. Athelgar put him in charge of the College last year, didn't you hear? You really do not listen enough, love." He turned her to face him, gripping her shoulders. Devilry danced in his eyes like quicksilver. "Darling, trust me! Athelgar has not paid his debts, so I'm going to stuff pebbles up his nose and make him sneeze diamonds."

"Spare a rock or two for the child bride."

Beau shook his head. "Oh, Tasha's not bad, just young and spoiled. Whatever happens, remember I'm doing this for you and our baby. I am *not* suicidal, and if I have to leave you for a while, I will see you are comfortable until I return. And I *will* return! Remember this!"

She could smell excitement on him, see it blaze in his eyes. For once this arousal was not about sex; he was foreseeing some very different sort of action. The long tormenting wait was over.

"I will remember," she promised "I have never doubted you. I never will."

⋄ 2 ⋄

She walked through the gate, past two men-at-arms who paid her no heed. They were tall and very pretty in their shiny breastplates—Household Yeomen, Beau had called them, sounding disdainful. When she reached the arch at the top of the steps she looked back, but he had gone. *Trust me!* he had said as they parted. *Whatever I say or do, trust me.*

Many people were coming and going under the bored eyes of brightly tabarded ushers. One of them floated over to her, haughty as a summer cloud.

"I have brought a letter for the Queen."

"It will be delivered." He reached.

Isabelle jerked it back just in time. "I must personally hand it to Her Majesty. It is written in Skyrrian, see? And very urgent."

"Her Majesty is not receiving petitions in her present condition."

Whatever was she thinking of, Isabelle wondered, trying to browbeat a young male? She smiled instead. The effect was immediate. Pupils dilated, nostrils flared.

"I am in the same fortunate state myself, as you can see. I feel a little . . . May I sit somewhere? Thank you." She let him help her to some chairs. "You are *very* kind, sir. Now, if you can just explain to Her Majesty that a lady has brought her an urgent letter written in Skyrrian, I do believe Her Grace will . . ."

Her Grace did. Late pregnancy was very boring and any diversion welcome.

The way into the royal quarters led past several groups of Blades in royal livery. Their raptor eyes scanned the visitor, but none showed signs of recognizing her. Why should they? Even those who had been present in the Bastion that day, more than a year ago, would have been concentrating on Beau.

She was led at last to the queen's withdrawing room, which was large and opulent and perfumed to suffocation. Only women inhabited it, one of whom was tinkling a dainty tune on the virginals.

Tasha was garbed in a cloud of lace and muslin and bright jewels, glittering like a spring shower. Matrimony had worked startling changes on her. Athelgar himself had worked the largest one, of course, for she was close to term, bulging like an overstuffed laundry bag, but she had acquired the mystic glow of impending motherhood and was certainly no longer the terrified child of Laville. She was a crowned queen triumphant, carrying the heir. The King doted on her.

She offered ringed fingers for kissing. "Isabelle? What a long time it has been! How do you fare? And your stalwart husband?"

The ladies-in-waiting paused in their needlework to inspect this unknown intruder. The music had stopped.

"He is well and will be honored to hear that Your Grace remembered him."

Scarlet-painted lips smiled. "What is he doing these days? I have not heard a word about either of you since our time together in Laville." That could be true—the former Sir Beaumont would not be Athelgar's favorite subject, even for conversation. The harpy audience frowned darker at mention of times before their own. Seniority mattered in royal circles.

"He works here in Grandon, Your Grace." Isabelle noted that she was not being invited to sit like everyone else. "He sends this letter, which I must warn you contains very serious news."

Tasha accepted the package with an appraising stare of

sapphire eyes. Despite Beau's snideness, the Queen of Chivial was no Lackwit where her personal interests were concerned. She had proved she could be tough, but Isabelle wondered what the official penalty would be for causing the royal consort to go into premature labor.

Her Majesty broke the seal and extracted a rectangular paper bearing handwriting in the bizarre script, plus a triangular one printed in heavy black type, which Isabelle was bewildered to realize was half of the forged warrant, cut diagonally. She had believed that to be on its way back to Ironhall by now. Had not Beau told Grand Master, *Take your gold and your warrant, too?* Yes, but he might have switched the documents while speaking for the sticky ears of Mistress Snider or others like her.

Tasha read. She changed color several times and there was a slight tremor in her fingers when she finished. She laid the documents in her lap. Her cheeks had lost their bloom; she was white with fury, yet she spoke with admirable calm.

"This is distressing! Ladies, bring a stool for Mistress Cookson, and perhaps you would do us the honor . . ." It was sweetly, gently done, but the ladies-in-waiting withdrew to wait out of earshot. How many of them were spies for the King or the Dark Chamber?

Isabelle settled on her stool and tried to look like a concerned friend.

Tasha, on her raised chair of estate, did not. "Come to think of it," the Queen said drily, "I recall that I did hear news of your circumstances. You were scrubbing floors and your husband shoveling horse dung. Is that where he found this filth—in a stable yard?"

"No, Your Grace. He was alerted to the problem by—"

"Yes?"

On the walk from Gossips' Corner, Beau had coached Isabelle in the sort of answers she must and must not give.

"By a man I did not recognize. He gave no name."

"But he expects a share of the loot, I dare say!" The Queen curled her pretty lip. "So how much do they demand for their silence, the thief and that stableman of yours?"

"Beaumont wants only to serve you, Your Grace, as he served you in the past. Surely you, of all people, do not question his loyalty?"

Tasha flushed scarlet.

Isabelle saw an opening and smote hard. "And certainly not his discretion!" Whose had been the "words of endearment" that Beau had refused to report to the King?

The Queen drew several deep breaths, a luxury not available to the tightly-laced Isabelle.

"Beau says, Your Grace, that he can put the matter to rights with a minimum of danger to you. He could not approach you directly, as you must understand. He begs private audience to explain his plan to Your Grace. That is all he asks."

"But if I refuse, the other half of that paper goes to my husband, I suppose?"

"I honestly do not know, Your Majesty."

"So where is he, this blackmailing stableboy of yours?"

"He said he was going to the Royal College of Conjurers."

Tasha was understandably startled. "That's the building behind the palace?"

"I believe so."

"Rosebud!" Tasha caroled, "ask the guardsmen to step in here, will you? Lady Patience?"

The entire pack of ladies swooped back to listen as Queen Tasha introduced her visitor to the blacksmith-sized Patience. Isabelle offered an unsteady curtsey. A drumming of boots announced the arrival of four liveried Blades who had been stationed directly outside. The one in charge was a pleasant-seeming man with twinkling eyes and a ready smile.

Tasha now showed that she had mastered the art of command. "Sir Modred, do you know a man named Beaumont, a former Blade?"

Surprise. Glance at Isabelle. Remembrance. Annoyance at having failed to recognize her sooner. "I know him, Your Grace."

"I understand he is skulking around the College. Fetch him!"

"Is he armed?"

"Mistress Cookson?"

"No, Your Grace. He is awaiting the summons."

Modred's smile returned. "Then I need not send stretcher-bearers. Sir Tancred, see he is fetched, but you return here."

One of his men headed for the door, gliding like a trout.

"You are kind," the Queen cooed. "Patience, darling, do see if you can find some refreshment for Isabelle and entertain her for the next half hour or so. Perhaps she would enjoy viewing the new winter garden. Sir Modred, you will keep an eye on the ladies? I should not want my guest to get lost."

She began reading the letter again. The audience was over.

✦ 3 ✦

*L*ady Patience dutifully regaled Isabelle with sickly pastries, a pitcher of milk, and some dispirited plants in a greenhouse, all under the supervision of three Blade jailers. When the visitor was summoned back to the royal presence, it was not to the withdrawing room. Tasha had moved to an uncomfortable-looking oaken bench in a library. This was a spacious chamber with walls of books and soft carpets on the floor, but it was cluttered with high, freestanding bookcases and massive sculptures in seemingly random array. Even an innocent kitchen maid could doubt the Queen had chosen it to pursue literary research.

There Tasha sat, incongruous in her misty lace and satin, with Beau on his knees before her and four Blades looming over him like hungry ravens waiting for battlefield casualties to stop blinking. He looked around as his wife arrived. He winked. The Queen noticed and pursed her lips in disapproval.

"You may leave us, Sir Modred. No, do not sulk! I entrusted my life to Sir Beaumont for months in much more dangerous surroundings than these. Begone!"

The Blades departed, silent on the rugs. A door was closed in the distance, but who could say from which side?

Tasha waved at an opposing bench. "Sit there, Beau, and you beside him, Isabelle. Now we can talk." The Queen smiled.

Were Isabelle a cat, one glimpse of that smile would make her back arch until it twanged. A woman facing ruin should not be smiling at all. Tasha was much more sure of herself now.

"How are the spirits treating you, Beau?"

"No better than I deserve, alas, Your Grace. But Belle will soon give me a beautiful daughter to make it all better."

"Or a son?"

"No, I ordered a daughter first and she never disobeys. May I say that the whole nation prays for Your Majesty's safe delivery?"

"Thank you. Now what is all this borscht about Dimitri?"

"I came to warn Your Grace. By your leave . . ." Beau rose and presented her with a roll of paper. Then he resumed his seat. "That is the other half of the warrant, as you see. I should not want Your Grace to think I was attempting extortion."

Tasha's jaw dropped.

Beau leaned back on the couch and crossed his ankles, not a proper courtly posture. "Eight days ago, here in Grandon, your honored brother embarked on a chartered Gevilian merchantman to cheerful sounds of military bands and in plain sight of a large number of persons, including a squad of the Royal Guard. A week or so later, he was observed riding on Starkmoor. There are several ways he could have managed that—sailing around the coast to Brimiarde, or taking a small boat back up the Gran to Abshurst and proceeding from there on horseback—but somewhere near Blackwater he was recognized."

"Wrongly!" Tasha snapped. "My brother was frantic to get home. His wife is due to be delivered of another child. He dotes on little Bebaia and grudges missing a single minute of her childhood. He was anxious to reach Treiden before winter storms begin. Why on earth would he change his plans and go cavorting around this Starkmoor place?"

Her Majesty was an astonishingly convincing liar.

Beau's response was as smooth as if had rehearsed for weeks. "He was recognized by two Blades of the Royal Guard, who must have spent hours in Prince Dimitri's presence this summer. He was accompanied by a young Blade, Sir Swithin, who before that day had been Prime Candidate at Ironhall and was thus equally well known to the Guard. Unfortunately, one of the Blade witnesses is a notorious tattler. He told everyone in Ironhall and will inform the rest of the world as soon as he returns to Grandon. The secret is out, Your Grace—Prince Dimitri bound a Blade before he left Chivial."

Tasha bit her pretty lip. "And if he did? What business is that of yours?"

"Certainly it is His Majesty's right to deed a Blade to any person he wishes," Beau conceded. "But he should not mistake his brother-in-law's name on the warrant."

The Queen flapped the fragment at him. "Then this is a forgery."

"That was the proposition put to me."

She colored. "I mean that this paper has absolutely nothing to do with whoever may or may not have been seen on Starkmoor."

"I have it on *reliable* authority that it does."

Now Isabelle could appreciate Lord Roland's cunning. As a nobody, Beau could be ignored or denied—or even disposed of, if necessary—but Grand Master was a legend, a national icon. Together they were a fiendishly dangerous team. Beau was making it clear that he was Grand Master's proxy, but deniably so. He exerted Grand Master's influence with the promise of not exposing it—the issue must be resolved, but face could be saved.

"So what exactly are you asking of me?" Tasha asked uncertainly.

A good question! Dimitri could never have pulled off the forgery without Tasha's help. If she had not known of the clandestine binding until now, then who was the traitor? And surely the only thing more dangerous than trying to blackmail the King's wife was trying to blackmail the King's wife on the basis of faulty evidence.

Yet Beau still seemed confident. "Your Grace, consider what has been done to young Swithin! To serve his king, he submitted to lifelong slavery, and he was given away to a monster. Igor is insane. We all know that. Your brother, his wife, his children, all are hostage. Even your sister the Czarina and her baby son—everyone is hostage to his madness, and now Swithin is, too. Igor wants Blades of his own and will stop at nothing to obtain them, but his methods cannot work. Swithin will be required to produce what he cannot produce. A Blade will die under torture before betraying his ward, and conversely he will betray anything or anyone to save his ward from harm. Yet even if Igor turns them both into beef soup, he cannot get what he wants!"

Tasha glared at him. "So you think Igor sent my brother to Chivial to obtain a Blade by hook or by crook, threatening the lives of Yelena and her children? You dare accuse me of betraying my husband by stealing his signet, forging his writing, committing treason and grand larceny, and spirits know what other crimes?"

"Oh, no!" Beau exclaimed. "I do not think that at all. I would never believe such terrible things of Your Majesty."

Tasha gaped again, and this time Isabelle discovered her own mouth hanging open too.

The Queen's gaze wandered desperately around the high bookcases that enclosed their nook. "Then I do not understand your reasons for coming here."

"I came to warn you that the slanders you describe are going around already and may be believed by people who do not know Your Grace as well as I have the honor of knowing you."

"But the accusations in your letter?" Tasha shouted. "The writing on the warrant, the post-dating?"

Beau shrugged. "His Majesty must have made out the warrant before your brother sailed, allowing extra time for the roundabout trip through Brimiarde, the possibility of headwinds, and so on. He wrote with a very bad quill, obviously, and perhaps in the grip of strong emotion. He was faced with the sort of intolerable royal decision that baseborn like me can hardly imagine. Three dozen of his subjects were held hostage by an imperial maniac and the absolute minimum Igor would accept for their return was a Blade. Gossip has it that he demanded six and Ambassador Hakluyt bargained him down to one, but from there the Czar refused to budge. Your royal husband was faced with giving away one to recover three dozen. A nightmare choice! I do not presume to judge my sovereign lord."

"I am gratified to hear that!"

"But others will. Alas, capricious elementals of chance have exposed the royal secret. The whole country will now learn what has been done to young Swithin, and may decide—rightly or wrongly—that it was a fearful injustice."

Tasha nodded mutely.

"What would you have had me do?" Athelgar roared, emerging from behind a bookcase. Fittingly, today he wore red and gold, the colors of flame and fury. "You do not judge me, you say. But when the Czar demanded that I turn you over to him for interrogation, what should I have done?"

Beau rose and bowed. "Complied, sire."

"Because the Wassail disaster was your fault, you mean?" The King acknowledged Isabelle's wobbly curtsey by waving her back to the bench. He paced over to the window.

Beau turned to him. "No, Your Majesty. Because I knew the situation and might have been able to do something. Not being bound, I would have had more freedom of action than Swithin has now."

"And what would your terms have been?"

"A pension for my wife in the event I did not return. Your Majesty's favor if I did."

Isabelle was biting her lip until it hurt. She had promised to trust him.

Athelgar spun around, with the light at his back. "Keep talking."

"And now," Beau said, "I am the only person who might convince Swithin of his peril. He knows me. He would trust me, I think. I beg you to let me go after him. If I can catch him in time, I can warn him. He will count his own fate as nothing beside his duty to Your Majesty, but he will see the danger to his ward, just as I did when Lord Wassail was in the same position. Give me ten minutes with Swithin and I can convince him to keep the Prince out of the Czar's clutches."

Tasha gasped and pushed a knuckle in her mouth.

The King glared. "For a stable hand you meddle in weighty matters, Cookson. Suppose you are correct. Suppose we did agree to assign a bound Blade to one of Czar Igor's subjects, you now instruct us that we should renege on our royal word?"

There were rats in that larder, and Beau hesitated before replying. "I venture to advise Your Majesty that he has carried out his part of the bargain. Because the warrant was made out in a false name, I assume that Swithin was not fully informed when he agreed to serve Your Majesty by being bound. Your Grace will forgive my frankness, but many will say that Swithin was tricked."

But Swithin would naturally trust Grand Master, so it had been Grand Master the King had intended to deceive. In doing so, he had inadvertently roused Grand Master's wrath against the Queen. If he confessed to the deception now in order to clear Tasha, Grand Master would resign and the Order would turn against the King. Potential scandal would become political crisis.

Beau continued, "Is it not just human decency to warn him now, so that he can weigh his actions? And provide a way out if he wishes to take it? Czar Igor, having demanded a Blade, can hardly object if the Blade performs his assigned function, which is to protect his ward."

Such questions should not be asked of a monarch, and Athelgar did not answer them. "The Queen's brother is long gone over the seas by now. How could you possibly catch him in time?"

"Good chance and ill even out in the end, they say, sire." Beau's smile showed that he was back on safer ground, with an answer ready. "Your Majesty does have a ship that could make the journey much faster than that lumbering Thergian carrack. You even have a crew to sail it, although some of them are presently in the Bastion."

"Blood and fire!" the King roared, as if tormented beyond endurance. *"Sig!"*

"You were right," announced another man, strolling out from behind another bookcase. "Such insolence truly is intolerable. Good chance to you, Beau."

Beau bowed. "And to you, Your Highness."

The newcomer was a big man in his late twenties, just starting to turn muscle into blubber. His hair and beard were a blazing red, his eyes green as grass, and his pudgy face wore a wide and amiable leer. Despite that and his exquisitely fashioned clothes, he was quite obviously a Baelish barbarian.

As Isabelle began to rise, the newcomer gestured for her to remain, flashing a lecherous smile. "Mistress Cookson, I'm a pirate and you are the most appealing piece of loot I have seen in a long time. I was told Beau owned the fastest sword, the sharpest wits, and the most gorgeous wife in Eurania. I'm not sure about the sword yet." He smirked across at the King. "Ath, the boy is sailing circles around you and always will. Why don't you just give up and let him have what he wants?"

◆ 4 ◆

Even as a child, Ath had been cold as an eel. The years had done nothing to warm him. For him to fly into a rage like this was historical.

Sigfrith, in contrast, regarded life as something to be wooed, not raped. Having observed his parents' endless worries and his two brothers' grinding ambition, he had concluded very early that kingship was simply not worth the candle. Lesser men got pretty girls too, and had lots more time to enjoy them.

Part of Ath's problem was that both his parents had been monarchs in their own right, and both were still alive to carp at him from the sidelines. Other rulers need not put up with the detailed nagging nonsense the Old Man wrote regularly to his errant firstborn. Having ruled Baelmark much longer than any other man ever had, Ex-King Radgar had decreed that Athelgar would inherit Chivial, Fyrbeorn would follow him as Lord of the Fire Lands, and Sig would do as he was told. Some of that had happened. Ath had graciously accepted the Chivian throne and very nearly lost it.

Second-born, second-rate Fyrbeorn had not managed even that much. Baelmark's kingship had to be won by merit, of which the first requirement was fighting ability. True, the lad swung a mean ax, but when they handed out brawn and brains, Fyrbeorn had put both hands in the same bucket. A shiplord's power grew from his own *werod,* but Fyrbeorn's shipmates had greeted news of his candidacy by asking to be excused because they had to attend a funeral that day—his. Thus fame had passed Fyrbeorn by and on Radgar's abdication, the crown had gone to a lesser royal family, the Nyrpings.

When the Old Man then cast a mean dynastic eye on son number three, Sigfrith had weighed anchor and vanished in pursuit of wine, women, and girls. Foolishly, a man got nostalgic sometimes and went home to check on the old folks in their dotage. The result, last time, had been an epochal, roaring row, in which the former king had openly accused his youngest of cowardice and lack of manhood, after having sneakily filled him brimfull of Hatburna mead. Sig had awakened the next day with a blurred recollection of swearing to put the crown of the Fire Lands on that part of him that presently held the thundering headache. At his age! Radgar would never let him forget it, either.

That was why he had dropped in on Ath a month or so ago, to see how Big Brother was making out in the ruling business and mend a few fences. Also borrow some seed capital. They had got along surprisingly well after so many years apart, once Sig had conceded that his own youthful high spirits on his last visit might have been a contributing factor to the unrest preceding the Thencaster Rebellion— while privately establishing that ladies of the Chivian court were still as intrigued by the untamed male Bael as they had been back in those days. Then a trivial disturbance in a beer shop had opened all the old wounds again and brought Sig's ambitions crashing down in dust.

Athelgar had gone storming off to Avonglade, leaving Sig to stew in his own juices on the flames of his crew's fury. Now Ath had returned, the brothers had been trying to negotiate a peace settlement when Tasha had waddled in spluttering that she was being blackmailed and had Dimitri truly been assigned a Blade? Although the Queen was not much smarter than Fyrbeorn, Ath was so infatuated with her at the moment that he had swallowed her story without chewing. On hearing the name of the criminals involved he had exploded in a tantrum so reminiscent of the Old Man in his berserker moods that Sig had come along to witness the entrapment and retribution. He had been standing next to Commander Vicious, the two of them peering through adjoining squints at the alleged extortion in progress.

The Beaumont boy was a classic, an absolute joy. Anyone who could knot up Ath's bowels the way he could was worth a *werod*'s wergild.

The final twist had turned Ath almost purple. "You two are acquainted? *You* are involved in this villainy?"

"Innocent as a virgin's tears," Sig said. "For once. Beau and I met briefly last week. He was serving beer in . . . in a tavern I was frequenting, and we had just begun discussing the possibility of fencing lessons when we were, er, interrupted."

"I had to go and help put out the fire," Beau explained helpfully.

"Gossips' Corner!" the King roared. "It's a plot! You dreamed this up to get your ruffians out of jail."

"I did not, brother," Sig protested, "but it's a good idea. What exactly do you need, lad?"

"Fast passage to Treiden, Your Highness," the pig-sticker said politely, "time there for Swithin to arrive so I can explain his problem, which won't take ten minutes. Then passage home—for myself and possibly two others, if Swithin makes the decision I think he will."

Beautiful! "Easy enough if I get my boys back. How about it, Ath? Seal that pardon we were discussing and I can be gone tomorrow. You scratch my ears and I'll scratch yours." Sig awarded his brother a family smile, the sort of silent communication only blood-relatives understand. It said, *And if you want this churl dropped overboard, just ask nicely.*

The King ground teeth for a moment. Then he glared again at Beaumont. "You think this would satisfy Grand Master?"

The boy evaded the trap easily. "Sire, Ironhall taught me never to try second guessing Lord Roland! But the Blades boast that they are born to die, so they cannot object to a candidate being given a dangerous assignment. Whether Swithin proceeds or withdraws his ward, as long as he acts in full knowledge of the situation, I cannot see how Grand Master or anyone else can protest."

Sig saw that Tasha had finally caught up with proceedings and realized that Athelgar had been deceiving her also, or at least had kept secrets from her. Her cheeks were dangerously flushed. "Darling, I think Beaumont's offer is both generous and extremely courageous. Dimitri should be warned, too. I doubt if he has fully realized the peril he may be in."

Sigfrith nodded to convey brother-in-lawful agreement. He doubted Dimitri could point south at noon.

The Queen sailed on. "Isabelle, you will be welcome to join my household until Beau returns so you won't be lonely. You and I can talk about motherhood!" She shot the King a smile with the impact of a battleaxe between the eyes.

Isabelle said, "That's exceedingly generous of you, Your Grace."

Realizing that he was cornered, Ath simmered down to a growl. "Very well. Your wife will be looked after until you return, Cookson. Sig, I will release your thanes, and you'll see that Cookson is transported where he needs to go."

His blood-relative smile meant, *And tie an anchor on his ankle.*

◆ 5 ◆

Ath was still Bael enough to be aware of tides, which was why Sig found himself shivering in a pre-dawn drizzle at the docks. He had spent the night in bed, several beds, saying his farewells, so he was wrung dry and lethally hung over. Fortunately, Bosun Plegmund had done his usual sterling job of readying *Eadigthridda* for sea. The last water barrels were just being manhandled aboard, so she lacked only one passenger and fifteen crewmen. Sig's head throbbed to a killer beat.

"Good chance, *ealda!*" Beaumont came out of the gloom with his smile glowing like a lantern. He wore a sword. Another man walked at his side and they were both bent under sizable bundles.

Sig grunted. "Who's he?" He peered closer and saw nothing smarter than clams. "I mean what's *that?*"

"Sir Arkell of the Blades. He was unlucky on the Skyrria junket. He answers to 'Lackwit.' "

Beaumont's sizzling good humor made Sig feel as grumpy as a Bael with a sore head, which he was. "I don't recall agreeing to take more than one passenger—outward bound, I mean."

"My pardon, *ealda,* I should have mentioned him yesterday. He needs a lot of attention and I could hardly dump him on Tasha, could I? But I promise we will find him very useful."

"We? Useful for what?"

Before the Chivian could explain, sounds of marching feet and clanking metal proclaimed the arrival of the missing Baels. *In chains!* Curse Athelgar! Sig stared in horror as the last traces of his political fortunes washed away in the cold rain.

Chain gang and escort clattered to a halt. The Yeoman officer saluted like a sapling whipped by the wind. "His Majesty assured me that you would have a mallet and chisel aboard ship, Your Highness, so it would be all right to load the prisoners as is."

Sig was very tempted to pick the sprig up and toss him off the dock, then loose the *werod* with orders to give no quarter. A good massacre would serve Ath right, but that creepy fish might have foreseen the move and prepared a countermove—archers on the rooftops, perhaps.

"No, it is not all right. Free them immediately." Ignoring a second salute, Sig jumped down from dock to deck. *Curse Athelgar! Burn him to eternity!*

The passengers had slipped aboard already, both of them. Beau did not wait to be challenged. "Pardon my ignorance, Your Highness, but are passengers allowed to wear swords on a Baelish vessel?"

"Don't recall a precedent, sonny. Any passengers I've ever carried were bound for the slave market."

"Then I'll be tactful and remove mine."

"What's all that junk?"

"Personal kit, *ealda* . . . and a few little conjurations a friend of mine ran up for me. We may find them useful."

That was the second time he had deliberately dangled a *we*, but Sig left it for later examination. "Stay over there, out of the way, you and your jellyfish friend." He spun on his heel and headed forward to begin his inspection.

Eadigthridda was larger than most longships, with thirty-two oars a side, and although she was still just an open boat with a single mast, her slender length let her outrun anything on the sea's face. Having handpicked seventy of the biggest, lustiest, most truculent young thanes in Baelmark as his *werod*, Sig had intended to begin his kingship campaign by polishing up his reputation as a raider. He'd lucked on a couple of easy merchant ships as appetizers and had asked Ath to advise him of some coastal cities in Eurania worthy of pillaging—to mutual advantage, of course, since Ath's nominees would undoubtedly turn out to be commercial rivals of Chivian ports.

Knowing from his pre-Thencaster visits that bringing Baels into a foreign city was dangerous, Sig had given strict orders about shore leave, but rules to thanes were like fence-posts to dogs. On that fateful night in Gossips' Corner, one of the hands had decided to liberate a pretty girl from her grubby landlubber companion. Some spectators had unwisely objected. Three other *Eadigthridda* parties had been close enough to hear the riot and come running; in moments the tavern had been professionally sacked. At that stage, with the score standing at two Baels and eight Chivians dead or wounded, matters had been serious but not beyond redemption. Then someone had decided that the furniture, having been rendered into kindling, might as well be lit, which it had been, but just as the City Watch arrived, backed up by a troop of Yeoman lancers. The final tally had been around forty men and five horses.

The sky was paler and the rain heavier when *Eadigthridda* slid smoothly out into the current, fifty oars swinging as one. Farewell, Grandon, may the spirits curse you! Plegmund held the steering oar in one hand and beat stroke with the other. Sig stood beside him and brooded on disaster.

This might be not merely his last departure from Chivial but the last time he shipped out from anywhere. A shiplord was expected to collect plunder without taking losses. If he did lose men, it had better be a whole mountain of plunder, especially if he hoped to stoke political ambitions with it. Sig had lost five men killed and two maimed in a *bar brawl.* Fifteen others had spent a week in a dungeon and been brought back in *chains.* He would be the laughingstock of Baelmark and no self-respecting thane would ship out with Atheling Sigfrith ever again. He might even have to keep Beaumont company on his record-breaking dive.

Which would surely be more fun than having to crawl to the Old Man and tell him he had been absolutely right—son number three was a total failure, good for nothing but debauchery.

When the handpicked brawn brought *Eadigthridda* down to the estuary, Plegmund hoisted sail and shipped oars. The wind was fitful, but at least the rain had stopped. Chivial melted into the horizon and an empty world rolled by in monotonous blue-greens. The thanes opened their sea chests to find warm clothing.

The swordsman was leaning on the side, watching the following gulls, while his idiot companion sat on the deck beside him, staring at nothing. Sig wandered over to their baggage nearby and took up the sword. Now would be a good moment to throw it overboard.

Beaumont turned to grin at him—bareheaded, smooth-shaven, bright-eyed, and smirking as if he was as stupid as his friend. "I brought a couple of practice swords in case you don't have any, *ealda.*"

"Huh?"

"You want fencing lessons, you said. No charge on board ship."

"I was drunk that night. Forget it."

The kid pursed lips. He must know he was about to die, and yet his only visible sign of tension was the way his eyes watched what Sig was doing with his sword; his voice was steady. "They do say that the reason Athelgar hates fencing is that his father stuffed it down his throat, day in, day out for years."

"So?" Sig growled.

"Of course it was King Radgar's Ironhall training that let him survive so many challenges over the years." Beaumont paused, as if waiting for comment, then continued. "So an atheling expressing an interest in brushing up his swordwork must have developed political ambitions. A little late in life, perhaps, but by no means unattainable."

Although the sea air was clearing Sig's hangover, he now understood how Ath felt about this upstart pest. It was going to be a real pleasure watching the briny billows close over those golden curls.

All the same . . .

"Sonny, you're smart. You must know how your sovereign lord felt about you yesterday."

The kid sighed. "I was trying to make on a weed."

"Huh?"

"Gaming slang—I was bluffing. Of course Tasha's unpopular just now as a foreigner and because she's her uncle's niece, but the moment she produces a baby prince, or even princess, then mobs will be cheering and dancing at the gates. Given time to think, your brother would have chosen to make a fast and fatal example of me and damn Grand Master from the boots up. I had to get him too mad to think."

"You did that very well," Sig admitted. No, it was going to be a real shame to watch the briny billows, &c. The boy had flair—and he did not seem to be suicidal. "You know what our final agreement was, concerning you?"

Beau arched a silver eyebrow. "Splash?"

"Exactly. Tie your neck to an anvil, he said. I even had to promise not to sell you in the slave market, in case you'd escape somehow. I swore you would definitely not go to Skyrria and on no account will you ever return to Chivial, not even washed up on a beach. I'm a Bael, sonny. I'm ruthless and brutal and I had fifteen men to ransom. You think I refused his terms?"

"I'm sure you did not, *ealda*. Were the chains part of the deal?"

"Now you're trying to get me mad!"

The boy grinned. "Yes, but not at me. It's such a shame your brother's like that. Constipation, is it?"

"Joking won't save you now."

"No, *ealda*. I have to bribe you, don't I?"

The words seemed to echo around inside Sig's skull like bells until he decided that he had indeed heard them correctly.

"Bribe me? You? With what?"

Beaumont contemplated the heaving sea for a moment. "Well . . . I can make you Lord of the Fire Lands. Will that do?"

✦ 6 ✦

ℬove-to offshore, *Birgit* rolled with an unpredictable, drunken motion, waving her masts in complex patterns. Swithin, perched high in the crosstrees, took a childish pleasure in being swirled around the sky like that, although the bitter subarctic wind that rippled the sails was slashing at him like sabers. He could see the pilot boat coming now, a speck of white between a pewter ocean and a leaden sky. Skyrria was a dark smear along the south. It had been a long time coming and so far wasn't worth the wait, just dunes and salt marsh braided with channels, the delta of the Dvono. He had expected Treiden to be visible, a league or so upriver, but the only landmark was a squarish tower on the shore. A fire burned on that tower by night; by day the pilots kept watch there for inbound ships in need of guidance.

Far below him the sailors were busier than usual, preparing for arrival and cursing passengers who got in the way. On the quarterdeck, Captain Magnus and the helmsman kept wary eyes on that lee shore. Dimitri, typically, was draped over the rail nearby. The slightest change in the ship's motion made that flabby lunk seasick, and his ethics were as soft as his carcase. Yes, he could babble about his wife and child being hostage, but a man was measured by his honor and courage, and Dimitri's did not inspire. He was not much to die for.

Swithin had always been a very active young animal. He ran up and down the rigging many times a day just to keep his sweat glands happy. Lately he had taken to sitting up here to think about his problem. It was a long way down to that hard pine deck, but was it far enough? Bound Blades were very hard to kill.

There were precedents.

*On winter evenings while the juniors were entertained
with games and singsongs in the hall, Grand Master would
gather the seniors in his study to discuss case histories.
Ironhall had four centuries' worth of such chronicles, each
one referenced by its year and the name of the Blade involved. Most dealt with mistakes and failures, of course.
YORICK, 337—should he have foreseen the possibility of a
Baelish raid? One candidate would be assigned to read out
the history and another to give an instant analysis, which
the rest would then rip apart. Some arguments dragged on
for days.*

BRUNO, 304—should he have left his ward unguarded?
Coming soon: SWITHIN, 402.

A hundred men in a carrack squirmed like ants. After
eight weeks at sea, Swithin would give anything to be free
of *Birgit,* and yet there was worse in store. He had waited
too long. He should have gone overboard one dark night and
let the freezing ocean make certain.

*HERON, 271—should the Blades have dropped their ward
out the window? But second-guessing was not the purpose
of Strategy Class. What-if answers were meaningless. Gradually, week by week, Grand Master would nudge each young
skull around until it stopped looking for answers and studied the questions instead. Ask not, "How could they have
gotten out of that mess?" but rather, "How did they get in
there in the first place?" Adding good tactics to bad strategy
was just polishing the brass on a sinking ship.*

Either it was the odd angle of view or some Blade instinct
for the unexpected . . . Swithin was no sailor, but there was
something . . . something odd about the little pilot boat. She
was riding very low, almost shipping water as she rolled.
Her cargo was hidden under tarpaulins, and with luck it
would include water and fresh victuals for sale to deprived
seamen. He would murder for a crisp apple.

Grand Master had warned him that there was something fishy about his binding. Osric was a complete unknown and King Athelgar had never assigned a solitary Blade before. Roland had even dropped a hint that Swithin could refuse the assignment, but that meant failure, expulsion, the waste of five years' labor, and Grand Master would just have to ask the next candidate and the next until one accepted. Swithin never turned down a challenge; he enjoyed being considered a daredevil. He had named his rapier *Sudden*.

Even after the binding, when ward and Blade were cantering along the Blackwater road with Dimitri still refusing to discuss himself or his mission, Swithin had been too intoxicated by the prospect of adventure to worry. His awakening had come when his sharper eyes identified two stray horsemen approaching as Royal Guard and the news sent his ward into a near-panic. Dimitri had galloped off over the moor on a wide detour to avoid a meeting. Swithin had necessarily followed, but he had recognized Hazard and Valiant and was sure they had recognized him.

HERON, 392: realizing that the King's sniffers were tracking his binding, he led the chase in the wrong direction. Was he right to desert his ward?

BEAUMONT, 400: why didn't he?

The boat tacked closer. She carried only two men, one of whom must be the pilot.

At Brimiarde Dimitri had taken his Blade to an elementary for a language conjuration before going to the harbor and *Birgit*. Once aboard he had admitted his identity—necessarily so, because she flew his pennant alongside the Skyrrian and Gevilian flags and her cargo was his train of servants and bodyguards, all bowing and scraping and addressing him as His Highness.

Thus Sir Swithin had learned that he was a going-away present for the Queen's brother. All kings of Chivial had assigned Blades to courtiers or nobles when they felt like it, and once in a while even to foreign royalty. Abandon dreams of danger and derring-do! He was only a medal, an emblem of royal favor.

It could be worse. Palaces could be dangerous, too. *SIR WYVERN, 361: four Blades shot down around their ward by Yeomen archers. Why hadn't they smuggled Queen Sian out of the country weeks before?*

And Skyrria was exotic, mysterious, perilous. Beaumont, of all people, who had been Swithin's hero once, had miscarried disastrously in Skyrria less than two years ago.

After *Birgit* had made her last provisioning call in Gevily and started on the long haul around the Iron Shores, Dimitri had made a more complete confession. Swithin had not been given away, he had been sold. He was Clause Four, Item One, in a secret treaty. Czar Igor wanted Blades of his own and needed a model.

So Swithin was to be the cadaver in an anatomy class. That was when the abyss had yawned.

BEAUMONT, 400: Although Grand Master normally knew anything any Blade knew, he conceded that the Beaumont file was incomplete, still mostly hearsay. Beaumont had at first refused to contribute, but in the spring he had sent in a report on a spectacular battle by Sir Oak, and this had opened everyone's eyes to the nature of Czar Igor. It was fairly easy to guess from that treachery that Lord Wassail's Blades had seen themselves as attracting danger to their ward, as in HERON, 392. Knowing their ward's precarious health, shouldn't they have left him behind in Kiensk and fled without him? Was the right answer for HERON, 392 the wrong one for BEAUMONT, 400? Why had they not researched their mission properly and foreseen the danger in time to prevent Lord Wassail from entering Skyrria at all?

The long voyage was over. Today *Birgit* would dock at

Treiden and the Temkin party would set off upriver by boat. Dimitri had admitted that from now on he would be a hostage for his Blade's cooperation, just as his wife and children had been hostages for his while he was in Chivial.

SWITHIN, 402: what did he do wrong?

He swore loyalty to a faithless king, that's what.

Princess Yelena was not Swithin's concern. His most obvious strategy was to prevent Dimitri Temkin from setting foot in Skyrria ever again, but one lone Blade could not take over a ship and force it to sail back to Chivial. Three or four might, but not one.

The only remaining solution showed up in only one chronicle that he could recall—*BURL, 356*—although no doubt more instances lurked in the full Ironhall archives. Every time he climbed up here to the cross-trees, he meditated on that other solution. His ward was in danger because a threat to Dimitri was a command to Swithin, but Dimitri's peril would disappear if Swithin did not exist. Far below him, the deck represented that ultimate solution. Splat. Czar Igor could have his Prince back, but he must not get his hands on the Prince's Blade.

The pilot boat was closing. Swithin scrambled into the rigging and began a fast descent. Swordsmen had too much need of their hands to slide down ropes.

The pilot boat swung in alongside, dropping its sail; Gevilian hands shouted and threw lines. Treiden was officially the only Skyrrian port open to foreign traders, but Dimitri admitted that it was the only town of any size still standing along this bleak coast. It was well fortified and could be approached only by such a maze of shallow, winding channels that even wily Baels could not reach it unobserved.

As the pilot came over the side, Swithin dropped to the deck and trotted up the steps to the quarterdeck. He almost tripped over the topmost tread when a voice at his back said, "Starkmoor!" He spun around wildly.

The pilot was a small youth wearing salt-stained sailor garments of oiled canvas, plus, oddly, a sword with a basket hilt and a white stone pommel. Then the grin behind that flaxen fur registered.

"Beau!" Beaumont had last been heard of serving beer in a slummy tavern in Grandon. *(SWITHIN, 402: why did he faint?)*

"Good chance, brother! I swear I'm here to help both you and your ward." Taking Swithin's arm, Beau hastened him over to the captain. "So please play on our team if it—" around the bosun—"comes to steel. Your Highness, you had a fair voyage?"

Dimitri made a strangled noise. The crew screamed in terror as ominous red beards appeared over the ship's side. Arriving within reach of Captain Magnus, Beau flashed out his sword and put the point at the Gevilian's throat.

Prospects of rescue struck Swithin like a hundred thunderbolts. Baels were swarming aboard now, all bare-chested and some stark naked. The mast of the pilot's boat swung madly from side to side as its crew heaved one another up. Dimitri began to move. Swithin slammed into him, bouncing him back into a corner of the rail, out of harm's way. The bosun jumped to help Magnus. Swithin kicked him hard at the back of his knee, sending him sprawling, then stepped in front of his ward with *Sudden* in hand.

"Surrender!" Beau shouted at the Captain. "Surrender and we will spare your ship!" The Gevilian grabbed at the sword. Against a rapier that would have been an excellent move—he was twice Beau's size and could have disarmed him easily—but a schiavona was two-edged. He screamed.

Beau said, "Damn!" and killed him with a quick upward stab.

It was already too late for a bloodless surrender. The rest of the ship was a howling riot with an army of Baels still boarding and crew scrambling for weapons, any weapons: pins, axes, daggers, cutlasses. The helmsman, starting out of his paralysis, drew a knife from his belt. Beau, as if he had eyes behind his ears, pivoted on a heel and delivered a slash that almost severed the man's arm. The bosun scrambled to his feet. He was a big man and had a dagger, so Swithin sadly ran him through from behind—a poor way to begin a career.

Then Swithin himself was taken from behind by his ward, grabbed in a clumsy two-armed hug.

"Idiot!" Dimitri roared in his Blade's ear. "They're pirates!"

(SWITHIN, 402: why did he help Baels kidnap his ward?)

Fortunately, Dimitri's bulk was all dough. Swithin slammed a foot down on his instep to distract him, then buried an elbow in the man's solar plexus. He dodged clear as Dimitri toppled to the planks.

That had felt quite refreshing.

Despite their nudity and bestial war cries, the Baels were well-drilled professionals, expertly wielding axes in the cramped melee. They had already seized the main deck, dividing the defenders. Twenty or so Gevilians, mostly unarmed, were being herded into the bow, while the rest made a fighting withdrawal aft, toward the quarterdeck and also the companionway, from which all hands below decks were now trying to emerge, greatly adding to the confusion. These newcomers were armed. So were Dimitri's four men-at-arms, who were heading to his rescue.

"Take the stair!" Beau yelled, and ran forward. Swithin snatched up the bosun's dagger and followed.

(SWITHIN, 402—did he not remember that a Blade unbound is no more trustworthy than any other man?)

Already a sailor armed with a heavy pin was coming up to the quarterdeck. He stopped when he saw *Sudden* pointed at him, and for a moment nothing happened. Swithin feinted, the man tried to deflect with the pin, but a rapier was far too fast for that. Swithin jabbed him in the arm. "Back!" But others were pushing the Gevilian forward; he swung again and tried to rush the deck. Swithin stabbed him in the eye, sending him tumbling back on his friends.

"Next?"

He had only the stair to guard, while Beau had taken on the entire rail, almost the full width of the ship. The balustrade was no more than head-height for the sailors, and they could have come over it ten abreast if anyone had organized the chaos into a mass assault. Unlike *Sudden,* Beau's sword had a sharp edge he could use to chop off fingers gripping the rail itself. Grips on the posts were harder for him to get at, but men who pulled themselves up to his level got slashed across the face. Meanwhile he must watch out for attempts to grab his ankles or cut off his feet.

Had Beau taken the companionway for himself and assigned Swithin the rail, *Sudden* would have been useless for slashing at fingers and would have been snatched from Swithin's grasp by the myriad hands of the mob. The rapier was the perfect weapon for one-on-one confrontations at the stair head, providing an unbeatable advantage in reach that a schiavona lacked. Beau had foreseen all that.

A man with a cutlass charged the steps, swinging up his arm to make a downward slash. Before he came within range, Swithin ran *Sudden* into his armpit. Two down. A thrown knife hissed past his ear like a mosquito, and he yelped. A man tried coming over the rail alongside him; Swithin swung a slash at him. A rapier was little better than a fingernail for cutting, but the threat to his eyes made him let go and fall back. Then another one on the steps—

Death and violence, screams of pain, not much blood. The ship rolled drunkenly, her sails flapping like thunder.

Suddenly *Sudden* jammed between two neck vertebrae. The falling body jerked Swithin forward, threatening to pull him down into the melee below. He had a momentary horror of the rapier's point being broken off, or the hilt being dragged from his hand, but fortunately the corpse was held up by the heap that now covered the steps and he was merely jerked to his knees. Rapiers rarely caught like that; it was more a saber trick. He sensed Beau leaping close to cover him as he worked *Sudden* free.

When he stood up, the defenders were throwing down their weapons. He had survived his first fight.

◆ 7 ◆

Gasping and sweating and still fizzing from the struggle, the two Blades could now spare a moment to look properly at each other. Simultaneously they yelled in glee and leaped into an embrace. Beaumont seemed smaller than he used to be; Swithin lifted him off his feet and spun him around. He was going to live! His ward was out of danger—or so he hoped.

"Congratulations," Beau said, when released. "You've really mastered that distribution of balance problem."

"What dist . . ." Swithin vaguely recalled a fencing lesson years ago, before Beau was bound. "Thanks. Winning the Cup was terrific. The whole school went mad. And what in the royal crap-house are you *doing* here?"

"Feeding mosquitoes in the delta for the last week, waiting for you. Grand Master sent me."

"Kind of him!"

"And the King, although he didn't quite understand the program. That fat joker is the King's brother, by the way. Atheling Sigfrith."

"I am honored."

"Here comes *Eadigthridda*." Beau pointed.

A square red sail was approaching, already close enough to show the dragon-head bow post and the white bite of foam below it. The pilot boat had been cast off and was drifting away.

"What does that mean?"

"*Eadigthridda?* Roughly, *Third Time Lucky!*" Beau chuckled. "I expect Sig chose it to annoy his brothers. That's typical of Sig."

"Is my ward—" Swithin glanced around at Dimitri, who was still lying on the deck, curled around his wounded belly—"now up for ransom?"

"Not if everything goes according to plan."

"You'll take us back to Chivial?"

"That's one option. You've realized that the Czar is a real threat to both you and your ward?"

"Yes," Swithin said bitterly. "And I couldn't see any way out." (He was going to *live!* Live, live, live!)

Beau dragging a blood-stained arm across his forehead. "There are several, but most of them don't bear thinking about."

Prince Dimitri was clearly in shock, barely able to stand. He had been assaulted by his own Blade so he could be kidnapped by King Athelgar's brother—a dissolute, womanizing barbarian he had left behind, as he thought, in Grandon—aided by a baseborn swordsman he had last seen two years ago at his sister's wedding. Such things should not happen to a prince who was brother-in-law to both a Czar and a King.

The sailors and passengers were being herded below, carrying their wounded. Many Baels were still swinging axes, but now they were attacking rigging. Two ran up the blood-stained steps to the quarterdeck, where one drove off the wounded helmsman and the other began demolishing the rudder head. Atheling Sigfrith was next to arrive—a nightmare figure, naked except for boots, a helmet, and much carroty body hair. His battleaxe was bloody. He looked chilled, as well he might, but too stubborn to admit it.

"Can't linger," he proclaimed. "You all right, Temkin?"

The Prince moaned. "Not much."

"Well, I need some information, and I need it soon. We're about to run aground."

Dimitri yelped. Swithin, too, had failed to realize that breakers were thundering on a beach less than a bowshot away. Beyond it, wind rippled grass of a startlingly bright green on rolling dunes. A Bael on main deck was being stitched up by a shipmate, and his language was louder and more violent than the surf.

"Alf's hurt," Beau said. "Doesn't sound as if his vocabulary was wounded much. No other casualties?"

"Course not," the Bael snarled. "From that Gevilian trash? Now you keep your jaw shut, Beaumont, just for once. Prince, we rescued you as a favor to this insolent, weasel-sized swordsman."

"Ransom!" Dimitri squealed. "I'll pay ransom!"

"Don't tempt me. I'm planning to let you go free, but you have to cooperate. Tell me what you know about Czaritsyn."

"What? Oh, it's the Czar's dacha. A hunting lodge, a retreat."

"Ever been there?"

"No. No one has . . . nobody knows where it . . . I mean, it's somewhere north of Kiensk, but that's all. I was told I was going . . ." Dimitri's voice tailed off uncertainly.

Another enormous Bael bellowed from the waist, "Prisoners secure, *ealda!*"

"Prepare to abandon ship!" Sigfrith roared back. "Keep talking, Dimitri. This hulk's going to be smashed to driftwood in about ten minutes. If you want to leave with us, you've got to pay your fare. Now—Czaritsyn?"

"What do you want to know? I was told there would be *streltsy* waiting in Treiden to conduct me there," the Prince babbled. "And Sir Swithin, of course. The Czar will, er, was to, meet us at Czaritsyn."

Sigfrith grunted and peered inquiringly at Beau.

Who pursed lips doubtfully. "It's possible, I suppose."

"No!" Swithin said. "My ward is no stalking horse. He'd never pull it off. You want this Czaritsyn place, you find it for yourselves."

"You got nothing to bargain with, either, swordsman," the Bael said.

"Don't bet too much on that, pirate." Swithin's dander was still up from the fight and rapier against ax would be no contest. Killing his king's brother might not be an astute move, though.

The Bael laughed contemptuously and resumed his interrogation. "How many men does Igor keep there? What are the defenses?"

"I dunno!" Dimitri bleated. "How could I know?"

"What does he do there?"

The Bael wrecking the tiller had completed his work and departed. The carrack was a hulk, drifting ashore broadside on, rolling nauseatingly. Rising sounds of terror and mayhem below showed that the prisoners had realized their peril. Even as *Eadigthridda* slid expertly alongside and grappled, Baels began leaping down to the longship.

"Do?" Dimitri wailed. "Who knows? There's crazy rumors of torture and bizarre witchcraft and fearful orgies.

And dogs. He keeps most of his dogs there, huge monsters he feeds on human flesh."

"That's all?" Sigfrith was glowering dangerously, mostly at Beau.

"What . . ." At last a ray of light—"Treasure!" Dimitri yelped. "He keeps his treasure at Czaritsyn! Chests of jewels, bars of gold!"

"But you're just quoting rumor? You haven't seen any of this?"

"Er, no. But they're very reliable rumors."

The prisoners were hacking at the companionway door with axes. *Birgit* shuddered, making everyone stagger. Her keel had struck bottom.

"Anything two people tell me must be true," Sigfrith decided. "Time to go." He led the way at a run, nimble for his bulk. Dimitri hobbled after him on his sore foot. Beau and Swithin brought up the rear. Again the ship struck, harder this time. Timbers creaked. The longship's shallower draft was keeping her safe for the moment.

Swithin saw a chance for a confidential word. "You bought our freedom with the Czar's treasure?"

"I bought something." Beau's old familiar grin twinkled like silver at him. "If I can't deliver the chests of jewels, you may be in ransom country after all. And if any more Baelish blood is shed, I will have to learn how to breathe water."

They ran down to the main deck. *Birgit* struck again. Four enormous Baels were holding the two vessels together with grappling hooks, but even they would not be able to keep that up very long.

"How can you possibly find the place if nobody knows where it is?" Swithin demanded. He was starting to wonder how much better his situation was than it had been half an hour ago.

"Trust me," Beau said.

nd dogs. He keeps most of his dogs there, huge monsters
e feeds on human flesh."

"That's all?" Sigfrith was glowering dangerously, mostly
t Beau.

"What . . ." At last a ray of light—"Treasure!" Dimitri
elped. "He keeps his treasure at Czaritsyn! Chests of jewels, bars of gold!"

"But you're just quoting rumor? You haven't seen any of
his?"

"Er, no. But they're very reliable rumors."

The prisoners were hacking at the companionway door
with axes. *Birgit* shuddered, making everyone stagger. Her
keel had struck bottom.

"Anything two people tell me must be true," Sigfrith decided. "Time to go." He led the way at a run, nimble for his
bulk. Dimitri hobbled after him on his sore foot. Beau and
Swithin brought up the rear. Again the ship struck, harder
this time. Timbers creaked. The longship's shallower draft
was keeping her safe for the moment.

Swithin saw a chance for a confidential word. "You
bought our freedom with the Czar's treasure?"

"I bought something." Beau's old familiar grin twinkled
like silver at him. "If I can't deliver the chests of jewels, you
may be in ransom country after all. And if any more Baelish
blood is shed, I will have to learn how to breathe water."

They ran down to the main deck. *Birgit* struck again. Four
enormous Baels were holding the two vessels together with
grappling hooks, but even they would not be able to keep
that up very long.

"How can you possibly find the place if nobody knows
where it is?" Swithin demanded. He was starting to wonder
how much better his situation was than it had been half an
hour ago.

"Trust me," Beau said.

"And the King, although he didn't quite understand the
program. That fat joker is the King's brother, by the way.
Atheling Sigfrith."

"I am honored."

"Here comes *Eadigthridda*." Beau pointed.

A square red sail was approaching, already close enough
to show the dragon-head bow post and the white bite of
foam below it. The pilot boat had been cast off and was drifting away.

"What does that mean?"

"*Eadigthridda?* Roughly, *Third Time Lucky!*" Beau
chuckled. "I expect Sig chose it to annoy his brothers. That's
typical of Sig."

"Is my ward—" Swithin glanced around at Dimitri, who
was still lying on the deck, curled around his wounded
belly—"now up for ransom?"

"Not if everything goes according to plan."

"You'll take us back to Chivial?"

"That's one option. You've realized that the Czar is a real
threat to both you and your ward?"

"Yes," Swithin said bitterly. "And I couldn't see any way
out." (He was going to *live!* Live, live, live!)

Beau dragging a blood-stained arm across his forehead.
"There are several, but most of them don't bear thinking
about."

Prince Dimitri was clearly in shock, barely able to stand. He
had been assaulted by his own Blade so he could be kidnapped by King Athelgar's brother—a dissolute, womanizing barbarian he had left behind, as he thought, in
Grandon—áided by a baseborn swordsman he had last seen
two years ago at his sister's wedding. Such things should not
happen to a prince who was brother-in-law to both a Czar
and a King.

The sailors and passengers were being herded below, carrying their wounded. Many Baels were still swinging axes, but now they were attacking rigging. Two ran up the bloodstained steps to the quarterdeck, where one drove off the wounded helmsman and the other began demolishing the rudder head. Atheling Sigfrith was next to arrive—a nightmare figure, naked except for boots, a helmet, and much carroty body hair. His battleaxe was bloody. He looked chilled, as well he might, but too stubborn to admit it.

"Can't linger," he proclaimed. "You all right, Temkin?"

The Prince moaned. "Not much."

"Well, I need some information, and I need it soon. We're about to run aground."

Dimitri yelped. Swithin, too, had failed to realize that breakers were thundering on a beach less than a bowshot away. Beyond it, wind rippled grass of a startlingly bright green on rolling dunes. A Bael on main deck was being stitched up by a shipmate, and his language was louder and more violent than the surf.

"Alf's hurt," Beau said. "Doesn't sound as if his vocabulary was wounded much. No other casualties?"

"Course not," the Bael snarled. "From that Gevilian trash? Now you keep your jaw shut, Beaumont, just for once. Prince, we rescued you as a favor to this insolent, weaselsized swordsman."

"Ransom!" Dimitri squealed. "I'll pay ransom!"

"Don't tempt me. I'm planning to let you go free, but you have to cooperate. Tell me what you know about Czaritsyn."

"What? Oh, it's the Czar's dacha. A hunting lodge, a retreat."

"Ever been there?"

"No. No one has . . . nobody knows where it . . . I mean, it's somewhere north of Kiensk, but that's all. I was told I was going . . ." Dimitri's voice tailed off uncertainly.

Another enormous Bael bellowed from th
oners secure, *ealda!*"

"Prepare to abandon ship!" Sigfrith roared
talking, Dimitri. This hulk's going to be smashe
in about ten minutes. If you want to leave with
to pay your fare. Now—Czaritsyn?"

"What do you want to know? I was told the
streltsy waiting in Treiden to conduct me there
babbled. "And Sir Swithin, of course. The Czar
to, meet us at Czaritsyn."

Sigfrith grunted and peered inquiringly at Bea
Who pursed lips doubtfully. "It's possible, I su

"No!" Swithin said. "My ward is no stalking h
never pull it off. You want this Czaritsyn place,
for yourselves."

"You got nothing to bargain with, either, swords
Bael said.

"Don't bet too much on that, pirate." Swithin
was still up from the fight and rapier against ax wo
contest. Killing his king's brother might not be
move, though.

The Bael laughed contemptuously and resumed l
rogation. "How many men does Igor keep there? V
the defenses?"

"I dunno!" Dimitri bleated. "How could I know?

"What does he do there?"

The Bael wrecking the tiller had completed his w
departed. The carrack was a hulk, drifting ashore br
on, rolling nauseatingly. Rising sounds of terror an
hem below showed that the prisoners had realized the
Even as *Eadigthridda* slid expertly alongside and gr
Baels began leaping down to the longship.

"Do?" Dimitri wailed. "Who knows? There's cr
mors of torture and bizarre witchcraft and fearful

Yelling, "Wait, wait!" Dimitri managed to catch Sigfrith just as he was about to go over the side, grabbing him by his fiery beard, since the rest of him offered no fair purchase. "You can't abandon all these people! They'll drown. I have servants down there—retainers whose families have worked for mine for generations. My guards—"

The Bael punched his hand away, but grinned as he did so. "Maybe there's more to you than I thought. Don't mourn your guards, Prince." A door burst open with a crash and the companionway began vomiting a screaming mob. "And don't worry about the others, either." He vanished.

Bleating, Dimitri followed, half thrown by his Blade. Swithin jumped after him, landing hard on the longship's gratings; Beau went with him, just escaping the furious Gevilians. The two ships rolled apart.

"You really needn't worry about them," Beau said calmly. "She'll run aground, but she'll need a few days to break up. They'll get ashore at low water."

"And then they'll freeze or starve?"

Beau shrugged. "I'm only the strategist. Baels make their own tactics. It's not far to the lighthouse."

"And what will they find there? A dozen dead pilots?"

"I did talk Sig out of that. They won't find any usable boats is what matters. We need some time to get ready. But Treiden will discover the situation fairly soon—and send word to Kiensk."

◆ 8 ◆

"**V**illain!" she said. "Who's a big villain? Got you!" Clutching him close, she pressed her lips against his neck and blew a loud slobber noise. He yelped with glee.

Sophie spent an hour or two every morning with Boris and let nothing interfere with this ritual. He could walk very well now, almost run, so catching him had become a serious challenge for a woman in long skirts down on her knees on a shaggy bearskin.

" 'Gain!" said the Czarevich.

"Go then! Momma catch you."

Boris screamed and hurled himself back in her arms. She glanced around, into the fangs of a giant hound, and almost screamed herself.

"Down, Leonid!" shouted the Czar. "Anfrei, down!"

By the time he was fully into the room, Sophie was in the far corner, clutching her son tight. The dogs had crouched as commanded. Anfrei and Leonid were not as huge as Vasili, but still two of the largest monsters in the pack.

"So how is my dear boy today?" the Czar demanded, shuffling closer. He had aged greatly since Fedor death's— beard white, eyes sunk in caves. He walked with a stoop, leaning heavily on a staff, and he always wore a sword, which he rarely had before.

Three men followed him into the Czarina's chamber— Chief Boyar Skuratov, Marshal of the Army Sanin, and sinister *Voevode* Stenka. Clearly government business was involved. Igor sometimes took a fancy to include Sophie in such matters now, which frightened her because his favorite method of disposing of aides he tired of was to accuse them of leaking secrets, a capital charge which could never be disproved.

"The dogs startled him, sire," she said. "Give him a moment, please." In fact, Boris was as terrified of his father as he was of the hounds and would scream hysterically whenever the Czar tried to hold him. She hoped Igor would not insist on doing so before witnesses.

He grunted angrily and settled on a chest. "Bad news. Or

maybe good news." He made a gruesome attempt at a smile. "Tell my wife what Unkovskii told us, Chief Boyar."

The old man *ahem*-ed and mumbled in nervous inaudibility.

"The noble astrologer proclaimed," Prince Sanin said, "that a time of justice approaches, a reckoning that will see terrible crimes terribly punished." He smirked at Stenka. Those two hated each other so much that it was incredible they both continued to breathe.

The *streltsi* sneered back. "He also said that defenders shall attack and attackers defend—an obvious warning against trusting the army."

Igor cut off the quarrel by ignoring it. "Terrible crimes!" he repeated, nodding and drooling. He caressed the hilt of his sword. "Like the murder of my son. Your brother is dead, wife. Or kidnapped."

"No! Dimitri?" Sophie sat down without permission. "Stars defend us! What happened?" Dear, harmless, well-meaning Dimitri! She rocked Boris, whose sobs were fading to sniffles.

"Baels!" The Czar bared his teeth. "They boarded his ship off the mouth of the Dvono. Took him away, ran the ship aground. Half the crew murdered or drowned. Treason!" he muttered. "Betrayal. Who knew when he was due home, Chief Boyar?"

"Er . . . Probably many, many people, sire," Skuratov bleated. "And if the secret was betrayed then it must have happened in Chivial. Or Gevily. Yes, probably in Gevily. If Baels saw—"

"But why just the Prince? There were others worth ransoming, treasure worth stealing, slaves for the plucking. And they took his Blade, too!" The Czar's eyes shifted restlessly, glittering brighter than the yellow jewel on the pommel of his sword. "Explain that! How do Baels kidnap a man who has a Blade?"

Mention of Blades startled Sophie. *"Dimitri* had a Blade, sire?"

"A gift from your brother-in-law."

That sounded unlikely, somehow, but she dared not show doubt.

Stenka spoke up. "I smell treason, sire." That was the surest way to catch the Czar's attention.

"Yes? Yes? Go on!"

"Obviously Prince Dimitri is in league with the Baels. Otherwise his Blade would have defended him. He conspired at his own pretended abduction!"

Igor nodded eagerly. "And why?"

"Because he wanted to escape from the scrutiny of those persons in his train who were truly loyal to Your Majesty."

He meant his own *streltsy* spies, of course. Sophie could think of nothing in the world less likely than Dimitri conspiring with anybody, but she knew better than to start objecting when the Czar was on a traitor hunt.

"And now what is he doing?" Igor demanded, slobbering like a hungry hound.

Again Stenka had an answer ready. How long had he needed to invent this rubbish? "Is he not Your Majesty's heir, second only to the Czarevich?" Who was currently snuffling in his mother's ear. "I suspect your nephew has been up to no good while abroad, sire. Very likely raising an army to attempt a coup. His troops are doubtless disembarking at Treiden even now."

Sanin snorted. Anything the *Voevode* favored, the Marshal scorned, and vice versa. Their hatred might be rooted in traditional rivalry between regular army and irregulars, but much of it was purely personal. The *streltsi* was even younger than the Prince and more beautiful—at least in his own eyes. Sophie neither knew nor cared if they were rivals for Igor's affections, but they certainly behaved as if they were.

"Or the messenger bringing the ransom note has been delayed by a tavern wench. There is absolutely no evidence to support such tarradiddle, sir."

"What of the Blade?" Igor demanded, scowling.

Sanin shrugged. "The Blade would have made the best of a bad situation. A hostage is worth more alive than dead; his Blade can do more good by accompanying him into captivity than being axed by a shipload of Baels."

"Blades!" Igor muttered, fondling the sword again. He was obsessed by Blades. "He will return, the witches say. Do you hear me, wife? The witches say that this is the very blade that killed Fedor and the Blade who wielded it will return to claim it!"

Sophie had heard this nonsense a hundred times. "Then Your Majesty must take great care, for Blades are dangerous."

But so lovable! In the dark loneliness of night, she thought she would give anything to hold Beau in her arms again just once, to taste his kisses again, to show him her son. She knew Beau had escaped the massacre, because Tasha had written that he and another Blade had escorted her safely to Chivial. The other was almost certainly Oak, because Arkell's sword had been found in the yard at Mezersk. Despite Igor's mad dreams, neither Blade would ever be crazy enough to return to Skyrria. Reunion could never be.

Stenka sneered. "His Highness is forgetting that the alleged abduction happened two weeks ago. However lusty his tavern wench, why did we not hear the news from the town *voevode* of Treiden before today?"

"Tell us why!" Igor demanded.

"Because Treiden is also in the plot, sire. Traitors have betrayed your city to the invaders."

From anyone else that suggestion would be moonbeam jam, but coming from Stenka it was pure horror. Igor's vengeance for Fedor's death had included the complete destruction of Morkuta, Dvonograd, and half a dozen nearby villages. Not one cat or dog had survived, and most victims had died very horribly. It was in that campaign that Stenka had emerged as Viazemski's successor, earning the Czar's favor by devising ever more fiendish atrocities. Now his lupine face glowed with excitement at the prospect of butchering Treiden also.

Sanin obviously thought as Sophie did, for his expression reflected her nausea. "Sire, that is manure. But if you do have doubts about what is happening in the Delta, then by all means send me and my lancers to investigate."

"To assist whom?" Stenka snapped triumphantly. "The stars warn us that the defenders are to become attackers! *Which side are you planning to attack?*"

Sanin noticed the Czar's expression and lost color.

"Indeed, yes," Igor mumbled. "It is time to give the boys an outing, *Voevode!*" He heaved himself to his feet. "We shall go and visit Treiden. The defenders shall indeed attack!"

Sophie and Sanin shouted, "Your Majesty!" simultaneously, which was an error, suggesting collusion. Hunched, and leaning on his staff, the Czar eyed them both darkly, while Stenka leered in the background.

"Sire!" Sophie said, "I beg you not to put yourself in danger!"

"Indeed, sire," the Marshal agreed. "Your life is too precious to risk."

"Oh, so now you agree that there is danger?"

Sophie rose, holding out Boris. "Husband, remember your years! Your heir is only a child, and you must live long to see him grow tall and strong like his father, so he can ascend the Ivory Throne!" Boris, understanding only that he did not like that smelly, hairy man, renewed his howls, but he had served to divert the Czar's thoughts.

"True, true. Well, I shall not go to Treiden until Stenka assures me my loyal *streltsy* have contained this plague of treason. Will that satisfy you, wife? I shall wait at Czaritsyn. You, Sanin, will guard my palace and my family." He reached out a twisted, spotted hand to touch Boris's silver curls. "Take care of him, Czarina! Beware the traitors, the witches. Remember how they killed Igor, Fedor, Alexis, Avramia, Leonid. Keep this last of my fledglings safe."

For a moment Sophie could almost feel sorry for him. "I will, sire, I promise."

"And yourself," the Czar mumbled, turning away. "They murdered Melania. And Ludmilla. And Irene." That was the first time he had ever admitted that Sophie's immediate predecessor was dead. Her death would not have been in any way his fault, of course, even if he had strangled her with his own hands.

His mad gaze settled on dithering old Skuratov. "Chief Boyar, you also will remember that my son's safety must come before anything else. You will consult the Czarina and heed her wishes!"

The old relic bowed acknowledgment.

Stenka was gloating. "To Treiden, then, sire? When?"

"Now!" Igor shuffled toward the door. "To Czaritsyn first. Come, Anfrei, Leonid! I know you enjoy the taste of traitors."

VIII

Paragon Regained

◆ 1 ◆

It had seemed easy when Beau explained it. Czaritsyn lay a couple of days' ride north of Kiensk and southeast of Treiden. Its exact location in the great forests of northern Skyrria was kept secret, but Arkell could always point to it. The garrison would certainly be complacent and probably small, except when Igor was there with his guards. Arkell could determine his whereabouts, too. All Sigfrith need do was bypass Treiden unseen, sail up the Dvono, and make a lightning raid overland—which required no more than the basic skills Baels inherited with their mothers' milk, began practicing as soon as they could walk, and admired more than anything else in adults. If the loot available came anywhere close to its legend, the atheling would return to Baelmark a national hero. With the swordsmanship his father had taught him sharpened up by lessons from Beau, he could confidently make a play for the throne of his forefathers.

In practice, things had not worked out quite that way.

Arkell's uncanny power had been no help in finding a path through the maze of the delta, and when the myriad channels had eventually converged into one, it was obviously a smaller stream than the Dvono itself, a tributary. Since it seemed to lead in the right direction and its banks were virtually uninhabited, the shiplord declared it good fortune and chose to press on. But water was low in the fall and Skyrria very big. *Eadigthridda* needed a week to cross the tundra and reach the vast conifer forest of the taiga. The longship had a very shallow draft and could even be manhandled overland for short distances, but she could not cross a bog and after a few more days the river shrank to a stream trickling out of an evil-smelling swamp.

Bael tradition required a shiplord to consult his *werod* before making decisions. Sigfrith jumped up on a chest and called a council.

"All hearken! Human Compass points southeast, a point east. Slow as we've been, he's changed the bearing every day, so Czaritsyn can't be far off. I'm going to leave a skeleton crew here, and lead the rest overland. Argue with that?"

Swithin was much inclined to. His only choice when Beau rescued him from *Birgit* had been to cooperate or drown, but he did have some leeway now. At first sight the answer was easy—to drag his ward off on a Baelish raid seemed the height of insanity. But second thoughts suggested that remaining with *Eadigthridda* might put Dimitri in worse danger. If the Skyrrians tracked down the hidden ship, or if Sigfrith never returned, then the skeleton crew might use the Prince as a bargaining chip to buy their escape, or else just treat him as consolation booty.

"Tricky one," Beau said. "I'd say bring him along."

Dimitri was close by, of course. He howled. "Why?"

"Because," Swithin said, "staying here may get you

shipped to a Baelish slave market. Besides, Czaritsyn is closer to home than this is."

The Prince grumbled, but an hour later, when fifty-one Baels and three Chivians marched off into the woods, he went with them.

Although the thanes were experienced raiders, they had not come equipped for a long trek in what was now early winter. They lacked tents and adequate clothing, especially proper boots. Beau insisted they take turns carrying his accursed mirrors, and it was an inescapable law of warfare that infantry burdened with weapons and equipment could carry no more than ten days' rations. There was nothing to eat in a spruce forest.

Six days from *Eadigthridda,* the expedition had still not reached its goal and its mood was ugly. Kiensk must know by now that there were Baels on the coast. Death had become a race between starvation and the Skyrrian army.

"A kopek for your thoughts," Beau said cheerily.

Chin on fist, Swithin had been staring morosely into the campfire, ignoring the terse, haphazard talk around it. "I was reviewing Ironhall chronicles. Like SWITHIN, *402—Whatever happened to that big oaf?*"

"Easy! He wandered into the woods and was eaten by wild geese."

"And isn't that the truth?" said a harsh Baelish voice from the far side of the circle.

"Wouldn't call that one *big,*" said another. "Stringy, yes."

"All feet and neck."

"And fists," Swithin muttered, but not too loudly. He had felt big, or at least lanky, at Ironhall; he did not here.

The night was too cold for sleeping. With the moon close

to setting, dawn must come soon, but so must snow, if this wind kept up. Sigfrith, Dimitri, and a few others were still snoring, but most had gathered around small fires, huddled together in search of warmth. Arkell, Beau, and Swithin were sharing one with six ill-tempered pirates.

The forest was noisy. Vast gusts of subarctic wind could be heard coming from afar, the sounds of thrashing boughs growing steadily louder until giant spruces overhead joined in the rampage, shedding a rain of cones and needles. Then flame and sparks would whirl up from the little fires and everyone would huddle closer until the violence passed and the storm song faded away to the south. By then another wave would be advancing from the north.

"Not eaten by geese," growled Erwin, whose skull was notably lopsided. "Eaten by Baels."

"Yuck!" Plegmund said. "We still got rations to get some of us back to the ship. It's just a matter of culling."

As second in command, the bosun should be staunchly supporting his lord. Swithin glanced uneasily at Beau, but Beau's inevitable smile was no help.

"Who do we need least?" asked Wulfstane. "Compass Man?"

"He'd be useful at sea."

"The midget who got us into this."

"But I eat so little," said Beau. "You and Erwin guzzle like pigs."

"We don't need him," Plegmund said. "He can eat his flaming mirrors. Who else? The useless fat Prince? Or Stringy, there?"

"Which useless fat Prince?" Erwin said. "The Skyrrian one we could ransom."

"That's mutiny," said Sigfrith, rising up in the shadows behind him. "Draw your sword." He drew his.

"Lads?" Erwin looked hastily around for support.

Plegmund sighed and told him, "You should have waited until tomorrow. One more day we can manage."

"Draw!" Sigfrith repeated. "Or die where you sit!"

Swithin's stomach clenched as he decided that the atheling was serious. A brief lull had settled over the forest, so that even the crackling fires could be heard. Erwin's neighbors scrambled away from him to escape the expected explosion of blood.

Without rising, Erwin extended both hands to the menacing figure outside the circle. "Just joking, lord! Passing the time. It was my old bang on the head talking, that's all."

"Can I claim first offence?" asked Beau quietly. "He called me a midget."

Some of the Baels muttered angrily, but Sigfrith laughed. "Very well. You go first and save me the trouble."

Erwin growled and leaped up, ax in hand. He must know he stood no chance against the Blade and it had been Wulfstane who used the m-word, but this challenge could not be refused.

Beau stayed where he was, cross-legged. "Tonight. If we're not at Czaritsyn by sunset, I'll fight you with axes. If we are, you ask my pardon."

"And if I say we do it now?"

"Then I'll cut your guts out."

While Erwin struggled with the decision, Plegmund said, "You won't feel hungry if you got no guts." The others laughed.

"At sunset with axes? To the death?"

"It's a deal," said Beau. "Let's strike camp, *ealda.*"

Before sunrise the raiders were on their way, limping along through more hummocky forest, full of ponds, ridges, and swamps. It was an hour before Swithin managed to shepherd his constantly grumbling ward forward to join Beau and Arkell, who always walked near the front.

"Well?" he demanded. "You really think you have a chance against Erwin with axes?"

Beau laughed as if he'd already forgotten his crazy challenge. "Don't intend to find out! We're almost at Czaritsyn."

"How can you know that?"

He flashed a quicksilver grin. "I have a compass. When we set out this morning Lackwit was pointing east and already he's at northeast by north. It's just over this hill."

Even last night, Beau must have known they were close. So, almost certainly, had Sigfrith and Plegmund. Before Swithin could make any well-pointed comments on the shortcomings of Baelish humor and Beau's participation in it, Atheling Sigfrith uttered a peculiar whistle. His men went down like scythed corn, carrying the non-Baels with them onto the spongy needle mat of forest floor. Somewhere a mirror shattered.

For a moment there was only the sound of the wind and Beau trying to hush Arkell's weeping—he did not like unexpected manhandling. Juniors in Ironhall had tended to laugh at the bookish Arkell, while secretly appreciating his cleverness and good humor. Now he was a terrifying warning of what might happen if Dimitri came to harm.

Then Swithin heard hooves. Two horses, no more, going fast. They went by without stopping, somewhere not far ahead of the raiders, and their sound faded away eastward. They would not be going at that rate if they had come a long way.

"Bosun," Sigfrith said, "send a man ahead to scout that road and two more up the hill."

An hour later the entire expedition was sprawled among the trees along the ridge top. The far face fell away steeply, giving them a clear view of Czaritsyn, which was surprisingly similar to what Swithin had expected—a village enclosed by a high palisade. The wide clearing around it was divided into fields by rail fences, providing pasture and an unobstructed view for the defenders. The timbered buildings seemed too large for private dwellings, and the two-story edifice in the center would certainly be the Czar's.

"See those horses!" Sigfrith said. "We can ride back."

"Would be easier to eat them here," Beau retorted. "There must be twenty chimneys smoking. How many inhabitants need so many fires at this time of year?"

Dimitri spoke up at Swithin's elbow. "The riders we heard were harbingers, so the staff is making ready for visitors." He smirked, understandably smug.

Some of the nearby Baels cursed luridly.

Beau said, "Lackwit, which way is Kiensk? Good man! And which way is Czar Igor?"

Arkell's arm swung around to the west.

"He's coming here," Dimitri said. "He never travels with less than fifty *streltsy!*"

"He may be on his way to Treiden."

"We'll soon know," Sigfrith said. "If worst comes to worst, we can eat horse and then head home empty-handed. Meanwhile we wait for nightfall, or that."

That was a black wall of storm sweeping in from the north.

What came first was a pack of hounds, a dozen of them, some as large as cattle. Even before they came into view, their baying had set the horses in the pastures racing and plunging in terror. It made Swithin's scalp prickle. Behind them rode a column of black-clad *streltsy* that grew longer and longer and yet still kept coming, so the dogs were almost at the gates before the last of the troop entered the clearing. Igor was somewhere in there, indistinguishable.

"At least a thousand," Dimitri remarked cheerfully. "Would you like me to send my Blade down with your challenge, Atheling?"

His Blade was wondering what would have happened if the raiders had reached their destination a couple of hours earlier.

Things could get still worse, so they did. Flurries grew to blizzard. The raiders set up camp in a hollow on the west side of the ridge, but they dared not light fires even there. Packed together like nestlings in every sheltered nook they could find, they ate a meager meal and grumbled, but there was no sign of mutiny, neither serious nor make-believe.

"Igor's on his way to Treiden looking for pirates," Sigfrith said stubbornly. "He's stopping in here to wait out the snow. When he leaves, we'll take over."

"Could fetch a horse for breakfast," Erwin suggested.

"And if someone's out walking the dogs?"

Nobody volunteered.

Beau said, "Is it true, Atheling, that the only Bael who ever starves is the last one?"

Someone said, "Shut up, midget."

· 2 ·

𝔐idnight, or thereabouts, found Swithin and his ward huddled together under a makeshift shelter of spruce boughs piled against a fallen tree. Snow continued to fall, and in the forest it tended to fall in huge wet lumps from high branches. Sometimes the soggy thumps would be followed by wild cursing. After hours of grumbling, Dimitri had taken up snoring instead, which was almost as irritating.

A faint sound nearby and Beau said, "Starkmoor?" softly.
"Ironhall."

"Time you and I discussed your problem."

"Yes." They had not spoken in private since the sinking of
Birgit. Dimitri continued to snore.

"You know," Beau said chattily, "he's not a bad man, that
ward of yours. Not clever, but honest. He loves his family,
he's loyal to his Czar. I'd guess he's a good lord to his people. You could have drawn much worse."

"Yes."

"Igor's the trouble. You, your ward, and Igor—the three of
you must never come together."

"Succinctly put."

"And killing any one of you is not an option."

"*BURL, 356?*"

"No," Beau said. "He was dying anyway, so he could be
no more help to his ward. Assassinating Igor, even if it were
possible, is out of the question—Blades are not assassins.
That just leaves exile. If Sigfrith storms Czaritsyn, he'll
want to take Dimitri along. That could be a good idea from
your point of view. If Dimitri can be branded a traitor for
being in league with the Baels, then he won't resist when
you want to take him back to Chival."

The thought was grotesque. *SWITHIN, 402* would be Ironhall's favorite farce, the tale of the Blade who dragged his
ward into a battle. Generations of seniors yet unborn would
roll on the floor in hysterics. "I'll consider it." It was a nasty
shock to realize that he might have been so wrong to trust an
old friend.

But Beau chuckled. "And you'll decide that it's impossible, just as I did. I'll back you on that. Wanted you to know."

Better! "I was hoping you might have seen a solution I'd
missed."

"Just the obvious one that if Sig can't take Czaritsyn, he'll try to cover his costs by selling us to Igor or dumping us in the slave markets. We'll have to make a break for it before we reach the ship."

"Tricky. He'll be expecting that."

"Yes," Beau whispered. "If I ever mention Good King Ambrose, that means I intend to skedaddle after dark. All right? Further plans to be announced." He vanished as quietly as he had come.

By dawn continuous snow had given way to flurries. Sigfrith set men to keep watch from the ridge top and two more down by the road; then he perched himself on a rock and beckoned everyone else to close in. Hungry, frozen, and furious, pirates gathered around, sitting or kneeling in the center, standing at the rear. They blew on fingers and stamped icy feet.

"All hearken! We can't hope to sink a garrison that size. If they're leaving today, they'll go soon and we'll move in when they're beyond recall. We'll be icicles if we sit here and wait for another night. Argue with that?"

No one did. Whiskered faces showed approval. When Baels suffered as these men had suffered in the night, somebody must pay.

"And if they don't go?" Dimitri demanded triumphantly.

He had found a good rock to sit on. Swithin stood at his back and worried.

Sigfrith shrugged. "Then it's a long walk back."

"It's an impossible walk back," the Prince said. "You have almost no food and it will take you twice as long in this snow."

"What's this 'you'?" the atheling bellowed. "I didn't notice you fasting on the way here. We'll rustle some horses after dark and make a race of it."

"You'll sneak fifty horses away unseen? And ride them

bareback? Without bridles?" After two weeks' captivity, Dimitri was clearly enjoying himself.

Sigfrith scowled. "Let's suppose the *streltsy* go but the Czar stays. Beau, tell us again about the dogs." The dogs had been a fairytale until yesterday. Now they were horrible reality.

Beau said, "The popular belief is that Igor bewitches men into hounds. One of my Blade brothers killed one and it turned human as it died. I consulted Grand Wizard about them—he's the King of Chivial's top conjurer, and he's had more than a year to think about this. He says they can't be dogs, only a sort of illusion. He said he can conjure a dog to grow very big and fierce, but it will sicken and die within days—which these do not. Thirty years ago evil conjurers tried combining men and animals into chimera monsters, but they were unstable and certainly not controllable. Their shapes kept changing and they never lived long. So Igor is turning men into mirages of dogs, not real ones. Admittedly, the difference matters only to a conjurer, because they look like dogs, smell like dogs, feel like dogs—they're quite capable of tearing your arm off—and they can probably follow a scent as well as real dogs. They believe they're dogs, which makes them loyal to their master. But it's sort of makeshift, like turning water into ice."

"And we explain that to them how?" Sigfrith prompted.

"That's where Grand Wizard had to do some guessing. He's most confident about those accursed mirrors we've been lugging along. He thinks they will destabilize the spirituality, although he suggested we don't try them in the dark. He also gave me some whistles he thinks may have a similar effect at close quarters, but may not, and some horrible-smelling biscuits. He warns that those will need time to act. Not much point offering Rover a cookie when he's eating your windpipe."

The answer was a sour silence.

"I did bring a few more tricks along," Beau admitted. "I can open doors and I have a rope ladder that will climb up the stockade."

"We can do that," growled Alfgar, the largest thane of all.

"You can kill dogs, too. Just remember these ones are smart."

"Listen!" Plegmund snapped.

It was less a noise than a trembling of the world. It was the thunder of many hooves. It grew louder, filling the forest, adding voices and jingling harness as the procession rounded the hill, then fading away westward along the road. It left all the Baels leering. Now the odds were better.

"Lackwit?" Sigfrith demanded, looking around. "Where's Compass Man?"

He-who-had-been-Arkell was crouched behind a tree on the edge of the hollow, pouting. He had fouled himself and so was worse off than any of them. He didn't understand the cold, the lack of shelter, the meager food.

"Lackwit, where is the Czar?"

Sulk.

Beau tried. "Brother, please show me where the Czar is. I really need to know." But even Beau could not cajole a response. *"Please,* Lackwit? For Ironhall? For Starkmoor, Lackwit?"

It was unbearable. "Oh, stop it!" Swithin screamed. "How can you call him that? He's a brother! Help him, for death's sake, don't *mock* him!" His own ward was in terrible danger. He might turn into a human mollusc too, very shortly.

Beau's stare was cold as lead. "Help him how? You think we didn't try?" He was in mortal peril, also, and for once he was not quite managing to hide his feelings.

"Why didn't they try a reversion spell?" Swithin said. "I know it doesn't always work, but anything would be better—"

"A reversion spell needs his sword, and he lost it somewhere here in Skyrria." Beau knelt and took one of Arkell's hands. "Brother, please help! You know which way the Czar is, don't you? Show me, please?"

Scowling, Arkell turned away to stare eastward, toward Czaritsyn.

Beau sighed with relief. "Thank you, brother."

Sigfrith chortled. "That makes things simpler!"

"It means another fifty defenders or more," Dimitri said, alarmed.

"But if we can take him alive our problems are over. We'll rush the stockade under cover of a flurry, find the Czar, and hold a sword to his throat. Let's get in position. Starboard watch, bring the mirrors. Prince, I want you along to—"

"Not me!" Dimitri squealed. "I'm no traitor!"

Swithin's hand reached for *Sudden*. This might be *it* . . .

The pirate snarled. "You could be real useful, Prince, making the Skyrrians see reason. I may call on the defenders to surrender and support the new Czar Dimitri; I may threaten to kill a prince if they resist. I would only be bluffing, of course! I can't afford to lose men when we're so outnumbered. Besides, bloodshed is a sign of incompetence. If anything regrettable happens to Igor you'll come out of this as Czar."

"I am not the heir." Dimitri peered around. "Swithin? Swithin? Where—There you are. You got me into this. Now get me out!"

Swithin met the Atheling's grass-green killer eyes. "I won't let my ward go into danger, *ealda*."

"We'll take good care of him," Sigfrith said. "I promise."

"No." Swithin would sooner trust a trapdoor when he had a noose around his neck. There were Baels all around him, no wall to back up to.

"He's worried about his ward," Beau said. "I'm worried about the Czar, so I won't help you, either."

"*Igor?*" Sigfrith scoffed. "Igor? You care about that murdering madman?"

"He's a crowned monarch," Beau said firmly, "and killing him would be assassination. Who's going to stoop to that? I won't, because Blades are not hired killers; if the Skyrrians didn't chop off my head, Athelgar would. Swithin can't, because the Czar's men will retaliate against his ward. And if you do it what is your own king going to say? Baelmark fought a twelve-year war once over an assassination. What is your father going—"

"You leave my father out of this!"

Beau glanced quickly around the other angry Baels. "Atheling, the plan didn't work! Admit it. It was a good gamble, but chance turned against us. We have to cut our losses and leave. Our agreement—"

"The deal I swore to, midget, was that I was going home to Baelmark and would drop you off halfway. You're with us or you're against us. Lackwit will be staying aboard. Now, you really going to cause me trouble?"

"Lackwit you can have," Beau said sadly. "He's as happy being a human compass as he ever can be, and he'll be so valuable that I know you'll take good care of him. For the rest, I suggest you put it to a vote of . . . Where *is* Arkell? Where did Lackwit go?"

"His tracks lead up the hill," Wulfstane said from that side of the group.

"His sword!" Dimitri yelled. "The Czar wears Arkell's sword."

✦ 3 ✦

The pirate gang went up the hill at the double and Dimitri managed to keep up with all but a few of the youngest. He felt pleased by that. Overall, he was proud of the way he'd stood up to his ordeal so far—no groveling or sniveling, just dignified defiance, worthy of his ancestry. Now he could look forward to watching the Baels being hanged in a row. He even hoped Igor would let them off with that and not get too creative.

They reached the crest in a streaming snow shower, which had been almost undetectable down in the forest. Up there on the exposed edge, even giant conifers faded to ghosts. The Bael sentries had not seen Arkell go past them; his tracks vanished down the steep face into blankness. The universal dismay was most satisfying.

"Death and fire!" Beaumont said. "You were right, Your Highness. He sensed his sword. He's gone to get it. Oh, spirits!"

"We must catch him," Sigfrith said. "He'll betray us."

"Too late."

They couldn't find him until they could see him and by then he would be out in the meadow, visible to the garrison also. Seeing that the Baels were doomed, Dimitri was tempted to scream in triumph.

"Now what?" he asked.

"We must attack at once," Atheling Sigfrith said. "The moment the Czar knows we're here, he'll send men to recall his main force of *streltsy* and hunt us down." He fancied himself as a great raider, but he was obviously sounding out Beaumont's opinion.

"Ambush," the Blade said absently. "Stop his couriers on the road. Oh, brother Arkell, what have you done this time?"

He sighed. "All right, Atheling, you win. There is one other thing we can try, although I don't like the odds. Brother?"

Swithin said, "Yes?" warily.

"You and your ward wait here. I'll be right back."

He led the Baels off, leaving Dimitri and Swithin on the ridge. In a few moments the sun emerged from the murk like a giant pearl, then the snow swirled away like a curtain to reveal the meadow below and the walled village within it. Horses were pawing the snow in the pasture. Dimitri could make out groups of men in the streets, but not isolated guards on the ramparts, although he knew there would be some. Igor always had guards.

"There he is!" Swithin looked sick with worry. "See him, down there? In twenty minutes he'll be rapping on the gate. Blast him!"

"What's Beaumont planning?"

"I have no idea. I don't think I'm going to like it."

Dimitri felt nauseous thinking about it. The astrologers and witches had predicted that the Blade who killed Fedor would return to claim his sword. That he had lost his mind would make no difference to Igor. That he had unwittingly betrayed the pirates would not stop Igor, either. Igor would destroy him by inches. Igor, who had been quite mad enough before Fedor's death and was much worse now, was still the Czar, so Dimitri must suppress such disloyal thoughts. If not for honor's sake, then for Yelena and Bebaia.

Beaumont came panting back up the hill carrying a sack that contained something large and flat and square. It would be one of the remaining mirrors, of course, and the thought of trying to stop Igor's monsters with that chilled Dimitri's blood.

"Let's go!" the Blade said.

"Go where?" Swithin said.

Was Beaumont's smile a little forced now? "To call on the Czar."

"No! You said—"

"Four's company."

Swithin turned even paler. "Never! You think that Igor will let me be if he has you and Arkell to torture? That's obscene! I won't stand for it."

Dimitri jumped over the lip of the cliff and went leaping and slithering down through the scrub, soon falling and starting his own avalanche. He was genuinely surprised to reach the bottom alive, although badly scraped and bruised, half buried in snow and dirt. His right knee and both elbows hurt like fire; he had torn an ear. As he lay there panting, he heard the two Blades following him down, but he was too battered to make any more effort to escape.

He had no need to. Without comment they helped him up and all three of them set off across the pasture—he limping, his lanky Blade plodding along on the left wearing an expression of grim fury, the shorter one being inscrutable. The slushy snow was calf-deep and flakes were swirling again. He could not remember the last time his feet had been dry.

"What's going to happen?" he demanded.

"You're going to report to your royal uncle," Beaumont said. "Tell him what a nice time you had, present your Blade. He knows me already."

"I will warn him about the Baels!"

Beaumont smiled politely. "You could not explain your presence here otherwise."

"And what are they doing meanwhile?" Getting no answer, Dimitri looked to his Blade.

"I don't know!" Swithin snapped.

Evidently those two were no longer on speaking terms. Could Beaumont truly be so crazy as to give himself up to the Czar?

They followed Arkell's track at first, but lost it as soon as they scrambled over a rail fence into the trampled pasture.

The weather closed in, returning the world to an eye-stinging white blur. This quickly disoriented Dimitri, but the Blades pushed on confidently until the stockade appeared as a vague grayness on their left; then they kept their distance, going parallel to it.

"You honestly think a mirror will save you from those hounds?"

"I honestly *hope* it will, Your Highness," Beaumont said. "As Grand Wizard explained it to me, a mirror is composed of silver, whose elements are earth and fire, and also love, which is why we see ourselves in it. He enchanted the mirrors he gave me with additional love, so that conjured hounds looking in them will see themselves as they should be, not as they are. Once they are reminded of that, Grand Wizard thinks, the conjurement will start to unravel."

Evidently Chivian conjurers were as crazy as Skyrrian witches.

"What about the other things?" Dimitri asked. "Whistles, was it? And biscuits?"

"His explanations of those didn't make a great deal of sense to me."

"Astonishing."

"It's too quiet!" Swithin said. "Why hasn't Arkell set off alarms and bugles?"

"If he merely wandered away for a leak, I will be seriously pissed," Beaumont muttered.

"Madman! Your Highness," Swithin said, "for your own safety you must insist your Blade remains armed."

"Nobody insists on anything around the Czar, lad."

"I will fight to keep my sword."

"I will try to explain."

The sun was coming out again when they turned toward the gate, fighting through drifts. They were seen, resulting in shouts and running footsteps. Helmets, pikes, and bows appeared over the palisade.

"Halt and identify yourselves!"

"Where is Arkell?" Swithin muttered angrily.

"I bring an urgent warning for His Majesty. I am Prince Dimitri Temkin, the Czar's nephew." A likely tale!—had he just wrestled ten goats in a pigpen, he could look no less like a prince.

After an understandable hesitation, the shouter commanded, "Wait there!" More voices, more running. At last a bugle sounded, calling out the full guard.

Just when Dimitri was certain he was going to freeze to death, a new speaker called: "The one who claims to be Prince Dimitri advance. The other two stay there."

"No. Where I go, my bodyguard goes. Now let me in and inform the Czar that his nephew is here and Czaritsyn is about to be attacked by Baelish raiders."

"Then advance and be recognized."

The visitors plodded forward to be inspected by eyes behind a grating. The timbers of the gate were thicker than a man's head.

"What color robe did Princess Yelena wear to the Czarevich's naming?"

"How the stars should I know?" Dimitri roared. "She wears a hundred gowns a year. Admit me or suffer the consequences."

The man laughed. "It was blue. Open the side gate for His Highness."

Dimitri vaguely recalled the officer's face when he saw it, but not his name. He evidently knew Dimitri and seemed to know about Blades, too, for he did not push the argument over their swords. Swithin said simply that he would not be disarmed and, while he could no doubt be overpowered, he would fight to kill. Beaumont had more of a choice in the matter, but no one said so and he retained his sword also.

"How many Baels, Your Highness?" the officer said.

"About fifty. I'm not certain they're going to attack, but they are in the vicinity and certainly dangerous."

"Thank you. Vladimir, escort His Highness and his men to the palace and ask them to wait in the throne room."

The Czar's secret dacha was the size of a small town, but tidier and cleaner, and laid out with rigorous straight streets between very long buildings like barracks or stables. Dimitri could hear voices, pigs grunting, men chopping wood, and even a mill grinding, yet he saw almost no one except the thirty or so of his pike-bearing *streltsy* escort.

The prospect of an audience with his ferocious and unpredictable uncle made him taut as a bowstring. He had obeyed orders exactly, delivering the hostages to Chivial and returning with a Blade, but obedience was no guarantee of favor in Skyrria. The day was still young; by rights he should soon be riding off to Kiensk with Swithin at his side to be reunited with Yelena. He kept trying to imagine that, but the picture refused to form.

The palace, predictably, was the high-roofed building in the center of the settlement. The honor guard lined up smartly on either side of an entrance, whose massive timber door stood open. Swithin's hand locked on Dimitri's shoulder.

"Wait! Beau, will you investi—"

The *streltsi* officer barked. Thirty pikes swung down to the attack position, a cordon of steel teeth enclosing the visitors. Swithin and Beaumont whipped out their swords.

"Stop!" Dimitri bellowed. "Are you crazy? Put those away! *We are being watched!* Not just watched by this rabble, I mean." He strode forward into the palace and heard the Blades' boots follow. The door boomed shut like thunder behind them.

A short, dark corridor led through to light, to a great hall, very high and rainbow bright. As soon as the visitors had entered, the corridor door shut behind them also, with a sound of bolts thudding home. There were several exits in sight, but all were closed.

This was the throne room, and very splendid in a manic, sinister fashion. Light poured down from stained glass windows to shine on mosaics of gold and precious stones on roof and walls—not all the walls, for some parts were not yet tessellated, and the presence of scaffolding, ladders, and buckets showed that workmen might have been evicted only moments before. The floor was paved with irregular black slabs, in stark contrast to the rigid, formal figures of the mosaics. A balcony ran the dull width of the hall at the far end, and on that stood a replica of the ancient ivory throne of Kiensk.

Beaumont said, "Oh, spit!"

He was undoubtedly commenting on the high steel fence that divided the hall into two, making it seem more of a giant jail than an audience chamber. Dimitri shuddered, remembering gruesome rumors about Czaritsyn. He wondered what sort of reception the Czar offered his visitors that he needed such a defense.

"Come forward, if you please, Your Highness." The low, hoarse words came from a tall man in *streltsi* black, standing beyond the central divider.

"Is this how my uncle greets all his guests?" Dimitri tried to bellow and achieved little more than a whimper. He strode forward and the Blades followed.

"Many of them. I am Boyar Kuraka Saltykov, having the honor to be castellan of Czaritsyn." Saltykov bowed; he had the bleached, drained features of a consumptive. "Your uncle requests that you wait here."

There was a gate in the fence, closed by a huge lock. Beaumont had said, *I can open doors.* Although he some-

times forgot his manners, the swordsman was admirably re-
sourceful. He had insisted he would not stoop to assassination, yet he must have some trick in mind, and Dimitri was
shocked to realize that he hoped it would work. His acquaintance with King Athelgar had made him aware of the
Czar's shortcomings. Yet even thinking such thoughts was
treason.

"The stains on the grout look like blood." Beaumont was
down on one knee, examining the paving. "Is this the famous torture chamber?"

"No, those quarters are elsewhere," Saltykov responded,
deferent as a flunky greeting important guests. "They contain much specialized equipment. His Majesty uses this
room for training and feeding his dogs, and for entertaining
visitors."

"Or entertaining himself with visitors?"

The castellan smiled without comment and coughed
thinly. Beaumont straightened up, leaving his sack on the
floor. He had untied the thong around its neck.

Side doors opened under the balcony and *streltsy* began
filing in, carrying crossbows. They lined up along the ar-
cade, and Dimitri realized that they were behind yet another
steel fence. There they had a clear field of fire at the visitors
but could not emerge to aim their weapons at the throne
above them. Igor trusted only his dogs.

"His Majesty will be here shortly," Saltykov said. "He is
most anxious to meet you."

"Tell him not to hurry," Beaumont retorted. "Our allies
need time to get into position."

"How many allies?" asked the Czar. He hobbled along the
balcony, trailing one hand on the railing, followed by two
great hounds. The sword that had killed his son hung at his
side with its gold jewel gleaming, and his silvery beard
shone in the shadows.

Very conscious of his wet and filthy clothes, Dimitri dropped to his knees and touched his forehead to the floor, close by Beaumont's sack. The moment Beau tried to use the mirror as a weapon, of course, it would be shattered by a cross-bow bolt. The stains on the grout did look like dried blood.

"Answer!" The Czar stood before his throne while the two great hounds sniffed around the gallery, showing little inter-est in the visitors below.

Dimitri rose to a kneeling position. "About fifty Baels, sire. Beaumont's allies, not mine, I assure you! I was kid-napped. I have no idea what they are doing at present."

"And Beaumont," the Czar muttered. "What a pleasure! The beautiful Beaumont once again." He removed his sword so he could sit, laying it across his lap. "Anfrei, Vasili, down." Then he took a longer look at the prisoners in the center of the hall.

"So what are your Baels doing, Beaumont?"

"Driving off your horses, sire. As a preliminary to other mischief, I expect—you know Baels."

The Czar's eyes glittered. He wiped his mouth. "Horses are unimportant. I have plenty of men to handle fifty Baels."

"Well trained in firefighting?" The Blade wore his cus-tomary confident smile.

"The raiders have no bows with them!" Dimitri shouted. But slings and spears were easy enough to make and would have enough range to make a fire attack under cover of a snow flurry.

"Was it you who killed my son?"

"No, Your Majesty," Beaumont said. "Fedor killed him-self."

Igor screamed, *"That is a lie!"* and the hounds leaped to their feet, snarling and growling.

"He struck at a man guarded by Blades. One of us made appropriate response."

"You will pay." Igor wiped his mouth again. "For years you will pay. Down!" he snapped at the dogs. "But this is not your sword. Why are you here, associating with Baelish rabble?"

"Ah," Beaumont said, changing mood. "I regret the necessity, Your Majesty. I wish I did not have to be the agent, but spirits of chance and death have decreed that—*Oh, spit!*"

Arkell had entered through the door behind the throne. "Mine!" He said. "*Reason!* Mine!" He snatched for the sword.

The hounds sent him flying, landing on top of him simultaneously. Igor jumped up, screaming at them, lashing them with the rapier. Beaumont put a whistle to his mouth and blew a long, shrill note.

"To the Czar!" Saltykov yelled hoarsely. "Quickly! Help His Majesty!" The bowmen started disappearing out the way they had entered. Saltykov himself ran to a side door and pounded on it.

Wild-eyed and foaming, the Czar continued to rage. "Back, brutes! Back! His death must be epic." He beat the dogs away from Arkell; they retreated, snarling and growling.

Beaumont drew a gasp of breath and began blowing another long, piercingly painful note. Arkell tried to sit up, but the Czar was standing over him. Igor turned in wild alarm to the bowmen who had appeared at the both sides of the balcony. "Scum! Vermin! Get those weapons out of here! I will flay every man of you. I will impale you, feed you your own tripes. You down there!—stop that accursed noise!"

Castellan Saltykov had left the hall, leaving the door open. Swithin was cursing in some tongue Dimitri did not know, Beaumont continued to blow, and now the hounds joined in with eldritch howls. From behind the throne came more muffled yowls, sounding like a whole pack of them.

Arkell punched Igor on the back of one knee, toppling the old man. They rolled together on the floor, wrestling for the sword. The bowmen stood at the sides and watched uncertainly.

"Stop that!" Dimitri yelled in Beaumont's ear. "Open this door!" He rattled the barred gate.

The Blade did stop whistling, but the hounds were making so much noise that the difference hardly mattered. "Good idea, Your Highness. Grand Wizard will be pleased to hear how well this worked."

The hounds were writhing as if in fearful pain, their baying growing louder and somehow less doglike. The black one, the giant one named Vasili, reared up on its hind legs. It was changing, melting, shedding hair.

Arkell, having struggled to his feet without releasing his grip on the sword, had succeeded only in hauling the Czar upright also, and still they wrestled for possession—Arkell mostly yelling, "Mine! *Reason!*" over and over, Igor now screaming in terror as he realized his peril.

The Vasili thing lurched unsteadily at them and all three toppled back to the floor. Castellan Saltykov appeared on the balcony also and stopped to stare in horror.

This time Arkell broke loose and rose, holding the sword. He drew it, then just stood there idiotically, admiring it and ignoring the frenzied struggle at his feet. The former hound was halfway back to being Vasili Ovtsyn. It tried to pick the Czar up. Unable to grasp yet with its paws, it swung a punch, discarded that approach, and went back to teeth. The Czar's screams bubbled horribly. The other dog-man, whom Dimitri now recognized as Anfrei Kurtsov's grandson, stumbled over to join in.

Beaumont did something to the lock, opened the gate, and then paused. "Where now, though?" he said. "I don't think we can do much to help up there."

"Might be hard to choose sides," Swithin said. "Hate to make a mistake."

"Let's just watch for now and decide later."

Dimitri could not tear his eyes away. Saltykov and the bowmen were clearly in no hurry to rescue a man who had so recently vowed to impale them. Anfrei still had to make do with teeth, but big Vasili had the use of his hands now, and was methodically breaking every bone and joint he could find. Several naked and patchily-hairy monsters shambled in from behind the throne and tried to join in. Vasili snarled at them to back off. He picked up the imperial corpse, lifted it overhead and hurled it over the balcony. Then he jumped after it, landing on it with both feet. Igor did not even twitch.

Dimitri felt a nudge.

"Say it, Your Highness!" Beaumont said. "Quickly! 'The Czar is dead—' "

Dimitri croaked out the words. " 'The Czar is dead, long live the Czar!' "

Other voices picked up the refrain: *Long live Czar Boris!"*

◆ 4 ◆

Several other dogs, now recognizably young men, followed Vasili down to worry the corpse. Swithin was not sure whether to cheer or be sick, so he did neither. He even resisted the urge to put himself between his ward and the bowmen on the balcony, because that would spoil the very necessary performance the dazed-looking Dimitri was now attempting, prompted by Beau's whispers.

"As the Czar's only male relative, I—"

"As the Czar's only male relative, I—"

" . . . will undoubtedly serve him as regent—"

" . . . will undoubtedly serve him as regent . . . during his minority . . . so I am certainly in charge here now . . . is that understood?"

"Of course, Your Highness." Castellan Saltykov bowed. His emaciated face did not reveal how he felt about this change of rule.

"You all bear witness . . . that the late Czar Igor . . . died when assaulted by his own dogs . . ."

Swithin's problem had been solved. Igor was no longer a threat, and he had not been assassinated. He had died in a horrible accident. So there would be no SWITHIN, 402 to bedevil the seniors at Ironhall, and yet there might well be a SWITHIN, 405 or a SWITHIN, 415, because now he was sole Blade to the Regent and Heir Presumptive, and had his work cut out for at least the next twenty years, or even forty.

As Beau had said, he might easily have drawn a shorter straw than Dimitri. Old Flabby was doing very well already—he certainly made a splendid ventriloquist's dummy.

" . . . lower the flag to half mast . . . as a signal to the Baels . . . in the area that . . . keep the guard on alert . . . proclaim Czar Boris . . ."

In a few minutes the Castellan came down from the balcony to attend the Prince in proper fashion. Commands passed from Beau to Dimitri to Saltykov and then one of the *streltsy,* who raced off to see it obeyed.

" . . . prepare His Majesty's body for immediate transportation to Kiensk . . ."

"Prince Dimitri!"

Swithin recoiled and almost drew *Sudden.* A naked, black-haired giant with a bloody mouth towered over him and his ward like a stallion over rabbits.

Dimitri was glassy-eyed, past blinking at anything now. "Welcome back, Vasili! It is a joy to see you restored."

"I killed the Czar!" The giant pointed a thick finger at the badly tattered remains. Some of the other dog-men were still tearing bits off.

Dimitri tried an unconvincing smile. "The bells of Kiensk will ring for you, Vasili. I expect to ride there very shortly and will be honored if you will accompany me as my aide."

Wild emotions twisted the big man's stubbled face in gargoyle shapes. "I'll need, er . . . clothes? That the word? And . . . horse?"

"Of course," Dimitri said. "Relax! It will take you a little while to recover from such an ordeal. Your parents were well, the last I heard."

"Prisoners, Your Highness?" Beau whispered.

"What? Oh, yes, Castellan, tell me about prisoners—"

"You're Swithin!" said yet another new voice. "Have I shrunk?" Arkell's eyes flickered alarm and bewilderment. "What year is this?"

Swithin smiled down at him. "It's 402, brother, Tenthmoon. You had a bad experience, but I think you're going to be all right soon."

Arkell glanced around, puzzled. "I don't remember this place. Is it Morkuta? My ward . . . yes, I think I remember that. Fedor? Viazemski? Where are we now?" Gory gashes on his face and neck showed how narrow his escape had been.

"Czaritsyn, brother. You lost your, er, sword . . . Lace up your lip and listen. Beau's making history."

The critical meeting came soon after, out at the gate, in sunshine and slush. Sigfrith and his Baels were drawn up outside, Dimitri and Saltykov and others inside, and Beau had deliberately taken up position under the lintel, between the two forces. He was no longer playing ventriloquist; he was dictating a settlement. Swithin watched in admiration from behind his ward's shoulder.

"We have no time for arguments, Your Highnesses. *Voevode* Stenka and his horde are on their way to Treiden, looking for Baels. If they hear of Igor's death, they will either return here or head for Kiensk, hoping to seize the new Czar. Prince Dimitri must be first with the news to High Town. You, Atheling, cannot take time to besiege this stockade, for you must return to *Eadigthridda* before the river starts to freeze, or she will leave without you. How many horses did you collect?"

"Thirty-two," Sigfrith said.

"The Castellan says forty-four."

The Bael shrugged. "Details."

Smiling, Beau shook his head. "Horses are the key. We must not allow any Stenka loyalist to ride out of here. There aren't enough mounts for you to ride back to your ship, so your men must walk; all you need are pack animals, for food and booty. So twenty-two for you, twenty-two for us."

The pirate guffawed. "And what do you pay me for these horses of mine?"

"We open the gates of Czaritsyn and let you help yourselves. Castellan, will you give him the bag, please?"

Saltykov walked out and handed Sigfrith a weighty sack.

"Just a sample," Beau said cheerily. "That alone will make your entire *werod* rich men. Twenty-two horses can carry enough to sink your longship. Or you can fight and take casualties."

The Atheling peered into the bag and then skeptically tipped out the contents. Jewels fell in a torrent of rainbow to the snow. He looked shocked when he realized that there were gems all the way to the bottom. His men screamed in excitement.

"I'll trade you a shovel for two more horses," Beau said brightly.

"Just a moment," said the spidery voice of Castellan Saltykov. "What happens to me and my men?"

Beau swung to face him, confident as ever. "The *streltsy* are finished. You know that, just as Stenka will when he hears the news. They will be disbanded, but I doubt many will ever be brought to justice. You and your men can help yourselves to whatever the Baels leave. Last one out burn it."

"I shall need a horse." The Castellan coughed painfully.

"We leave no horses here. We will send some once the government is secure, but Prince Dimitri will give you a written pardon before he leaves here—obviously it will be worthless if he does not reach Kiensk safely."

"I will?" Dimitri muttered, but probably only Swithin heard.

The Castellan shrugged as if his future did not matter very much any more.

"And I get Lackwit!" Sigfrith shouted.

Beau turned again to him. "Lackwit is dead. You know *Eadigthridda* lies nor'-west by a point west. Arkell, which way is Kiensk?"

"How the vomit should I know?" Arkell said indignantly.

Beau laughed. "It is so good to have you back, brother! My lords, time flies! Do we have a treaty?"

✦ 5 ✦

That a bound Blade needed no sleep did not mean he was tireless, and the ride to Kiensk taxed Swithin to limits he had never tested before. Dimitri, a superlative horseman, set a breakneck pace that even the three Blades were hard put to match. None of the restored dog-men and the prisoners rescued from Czaritsyn's dungeons were in fit shape for such an ordeal, so they were left to follow as best they could.

The going was hard, with sunshine turning snowy trails to quagmires. Skyrria had no system of post houses as Chivial did, but Igor had not completely wiped out the princely families and Dimitri called in on several on the way, breaking the news to men he trusted, gathering fresh mounts and promises of support. Close to curfew on the second day, he and his weary swordsman rode in through the gate of Kiensk unchallenged. Swithin was too tired even to gawk at his first sight of a great city.

So far so good. They had outrun the news and the capital was calm; but the entrance to High Town was guarded by *streltsy*. Although they recognized Dimitri, the sergeant insolently refused admittance to an armed band lacking an imperial warrant.

The Prince backed his horse away and waved the Blades forward with a bellow: "Swordsmen! On the count of three, kill that trash for me. One!"

This was not the aristocratic rabbit the sergeant knew. He gaped. Three swords flashed from their scabbards, three horses advanced.

"Two!"

Some of the onlookers cheered.

The trash took to its heels, with the sergeant well out in front.

So the news that *streltsy* were no longer sacrosanct was out, and the firestorm lit by that spark went flaming across the capital, somehow even racing ahead to the doors of the Imperial Palace itself, where the guards of the Household Regiment cheered the Prince. A rising tide of supporters and excitement swept him along corridors toward the imperial quarters and the Czarina. All the way there, Dimitri barked orders at any page or herald who came near enough: Fetch the Chief Boyar, summon Marshal of the Army Sanin, inform my wife, get Boyar This, find Boyar That . . .

A page opened the final door, but Swithin claimed his right to enter ahead of his ward, stooping through the tunnel. The appearance of this muddy vagabond set off a chorus of alarmed shrieks from the ladies within, who had obviously been amusing a group of small children. The children added their startled cries to the hubbub and fled to their respective mothers.

Swithin stopped dead in his tracks, blocking the doorway. Women! It was years since he had been in a room full of women, and never such splendid scented ladies in silks and jewels. He gaped. He gawked. He picked out the Czarina instantly, for she was not merely the best dressed and incomparably the most beautiful, but her authority glowed like a sun. She caught up a small, flaxen-haired boy, drew breath to hurl a thunderbolt at the intruder, stayed it in shock when she saw his cat's-eye sword.

Dimitri thrust him aside and strode forward. He started to speak, stuttered, and then, overcome by the unexpected sight of the Czar, fell on his knees and touched his face to the floor. That was not the most tactful way of informing his sister that she was now a widow, but it served. The other women cried out and sank down also. More men came scrambling in and followed suit. Pale but calm, Sophie stood in the center of the chamber holding her son high as the number of upturned buttocks multiplied.

Swithin, struggling not to laugh at the spectacle, was left the only other person on his feet. Chivians did not kowtow! Besides, the death of kings could raise passions to perilous levels, so he must remain on guard—*BURL, 356.* The Czarina glanced at him again. He made a slight bow; she nodded acknowledgment. Still nobody spoke. Or wept.

The room was almost full. Arkell entered and knelt just

inside the door. The Czarina's eyes opened very wide. Then the reality of the new situation finally caught up with her. She gasped and staggered. Swithin made a fast leap to steady both her and the child. He guided her to a chair, muttered an apology for his effrontery as he released her.

"No, I am in your debt," she murmured. "I am fortunate that you Blades are so quick." She sat down. "Welcome home, brother. I fear you bring sad tidings?"

Heads rose all around as Dimitri hoarsely made formal announcement of the new monarch. Backing away from the Czarina, Swithin caught Arkell's eye and just for a moment—

Then the gleam was gone and everyone was scrambling up to join in hailing Czar Boris the Third, frightening His Imperial Majesty very much.

Swithin alone was stunned to silence. *It couldn't be!* But it was. It had not been the news of her husband's death that had driven the Czarina close to fainting, it had been the sight of the third Chivian swordsman. Swithin took a harder look at the infant who was now Czar of all Skyrria—pretty little scrap, he was, with his silver curls and wide gray eyes.

Beau was standing beside Arkell. They were both exhausted by the long ride, of course, but Arkell did not look nearly as pale as Beau did, staring at the new emperor.

It couldn't be. It mustn't be!

But it might be.

◆ 6 ◆

A woman should display distress on learning that her husband had just been torn to pieces. Sophie wanted to burst into song.

And Beau was back. Beau was back. Beau was back . . .

But if Igor's dread grip on Skyrria had been a curse, it had also provided stability and security for her son. Now he was Czar, poor mite, his safety must be her prime concern.

The solar was crammed almost to suffocation and the most probable conspirators had arrived like ravens descending on carrion: Marshal of the Army Sanin, Court Conjurer Ryazan, Chief Boyar Skuratov, even sly Imperial Astrologer Unkovskii. She handed the Czar to Princess Nikon, his governess, a bleak but trustworthy woman of an ancient family so fallen from greatness that even Igor had seen no threat in it. Boris, thankfully, did not complain.

"We must leave you to your grief, Sophie," Dimitri said. "Many urgent matters require attention."

She nearly laughed aloud—Dimitri as regent would not last a month. She would never trust her son to him. "You are so kind, brother! Grief, I fear, must wait. You have your own family to console, and we shall release you as soon as we possibly can. Chief Boyar, let us hasten to the Hall for the oaths of allegiance."

Ignoring Dimitri's bewildered expression, she led Nikon toward the door. "Bring His Majesty," she said. "Your charge is doubly important now. We must increase his guard. Ah, Marshal Sanin!" She flickered the helpless-damsel smile that worked best on Sanin's inflated views of his own worth. "Our safety is in your hands."

His eyes glittered. No doubt a new ambition had just presented itself. "Your Majesty may rely on me absolutely."

She drew him out of the crowd also, as everyone else cleared a path, bowing and curtseying to Princess Nikon's burden. "We must take every precaution. And here may be an answer! Sir Beaumont, Sir Arkell! Would that your return had found happier times, but you are both welcome back."

"Your Majesty!" They saluted by tapping the hilts of their swords. They had both grown beards.

"Marshal, here are the two best swordsmen in the realm, unburdened by other loyalties. Would you two noble gentlemen consent to head up His Majesty's bodyguard—for the time being at least?"

Such brazen, blatant, crazy effrontery would destroy her if anyone ever suspected her motive, but today she could hope it would be dismissed as the whim of a scatterbrain unhinged by sudden bereavement. She had never seen Beau astonished before.

"We should be honored beyond words, Your Majesty."

"Then pray make arrangements with Marshal Sanin, here."

Sophie dived into the doorway before she went totally insane and kissed him.

Speed was essential, for possession was nine points of a coup. When she set Bo on the throne and knelt to him, he thought it was a game, and laughed. She repeated the oath very loudly. Then she took the throne herself, sat him on her knee, and nodded to Dimitri to come forward. Then Skuratov, Sanin . . .

When the Czar began to tire of this new play, Nikon gave him his favorite toy, a stuffed wolf, which he used thereafter to wallop each bearded head as it bent before him, yelling with joy. Perhaps there was some of Igor in him after all.

"I think His Majesty should retire now," she said, handing him to Nikon. "Chief Boyar, Marshal . . . you will confirm for the others that my husband left me in charge in his absence?"

"Certainly, Your Majesty," Sanin said soapily.

Old Skuratov agreed. During the past few months, as Igor's strength waned, Sophie had cultivated both of them and others also. She had not expected to need their support so soon, but those parting words of Igor's were enough to carry her over the quicksand. Dimitri looked shocked, but more relieved than affronted. Yelena, at his side, seemed less pleased, but she was no threat.

"Then my preliminary nominations for my council are as follows—"

Dimitri, of course, but she could send him back to Faritsov in a few weeks. She pronounced seven names and decided those would do for now.

"All others may now withdraw. Dear brother, will you please relate to the council the circumstances of my husband's death?"

She ordered the knell sounded, Czar Boris proclaimed, the corpse fetched, funeral arrangements made, foreign ambassadors and *voevody* of provincial districts notified, Marshal Sanin to march on Treiden and disperse the *streltsy*—as permanently and fatally as possible, but she need not tell him that—Unkovskii to cast the new reign's horoscope, which she knew would be sensational . . .

And so on. Every order given and accepted settled her more firmly on the throne. Mother Tharik's great voice made the palace tremble: *Klong-ng-ng!*

By nightfall, when the knell ended, she had signed a hundred documents, two of which were commissions in the Household Regiment. Senior officers of His Majesty's bodyguard had access to the imperial quarters.

She paced her chamber by candlelight. Old Skuratov must go. Prince Grigori Ovtsyn would make a good replacement, she thought. The army should be safe under Sanin as long as he believed she lusted after him. She sat down to make notes, only to find herself pacing again. It was well over an hour before the door opened and Beau slipped in. He was in uniform, wearing a sword with a white stone on the pommel. He had removed the beard.

They stared at each other and she guessed exactly what he was going to say: "Sophie, I cannot stay."

She nodded, not even trying to hide the pain.

"I never meant to come here and open half-healed wounds," he said. "It is cruel. I wanted only to rescue Swithin."

That must be the gangling boy who had been following Dimitri around. "Even if you could stay, it would be too dangerous," she said, and yet her heart screamed that there must be a way. "Did you cause Igor's death?"

"Not directly. That was not my purpose, either."

"It was well deserved. Would you hold your son?"

He flinched and went over to the crib, warily as if he expected it to attack him. She joined him there, very conscious of his nearness. He was staring, transfixed.

"Pick him up. He won't waken."

"Better not, not tonight. Later, when he's seen me around." Beau's hand on the rail ignored hers beside it. "He is very beautiful, takes after his mother."

"No, he takes after his Great Aunt Euphrosyne, of blessed memory. She had no lobes to her ears either."

Beau's smile flashed, brightening the room, then vanished into sadness. "Oh, Sophie, my love! We broke each other's hearts once. Would you go through all that again?"

"Gladly."

"Me too." There were tears in his eyes. "But, Sophie, I cannot. If for no other reason, because it will endanger Boris. No one cared if Igor's wife was unfaithful. No one would have dared tell him. But High Town is full of eyes. Your son needs you, and you will have many enemies, if you do not have them already."

That made sense, but there *was* another reason, she was certain.

"Not that you can't have lovers," Beau said, turning again

to study his son. "In fact, lovers will probably be essential, so you can play the great houses against one another, but nobles. A baseborn foreigner gigolo would be certain suicide."

"You're married," she said sadly.

He nodded.

With any other man that would not be a problem, but Beau was Beau.

"To a woman of my own station, Sophie."

"She can't possibly need you more than I do for the next few months! If I can just hold on until spring, until everyone gets used to a Czarina Regent . . . I must find able ministers— Igor trusted only fools, but I need strong, ambitious men, at least four of them, who will struggle against one another and not gang up on me and force me into some frightful marriage at sword point. Bo needs you! The Chief Boyar is useless, but fortunately he has no son to inherit his post, so I shall appoint a chancellor, Euranian style. And finance—"

He took her hand. "I can't help you with those decisions, love, but I didn't say I was leaving immediately. They say civil war has broken out in Dolorth, and every ship in Treiden will have fled the Baels, so I cannot go before spring. Until then, I will keep Bo safe for you, I promise. No harm will come to him while I am here. Go ahead and build your government without that worry, at least." He smiled sadly down at the sleeping child. "I will recruit and train a Royal Guard for him, one that you can trust. It is the only gift I can give him."

"No. You will have given him courage and honor, for those are in the blood. The Tharik line has been tainted by madness for over a century. If Skyrria gains a sane and dutiful Czar, then that is your gift to all the land."

"Being what I am," he said with an attempt at a smile, "I prefer to believe in upbringing. If he is worthy, the credit will be yours." He raised her hand to his lips.

They stared at each other for a long, sad moment with the issue balanced on an edge of pain. *Two proud people,* she thought—an empress too proud to beg and a nobody with nothing but his hard-won fighting skills and his damnable honor. If she did beg, he might give up even that for her, but she loved him too much to demand such a sacrifice.

He bowed jerkily and went away.

◆ 7 ◆

Spring came late to Chivial that year, but Grandon's weather had no influence on the sea lanes to Skyrria. The first ships usually returned about the end of Sixthmoon—so Isabelle had been informed—and every day she reminded herself she must be patient. She had Maude to care for, she trusted Beau. In the lonely crypts of the night, it was her mantra: "I trust him, I trust him."

All she knew was that he had sailed off to Skyrria with Baels and the last ships to return before winter had reported Baels raiding there. King Athelgar had been very wroth over that, for some reason.

Sixthmoon ended and there was still no word. Maude was four months old, thriving better than Prince Everard, who was half a year older. Palace life was deadly—at times Isabelle could almost wish she was back in Gossips' Corner, where there were real people, not just vaporous ladies-in-waiting floating high above any jumped-up kitchen maid. Curiously, the only person at court who came close to friendship was Queen Tasha herself, probably because they were both foreigners and both had babies. Also, neither of them bothered to play the nasty little spite games of the

Court. Isabelle could never hope to set foot on that ladder, while Tasha was already at the top and could rise no further.

One morning, when Isabelle had just nursed Maude and laid her down for her midday nap, the door swung open without warning. She jumped and hastily moved to close her gown.

"Don't," he said. "I was enjoying the view." He dropped his pack and caught her on the first bounce.

Neither said anything for a while. Then they made a few incoherent noises and went back to kissing. Husbands returning from long voyages were expected to be urgent and she had no desire to slow him down. He was gaining speed rapidly when a loud rap on the door intervened.

A very flushed Beau said, "Who is it?"

"Royal Guard. You're wanted."

"Fire and death! I just got here."

"Tell that to the Pirate's Son."

"Tell him I'm dressing as fast as I can." Beau discovered his daughter. "That's very nice, too. Is it a boy or a girl? Why didn't you give her earlobes?"

Isabelle had not been included in the summons, but she called in Maisie the laundry girl to keep an eye on Maude and went along with Beau. Sir Calvert made no objection. Normally a cheerful, talkative type, he answered Beau's questions with monosyllables.

"The dispatches have arrived already?"

"Yes."

"His Majesty's demeanor forebodes?"

"Yes."

"I hear Vicious was granted release at last."

"Yes."

Calvert halted at an inconspicuous door and held out a

hand. Beau started to draw his sword, then stopped, frowning.

Calvert smiled for the first time. "I will see you get it back, brother . . . on one condition."

Beau passed him *Just Desert.* "Namely?"

"Remember the day we found you on the Blackwater road and I gave you a ride into Ironhall?"

"As it were yesterday."

"Just don't tell the King it was me!" He chuckled. "Good luck, brother."

"Brother?" Beau repeated softly as he and Isabelle went out to the Queen's Garden, a dainty place of flowers and shrubs, sheltered from both wind and prying eyes.

There Tasha sat on her favorite bench beside the hollyhocks, wearing one of her absurdities of lace and osprey feathers, which made her seem like a large white cat sunbathing. Commander Florian stood in the background, being unobtrusive. The King was pacing back and forth on a paved path, from the irises to the tea roses and back again. He carried a rolled paper, tapping it impatiently against his other hand.

"Rise!" the King said. "We have just learned that Czar Igor died last fall."

"That is correct, Your Majesty," Beau said.

The royal eyes narrowed. "A gruesome accident, we understand."

"Extremely gruesome."

"And where were you when that happened?"

"Beside Prince Dimitri, sire, about as far from the Czar as . . . he would have been about at the top of that apple tree. We were behind a steel fence."

"So you had absolutely nothing to do with his death?"
Silence.

Not again! Questions that need not be asked . . . Isabelle resisted an urge to scream at the top of her lungs or punch her husband in the kidneys. Athelgar glared.

Then Beau said, "How could I have, sire?" It was not an answer but it came close enough.

"I will not be known as a barbarian who employs assassins!"

"Certainly not, sire. Did Ambassador Hakluyt report rumors to that effect?"

"No." The King took a turn the other way, as far as the lilies.

"My sister is doing well as regent, I gather?" Tasha remarked sweetly. She, too, held a letter.

"She has Skyrria eating out of her hand, if I may be so bold."

"You are always bold, Sir Beaumont. She is well?"

"Extremely well, Your Majesty."

"She speaks highly of your service." Smiling, Tasha went back to reading.

The King returned, quietly fuming. "You intercepted Swithin?"

"I did, sire. He . . . I may continue?" Beau's unusual caution was a reminder that his two previous audiences with his sovereign lord had ended stormily.

"Tell us."

"He fought most valiantly when Baelish pirates boarded the Prince's ship. Your royal brother commended him. I have prepared a report for Grand Master, who may well choose to enter the encounter in the *Litany*."

For the first time the King smiled. "Swithin fought the pirates? How many—"

"Um, no, sire. He fought the crew." Beau winced at the royal glare. "He seemed very content the last time I saw him, sire. He has sent a letter to Grand Master reporting on his assignment, and I know it was favorable. He and his ward share a devotion to horseflesh. There were even hints of a romance . . .

". . . or two."

King Athelgar pretended not to hear that postscript. "And Sir Arkell?"

"Completely restored to health, sire, and extremely happy. He serves the Czarina Regent as both Imperial Librarian and *voevode* of the Czar's bodyguard."

"How many romances is he pursuing?" asked Queen Tasha pertly.

"I did not obtain an exact count, my lady."

Athelgar said, "You are aware that my brother is now King of Baelmark?"

"No, I had not heard that, Your Majesty! That is wonderful news!"

"Is it?" The King uttered a royal grunt and stalked off to inspect the lupins. Tasha was smirking about something.

Athelgar snarled at some forget-me-nots and strode back. "Beaumont, I am persuaded that I treated you harshly. We never paid the debt we owed you for your escorting our dear wife from Skyrria."

"It was my honor to—"

"Silence!" Athelgar strode closer to glare down at the offender. *"You also rile me more than any other man in the kingdom!"*

Beau tried to appear contrite, not very convincingly.

"You will be reinstated in the Order. Lend me your sword, Commander."

Beau sank to his knees. Sir Florian's sword tapped his shoulders and the King almost threw it back to its owner. This was mere formality, not ritual, because Beau's binding had ended with his ward's death.

"Rise, Sir Beaumont. We need a consul for the southern Isilondian city of Mardeau. Consular salaries are modest, but the perquisites let the incumbents live like, um, gentlemen. It is reputed to be a very pleasant place, and has the laudable advantage of being very far away. Have you ever been there, Lady Beaumont?"

"No, sire. But I have a brother there who tells good tales of it."

"Beaumont?"

"Your Majesty is most generous. I am deeply honored."

"So you should be. You have our leave to withdraw." King Athelgar turned his back and gave his wife a *now-are-you-satisfied?* scowl.

In its own mysterious fashion, the Guard had heard the news, even to knowing that Arkell was restored and Oak avenged. A dozen Blades pounced on Beau the moment he left the garden—back-thumping, hand-wringing, congratulating.

Sir Calvert proffered *Just Desert* in formal fashion, across his forearm. "If you drop by Ironhall, I'm sure that Master Armorer will find a suitable cat's-eye to fit."

Sir Cedric laughed. "It's probably been in Grand Master's pocket all this time."

"Let the man go," said Sir Modred. "Can't you see he has more urgent business to attend to than listening to our chatter?" Faces leered knowingly at Isabelle.

"I do have to meet my daughter," Beau said. He offered Isabelle his arm and set off along the corridor, humming a happy tune while his wife silently whetted her gutting knife. "I don't think I will," he said. "Change the pommel, I mean. The pebble brought me luck and a cat's-eye won't make any difference if we go to live in Isilond." He slid his arm around her as they turned the first corner. "You are happy about this Mardeau?"

"The climate is said to be clement." *Mardeau was not the problem!*

"I always told you Tasha was all right."

And who did he think had made Tasha see reason?

"I'll be happy wherever you are, my love." His voice was throaty, his grip tight around her. "We can do anything we want now. We won't ever have to eat in the kitchens again! You don't ever have to cook."

"I enjoy cooking," she said through clenched teeth.

He chuckled. "Just dessert, then."

Back at the room, they found Maude still asleep. Beau flashed Maisie a smile that turned her pink to the tips of her ears, bolted the door behind her, and fumbled with the ties on his pack. "Remember I promised you gowns and some small jewels?" He pulled out a leather sack and tipped a river of gold out on the bed beside the sword he had left there. It was a fortune. It would buy a farm, or a hostel, or a fencing school. For a moment Isabelle was stunned. And then the hurt returned, worse than ever.

"For services rendered, I assume? Yeoman service! You must have pleasured her greatly!"

"My love?" Beau said warily.

"Yes, your love!" she shouted. "Czarina Sophie!"

Isabelle knew Tasha very well now and no doubt Tasha knew her sister. Tasha was not quite certain—she had been probing—but obviously the Czarina had dropped a hint or two of what had been going on.

"You are my love, Lady Beaumont . . ." Beau advanced with carnal intent.

"Don't touch me!" she said, backing away. "Is she so very beautiful?" Soft hands, white skin. Rich and cultured. Clever.

Beau smiled wistfully. "She is very fair. But she is snow, she is ice. You are fire and earth. I came back to you, love."

"And you can go right back to her again!"

"Let me show you something." He began unlacing his jerkin.

"I have seen your manly body before! You expect me to melt with desire at the sight of it?" If she didn't keep yelling she would start weeping. "Did it have that effect on your precious icy Czarina?"

"That wasn't what I had in mind *just* yet. She sent this to you."

He wore a gold chain around his neck. Suspended from it, close to his white binding scar, dangled a ruby the size of an egg yolk, cut in the shape of a heart. It burned like fire, like blood. Isabelle stared at it in utter disbelief. Even Tasha owned nothing to compare with that.

All she could think to say was, "Is it real?"

"Certainly." He lifted the chain over his head and stepped close to loop it over hers. "When she heard that I was married, Sophie said . . . I mean, Her Majesty the Czarina Regent sent that for you."

"Oh." Isabelle had never heard of quite such a situation before. Rent for one husband? She wasn't sure what she was supposed to do—write a thank-you note or a receipt? Ask for advice on technique?

"She sends me her heart?" she yelled.

"She is a very sentimental lady . . . as well as being icy, of course."

"She rewards all her flunkies with pickings from the crown jewels?"

"Only the very beautiful ones."

Before Isabelle could answer that, Beau kissed her, taking her unaware. She did not refuse. Nor did she cooperate. After some time he pulled back just enough to give her a worried look and murmur, "Better now?"

Mmph!

"You're staying this time?" She ought to make him suffer much, much longer! He should pay for all the months he had spent fornicating with his fair Czarina, never thinking of the wife he had left languishing alone, here in Greymere Palace. But then she would suffer too.

"I shall stay with you forevermore, I swear."

After all, he *had* come back.

It wasn't as if That Woman was accessible, just around the corner.

And he *did* look worried. She had never seen him look so worried.

She had promised to trust him.

"Oh, very well," Isabelle said. "Clear that trash off the bed."

If you've enjoyed
Paragon Lost,
don't miss the next exciting
King's Blades adventure,

Impossible Odds,

coming in hardcover
from Eos in November 2003!

Turn the page for an excerpt.

Prologue: Awaken the Dead

The night was unusually dark. The day had been hot and clear, but heavy clouds had rolled in after sunset to blot out the stars. There was no moon. In Chivial such nights were called *catblinders*.

The guard changed at midnight. In pitch darkness Mother Celandine, Sister Gertrude, and their escort paraded through the grounds of Nocare Palace. Nocare's gardens were deservedly famous and especially lovely now, at the start of Eighthmoon, except that they were totally invisible. Trudy caught enough scents of night-flowering plants—stock, evening primrose, possibly moonflower—to tell her what she was missing. The two footmen leading the way carried lanterns, but those illuminated only the paved path underfoot and hints of shrubbery nearby. Four men-at-arms of the Household Yeomen marched noisily at the rear. Trudy privately considered them an unnecessary precaution, because any evil-intentioned intruder who glimpsed her and the majestic Mother Celandine in their voluminous white robes and steeple hats was likely to run screaming off into the darkness, gibbering about ghosts.

The White Sisters were rarely required to use their conjuration-detecting skills in the middle of the night. Nighttime security was normally a male sport—the Yeomen guarding the gates and the grounds, the Blades patrolling the inside of the palace—but now the King was entertaining an important guest and either he or someone in his train had been tactless enough to include conjurements in his baggage. Anyone else would have been reprimanded and made to turn them in, but a Grand Duke had to be humored. So the White Sisters' help was required, and Sister Gertrude was the most junior Sister in attendance at Court. Tonight Mother Celandine would supervise and instruct. Thereafter Trudy would have the night honors all to herself.

It was only a formality.

Two lights came into view and soon resolved themselves into torches set in sconces, on either side of an imposing doorway, the entrance to Quamast House. The Grand Duke had been lodged a long way from the main palace, and Sir Bernard had assured Trudy that this was the Blades' doing. Most visitors were bunked in the West Wing, but the Blades never took chances with unidentified spirituality.

Under each sconce stood a pike man in shiny breastplate and conical steel hat. The one on the right stamped his boots, advanced one of them a pace, lowered his halberd, and proclaimed, "Who goes there?"

"The nightingale sings a sad song!" Sergeant Bates proclaimed at Trudy's back. That was not true, because nightingales had finished singing back in Fifthmoon, and he said it loud enough for any skulking trespasser to overhear.

The man-at-arms resumed his former position, slamming the butt of his halberd on the stone. "Pass, friend."

One of the footmen opened the right-hand flap of the double door. As Trudy followed Mother Celandine through it, she caught a startling whiff of . . . of she was not sure what. She did not stop to investigate.

A voice at her elbow said, "Good chance, Trudy."

She jumped and turned to meet his grin. "Bernard!" He had not told her he would be here!

He smirked. "A last-minute roster change."

Obviously he had arranged this so he could surprise her—and embarrass her! Mother Celandine was frowning and three other Blades had emerged from the darkness to leer. All Blades looked much alike—lean, athletic men of middle size, mostly in their twenties. The conjuration that bound them to absolute loyalty to the King showed to her senses as an ethereal metallic glow, which she found very becoming.

"He's a fast worker, our Bernie," one said.

"Gotta watch those rapier men."

Horrors! Her face was on fire.

"That will do!" The fourth Blade was a little older and wore a red sash to show that he was in charge. He tapped the cat's-eye pommel of his sword. "Good chance to you, Mother Celandine."

"And to you, Sir Valiant."

"Do you know Sir Richey? Sir Aragon? And our expert breaker of hearts, Sir Bernard?" The men saluted in turn.

Mother Celandine nodded crisply to each salute. "This blushing maiden is Sister Gertrude."

Jealous old hag!

"Known as Trudy to her friends," Aragon remarked in an audible aside.

"We asked for White Sisters, not red ones," Richey countered.

Mortified, Trudy caught Bernie's eye. He winked. She realized that he was showing off. The others' crude humor was a form of flattery. She winked back.

The old lady sniffed. "Well, let's get it over with. Carry on, Sister."

Trudy led the way back to the door to begin. The lantern-bearing footmen followed and the Blades retreated to the staircase in the center, so their bindings would not distract the Sisters. Trudy closed her eyes and listened. She inhaled, licked the roof of her mouth, queried her skin for odd sensations . . . did all the curious things that promoted her sensitivity to the spirits, tricks she had been taught at Oakendown. She missed Oakendown and all her friends there, although it had been seriously deficient in boy-people, who were turning out to be just as much fun as she had dreamed.

"Nothing here, Mother." She began walking around the edge of the hall, stopped at the first corner. "There is something above here, though! Mostly air, some fire and water. And love." Except for trivia like good luck charms, conjurations were forbidden within the palace.

With the footmen in attendance, Sister and Mother paraded around the ground floor, through deserted kitchens, a dining room, an office. Trudy detected nothing untoward until she was almost back where she had begun.

"There's something here! Upstairs, I mean." This one was much harder, and she struggled for several minutes, but the jangle of elementals defied analysis. "There's more than one conjuration. I can't make them out. A lot of them, all mixed up." Her skin crawled. "I think we should go up and have a close look at that!"

"It is Baron von Fader's medicine chest," Mother Celandine said. "Or, at least, that was what they were in when they arrived. He is His Grace's physician, as well as his Foreign Secretary and Treasurer and spirits know what else. We scanned it carefully. The Prioress decided not to ask for the chest to be opened."

"Why not? There's death in there!"

"Sister! There's death in almost anything, as you well know. Were you never taken to an apothecary's when you were at Oakendown? Many drugs and simples are dangerous in large amounts. And Grand Dukes are entitled to the benefit of small doubts. Now, have you done?"

"I am uneasy about this one, Mother," Trudy said stubbornly.

"It was approved only this morning. But remember it carefully. If you sense any change in it tomorrow, or any other night, then tell the Guard right away. Don't be afraid to ask for my help if you're in doubt. Come!"

She led the way back to the waiting Blades.

"You wish to go upstairs now?" Valiant asked.

"No, we are satisfied. Anything really dangerous we could detect from down here.

You know where we are if you need us, Sir Valiant."

As they headed for the door, Bernard pulled another of his tricks. Right behind Trudy's ear, but loud enough for everyone to hear, he said, "Breakfast as usual, Trudy?"

"Of course," she shot back. "My place this time."

Sir Aragon said, "Oooooh, Trudy!"

"We will come and chaperone you, Trudy," Sir Richey added.

Before her face could even think about blushing, she followed Mother Celandine into the dark vestibule, then outside. She went down one step and stopped so suddenly that Sergeant Bates almost slammed into her. She looked inquiringly at the guard who had challenged them on their arrival. He was playing statue again, but . . . but . . .

"Something wrong, sister?" Bates asked.

"I'm not sure." She was sensing something. "Are you all right?" she asked.

"Answer her, Elson!" the sergeant said.

The sentry was very tall and had an untidy blond beard. He blinked down at her stupidly. "Right? Yes, mistress, I mean Sister."

Trudy shivered. She recalled noticing this same oddness on the way in, and now it was stronger. Very strange. Nothing familiar. Air? No fire. No love or chance. Time, no water. Death. Yes, definitely quite a lot of death.

The Blades approved of Quamast House, calling it Quarantine House because they knew that any questionable guests billeted there would not go sneaking out any secret passages. No assassins were going to sneak in, either. It had been built by King Ambrose, back in the days when the great Durendal, now Grand Master, had been Commander, and he had made sure that it was built right. With the outer doors and windows securely barred, as they were, Valiant and his little squad had nothing to do except stay awake at the bottom of the staircase. From there they had a clear view of the upstairs balcony and the doors to all the bedrooms.

It was an easy chore and tonight they even had a rookie with them, who must be introduced to some of the fiendish dice games the Blades employed to while away their stints. No charge for instruction. IOUs accepted without limit. Some recruits needed years to pay off their initiations.

Of course Cub Bernard first had to be baited about that slinky White Sister he had acquired. It was unseemly that a freckle-faced tyro, not two weeks into the Guard and barely through his orgying lessons, should collect something like that when better men hankered in vain. They quickly discovered that young Bernard was not the average run-of-the-mill Ironhall innocent. He could see that they were all as jealous as stags with glass antlers. He gave back as good as he got, inventing much lurid detail.

Abandoning that game as unwinnable, Valiant, Aragon,

and Richey got serious. They found a massive oaken dining table and, with some difficulty, dragged it to the bottom of the stair. They tried to move the two colossal bronze candelabra closer to it—however exceptional a Blade's night vision, in monetary matters he liked his brothers' hands well lit. Finding the monsters immovable, they settled for the existing illumination and got down to concentrated instruction.

"You know Saving Seven, of course?" Valiant asked.

The kid said he didn't, so Richey demanded to see the color of his money and Aragon produced a bag of eight-sided dice. Each face represented one of the elements, he explained, and you rolled them four at a time. The object was to roll seven elements but not the eighth, death. Roll a death and you had to start collecting from the beginning.

"First player has a slight edge," he added, "so we'll give you the honor. After that the winner starts the next one. Put a farthing in the pot and roll four."

On his first try the kid rolled two airs, a water, and a chance, so he counted three. Sir Richey paid his farthing and rolled two deaths, which put him out of that game altogether. The other two scored four elements apiece.

"Just keep going," Richey said. "You can fold, pay the same price as the last man, or double it."

Nobody doubled on that round, which saw the kid roll love, time, and fire, while Valiant and Aragon added one element each. Being ahead with six, lacking only earth, Bernard doubled the price, but failed to improve his score. The others paid when their turns came, with the same lack of progress, so he doubled the price again. He had spirit. With the pot starting to look interesting, he rolled a triple death. Valiant and Aragon exchanged angry glances. Richey guffawed.

Bernard brightened. "What does that mean?"

"It means you win," Richey explained quickly, before the

other two could invent a new rule for the occasion. "Roll a *quadruple* death and everyone who was in the game at the beginning has to pay you the final amount of the pot. That's called the 'massacre.' Another game, Freckles?"

"Why not?" Bernard raked in the coins.

It is regrettable that skill, virtue, and experience are no match for fickle chance. The brat won four games in a row, two of them with triple deaths. The next game turned out to be a never-ender, where everybody kept rolling single deaths and no one could reach the magic seven. With the pot growing enormous and three sharpies' reputations at stake, the betting grew desperate, until eventually they had the kid cornered. They were all sitting on winnable arrays and he was back down to two. All three of them in turn doubled the bet, expecting to price him out of the game. Perhaps he was too dumb to see that he could not win from there in a single roll. Or perhaps it was just that he was playing with their money and they were all writing IOUs. He not only stayed in, he doubled yet again.

Then he rolled a quadruple death.

The appalled silence was broken by a yell from Valiant, who had his back to the staircase and was facing the main door. He leaped to his feet, whipping out his sword. "Intruder! Richey get him. You two come with me." He ran seven or eight steps up and turned to survey the hall.

"You're seeing things!" Aragon said, but he went to join his leader, blocking the way to the guests above. So, to his credit, did Bernard, who might reasonably suspect a trick to cheat him out of half a year's pay.

Sir Richey strode forward to the main entrance carrying his saber, *Pain,* at high guard. The little vestibule was dark, but when he reached the line of pillars, he shouted, without turning his head, "The door's still barred!" He stopped. "I can smell blood! There's blood on the—" Something standing behind the nearest pillar lurched out at him. Possibly the stains on the floor had distracted him, but he parried the halberd thrust admirably, caught hold of its shaft in his left hand and swung *Pain* at his assailant's neck.

A Blade had little to fear in such a match and Valiant wisely did not send him reinforcements. The staircase was still the key. He said, "Aragon, waken the Duke and the Baron and get back here." Aragon went racing up the stair.

Richey, having almost decapitated his assailant, let go of the halberd. That was a mistake, for the intruder did not drop. Instead he swung the halberd at Richey's midriff. Richey leaped back, parrying. His opponent shuffled after, repeatedly stabbing at him. As they came closer to the stair and the light, Bernard cried out in horror. Now it was clear that the intruder was a walking corpse, for its head hung at an odd angle and it was soaked in dried blood from cuirass to boots. The gaping wound Richey had made in its neck was almost bloodless, but there was another, a crusted black gash. Its throat had been cut twice, and it was still fighting.

Nearer still they came until, incredibly, Richey started to laugh, albeit shrilly. The apparition continued to thrust at him with the point of its halberd, which he parried effortlessly, as if it were made of stiff paper. He tried a few cuts of his own, knocking the apparition aside like straw. It kept coming back, but was obviously harmless.

"It's only a mirage!" he shouted.

Upstairs, Aragon was yelling and beating on doors.

Another Yeoman wraith came into view around the staircase, from the kitchen quarters. It moved with the same awkward walk and it had a dagger hilt protruding from his left eye. When it reached the table it dropped on all fours and crept underneath.

"Leave it alone," Valiant said. "Ghosts can't hurt us."

Richey had almost reached the stair and his opponent was

transparent, barely visible at all. He was letting its clumsy strokes go, for they passed clean through him as if he were not there. Likewise, *Pain* was useless, whistled through the shadow without any effect.

The table tilted, spilling dice and money. Valiant and Bernard watched in amazement, for all four Blades had barely managed to shift that monstrosity. For a moment it stood on edge, then tipped over, impacting one of the candelabra. They went down together with a crash that shook the hall. Most of the candles winked out. Darkness leaped inward.

Richey screamed as his opponent's halberd impaled him. *Pain* went skittering off across the marble floor. Richey fell; the corpse withdrew the halberd and stabbed him again. Then again. The second intruder clambered off the fallen table and went lurching toward the other candelabrum with both arms held across his eyes.

"Save the other candles!" Valiant yelled. He and Bernard went plunging back down the stairs.

Bernard got there first with a couple of giant, reckless, ankle-risking strides and made a spectacular lunge, thrusting his rapier into the armpit gap in the side of the dead man's cuirass. He did not stop there. Sword and Blade together went clean through the smoky figure. Bernard hit the floor in a belly-flop and slid past Sir Richey and the thing that kept stabbing at him. He lay as if stunned. His heroics had been unnecessary, for the corpse he had been attacking had faded to almost nothing beside the candelabrum.

Upstairs, doors were flying open. Unfortunately the light pouring out of them did little to brighten the deadly gloom below.

Valiant took station under the remaining candelabrum, parrying the efforts of the second shadow to throttle him until he realized that it could not harm him. A third intruder shuffled in from the kitchens, completely enveloped in a heavy carpet. Valiant waited until it was close and then charged it, ramming *Quietus* through the rug and feeling it jar against a steel cuirass inside. The occupant retaliated by tipping the carpet over him and body-checking him. He was thrown over backward by the weight of a big man in half armor, but by the time he hit the marble, the load on top of him was no more than that of the rug alone.

He struggled free of it. Now two of the wraiths flitted around him, struggling to injure him with no more success than he would have fighting mist.

Voices upstairs shouted that help was on the way. Out in the shadows Richey lay on his back, obviously dead. Bernard sat up. The first Yoeman corpse swung its halberd at him. Bernard rolled nimbly aside. Steel rang on stone where he had lain. His move put him within reach of his rapier, *Lightning*. He grabbed hold of her hilt, but was not quite fast enough getting back on his feet. Still off-balance, he parried the halberd aside with his left hand and drove *Lightning* through the corpse so that two-thirds of her stuck out of its back. That stroke would certainly have ended any living opponent, but the dead one ignored it and fell on top of him. They went down together, with the corpse clawing at his throat.

Valiant reached him, swinging *Quietus* like a broadsword. He chopped the thing's head off with one stroke, executioner style. The helmeted head hit the floor with a clang, but the decapitated corpse paid no heed and continued its two-handed throttling of the boy.

The third wraith was going up the stairs, at first flitting like flying ash, gradually slowing and growing solid as it reached the darkness. Aragon and the fat Baron were coming down to meet it, brandishing candlesticks and lanterns, and it faded back to harmless, flickering shadow.

Struggling to save Bernard from strangulation, Valiant went to work on the monster's arms. He had almost cut through one when he was hurled to the floor. He looked up to see the corpse with the dagger in its eye. It lashed out with its boot. He tried to roll away and it followed, kicking him with bone-breaking impacts. He couldn't breathe; he was as good as dead.

Then Aragon and Baron Fader brought their lights and it again faded to smoke.

"Quickly!" the Baron shouted. He was a gruesome apparition himself, with a voluminous white nightgown billowing around his great bulk and spikes of white hair and beard sticking out in all directions. "Before they escape! We must pen the shadowmen in here. Come, come!"

"Bernard!" Valiant croaked gasping at the pain in his ribs.

"He is dead!" Aragon shouted. "Can you walk?" He had both hands full of lanterns, four of them.

"Hurry, hurry, hurry!" the Baron screamed in his squeaky voice. "They will escape. They will attack the palace! Hurry!"

Bernard was starting to rise, his throat in shreds and his eyes like blank white pebbles. Valiant struggled to his feet and recovered *Quietus*. He trotted back to the stair between the other two men. The shadowmen followed, five ominous, barely-visible shapes at the edges of the brightness, one of them headless.

Wrapped in a heavy red robe, the Grand Duke was struggling to overturn the candelabrum. His two menservants were coming down, half naked, but bringing more light.

"Stop!" Valiant shouted.

"No!" the Baron retorted. "These must go." He threw his great weight into the argument. The candelabrum shivered. Only when Aragon joined in did it rock and then topple, hitting the ground with a noise like a falling smithy and snuffing out most of the candles. The Baron stamped on the others, dancing grotesquely while waving his many-branched candlesticks, in danger of going up in flames himself. Then the six living men hurried up the stairs together, leaving the lower floor to darkness and the dead.

They piled into the ducal bedroom and slammed the door. The Baron slumped down on a chair, which creaked alarmingly. The Grand Duke fell on the bed and buried his face in the covers.

"We must warn the Palace!" Valiant whispered. His bruised chest was an agony.

"No, it's all right!" Baron Fader proclaimed, wheezing after his exertions. "*Schattenherren* are deadly in darkness, but then they cannot pass through walls."

"Can't they just open the doors and walk out?" Aragon demanded.

The fat man shrugged. "Hope they won't. They want us and will stay close to us. Of course if someone else comes or goes by too near the house . . . Then they might. Daylight comes, they will die."

Richey had died. Bernard had died. Valiant wished he had.

Sister Trudy would breakfast alone.